THE CHAIWALLAH'S APPRENTICE

SANJEEV BAKSHIM

MOONBEAMS PUBLISHING

For Frances
Thank you for being you

© Copyright Sanjeev Backshim 2020
The right of Sanjeev Backshim to be identified as the author of this work has been asserted by him in accordance with the Copyright, Design and Patents Act 1988
This book is entirely a work of fiction. All characters, companies, organizations, products and events in this book, other than those clearly in the public domain, are fictitious or are used fictitiously and any resemblance to any real persons, living or dead, events, companies, organizations or products is purely coincidental.

Cover images licensed from
Nilaya @ Depositphotos (Delhi)
Zmei Photo @ Depositphotos (Man with gun)

First Edition

Paperback ISBN: 978-0-9552216-1-3

1

Ajay ran out and grabbed Nitesh by his top, dragging him off the boy he had pinned to the ground and was relentlessly punching.

"He called me a bastard! He called me a bastard!" Nitesh shrieked, his body fuelled with rage.

Ajay hugged Nitesh from behind as he struggled. Nitesh was determined to carry on pummelling the boy, who now slowly got up.

"Calm down, Nitesh. It doesn't matter," Ajay gently whispered in his ear.

"He called me a bastard!"

"Calm down, little brother. He's not worth it. You're better than him."

Ajay gradually loosened his grip as Nitesh's heart began to pound less ferociously and he stopped struggling. Ajay turned him around, pointing him towards the house. He obediently went inside, not wanting his rival to see the tears that would soon start to flow.

"Your brother's a stupid bastard," muttered the boy, who was shaking as he touched his bleeding lip.

"What are you?" sneered Ajay. "King of Paraharavi? Or a little turd who's just got his arse kicked?"

The boy fought back tears as he yelled, backing away: "You're a bastard, just like your brother!"

Ajay took a deep breath, managing to control the urge to smash this little rat's head into the nearest wall. "Fuck off before I let my little brother kill you." He did not raise his voice, but it was filled with venom. There was no mistaking that he meant what he said.

The boy turned and ran off.

Ajay watched him disappear before going inside. Nitesh was sitting on the floor, rocking back and forth, trying to control the tears flowing down his cheeks.

Ever since their father had died three years ago, Ajay had taken on the role of the man of the house. Nitesh, on the other hand, had become bereft and full of anger. Ajay sat next to him. He knew, somehow, that it would not be right to hug him. Nitesh needed toughening up if he was to cope with life in Parharavi slum.

"You showed him."

Nitesh carried on crying.

"I don't think he's coming back in a hurry…"

Nitesh began to regain some control.

"Would *you*?" Ajay said it with such comic effect that Nitesh could not help but burst out laughing.

"Come on, let's have one of mum's samosas."

Nitesh immediately got up. Their mum's samosas were legendary across Parharavi. To have one was a rare treat.

Nitesh savoured the samosa, eating it slowly and tasting every mouthful, just as Ajay had shown him. His big brother was right – you get more out of it that way.

After they had finished, Ajay smiled down at Nitesh and kissed the top of his head. "If anyone else gives you grief, just kick their arse."

A grin spread across Nitesh's face as Ajay left for the temple.

∼

Mr Joshi had started setting up his chai stall at the temple at 6am. He always did things in the same, ceremonious order. He put a flat cushion on the ground. On top of it he put a beautiful, embroidered gold cloth. The embroidery was the same shade as the cloth, but its rich, complex paisley pattern made it stand out. This was his seat. In front of the cushion, he placed a compact kerosene fuelled cooking ring. On his right, within easy reach, was a large stainless steel jug full of water, a smaller one half filled with milk and a much smaller one full of mixed spices. He reverentially put a small statue of Ganesh next to the jugs, saying a short, silent prayer as he did so.

Mr Joshi had taken Ajay on nearly three years ago because, instead of trying to beg at the temple like all the other ragged children (and subsequently playing cat and mouse with the temple security guards), Ajay went every morning from stall to stall, asking for work. Mr Joshi had always sent him away with a sharp flick of the hand. Eventually, Ajay had stopped asking him. The boy had dignity and was no fool. Mr Joshi had seen him work on the other stalls. He worked hard, was respectful and seemed never to steal.

After several months of watching him, Mr Joshi called him over.

"What's your name, boy?"

"Ajay, sir."

"Ajay, would you like to work for me every day?"

A look of delight spread over his small face. "Yes, sir. Very much, sir."

"Start tomorrow at eight. Don't be late." There were very few customers before 8am. The pious who came early rarely partook in the frivolities of chai so close to praying.

"Yes, sir."

Mr Joshi had been harsh in the way he spoke to him at first, ordering him to be quick whenever he gave him a task. However, he had soon found that not only was Ajay respectful, but also surprisingly quick and efficient – far more so than could be expected from someone so young. After a few months Mr Joshi had mellowed. Now he talked to him almost like a grandfather. He paid him every night but also warned him not to be late the next day. He gave him a bonus every month. It was his way of keeping Ajay loyal and showing he cared. It had worked: Ajay had never thought of going elsewhere in all the time he had been with him.

Ajay arrived at the chai stall a little out of breath, but on time. He had never been late.

"Namaste, bapuji," said Ajay.

"Namaste, Ajay."

"Shall I fetch some water?"

"Not yet, beta. It's been a quiet morning."

This was unusual – it was a Saturday. There should have been some sales to the families that frequented the temple early every Saturday – the middle-class people who gave thanks for all they had been granted.

"I'm sorry, bapuji."

"It's OK, beta. I'm sure Ganeshji will look after us."

Ajay knew that whenever Mr Joshi said this, he was worried. It had been quiet for a few months. Last month Ajay had not received his usual bonus. His mother had struggled without that extra money. Since his father had died things had been very hard.

"Is there anything I can do, bapuji?"

"No beta, nothing…"

Ajay hesitated. He had an idea which he had kept to himself for some weeks now. Maybe it was time to voice it. He knew scrawny boys like him were plentiful on the streets of Delhi. He also knew the middle classes despised them, thinking of them as vermin. He wanted to help but, looking the way he did, if he tried to promote Mr Joshi's business, it would have the opposite effect.

"Can I borrow the gold cloth you sit on, bapuji?" Ajay asked tentatively.

"What!?" exploded Mr Joshi.

"I can use it for a turban," Ajay replied, talking quickly. He was apprehensive but determined. "I'll look both cute and magnificent at the same time. I can say to tourists a 'namaste' as they walk past. Maybe they'll see us and stop."

"Don't be silly," muttered Mr Joshi.

"But, bapuji, you see the tourists. They just talk to each other. So few even look at us. All I ask is that I try just for today. I will treat your gold cloth with complete respect."

"Are you saying my chai isn't good enough?" asked Mr Joshi, his voice rising with anger.

"Bapuji, you make the best chai in Delhi. But the tourists just fly by. They hardly ever look. I respect you, bapuji. All I want to do is help."

Mr Joshi looked reluctant but torn. Ajay stayed silent while Mr Joshi thought.

"I've always said you're a bright boy... Very well, take the cloth and put it on. But look smart."

"Yes, bapuji," Ajay replied meekly.

Ajay formed the gold cloth into a turban. Although a little gaunt, he did indeed look cute and magnificent. Mr Joshi smiled and nodded in approval.

Ajay stood in front of the stall and, as people walked past, he put his hands together in a prayer gesture and said "namaste". After the first hour of this, his throat was beginning to hurt and no one had stopped. The problem seemed to be that, by the time they were next to the stall, it was impossible to get their attention other than by physically touching them or calling out loudly. But, obviously, if he did this he would drive them away, as well as draw the attention of the temple authorities.

He stood where he was for a few minutes, watching and thinking. He quickly realised people were looking at him, but from a distance, often just as they entered through the temple gates. When he looked at them, he found the men looked away. However, the women generally did not, especially the white European and American tourists. He tried smiling at them. Most looked away – especially the Indian women. But, for the ones who did not, he put his hands together in a namaste greeting and inclined his head slightly. This often resulted in an even broader smile and, from the white tourists, a return of the same gesture.

The problem was that it did not translate into chai sales. They just walked past the stall. If he was lucky, he would get a smile from them.

After a while he took a risk and asked: "Chai, madam?" as his potential marks went by.

He had done this more than ten times and was beginning to lose hope, when a middle-aged white woman said in an American accent: "Thank you, young man. I think I will. Would you like one, dear?" She was addressing her husband.

Her tip was over three times greater than the price of the two chais. It was by far the largest tip Ajay had known anyone to give. As always, he passed all the money straight on to Mr Joshi. He did not resent this arrangement – he knew no better. But he did know that the more money Mr Joshi made, the bigger his bonus.

As the day progressed, Ajay found his tactic was working: they had never been busier. He also noticed that the tips from the Americans were far bigger than usual (Europeans hardly ever tipped). He had learnt a long time ago that Americans nearly always tip and, if they really like the service, they tip generously. They must really like what he was doing. This pleased him.

At the end of the day Mr Joshi was smiling uncontrollably. Ajay stared at him, slightly shocked. It was something he had never seen Mr Joshi do. The very occasional smile when trying to ingratiate himself with a customer maybe, but only brief and when absolutely necessary.

"Well done, beta. Go to Ramesh bhai's shop and get yourself two white pyjama suits. Only wear them at work. Make sure they're always clean." Mr Joshi instructed. "Tell him I sent you and I'll pay him later."

It was now Ajay's turn to smile uncontrollably.

As he walked home with his suits in a carrier bag, he was looking forward to telling his mum and little brother and sister what had happened today. Soon it would be all over Parharavi. That thought made him happy.

He felt tired – more so than usual. Hopefully, he would get used to it. Every night he spent an hour teaching his brother and sister how to read and write English before doing his own studies to further develop his Hindi and English (although money was tight, you could get used school books for next to nothing in Parharavi). However, tonight he would just go home, eat, talk to his mum, brother and sister, and go straight to bed.

The next day he turned up with one of the pyjama suits on. As soon as he was at the stall, he transformed the gold cloth into a turban. Mr Joshi couldn't help staring at him. "Go and look in Ramesh bhai's mirror," he told Ajay.

Mr Joshi looked up and took in the scene. He may have been an old man, but he was no fool – he knew what Ajay was trying to do. He filled two of the disposable earthenware cups to the very top and handed them to Ajay. Ajay handed them to Deepika's mum and dad.

When Ajay turned back, another cup was waiting, but this time only filled to the usual, manageable level. As her parents struggled with the hot, overfilled cups, Ajay handed Deepika hers. They smirked at each other, both sharing the joke. His hand brushed hers. She blinked, holding her eyes closed a little longer than necessary, and smiled.

She quickly opened her eyes, looking embarrassed as she turned away just before her mother looked over to see what was going on.

"I want you to take two breaks every day," Mr Joshi told Ajay one morning. "One at eleven and one at three. Go for half an hour each time. We're both getting tired – we can't carry on like this. I can manage the stall when you're not here."

Ajay looked worried.

"I will pay you the same."

Ajay smiled.

Ajay liked the new arrangement. It meant that, when he got home, he was far less tired and was able to teach his brother and sister, as well as carry on with his own studies.

As time went on, Ajay developed a routine during his breaks of sitting in a hidden, shady part of the temple grounds without his turban on, reading and eating the food his mother had made for him. Where he sat allowed him to discreetly keep an eye on the stall just in case Mr Joshi needed him. He never did, but he might one day.

After a couple of months of doing this, one morning he noticed two men approach Mr Joshi. Ajay had seen them visit other stalls. Whenever they approached the stallholders always looked terrified or unhappy or both. They never stayed long. One was middle-aged, the other probably in his late twenties. Both men were stockily built. Ajay watched intently. Mr Joshi stood up, and there seemed to be an argument. Although the middle-aged man was trying to hide it, from the angle Ajay was at he could see that the man had taken out a knife and was pressing it into Mr Joshi's side whilst whispering something in his ear. Mr Joshi seemed to almost melt as he sat down sharply. He got out some money and handed it over. Both men left the stall.

Mr Joshi looked shaken. Ajay was going to see if he was OK, but decided against it – Mr Joshi looked too upset to talk to anyone. Instead, he waited until his break was over.

"Is everything OK, bapuji?" Ajay asked.

Mr Joshi said nothing. They worked hard that day, but Mr Joshi spilt chai a few times and put too much sugar in it once. These were things he *never* did.

At the end of the day Ajay asked again, but this time with more concern. "Bapuji, is everything alright?"

Mr Joshi just smiled at him weakly and said: "I won't be able to give you many bonuses from now on, my dearest child."

Ajay nodded. He might only be 13 years old, but it was obvious who those men were. Gangsters running a protection racket.

Over the next few weeks, he saw them visit Mr Joshi about twice a week. They always approached when Ajay was on his break. After each visit, Mr Joshi seemed to look older. Also, Ajay's bonuses, which Mr Joshi had begun to give him weekly, were cut to virtually nothing.

At his age the strain would kill Mr Joshi. He could not allow this to happen to the only person he had ever looked on as a grandfather. But what could he, a mere child, do?

There was no way he was going to give in that easily...

In Paraharavi there were many with smartphones. Ajay was not one of them. All the money he earned went straight to his mother, who used virtually all of it for food. The recent bonuses had meant that she had been able to buy a couple of new cooking pots (new to her – not brand new) – the old ones were so worn that they had developed leaks. He had kept on telling her to buy a new saree, but he knew they did not really have the money. He had stopped saying it when the extra money had all but dried up.

After Mr Joshi gave him a rare bonus, on the way home Ajay approached Bhatti the phone wallah, who had his shop on the next street to where he lived.

"Do you rent out smartphones?" Ajay asked.

"What do you want with a smartphone, boy?" Bhatti asked dismissively.

"To hire it from you."

"You don't have the money. Go and look after your mother."

"How much for one week?" Ajay persisted.

Bhatti told him.

Ajay nodded. He took out the exact money and handed it over to Bhatti.

Bhatti looked surprised but said nothing. What business was it of his if Ajay's family starved? Vermin like that were everywhere. Good riddance.

That night, when everyone was asleep, Ajay familiarised himself with the phone, especially the camera part of it. He had seen so many other boys of his age use one but, apart from the rare occasion when someone let him play with theirs for a few minutes, he had never used one before. Despite this, he had always known it was something he would be at home with.

He learnt to navigate around it quickly, but did so mainly on airplane mode to minimise use of his credit. He would need that for later.

On his breaks Ajay watched the stall intently. On the second day the gangsters approached. He quickly got the phone out and started videoing them. As soon as he was able to get a full view of both their faces he put his phone away. There was no one around, and no one was looking at him. Good.

That night he isolated the images of both the gangsters' faces and searched the internet. It took quite a bit of time, but he was eventually rewarded – there were newspaper articles about both of them.

The younger one was a petty thief. According to an article Ajay found, he had been caught several times trying to shoplift and burgle. Obviously not very good at it. Just over four years ago he had been given an 18 month prison sentence for breaking into a shop at night. His name was Mahesh Bakshi, and he was 32 years old.

The older man had only one report about him, but in several newspapers. It was dated three months ago. His name was Daksh Anand, and he was 51 years old. He had been on trial for dealing in heroin, but was acquitted. The police had been watching him for over two years and had plenty of proof, but he had been found not guilty. His expensive lawyer had been more convincing than the evidence.

Anand was obviously the brains. He had also looked as if he

would be good in a fight. Bakshi was there just for show – it was much more frightening if two big men approached you.

A few of the reports gave the name of the street Anand lived on. Ajay looked it up. It was in Greater Kailash, a posh area towards the south of the city centre known for its mansions.

So, he knew where Anand lived, but now what? He could not go and threaten him. No matter how good an act he put on, Anand would laugh at an emaciated street urchin trying to put the frighteners on him. After he had finished laughing, he would probably torture him before killing him.

Anand lived about two hours walk away. Ajay decided to visit. He waited until the others were asleep and then crept out of the house. He did not want them to know what he was doing. Also, it was best to go when respectable people had retired for the night – boys like him were not welcome in posh areas.

Ajay walked down Anand's street, taking in all the grand abodes. He had seen a few similar but smaller places not too far from Paraharavi. He was trying to work out how he could find out where Anand lived when he came across a truly magnificent house, the likes of which he had never laid eyes on before. Four stories, with balconies on every level above the ground floor. Each balcony had railings in the shape of peacocks and elephants, and archways reminiscent of Mughal palaces. No two balconies or archways were identical. The wall around the roof terrace seemed to glimmer in the moonlight. Ajay wondered if it was marble. He wished he could live here.

He stood staring. At last, he was able to shut his mouth, which he did just in time to hear a car pulling up. He quickly dodged into some shadows and crouched down. The large gate to the house silently slid open, and the car entered. Anand passed within a few feet of him. He held his breath. But, short of getting up, running over and banging on the window, Anand would not have noticed him. His eyes were bloodshot and he could only just keep his head upright. Ajay saw men like this all the time in Parharavi. He was drunk.

Only when he heard him come out of the car and go into the

house, did Ajay silently and speedily leave his hiding place and walk home.

Ajay made similar trips to Anand's house over the next two days but stayed well away from it, hidden in the shadows.

Anand came home at about midnight on both occasions – the same time he had on the first night. He appeared to be thoroughly intoxicated each time.

Slowly, a plan formed in Ajay's head. From his hiding place he had been able to see Anand approach the house. On both occasions, he had sped straight up the road (which was deserted at this time) and slowed down to negotiate the bend just before his house. The swerve in the road was only slight, but it seemed to have been designed to give the house a bit of exclusivity. The house was not quite out of sight (what was the point of having that much money and not showing off?). Instead, it was aloof, as if it was sneering at everything and everyone around it.

The plan was simple. Ajay would put a piece of wood with nails in it on the bend. When Anand ran over it, it would puncture his tyres. He would then get out of his car to see what had happened. Because he did not have a straight view down the road, it would allow Ajay to approach him unnoticed from behind and stab him in the back, through the heart.

The next night Ajay let himself into Saksham's (the furniture maker) workshop. It was four streets away from where he lived, but he knew it well. Saksham and his father had been good friends. He knew Saksham kept the front door locked, but the lock could easily be picked.

"What have I got to steal?" Ajay had once heard Saksham say to his father. "A few nails and some wood? If anyone tries to take any furniture, I'll hear them. Also, if they're caught, anyone around here would kill them – they wouldn't dare."

That visceral threat had stuck in Ajay's head.

He carefully picked the lock with a bent, rusty paperclip. He very slowly opened the door, just in case it creaked. It didn't. He breathed a sigh of relief and shut it behind him. He listened. Nothing. Good.

The entire downstairs was a small workshop, with a flight of stairs leading to the living area upstairs. He crept over to the corner with all the scrap bits of wood. They were all tiny – not more than four inches long. He needed something far more substantial. He slowly looked around from where he stood. There were some very large pieces, but they were way too big for what he needed. Finally, his eyes fell on a sound-looking but weather-beaten plank leaning against a wall. It was about two and a half feet long. One of the local kids had probably found it and sold it to Saksham for a few rupees.

Quietly, he approached the workbench, grabbing two handfuls of two-inch nails and silently pocketing them. He then picked up a hammer before making his way over to the plank. He rested for a moment, trying to get his breathing back to normal. Silently, he let himself out.

A major road was only five minutes' walk away. Even from where Ajay stood, he could hear the rumble of lorries as they ran along it, carrying their goods into the heart of Delhi.

He stood in a secluded area at the side of the road, hammering the nails into the wood. He had seen someone do this in a film once. "Put lots of nails in," the man had told his son. "We don't just want a puncture, we want his tyres torn to pieces." Ajay put lots of nails in.

He left the plank hidden in some undergrowth. On the way home, he carefully placed the hammer outside Saksham's front door.

The next day Ajay was both tired and nervous. Would he be able to carry out the plan? Could he stab Anand deep enough to kill him? Of course he could! But every time he thought about it, he felt sick. But he either had to kill Anand, or watch his own family starve. Anand was evil. He deserved to die.

Ajay tried to put it out of his mind by getting into his role of cute chaiwallah's assistant, but it kept nagging at him. He smiled as broadly as he could, but the temple goers were not coming to the stall like they usually did.

Luckily, Mr Joshi did not seem to notice. Ever since that first visit from Anand and Bakshi, he had seemed to lose all interest. His movements had become stiff and slow, as if he was forcing himself to go through the motions. He had never smiled much before, but now he looked even more miserable and angry. He hardly ever spoke to Ajay or anyone else.

Ajay looked sadly at Mr Joshi as he sat in the shade during his afternoon break. He had to do it for Mr Joshi's sake.

Ajay was outside Anand's house by 11.30. He crouched down at the outer edge of the bend in the road. Although he was more visible here, it gave him a better view down the road.

Within 15 minutes he saw the familiar blaze of Anand's headlights. He put the plank on the road and crossed over to the inner edge of the bend. He had his mother's best knife in his hand. He could do this. No, he *had* to do it. He had no choice. As soon as Anand ran over that plank, his tyre would burst, he would come out, look at it and, even though he was so drunk he could hardly stand, he would know exactly what had happened. He would find out who had done it and make them *suffer* before killing them. There was no turning back now.

The car approached, its powerful headlights illuminating everything in front of it. Even before it entered the bend, the light glinted off the nails. Ajay suddenly doubted he would have the power to kill such a large, muscular man. It was too late now. He had to do it or die trying. He hoped his mum, brother and sister would be OK without him. But how would they be? He could not bear the thought of his mum going into prostitution, like too many of the women in Paraharavi did. He could beat this bastard. He *had* to beat him.

He was ready to spring into action, when the car suddenly swerved as if to avoid the nails. It seemed to speed up as it hurtled forward and went off the edge of the bend and into a sharp ditch. It flew through the air, turning upside down before landing heavily on its roof and gradually sliding to a halt.

Ajay stood there, stunned. He quickly came to his senses and ran and grabbed the plank, taking cover in the shadows before anyone came. But no one did. The ditch was deep, meaning any sound emanating from it was muffled. Add this to the slightly secluded area at the end of the road, and the crash would have been barely audible in the surrounding houses.

After a few minutes, Ajay emerged, knife in hand. He clambered down the side of the ditch and, as stealthily as he could, approached the car. Anand had not been wearing a seatbelt, and he lay motionless, in a crumpled mess, with his bleeding head at an awkward angle. His eyes were open. Even to Ajay it was obvious what had happened: his neck was broken.

As relief swept over him, Ajay was barely able to control his bladder. He toyed with the idea of taking Anand's wallet, but if that was missing, the police might suspect something. But Ajay had seen Anand take out his wallet when he had taken money off Mr Joshi. It had always been thickly crammed with cash, enough to last Ajay's family a long, long time. He could not just let that go.

He looked around. No, no one about. He pulled his sleeve over his hand and opened the door. He clambered in, careful not to make a noise, leave any marks or touch anything. He tapped Anand's back trouser pocket. It was there. Holding on to his sleeve, he extracted the wallet. Just as thick as he remembered. He took out about three-quarters of the notes and shoved them in his pocket before replacing it.

As he began the walk home he felt relieved. Waves of happiness washed over him as he relaxed more and more. It was as if he had been blessed a thousand times over. He looked at the money – more than he could earn at Mr Joshi's in a year. But he would not quit. He would still work there but, as far as his mother was concerned, his bonuses had just got much bigger.

He threw the plank into some wild shrubs about halfway back.

He entered his house silently. If it had been raining, this would have been far easier as the sound of it on the corrugated metal roof drowned out all but the loudest noises.

He knew he was luckier than most. His father had built this place, and built it well. Two rooms, one of which was the kitchen. He crept through it and went upstairs, careful not to disturb his mum and sister, who were asleep on a mattress on the floor. His brother was sound asleep on the mattress upstairs. It was a big room – enough space for another two double mattresses with some room left over. His parents had planned for another three children, but then his father had died. The only other piece of furniture was a plastic chair in the corner, on which he now stood.

He removed a small piece of wood. If you had looked at it, it appeared to be supporting the roof. Ajay had seen his father put it there when he was building the house. He had been called away when a neighbour came around for chai, and had forgotten to nail it into place. Ajay had discovered that, if you removed it, there was a small space behind it to hide things. He now put the money there. It was wrapped in a small plastic bag – these were in plentiful supply, littering the streets of Delhi.

The late nights added to the incredible events of last night meant that Ajay could hardly get out of bed in the morning.

He reached the temple on time, but was still dreading Mr Joshi's reaction. No matter how much Mr Joshi was caught up in his worries, there was no way he would not notice the state Ajay was in.

But, instead, he felt a buzz as soon as he entered the temple grounds. The traders were all huddled together in a mass, talking excitedly. There was lots of laughter. Mr Joshi was the only one who had not joined the throng. He was sitting by himself at his stall. He was smiling, which was so unusual these days that it was almost disturbing.

"Ajay, my son!" was his warm greeting as soon as he saw Ajay.

"Hello bapuji," Ajay answered nervously.

"Today is a great day!"

"Is it bapuji?"

"Yes," replied Mr Joshi. "Ganesh has smiled down on us all."

"What has happened, bapuji?" Ajay tried to sound curious and excited. This was difficult – he could hear the tiredness in his voice.

"Did you ever see those two big men come to my stall?"

"Which ones?" Ajay asked innocently.

"You probably never saw them. They came when you weren't here. They always asked for money, lots of money…" Mr Joshi's voice trailed off sadly.

"Did you give them money?" Ajay was doing a good job of sounding confused.

"Yes, beta," Mr Joshi replied gently. "I had to."

"Why?"

"You don't say no to people like that… But it doesn't matter anymore!"

"Why not?" Ajay had now fully woken up and was getting into the role. Maybe he should be an actor…

"They've left Delhi for good and will never come back!" Mr Joshi almost shouted with pleasure.

So the news had already reached the temple? Ajay was stunned. Somebody must have found Anand's body this morning and put it on the internet. That reminded him – he needed to return Bhatti's phone. He would go through it tonight and get rid of the photographs and videos before taking it back. He had carefully researched how to completely erase any signs of activity – he had frequently heard other kids refer to "cookies" and "search history".

That day was busier than usual. The temple goers seemed to pick up on the joy of the traders, and stayed longer and spent more.

Ajay went home happy but thoroughly, thoroughly exhausted.

On the way back, he erased the photos, videos, search history and cookies. He had to walk past Bhatti's shop, so it was just a matter of dropping it off.

When he got there, he found Bhatti busy chatting to someone. Ajay stood there awhile whilst Bhatti ignored him. Ajay quickly grew irritated. It was not a feeling he was prone to, but the tiredness combined with Bhatt's ignorance was too much.

"Hey Bhatti, here's your phone!" he called sharply, putting it on the counter.

"That's Mr Bhatti to you, pipsqueak!"

Ajay turned and left the shop, leaving Bhatti glowering at his retreating form.

Ajay went to bed very early and slept soundly, waking at his usual time. He felt refreshed.

The next two days went well. Although the excitement in the temple died down, everyone was still in a good mood.

It was on the way home after that second day that Bhatti stopped him by standing in his path.

"Hey boy, I know what you've done."

Ajay looked at him questioningly.

"I found your photos and your search history."

Ajay felt a jolt go through him and wanted to throw up, but he managed to regain control. "*What?*" he said at last, trying his best to sound as if he did not know what Bhatti was talking about.

Bhatti smirked at his discomfort. "Daksh Anand, the dead gangster, I know what you did."

Ajay shrugged. "So, you found a few photos. Anyone could have taken them."

Bhatti snorted derisively. "What, six days ago? And how about the internet search and the GPS that showed you were at his house for three nights in a row – and the night *you* killed him." He pointed at Ajay when he emphasised the word "you".

He grinned as Ajay looked worried.

"You don't know as much about phones as you thought, pipsqueak. How much do you earn at Joshi's?"

Ajay looked at him sharply. How did he know he worked at Mr Joshi's? Paraharavi was a small place. Everyone knew everything about each other.

"How much do you earn?" Bhatti said more forcefully.

Ajay abruptly lifted his chin towards him, as if to say: "What's it got to do with you?"

"You're going to give me half of it."

Half! Was he mad? Everyone knew his mum was too ill to do anything but a little bit of cleaning at some nearby flats, and they just about got by. How was he supposed to give him *half*? The idea of giving Bhatti some of the money he had taken out of Anand's wallet briefly flashed through his mind, but he knew that would not be enough for Bhatti. He wanted to make Ajay *suffer*. All because of what – he had shown him a little disrespect when he was tired? This was not fair. Life was not fair. Sometimes, you just had to fight scum, which came in all forms, from big men like Anand to this slimy rat in front of him.

"So you think I killed Anand?" Ajay said at last.

Bhatti snorted.

"How do you think I did it? A little boy like me against a powerful man?"

"That's up to the police to work out."

It was Ajay's turn to laugh. "The police! Are you joking? Do you really think they'll believe that a 'pipsqueak' like me killed a giant like that?"

Bhatti reddened. "They will when I show them the phone."

"I'll tell them that I don't know anything about it. It's your phone – you must have done it."

Bhatti laughed. "It's got your fingerprints on it."

"I'll tell them I looked at the phone, but you're such a thieving bastard, I decided not to take it." The words were out of Ajay's mouth almost quicker than he had thought of them.

Bhatti looked like he was going to explode. He did not know what else to say except: "I'm going to the police."

Ajay was beginning to enjoy himself. He could get used to cutting bullies down to size. "It's my word against yours. Who's more likely to kill Anand – a big man like you or a 'pipsqueak' like me?" he asked, looking at Bhatti's protruding belly. The 'big man' certainly was not a reference to his musculature.

Bhatti stepped towards Ajay, looking ready to clout him. Ajay just stared at him, not budging an inch. Suddenly, Bhatti's temper dissipated as a thought slowly entered his near Neanderthal brain. "Prakash bhai was here when you brought the phone back. He'll tell the police." He smiled in sly self-satisfaction.

Ajay nodded. This was a good thought, but anyone could see that this lumbering elephant was no match for him. "They might look for me. They might take me to the police station for my fingerprints, but they'll let me out when I tell them you and Prakash bhai must have put the phone there on purpose, so someone would pick it up and you could blame them. They'll arrest both of you then. Who do you think they'll believe, a sweet, hardworking boy like me who everyone at the temple adores or a fat, thieving bastard like *you*?" He said the word 'you' in the most derisive way he could manage.

Bhatti took another step towards him. Ajay just laughed. Bhatti was only inches away from him now.

"You say I killed Anand. What do you think I'll do to someone like *you*?" Ajay snarled in a whisper.

It was almost comical to watch the dark clouds of anger on Bhatti's face turn into terror. Bhatti stepped back. Ajay didn't move. Bhatti scurried into this shop like a frightened little mouse. Ajay grinned broadly and walked the rest of the way home, a spring in his step. Could things get any better?

2

When Ajay got home, he hugged his mother, Nitesh and Bimala. He looked at them adoringly. They gave meaning to his life. But looking at their emaciated faces also made him sad. Nitesh was eight years old but, at barely more than three feet six inches tall, he was short for his age, even by slum standards. Bimala was nine years old and a little taller, but also far too short. At four feet six Ajay was head and shoulders above them, but still small for his age. His mum was a little over five feet tall, but looked shorter, as if she was weighed down with a massive burden. She was not even 30 years old, but her hair was beginning to turn grey. Ajay remembered how youthful and full of life she had been when his father had been around. Now she had a crease in her forehead, running vertically between her eyes. He noticed that the more she worried and the more tired she became, the deeper it got. She worked most mornings as a cleaner, which he knew exhausted her and increased the pain in her bad leg, but they needed every rupee they could get. They needed more food. This made him feel useless and miserable when he dwelled on it.

But today was not a day for misery. It was a day to celebrate. All three of them gasped in delight when he brought out a small cardboard box. They all knew the mataiwallah's shop at the end of the street, with the delicious looking sweets in his window. The small squares in their bright colours denoting chocolate, besan, pistachio or just plain milk. The top layer of silver, or the sprinklings of coconut, chopped pistachio and chopped almonds made them look even more irresistible. They frequently stopped to look in the window, but never got too close – the mataiwallah's wrath was legendary. They would look with longing as they saw people come out of the shop with the small boxes emblazoned with his logo. The last time any of them had been able to partake in those pleasures was when their father was alive.

He opened the box. In it were four pieces of jalebi and four besan ladoo.

A tear ran down his mother's cheek. "Beta, you are good to us. Your father would have been proud of you."

He went over to her, wiped away the tear, and kissed her gently on the cheek. "Mummyji, why don't you make some chai?"

He's old before his years, his mother thought. *It's not fair to steal the childhood of someone that good.* Before she burst into floods of tears, she busied herself with sugar, water, spices, tea and milk as she made four very generous cups of chai.

Ajay told them about the day he had had, but with more vigour than usual. Things had got better and better, and Mr Joshi had given him an extra bonus today.

Nitesh and Bimala asked him to tell them about the foreigners at the temple.

They giggled and his mum smiled as he told them – not for the first time – about the rich American tourists who all looked the same with their perfect teeth, manicures, immaculate hair and designer clothes. They were all ever so polite and tipped generously.

The hippies were more interesting. They all thought they were different, but they had uniforms, just like the rich Americans. Some wore colourful clothes they had bought since landing in India – the kind of clothes that had some Indian influence, but were aimed at

Westerners. Others were dressed in what they had got in Thailand, Indonesia and all the other places they had gone to before getting to India. There was another set who wore half-ragged t-shirts and shorts. The young ones hardly ever tipped. Some of the middle-aged ones were as hard as nails as well. Hippies fell into two camps. The ones who would never spend money if they could get away with it – these ones would haggle over a couple of rupees and go wherever there was free food. Then there were the ones who really wanted to make the world a better place – they were the ones who tipped. They were easy to spot – they looked good-natured, were mainly middle-aged and often a little plump.

His mother, Bimala and Nitesh all laughed more and more as he spoke. He told them how he paid extra attention to the big tippers, but was careful not to be rude to anyone. His sister and brother carried on laughing, but his mother just smiled and nodded. He was clever. How had someone that young have such wisdom?

They carried on laughing until Ajay realised it had gone 10pm – well past Nitesh's and Bimala's bedtime. With the giddy state Nitesh especially was in, it would take ages to calm him down enough to get him to sleep.

They were all settled down by 10.45. Ajay could hear Nitesh's rhythmic breathing as he slept soundly.

Ajay could not sleep. His mind was racing. At last, life was good. Initially, he had felt incredibly guilty about killing Anand, but the joy it had brought everyone at the temple had lifted a lot of his misgivings. He still felt bad, but what choice had there been? It was either Anand or Ajay and his family. Even if he had begged Anand, it would have made no difference – Anand would probably have killed him for daring to speak to him. However, no amount of reasoning completely shifted that horrible feeling in the pit of his stomach.

He tried to put it all to the back of his mind by thinking about what he could do with the money. Maybe he would get Saksham to make a bed for the mattress he and Nitesh slept on. He could buy a couple of chests of drawers, so all the clothes would not be in piles on the floor – it would be nice not to have them saturated with the smell of cooking. Maybe he could paint downstairs where his mum and Bimala were and, in time, upstairs where he and Nitesh were. It would be much nicer than the chipped mess that was currently on the walls. A TV would be good for his mother, whose bad leg meant she could not get out much...

He was drifting in and out of sleep, dreaming, day-dreaming, thinking, when he was suddenly woken up. He quickly realised he had heard glass breaking. He sat up and looked at the window in his half-dazed state. Moonlight was streaming through the threadbare curtains, but they were not moving. It must have come from downstairs. He sniffed involuntarily. The air smelt acrid. Smoke. Then he noticed a yellow light coming from downstairs. Fire! In the name of Ganeshji...

Quick! Move! Hurry – no time to lose...

He shook Nitesh roughly awake, who opened his eyes sleepily. Ajay forced him to sit up by grabbing his shoulders and wrenching him upwards. Nitesh looked at him as if to ask "What...?"

"Fire! Get out! Fire!"

Nitesh came to his senses and ran downstairs. Ajay followed.

"Go into the street and shout for help!" bellowed Ajay.

The fire had only caught hold at the far end of the room, where it had engulfed the kitchen area and was beginning to lick up the wall. The fire starter had a good throwing arm.

Ajay ran over to the mattress and knelt on it, grabbing his mother's and Bimala's shoulders. He shook them awake. They both sat up and coughed.

"The house is on fire! Get out!"

He did not have to repeat himself. His sister ran out. He helped his mother up and half helped, half dragged her to the door.

Nitesh was shouting, "Help! Help!"

The crowd outside was getting bigger.

Someone shouted: "The roofs. Pull down the roofs!"

"Pull down the roofs! Pull down the roofs!" came the echo.

It was the first thing you had to do. Pull down the roofs of the neighbouring houses. If you did not do it in time, the fire would spread through the roof timbers and the whole street could go up.

Ajay went back in. He hesitated, but only for a second. Should he go upstairs and get the money? He could probably just about get it before the fire ripped through the floor, but, if he did, it meant leaving the butane cylinder where it was in the kitchen. If that went up, it would blow the house and a few of the nearby houses to pieces, and kill and injure a lot of the crowd outside. He had no choice.

He ran to the cylinder, which was still attached to the double cooking ring. He turned it off and looked around frantically for a knife. The wooden cutlery drawer was ablaze. There was no alternative but to drag the cylinder with the cooker attached. As he did so, the cooker, which was covered in flames due to the accelerant from the arsonist's bomb, flew off the built-in concrete worktop and bounced on to the mattress, on which it poured burning liquid. The mattress went up in a sudden roar. Ajay kept on dragging, eventually getting the cylinder and cooker outside, where several of the people who lived nearby beat out the flames with dampened cloths.

Ajay and nearly everyone else looked up as the roofs of the two neighbouring houses came crashing down. Just in time. Flames began to lick around the metal roof of the Pandey home.

Buckets of water began to get passed down through the crowd. Ajay was one of the many who threw them on to the flames.

The fire quickly died down, partly due to the water, but mainly due to the lack of fuel. Thank god that his father had built this place well, otherwise the whole street would be ablaze by now.

He turned to look for his mother. She was just behind him, with Nitesh and Bimala cuddling up to her. All three were crying.

"What happened?" she asked.

Ajay shrugged.

"How did it start?" she persisted. Ajay shrugged again, but he knew this was not enough. "I smelt smoke and, when I came downstairs, the cooker was on fire."

Mrs Pandey started to quake as she cried uncontrollably.

Ajay felt sick. How could he let her feel guilty? But how could he tell her that gangsters wanted to kill him and his family?

"Don't feel bad, mummyji. It could have been anything."

"You just said it started on the cooker. I must have left it on," she replied through sobs.

"*It's OK*. Everyone can make a mistake. Nobody was hurt."

"But where will we live?" She was barely audible through her tears.

"We have a spare room."

They all turned to see who had said that. It was a tall, skinny youth who lived down the street. He had never talked to them before, but they knew his name was Ranveer Kaushik.

Ranveer lived six houses away. He, his mum and his dad had moved into that house a year ago. Everyone down the street wondered what they did with all that room – previously, an extended family of fourteen had lived there.

There was also speculation about how they managed to afford such a big place. If you kept your ear to the ground, you might hear that the son may have some connections with Delhi's underworld. But these rumours were only ever whispered. When it came to people like that, it was best to stay out of their way.

"Thank you," replied Ajay. Out of the corner of his eye, he could see a look of terror spread across his mother's face, but she quickly covered it up. What choice did they have?

The next day, all four of them went to look at their house. The bricks were soot-ridden and the inside was non-existent. The roof had mostly collapsed, and the formerly part shiny and part rusty corrugated metal sheets were now completely blackened. So much for any hopes of retrieving the money. Bimala, Nitesh and their mother cried openly. Ajay fought back the tears – how could he have done this to his family?

By the time they got back to Ranveer's house, there were three sets of clothes waiting for each of them on the dining table. Two of the outfits for Ajay were white pyjama suits. They were all speechless. Mrs Pandey started crying again. Ajay looked up sharply at Ranveer, shocked and with a face full of questions.

"I see you coming back from work at the same time every day, looking good in your spotless pyjama suits," Ranveer answered.

"Thank you, bhaisaab," Ajay whispered, a tear rolled down his cheek. The first since the fire.

Ranveer nodded and smiled. "Stay as long as you like. It will take time to rebuild things."

"Thank you, ji," said Mrs Pandey. She went over to where he was sitting, bent over, and touched his feet. The ultimate sign of respect.

Ranveer just smiled and nodded. "Please sit down, mataji."

They all sat down at his command.

"Is the room OK for you?"

"It's wonderful!" Mrs Pandey said before she could stop herself.

When Ranveer had said "spare room", they had expected a small place where all four of them would just about be able to sleep on the floor. Instead, it had a double bed, a chest of drawers and a wardrobe in it. Mrs Pandey and Bimala had slept on the bed. There had been more than enough room on the floor for Ajay and Nitesh.

"I've put a double mattress on the floor," Ranveer said.

There was a stunned silence before Ajay was able to whisper: "Thank you, bhaisaab." Mrs Pandey went over and touched Ranveer's feet again. So did Nitesh and Bimala.

"We will move out as quickly as we can, bhaisaab," reassured Ajay.

"There's no hurry. It will take time to rebuild."

They all chatted for a while. Ranveer's mother and father came into the room for a bit. It soon became clear that they were intimidated by Ranveer. He almost talked down to them. Ajay was shocked – how could he act like that? Even if those rumours were true, he did not have to disrespect his own parents. Still, it was none of his business. Ranveer was helping him and his family in a way no one else could. That was what mattered most right now. He just hoped Ranveer would not want too much in return.

Eventually, the Pandeys went upstairs to their room. Ajay quickly got changed and hurried to the temple.

It was gone 12pm by the time he arrived. Mr Joshi looked stressed and angry.

"Where have you been?" he said with a simmering rage. He would have yelled if he could have without causing a scene.

"Sorry, bapuji, my house caught fire last night. It's completely burnt."

Mr Joshi's expression of anger was replaced by shock.

"Burnt?"

"Yes, bapuji. We've lost everything."

"I'm sorry, beta." Mr Joshi looked at a loss for words.

"It's OK, bapuji. A very, very kind neighbour has taken us in."

Mr Joshi was dumbfounded.

"I will work very hard, bapuji. I will not take any breaks."

"I will pay you what I can, my son."

"Thank you, bapuji."

That day, Mr Joshi paid Ajay twice his usual amount. Ajay smiled broadly and thanked Mr Joshi profusely. But he knew this was a one-off payment. Mr Joshi may give him a little extra each day, but it would not be enough to pay for a new home. They would have to rent now, and Ajay alone could not earn the money for it. His mother was in too much pain to work any more than she did. It broke his heart, but Nitesh and Bimala would have to leave school and start working.

When he got back, Ranveer took him through to the downstairs back room.

Ajay was stunned. Not only was there a gleaming white fully fitted kitchen with a proper cooker and microwave, but also the most incredible dining table he had ever seen. It was chrome-framed with a clear glass top. The six chairs that went with it were also chrome-framed, and had sumptuous white upholstery. The chrome and glass glinted under the overhead LED lighting. The upholstery didn't have a mark on it. Although designed for six, the table was large enough to comfortably accommodate another couple of settings.

Mrs Pandey, Bimala and Nitesh were sitting around the dining table with Ranveer's mum and dad. Ranveer pointed to a wooden chair that had been placed at the table between Mrs Pandey and Nitesh, before taking his seat at the head of the table.

"How was your day, beta?" Mrs Kaushik asked.

"It was good, thank you, auntiji," Ajay replied, slightly taken aback.

"Your mother says you work very hard," Mr Kaushik chimed in.

Ajay blushed. "I just work at a chai stall, uncleji."

"That's good, honest work – especially at a temple. Your mother's told us that you have some tales to tell about it..." There was an expectant, mischievous glint in his eye as Mr Kaushik said this.

Ajay needed no more prompting. He immediately launched into his descriptions of the tourists. Everyone laughed and listened in fascination as he regaled them with tales of the hagglers and the tippers. He spoke of Mr Joshi with a reverential respect, which was well received by Ranveer's parents.

The chit-chat continued across the table as they all got to know each other. It was like when the Pandeys ate together, only better. However, Ajay could feel Ranveer carefully assessing him all the time they were sitting there.

Eventually, the food and the conversation ran out. Mrs Pandey made some excuses and was about to shepherd her family upstairs when Ranveer said: "Ajay, stay. I want to talk to you."

The command could not be disobeyed. A shot of adrenaline put Ajay's teeth on edge. He managed to nod and smile. Everyone else left the dining room.

"What happened last night?" Ranveer asked with no preamble. His usually harsh voice took on an increased underlying menace.

"We're not sure. Maybe mummyji left the cooker on and it set fire to -"

"I was playing on my PlayStation with the volume low. I heard glass breaking and, two minutes later, your brother is shouting in the street. Tell me what happened."

Ajay sighed. "I think someone threw a petrol bomb into the kitchen."

"Why?"

Ajay shrugged resignedly. "I don't know."

"Things like that don't happen here. Nobody tries to kill you – especially your whole family – for no reason. You must have upset someone."

Ranveer looked even more intimidating than usual. Ajay could not think of any more lies to tell him. If he tried, it would come across as childish and almost rude. He could not afford to have Ranveer throw him and his family out on to the street.

"I think it was Bhatti the phonewallah," Ajay said at last.

"What, that fat idiot with the phone shop!" Ranveer quietly exploded, looking even more angry.

Ajay nodded, trying not to grin at Ranveer's description of Bhatti.

"Why?" asked Ranveer.

Ajay hesitated. He could weave an elaborate tale, but that would take some doing. If he tried to do it off the cuff, there would be holes in it which anyone with half a brain would see through. It was best to tell the truth.

"Have you heard of Daksh Anand the gangster?" asked Ajay.

He was surprised when Ranveer nodded. Was Anand that well known, or was Ranveer even more well-acquainted with Delhi's underworld than people said he was?

"Well, he began to threaten Mr Joshi. He's an old man, and Anand was demanding protection money which Mr Joshi can't afford. It meant he had to cut my pay. We need the money – mummyji's too ill to work much."

Ajay looked up at Ranveer, who nodded. Those hard eyes had some sympathy behind them, that same humane glint Ajay had seen the previous night.

"So I found out where he lived -" Ranveer looked startled. "And I went to his house late at night. I rented a phone from Bhatti, and he was able to see I was there when Anand died. Bhatti reckons I killed him."

"Did you?"

"No! I was just watching when his car came off the road." Ajay's heart was pounding as he said this. He hoped Ranveer could not hear it.

Ranveer nodded grimly, staring at Ajay.

"Honestly, I had nothing to do with it. I was just watching." There was no way Ajay was going to confess *that* to anyone.

"What did Bhatti want?"

"Half my wages."

"The thieving bastard!"

"That's what I called him," grinned Ajay.

"Did you?" Ranveer said, smiling uncontrollably.

"I told him that I'd tell the police it was him who did it - it was his phone."

Ranveer nodded, clearly impressed.

"I also frightened him off," Ajay continued, getting into his stride. It was such a relief to feel good about himself after all that had happened.

"How?" Ranveer looked bemused.

"I told him that, if I murdered a powerful gangster like Anand, what did he think I'd do to someone like him?"

Ranveer looked shocked, and then impressed. "What did he say?"

"He just looked like a frightened, fat mouse."

Ranveer grinned and nodded again. "You're good at this... I'll talk to Bhatti."

Ajay took this as a dismissal and left the room after saying "Thank you, bhaisaab." He should really have touched Ranveer's feet, but there was no way he was ever going to do that for anyone.

Ranveer nodded again, but to himself. This boy had guts and dignity...

∼

All the Pandeys slept well that night. The events of the last two days had exhausted them in every way possible.

Ajay crept downstairs the following morning, careful not to disturb Ranveer's family as he let himself out to go to work. As he stepped outside, a rat ran over his foot. It made him shudder. Normally it wouldn't have bothered him, but, after the relative comfort of Ranveer's house, it was too much.

When he got home that evening, the two families were gathered around the dining table again. Ajay expected that things would be a little subdued compared to last night, but he found the opposite. Mr and Mrs Kaushik seemed to love having Nitesh and Bimala around.

Again, Ranveer told Ajay to stay behind.

"Your brother and sister are making my parents very happy," he said.

Ajay hardly dared breathe. What was he supposed to say? "Yes, they are."? All the replies he thought of could be looked on as arrogant. He just kept his mouth shut.

"I visited Bhatti today."

Again, Ajay said nothing.

Ranveer threw a wad of rupee notes tightly bound with two elastic bands on to the table. Ajay stared at it.

"He gave you this."

Ajay's eyes opened as wide as saucers.

"I had to persuade him, but it didn't take long."

Ajay felt slightly sick. He was pretty certain that Ranveer's methods of persuasion would not have been gentle. But it was no more than that bastard Bhatti deserved.

"He told me what happened. He didn't burn down your house. That chicken shit wouldn't have the balls. He told Mahesh Bakshi – Anand's enforcer – that you killed Anand."

Ajay nodded.

"He actually gave you twice that." Ranveer pointed at the bundle. "But I kept half."

Ajay nodded again. This seemed fair. A little on the high side, but half of a lot was better than all of nothing.

"What will you do with the money?" Ranveer asked.

Ajay picked up the bundle and flicked through it. There was more than twice as much as he had taken from Anand's wallet. It would probably be enough to rebuild the house.

"We'll use it to rebuild," Ajay answered.

"What then?" Ranveer asked.

"I'll work for Mr Joshi." Ajay looked confused. What else would he do?

"And how about Bakshi?"

Ajay looked even more confused. What about Bakshi?

"Do you think someone like that won't burn your house down again? Or do worse..."

Ajay physically flinched. He had not thought of that.

"That's a lot of money," Ranveer said, nodding to the bundle in Ajay's hand. "You could move out of Delhi."

That thought made Ajay sad. His parents and grandparents had lived here. Everyone and everything he knew was here. He could not just go somewhere where no one knew him and he had no friends. This was a slum, but it was his life.

"I don't move because everyone I know is here," said Ranveer. "I could easily rent one of those fancy apartments that are everywhere now, but what would be the point? Those high caste bastards with their fancy jobs would despise me – a dalit drug dealer."

Ajay looked shocked.

"You've heard the rumours?" Ranveer asked.

Ajay slowly nodded.

"Here I'm a big shot. Because people are scared of me, they respect me. In the fancy apartments people would be scared, but they'd hate me. A dalit, whose very shadow sends you to hell," he sneered.

Ajay nodded again. It made sense.

"Do you want me to take care of Bakshi?"

Ajay stared at him, wide-eyed, mouth open.

"I could kill him. Nobody would know," assured Ranveer.

"Mahesh Bakshi is stupid," Ajay said.

"*What?*" Ranveer was confused by the reply.

"He's very stupid. May I have your phone for a minute please, bhaisaab? There's an interesting bit in a newspaper I want to show you."

Ranveer handed the phone to Ajay. Ajay brought up the article he had found on Bakshi and handed the phone back. Ranveer read it with interest.

"Only somebody stupid would be caught that much," observed Ajay. "Can I have your phone again please, bhaisaab?"

Ajay located one of the articles on Anand.

"Do you know who's running Anand's gang now, bhaisaab?" Ajay asked after Ranveer had stopped reading.

"Bakshi – he was Anand's deputy."

"It looks as if Anand took him on because he's not cunning enough to be a threat," Ajay said after a short while.

Ranveer snorted and shook his head in astonishment. "Bhatti said you were nothing but a pipsqueak. But he couldn't be more wrong. You're a smart guy."

Ajay continued, buoyed by the compliment. "Do you know what types of business Anand did, bhaisaab?"

"Drugs and protection. Mainly drugs – heroin."

"Was he a big deal in Delhi?"

"One of the bigger ones," Ranveer replied.

"Bigger than you, bhaisaab?" Ajay asked tentatively.

Ranveer nodded.

"Why don't you take over?" Ajay suggested.

"What!... *How?*"

"If Bakshi's in charge, he's probably the best leader they've got, but he's stupid. If you kill him, there won't be anyone else to take over. Whoever takes over will either be too weak or even more stupid than Bakshi. The gang will fall apart, and someone else will move in. Better you take over than let that happen."

"How old are you, Chotu?" Ranveer demanded.

"13, bhaisaab."

"Were you an army general in a previous life? I've never spoken to anyone like you before."

Ajay couldn't help the grin that spread from ear to ear. But then he began to look worried.

"Will you take over the protection rackets, bhaisaab?" Ajay asked pensively.

Ranveer shook his head. "Why would I? You spend a whole morning wandering around, getting a few rupees here and there. At the end of the morning, you end up with virtually nothing. What's the point? It's better to spend the time on the PlayStation."

Ajay's relief was palpable.

3

Ranveer's parents were overjoyed when he was born, even though his mum nearly died giving birth to him. Some doctors who occasionally visited the slums for free, but not many. Mrs Kaushik was lucky that one was nearby that night. He was able to stop her bleeding and save her life. But it meant she was not able to have any more children.

Ranveer loved playing with the other children in the area. They nearly all had brothers and sisters. Ranveer liked to watch when the older ones looked after their little brothers and sisters. He often wished he had a little brother to look up to him.

He could never understand why, but he always felt angry. It was an irritation in his head which he could never get rid of. When he played cricket and was bowled out or dropped a catch, he cried. He felt embarrassed, but he could not help it. As he grew older, he managed to control the crying, but he would argue and shout. One time, when he was bowled out, he threw the bat at a boy who was laughing at him when he saw how angry he was. It just missed his head. The boy whose bat it was took it and ran home. The others went off as well. He had managed to destroy a nice day. But he did not care – he felt angry.

After that, the children did not let him play with them. They would tell him they did not want him because he spoilt the games by arguing and fighting.

One or two, however, seemed to respect him. They were frightened of him, but it was as if they wanted to be with someone powerful. One of them was Dev.

School made Ranveer even more angry. Why did so many kids have to be nasty just because he lived in a slum? They had more than he did. Wasn't that enough? It was not his fault. It got to the point that, if anyone said anything at all about him being from a slum, he would punch them. Some kids did it even more just to bait him. He was always in trouble for fighting.

When he was ten years old, his parents were called in. He always remembered the headmaster saying: "We try to accommodate all children from all backgrounds, but there are some behaviours which children come here with that we cannot tolerate."

In other words, slum children were savages. Ranveer wished he had punched him in the face.

He lasted at school until he was 12 years old. By then he had had more than enough.

He was big for his age and managed to get a job in a dhaba, clearing and cleaning the tables. Most of the customers ignored him, but some treated him like vermin.

"Hey, boy, clean this table again," was the line that riled him the most. But, by now, he had more control over his temper.

The owner was OK, but Ranveer *hated* being told what to do.

He had been there two years, and he was telling Dev how much he disliked it, when Dev told him about a friend who had talked to him about heroin dealing. It was easy money. All you had to do was stand in your place, and customers came to you. At the end of the night, you gave the money to the gangmaster, and he gave you your cut. Apart from that, you were left alone. Dev's friend could introduce them to a gangmaster.

They met the gangmaster the next night. He said he was after two boys. You could make more money in one night's dealing than one week at the dhaba. They listened to every word he said.

Ranveer did not go to the dhaba the next day. Instead, that evening he met up with the gangmaster. He took Ranveer to what he said was his spot at Sadar Ganj. That night, Ranveer made what he could have made in four days at the Dhaba. Easy work, fewer hours and four times as much money. He never went anywhere near the dhaba again.

He got used to the desperate junkies with hollowed-out eyes and skeletons for bodies. Some craved it so badly that they shot up right in front of him. Ranveer always found it fascinating how they could control their shaking long enough to inject directly into one of their few veins that had not collapsed.

The gangmaster (nobody knew his name – they all called him Cheenee Wallah) had told Ranveer and Dev to get a knife and *practice using it* if they wanted to work for him. Best advice Ranveer ever got.

The shakers were OK. If they did not have any money, all they did was plead. They offered to pay you next week or suck you off for a fix. Ranveer just ignored them. They soon moved on.

The ones you had to worry about were the ones who looked crazy. They were on edge like the shakers, but you could see they were going to do more than just beg. If they came too near a kick in the bollocks would usually be more than enough to send them crawling away. But then there were the few who were able to dodge that (probably through experience). They would rush you, with a gleam of victory in their eyes. The first time that happened, Ranveer stepped to one side, got his knife out and slashed the junkie's arm as he flew past. A deep cut. He shrieked.

"Shut up and get lost before I cut your balls off!" Ranveer rasped. He never came back.

The trick was to make your mark, but not to kill. You did not want a dead body on your hands.

Within a month, Ranveer moved his family from one room to two rooms. His father asked him where he got the money. Ranveer told him it did not matter: they were eating properly now. Mr Kaushik simply nodded.

Ranveer saw other boys come and go, but he and Dev stuck at it. As you got the reputation of always being there, you got more regulars, meaning things got easier and the money got better.

After three years, Cheenee Wallah got a machete in the head. It was a risk everyone in that trade took, but the bigger the fish, the greater the danger.

Mr Anand came down himself to sort things out. Ranveer had heard rumours about this Mr Anand, but it was the first time he had ever seen him.

"Ranveer?" he said as Ranveer came to Cheenee Wallah's bungalow at the appointed time.

"Yes, sir," Ranveer replied.

"Have you heard what happened?"

"Yes, sir."

"I need a replacement." Mr Anand looked him straight in the eye as he said this. (Cheenee Wallah's assistant looked at Mr Anand – he obviously thought that the job would be his. Fat chance – he had all the presence of a maggot.) Ranveer knew if he broke eye contact or said the wrong thing, he would be finished.

"Do you want me to start now?"

Mr Anand nodded.

Ranveer soon found that there were more than enough hungry kids who wanted to make good money. But most did not have the stomach for it. They were the ones who looked innocent and nervous. You could toughen up the innocent ones. The nervous ones got over it by turning into psychopaths. But when they were both, they did not have a hope.

Others would try to run off with the heroin. You soon got a feel for who they were as well. They looked sly and were always incredibly "friendly" as soon as you met them. This was not a social club.

Cheenee Wallah used to take anyone. That meant a massive turnover of staff and a fair amount of lost product. Ranveer found that a bit of patience worked better. The hungry kids kept coming. It mostly didn't take long before suitable replacements for the inevitable casualties turned up. It meant some pitches were not staffed at times, but when they were, they produced far more money.

Ranveer and Dev increased profit by 25% in less than a year. Mr Anand was impressed. Ranveer's family moved again, but this time to a whole house, where the rooms were much bigger. A bedroom for him, one for his mum and dad and a spare one which Dev sometimes stayed in.

His mum was happy. She quit her job repairing motorcycle tyres and spent her time looking after the house and mixing with the women in the area. Life was good for her. But his father refused to stop working at the laundry. Ranveer often saw him out of the corner of his eye, looking at him. He probably resented Ranveer taking over as head of the house. Hard luck. Anyway, he had nothing to complain about. He ate better than he ever had, and he had a proper bed to sleep on instead of a mattress on the floor.

Who would have thought that the next major change would have been due to a 13-year-old kid? But it was.

A buzz had started when Anand had died. His car had come off the road. Everyone was talking about who could have done it, but the next day, the police said that it had been an accident. Nobody believed this. Of course Anand had been murdered – there were so many people after him. But then the police report was leaked, and the word on the street was he was drunk and took a corner too fast. The car flipped over and, being too arrogant to wear a seatbelt, Anand had fallen on to his head and broken his neck. There were no punctured tyres or any other signs of foul play.

Everyone was gossiping about who would take over – Mahesh Bakshi was bound to. He had been like some kind of faithful Doberman, but more so. When Anand could not be bothered or was too busy to do something, he would send Bakshi, who would carry out his orders meticulously.

Within 48 hours, word was out that Bakshi was in charge. No doubt, in time, he would come around trying to make his mark. Ranveer wondered what he was like. He had only seen him once, and then he did not say anything.

Sure enough, before a week was over, all the gangmasters got messages saying Mr Bakshi would be visiting them over the next few days.

Even though he was only 13 years old, Ranveer discussed this with Ajay. He knew he would get the best advice from him.

"Treat him with respect, but put a GPS tracker under his car," was Ajay's considered opinion.

Ranveer looked at him, confused.

"You don't want him to think that you don't respect him..."

Ranveer nodded. That bit was obvious.

"By putting a tracker on his car, you'll see where he goes, and the best place to kill him." Ajay's heart was beating hard as he said this. He could not believe he was advising on how to murder. But, if he did not, Bakshi would murder him and his family.

"I looked at trackers on the internet when I was staking out at Anand, but they were too expensive for me. You can get them at Sharma's Electricals on Main Bazaar, Paharganj."

Ranveer sent Dev to Paharganj the next day.

As promised, Bakshi turned up a couple of days after that. Of course, Ranveer was told when he was going to turn up and to make sure he was there, ready and waiting. Bakshi was *far* too important to be kept waiting.

Ranveer got Dev to wait outside the bungalow (which they had taken over after Cheenee Wallah's death), hidden out of sight. They both knew what Bakshi looked like. They would both keep a look out for the car arriving. As soon as Ranveer saw Bakshi, he would send Dev a text.

Bakshi turned up just after 8pm. Ranveer sent the message. But there had been no need to – Dev had already spotted him.

Bakshi was alone. Before he had time to reach the door, Ranveer had opened it. Bakshi came straight in. As he shut the door, Ranveer saw Dev emerge from his hiding place.

"You know Mr Anand is dead?" Bakshi asked without preamble.

"Yes, sir," replied Ranveer.

"I've taken over," Bakshi said, prodding himself in the chest. "And things are going to be different." He paused for effect.

"Mr Anand was soft. He let you lot get away with too much. If you don't sell enough, you pay for it. If someone runs off with what I give you, that's your fault" – he jabbed his fingers towards Ranveer's face – "and you pay for it. If it happens too much, you're out."

"Yes, sir," Ranveer said meekly.

"You're not as bad as some," Bakshi conceded, "But don't let it slip."

"Yes, sir."

"Where's your sidekick?"

"Dev – he's out making sure everything is OK with the boys, sir."

"Good. Keep up the good work, and we'll get along fine." This was supposed to sound authoritative but Bakshi came across as if he had a bit part in an amdram gangster play.

"Yes, sir."

Pleased with his performance, Bakshi left without another word. He drove off, presumably to perform his set piece in front of another gangmaster.

Dev waited until Bakshi was well out of sight before letting himself into the bungalow. The building was small – the front door opened directly into the living room/kitchen. At the back was a smaller room and a bathroom. It was in a fairly secluded spot. Anand had bought it for the sole purpose of giving the Sadar Ganj gangmaster somewhere to conduct his operations from. The windows were barred, and the front and back doors reinforced. When Ranveer had taken over he had put in cameras to cover the outside so they could spot machete-wielding maniacs. The place was sparsely furnished. Ranveer made sure that it was well known that nothing was kept there overnight, and that the inside and outside were monitored with cameras that linked straight to his phone. It was basically little more than a shell of an office from where to do business.

The following evening, Ranveer played an audio recording of the conversation between him and Bakshi to Ajay. Ajay burst out laughing.

"He sounds like he's 12 years old – he's *playing* at being a gangster."

Ranveer grinned – that hit the nail on the head. There was no way anyone would take Bakshi seriously.

"You will have to move fast though, bhaisaab. People will be laughing now, but they'll get used to him and he'll slowly learn what to do. He'll build up loyalty."

As always, Ajay was right.

Ranveer looked at the app on his phone which told him exactly where Bakshi had been ever since Dev had attached the tracker.

The previous night, he had made another 17 stops, all in Delhi, and all to the east of the River Yamuna.

Over the next three days, Bakshi visited a unit on an industrial estate in Greater Kailash a couple of times a day, often spending a long time there. He used most of the rest of the time going to shops and bars in East Delhi – maybe these were the most lucrative when it came to extorting protection money. At the end of most days, he went to a residential address just outside Greater Kailash – presumably where he lived.

Ranveer considered leaving a car with a camera across the street from the industrial unit, but he quickly decided against it. It was too obvious: even Bakshi would be able to spot that.

In the end, he drove past the unit on his motorbike, wearing his helmet with the darkened visor. It was only a small unit, but why would he need a large one? The one next door was a bit of a mess with a few rusty fridges dumped outside it. Perfect...

Ranveer's next stop was Sharma's Electricals. There he bought a standalone camera with night vision and a five-day battery life. All it required was a SIM card, and then he could have continuous transmission straight to his mobile phone. It was a little bulky, but it was black.

Much later that night, with his bike parked well away from the industrial estate, Ranveer crept into Bakshi's neighbour's yard. He had his hood up, just in case. He put the camera amongst the fridges. He looked at it from a distance. It was completely camouflaged amongst the mess. He checked the image it transmitted to this phone. The whole of the front of Bakshi's unit was visible.

Whenever he had a moment, Ranveer reviewed new footage of the unit. He fast-forwarded through, looking for any activity. Apart from Bakshi's two daily visits (about 10am and 6pm), there were always two men in the building. One pair worked from 8am to 8pm, and the other pair covered the night shift. All four were muscular giants.

The first thing of real interest was when a larger Mercedes pulled up to the unit two days into the surveillance. The shutter was opened immediately. This gave Ranveer his first view of the inside. From the angle the camera was at, a bank of four screens was visible – they seemed to be connected to two cameras at the front and two at the back of the building. Bakshi could be seen sycophantically greeting the emerging driver of the car just as the shutter went down.

Later that day, a Maruti pulled up to the shutter and, again, was let in straightaway. Ranveer recognised it as the car that was used to deliver his supplies every three days. Sure enough, he got a delivery within half an hour of it leaving the unit.

Business went on as usual for the next few days. However, when the Maruti next dropped off supplies to Ranveer, Dev was ready with a tracker. Not surprisingly, it visited the same addresses Bakshi had visited after giving Ranveer his "pep talk".

The next time the Maruti did its rounds, Ranveer could see that it made one drop before it got to him. He had nearly all the information he needed. Time for action...

It was 8pm. At this time, Bakshi often went to a bar in Hauz Khas. When he was there, he did not leave until at least 11, and then he would head home. Ranveer checked the tracker – he was at the bar. Ranveer and Dev got into Ranveer's car at about 10.30 and headed towards Bakshi's flat, parking a little way away from it. They waited patiently, with Ranveer watching his phone. Bakshi left the bar at 11.18. Ranveer waited until he was quite near home before driving into the car park serving the complex Bakshi lived in.

Bakshi parked in his allotted space. Ranveer and Dev got out of the car and headed towards him as quickly and silently as possible. Ranveer reached him just as he turned around, aware that someone was approaching. Ranveer stabbed the prongs of a stun gun into his chest, just above where his shirt was unbuttoned and pressed the trigger. He kept it pushed into him as he collapsed to the ground. He did not remove it until he had stopped spasming and his eyes were closed.

They quickly covered the inert body with a dark cloth and dumped it into the boot of Ranveer's car.

Ranveer watched him slowly come around. He was naked except for his boxers. His ankles were each tied to the legs of the chair, forcing his legs apart. His wrists were tied together in front of him. A rope securing them to the bottom of the chair meant he was covering his groin. Yet another rope was tied to his neck, forming a noose. Ranveer now went behind him and pulled on that rope, forcing him to sit up straight. He then secured that rope to the back of the chair.

Bakshi blinked. He looked at Ranveer. Surprise registered on his face. He did not say anything – the gag was stopping him.

"Hello, Mr Bakshi, sir," Ranveer said without the slightest hint of irony in his voice. "I hope you are comfortable."

Bakshi tried to say – or, rather, shout – something, but the gag muffled his efforts. He tried to struggle but soon gave up. He looked drained and, no doubt, the effort would have sent pain shooting through his chest, as well as cause the noose to restrict his breathing.

"Would you like some water, Mr Bakshi?" Ranveer asked.

Bakshi glared at him, but then seemed to melt. He nodded as best he could.

Ranveer cracked open an ice-cold bottle of still water, inserted a straw and went over to him.

"I'm going to remove the gag so you can drink. Don't shout for help or try to bite or spit. Do you understand?" The question was delivered with a sharp slap to the chest at the exact spot where Ranveer had used the stun gun, which had left behind two small, deep burns.

Bakshi jerked violently as pain tore through him.

"Do you understand?"

Sweating and eyes watering, Bakshi nodded.

Ranveer removed the gag and put the straw into Bakshi's mouth. He did not stop drinking until the bottle was empty.

"If I leave the gag off, will you behave yourself?"

Bakshi nodded.

"The correct answer is 'Yes, sir'." Ranveer raised his hand as if ready to slap Bakshi's chest as he said this.

"Yes, sir!" Bakshi said quickly, wincing.

Oh, good – he was a coward. It would make life much easier. Ranveer sat back down opposite him.

"Do you know why you're here?"

Bakshi shook his head.

Ranveer raised his hand.

"No, sir!"

Ranveer smiled.

"It's simple. I want your business. We can either do this the painful way, or the easy way. It's up to you."

Bakshi glared at him.

Ranveer got up and slapped him on the chest, a little harder than last time. He cried out in pain, but was careful to arch his back. The rope around his neck had nearly choked him last time.

By the time he was able to sit still, he looked exhausted.

Ranveer picked up Bakshi's phone from a small table to the side of him.

"Don't you love these modern phones? All you have to do is remove someone's thumb, and you've got permanent access to them."

Bakshi looked terrified.

Ranveer laughed. *"Don't worry* my dear boy," he reassured. "I've unlocked it and put in a four-digit pin. It's now more my phone than yours."

Bakshi glared at him again.

"You must stop doing that, or I'll have to slap you again. Would you like that?"

Bakshi winced.

"Well, would you?"

Bakshi shook his head slightly.

"I can't hear you."

"No, sir," he whispered.

"Sorry?"

"No, sir," he said clearly, any signs of hostility flattened out.

"I've found out a lot from your phone. Who the gangmasters are and where they live. You were kind enough to put your accounts on it as well. Useful, if a little incomplete. But I won't hold that against you. It's bound to take a little time to get up to speed after Mr Anand's death."

Bakshi glared at him again. Ranveer ignored it and carried on.

"You were also kind enough to put your mum and dad's address in here as well."

Bakshi froze. He was no poker player.

"Ahhh, you care for them, don't you? I've no doubt, if I torture your mum in front of your dad, they'll tell me about any brothers and sisters you have."

Bakshi was about to shout when Ranveer put his finger to his lips. Bakshi said nothing.

"Now, my dear boy, remember what I said about shouting?"

Bakshi was silent.

"Do you?" Ranveer was talking to him in the same gentle manner you would use to kindly tell off a small child.

"Yes, sir," he whispered.

"Good. Now, the problem is there are hundreds of names on your phone. I could go through them all and find out who your suppliers are and get the phone numbers of the gorillas you use to guard your nice little industrial unit, but that'd be tedious. So, why don't you make my life easier and tell me who they are?"

In reality, time was of the essence. If nobody contacted Bakshi's security, they would smell a rat when he did not turn up as usual in the morning.

The glare was back again.

Ranveer got up and slapped his chest. But he seemed ready for it this time. He jerked briefly and his back arched, but he made no noise. Sweat poured down his face and dripped on to his shoulders and chest, but he looked defiant.

Ranveer grabbed hold of his hair, pulling his head backwards, and forcing the gag into his mouth. He then left the room.

He came back a few moments later with a blow torch. He sat down and lit it.

He stood up, went over to Bakshi and held it in front of his eyes. Bakshi pulled away the best he could, a look of utter terror etched into his face.

Ranveer lowered it. It hovered an inch away from Bakshi's belly, which Bakshi involuntarily pulled in. Ranveer singed a few hairs on it, allowing the heat to travel upwards to the wounds on his chest. Tears began to roll down Bakshi's face. Ranveer lifted the blow torch up to level with Bakshi's eyes, and turned it off. He then quickly brought it down, so the hot, glowing end made contact with Bakshi's left thigh. He screamed through the gag.

Ranveer sat down and patiently waited for Bakshi to stop screaming and writhing about. He then went over and removed the gag before sitting down again.

"Those names, please," Ranveer said gently.

Bakshi just closed his eyes and tilted his head backwards.

"Next time I won't *play* with the blow torch!" Ranveer rasped as he kicked Bakshi in the left shin. Bakshi jerked his leg, causing the burning on his thigh to multiply. He screamed.

"If that doesn't work, I can get your mother in here and torture her to death in front of you and your dad."

Bakshi stared at him, too shocked to look scared.

"You're an amateur Bakshi," he rasped. "Now tell me what I want to know."

Bakshi looked defeated. Ranveer was careful not to grin. Any sign of gloating may give this bastard more fortitude.

Bakshi told him the names of the four security guards. Additionally, he gave him the name of their supervisor, Dilip, who also made the deliveries to the gangmasters. Ranveer knew him by sight, but had never known his name. Bakshi had one supplier, Dewan, whose courier visited once a month. The next visit was due tomorrow.

It was nearly 3am. Ranveer put the gag back into his mouth and left the room, closing the door behind him. Dev was asleep on an old, wooden-framed manji (cot). Ranveer woke him up.

"Get yourself a coffee," Ranveer ordered. "I'll tell you when to come in."

Ranveer went into the room and looked at Bakshi, who closed his eyes in response. Ranveer went over and untied the end of the noose so it was no longer fastened on to the chair. Bakshi let his head fall forward, grateful that he could stretch his back, which cracked.

Ranveer got an ice-cold bottle of water from the cool box next to the table. He held it against the burn on Bakshi's thigh. He watched as some of the lines lifted from Bakshi's face. He then opened the bottle, inserted a straw, took out the gag and allowed Bakshi to drink.

After he had finished the water, Ranveer took a couple of Snickers bars out of the cool box.

"Do you want to eat?" Ranveer asked, holding the bars up.

Bakshi slowly nodded.

Ranveer unwrapped a bar and held it up, allowing Bakshi to bite into it. He ate that bar quickly, only marginally slowing down for the second one.

"Do you need the toilet?"

Bakshi nodded. Ranveer took the stun gun out of his pocket. Bakshi looked at it, but there was no fear in his eyes, only resignation.

"I'm going to untie your legs. If you try anything..." Ranveer held the stun gun in front of Bakshi's face.

Bakshi did not say anything.

He did not need to.

Ranveer gagged and blindfolded him before cutting the ropes securing his ankles. Finally he severed the rope tying his hands down. His wrists were still bound together.

"Up!" ordered Ranveer, taking tight hold of the noose at the back of his neck.

Bakshi slowly got up.

"Walk!"

Bakshi managed to put one foot slowly in front of the other, but there was a pronounced limp on his left leg.

Standing behind him, Ranveer used his grip on the noose to guide him to the bathroom, where he manoeuvred him to stand with his back to the toilet and pulled his boxers down.

"Sit."

When Bakshi had finished, Ranveer put some toilet paper in his hands. Reaching down, Bakshi wiped himself. Ranveer smiled. The ultimate in humiliation. This was a broken man.

Ranveer led him back and secured his hands and ankles again. He did not bother with the noose. He then sat in his chair and just watched Bakshi.

Bakshi closed his eyes and was asleep in seconds.

Ranveer got Dev to sit guard, set his alarm for 7am and fell asleep on the manji.

∼

When Ranveer woke up, he had to force himself to sit up. He was exhausted. He opened the door to the back room. Dev turned around. Bakshi was still asleep.

Ranveer closed the door and made four cups of coffee. He took one into Dev.

He then sat by himself, slowly drinking a cup. He began to come around. He then drank another cup. He was feeling better. Much better.

Picking up the remaining full cup, he went into the back room.

"Go and get his shirt."

Dev scurried off, and was back in seconds with Bakshi's shirt on a hanger. He hung it on a hook on the back of the door, and went to sit on the only other chair in the room, in the far corner, behind Bakshi.

Ranveer put a straw into the coffee before putting it on the floor next to Bakshi.

He removed the blindfold and shook Bakshi until he woke up. Ranveer waited until he came round a bit. He sat up and stretched the best he could.

"Good morning, my friend," Ranveer said, removing the gag. "Coffee?"

Bakshi looked at the cup Ranveer was holding in front of him and sipped at it. When he realised it was cool, the whole cup disappeared at remarkable speed. He belched afterwards. Ranveer grinned.

"OK, time for business, my friend." Ranveer took a lighter out of his pocket, ignited it and held it two inches from the now blistered burn on Bakshi's thigh.

Bakshi began to sweat. "Please…" he desperately murmured.

Ranveer put the lighter away. "No problem. All I need you to do is video WhatsApp your head of security and tell him you've sold the business to me – Ranveer Kaushik. I'll be stood here so you can show him my face. Do you understand?"

Bakshi nodded.

"What's my name?"

"Ranveer Kaushik, sir."

"Drop the sir. We don't want any mistakes when you're speaking to your head gorilla.

"After that, you're going to phone your supplier and tell him the same thing. You're going to tell him I'm taking over straightaway and the delivery is to go ahead tonight."

Bakshi shook his head.

Ranveer got his lighter out.

"No, I don't mean that!" Bakshi said in panic. "I mean he won't deal with you unless he knows you! You could be the police."

Ranveer looked thoughtful. "Hmm... How do I convince him?"

Bakshi shrugged.

"Your head of security knows I'm a gangmaster," Ranveer said suddenly. "He's seen me often enough. Would Dewan listen to him?" Ranveer was now sitting opposite Bakshi.

Bakshi shrugged. The shrugging was beginning to irritate Ranveer. "Mr Dewan has never met him. The courier has seen Dilip, but they've never spoken."

Ranveer was silent for a while. "It's up to you to convince Dewan. Tell him I'm a gangmaster and I worked for Anand for a long time.

"Where do you keep your money?"

Bakshi looked up at him sharply. A look spread across his face which seemed to say, "You must be joking."

Ranveer got out his lighter.

A bead of sweat dribbled down Bakshi's forehead. "At my flat."

"Where in your flat?"

"In the living room. There's a safe underneath the rug."

How original.

"Key or combination?" asked Ranveer.

"Key."

Ranveer looked at him questioningly.

"It's in the kitchen, in a bag of frozen peas in the freezer."

"Looks like we're in business. Get the shirt," Ranveer ordered, turning to Dev.

Ranveer took the shirt and handed Dev the stun gun.

"Dig it into his thigh next to the blisters."

Bakshi took a sharp intake of breath as Dev did as he was told.

Turning to Bakshi, Ranveer said: "I'm going to take the rope off your neck and release your hands. I'm then going to help you on with your shirt, and then I'm going to tie your right hand down. You're going to make a video call to Dilip. You're then going to phone Dewan. Do you understand?"

"Yes, sir," Bakshi replied, almost automatically.

"If you try anything, Dev here will stun you. If you fuck up the phone calls in any way, I'm going to torture your mum to death in front of you, and then torture you to death in front of your dad. OK?"

"Yes, sir."

Dilip answered straight away. "Hello, sir."

"Dilip, this is Ranveer Kaushik. He's a gangmaster, and worked for Mr Anand for a long time. I've sold my business to him." Ranveer stood there, stony-faced, as Bakshi positioned the phone so Dilip could see him.

"Is everything OK, sir?" Dilip sounded concerned, with a slight edge of suspicion in his voice.

"Oh yes, yes," Bakshi said a little too enthusiastically, repositioning the phone so Ranveer was out of shot. "Like two sweet ludoo."

Dilip nodded.

"It's too much for me. I'm retiring," Bakshi continued in the same light tone. He might not be the sharpest of guys, but he was not a bad actor.

Dilip nodded again. It was clear from his expression that even Bakshi's own head of security thought of him as thick.

"Mr Kaushik will be in later today." With that, he ended the call.

Ranveer took the phone from him.

"What was that about ludoo?" asked Ranveer, sitting down.

"It's our code," replied Bakshi. "Two sweet ludoo means everything is OK. Three ludoo means I need help."

"OK. Dewan next."

This was a voice call.

"Yes," answered a clipped, angry-sounding man.

"Hello, Mr Dewan, it's Mahesh Bakshi here."

"I know. What do you want?"

"I've sold my business."

There was a silence.

"Who to?" Dewan said at last.

"Ranveer Kaushik."

"Who's he? Never heard of him."

"One of my gangmasters."

"*What?*" bellowed Dewan.

"He knows what he's doing. He worked for Mr Anand for many years." Bakshi was beginning to look bewildered.

"Where did a gangmaster get the money to buy you out?" Dewan demanded.

"He knows what he's doing -"

"You've just said that."

"I've got to leave town," Bakshi said desperately. "I'm in trouble."

"You're so stupid, Bakshi. What have you done?"

Bakshi didn't know what to say.

"Is he there?" Dewan demanded.

"Yes, Mr Dewan."

"Put him on the phone."

"Hello, Mr Dewan," Ranveer said.

"Which area do you manage?"

"Sadar Ganj."

There was a silence. Dewan was probably looking at a map.

"Give me your address."

Ranveer dictated the address of the bungalow.

"Your phone number."

Ranveer gave him that as well.

"OK. Somebody will be there this afternoon. Have the money ready." With that, he was gone.

That gave Dewan enough time to make some enquiries. It would also give Ranveer enough time to meet up with Dilip and then pick up the money from Bakshi's flat.

It was becoming more and more obvious that Anand had not been a big shot. He was just one of the minions in the heroin hierarchy, only one level above Ranveer. Ranveer had looked on him as some kind of unassailable god, just like the street boys looked on Ranveer. But he had only been marginally less expendable than Ranveer. It did not matter, though. Ranveer made more than five times as much as he paid all his street boys, and it looked like Anand had made many more times that. That was all now Ranveer's.

The meeting with Dilip was brief. There was nothing much to see. The main part of the industrial unit was empty, apart from the small bank of screens and a couple of chairs. There was an office at the back, to which he had the key. He unlocked the smallish safe in the corner of it. It contained 23 100g bags of heroin. Tonight's order would boost that to 73. Most of the 19 areas got through about a bag every three days – only a few did more than this. That made just under 5kg a week. To the uninitiated, that did not seem like a lot – by volume, it was no more than a small bag of chapatti flour - but it would make Ranvier rich very quickly.

Next, he went to Bakshi's flat. He emptied the crammed safe – it contained more than three times what he needed for tonight's order. He also helped himself to a couple of blankets.

When he got back, he fed Bakshi a couple more Snickers bars, gave him some water and took him to the toilet. He then forced Bakshi into the attic, where he made him lie down close to the edge of the hatch on the blankets he had got from the flat. He tied his ankles and wrists together, gagged and blindfolded him. He then got Dev to sit on a chair placed directly below the hatch, stun gun in hand, after issuing him with very precise orders, which he got Dev to repeat back to him three times.

They had to wait more than four hours before the same Mercedes that had visited the industrial unit pulled up outside the bungalow.

Dev immediately stood on the chair, stabbed Bakshi in the back with the stun gun and pulled the trigger until Bakshi was completely inert. He then gave Bakshi a hard shove, so he rolled well out of sight into the darkness. He pulled the cover over the hatch, jumped off the chair and tucked it under the small dining table. A few seconds later, the doorbell rang.

Ranveer opened the door. A man in a suit with a briefcase glared at him.

"Mr Dewan sent me."

Ranveer let him in.

He walked in and stood briefly, looking around. He opened the bathroom door and looked in. He then went to the spare room, which he, again, examined from the doorway. He looked up at the hatch to the attic. He glanced down at his suit. He looked at Ranveer, carefully watching him. Ranveer tried to maintain a neutral expression, even though he was aware was beating slightly faster.

"Open it."

Ranveer stood on a chair and slid the hatch cover open. He jumped down and stood on one side, hoping that this open invitation to clamber into the attic would have the opposite effect.

Dewan's associate approached. Maybe this had not been such a good idea...

Luckily, a small cloud of dust floated down before the associate reached the chair. Instead of climbing on to the chair, he took his phone out and, using it as a torch, examined the attic from where he stood. When he had finished, he switched off the torch and made a call.

"Everything seems to be OK."

Ranveer and Dev could hear a voice speak into his ear, but could not make out what it was saying.

The associate took the phone from his ear, glared at Ranveer and held it out towards him. Ranveer, slightly put out at this idiot's arrogance, came over and took the phone.

"Hello."

"Have you got the money?" It was the familiar harsh tones of Dewan.

"Yes."

"Give it to him. He'll give you the product. I'll phone you on Wednesday 12 o'clock. Minimum order 2kg. Delivery on Thursday at the unit. *Always* have the money ready."

This was not the kind of person you asked, what would happen if you did not have the money ready? If before Ranveer had played with wolves, he was now playing with tigers.

"OK."

Ranveer gave the money to the man, who did not bother counting it. Instead, he opened his briefcase, put the money into it, and took out a carrier bag full of small packets wrapped in brown parcel tape, each about the size of a pack of playing cards. He left it on the table, walked out of the bungalow and drove off.

Ranveer went over to the carrier bag, took out one of the packs and whistled. Dilip's next round was tomorrow. That should bring in 30% more than Ranveer had paid out. He was rich. A grin spread from ear to ear.

"What are we going to do about...?" Dev pointed to the ceiling.

"Get me a chair," ordered Ranveer.

He got on to the chair and clambered into the attic. Dev moved the chair in anticipation of what was about to happen.

Bakshi's inert body came flying down. Dev rolled it out of the way and put the chair beneath the hatch. Ranveer let himself down.

Ranveer went into the back room and got a piece of rope. He wrapped it around Bakshi's neck and pulled on both ends as hard as he could. He only let go when Bakshi had stopped breathing for well over two minutes.

Ranveer sat on a chair. Dev was sitting on the other chair, from where he had been watching. Neither made a sound.

Dev closed his eyes. He got up, went to the toilet, to which he did not shut the door. Ranveer could hear him retching.

What was the big deal? Dev had regularly taken care of violent junkies on the street. This was just one step further. It was just business. You had to break a few eggs to make an omelette.

Ranveer made two cups of coffee and put one on the dining table in front of Dev. Dev gently rocked back and forth as his coffee went cold.

Ranveer stood, perched against the sink as he sipped at his coffee, searching through Bakshi's phone for any more useful information, and occasionally glancing up at Dev.

The light began to fade. When it was dark, Ranveer got the same dark cloth they had used the night before, and covered the body.

"Help me move him," Ranveer ordered.

Dev stopped rocking and looked up. He seemed to come to his senses.

He helped Ranveer load the body into the boot of the car.

They went back into the bungalow. Ranveer picked up the delivery.

"I'm going to Narora reservoir. I've told the boys not to come tonight," he said gruffly before disappearing into the darkness, wondering whether it had been a good idea to tell Dev his destination.

4

They had been at Ranveer bhaisaab's for nearly a month. The meals together were lovely. Ranveer's mum and dad absolutely doted on Nitesh and Bimala. But Ajay felt guilty and ashamed.

Mr Joshi was being very generous with his bonuses, but the Kaushiks refused to take any money from Ajay or Mrs Pandey. They both tried offering at least every few days during the evening meal, but all three Kaushiks would turn them down in unison. Ajay tried approaching each of them individually, but it made no difference.

Ajay's father had always worked hard, and had frequently told Ajay never to be indebted to anyone – that way, you leave the door open for them to treat you with disrespect. It is better to be poor with dignity than be someone's monkey on a chain.

Would they ever be able to move out? Ranveer was right about Bakshi – it was only a matter of time before he tried to kill Ajay and his family again. The safest place they could be was right here. Ajay felt guilty and frightened. How could he have put his family in such danger?

Nitesh and Bimala quickly adapted to the situation, loving the attention they got from Mr and Mrs Kaushik. They also loved playing on Ranveer's PlayStation.

However, Ajay could see how devastated his mother was. She had lost *everything*. When he came home, he would frequently find the children on the PlayStation but, when he went upstairs into their room, he would find Mrs Pandey with red eyes. She smiled whenever she saw him, but such sadness lay beneath those smiles. The crease between her eyes had become even more pronounced – she looked much older.

Ajay's work was suffering. He could not attract customers like he used to. He tried his best to smile brightly and be engaging, but he was too distracted to make anything other than a superficial effort. Mr Joshi tried to be patient, but Ajay knew it was only a matter of time before Mr Joshi lost his temper, and it would not be long after that that Ajay would lose his job.

He had to do something about it.

With a supreme effort, he managed to control the horrible thoughts that constantly circled around in his head. He would silently shout "Stop!" to himself when they occurred, blinking and sharply shaking his head when he did so, in order to drive them out. It took a few days, but they gradually began to fade.

His improved mood meant he was able to better engage with the temple goers. Sales went up, and Mr Joshi's frown lifted. Mrs Pandey seemed to emerge out of her darkness at the same time – her eyes were red less often, and her smiles became like they used to be.

It was shortly after this that Ranveer asked him to stay behind after the evening meal – something which he had not done for a couple of weeks.

"You can rebuild," Ranveer said.

Ajay looked up at him. "Bakshi...?"

"He'll never bother anyone again."

Ajay could feel the worry which he had managed to temporarily sit on almost immediately evaporate. This meant they could be back in their house within a month.

"Thank you, bhaisaab." Ajay said, simultaneously sighing away that burden that had sat deeply inside.

"What will you do now?"

"Rebuild," Ajay replied.

"How?"

"Get someone to do it. I've heard Kamal does a good job -"

"Do you think he will?" asked Ranveer.

"Everyone says he's good."

"You're 13 years old. What makes you think he'll be honest with you? He'll use bad materials and cut corners. It'll fall down in two years. He'll laugh at you, and so will everyone else."

Ajay was silent. Ranveer was right. He could feel the worry creeping back in.

"Let me take care of it," Ranveer said.

Ajay looked up at him.

"I'll get Kamal to do it, but I'll make sure he does it properly."

Ajay grinned. With the reputation Ranveer had there was no way Kamal would not do a perfect job.

"Thank you, bhaisaab."

Within two days, building work had started on the house. The first thing Kamal and his men did was tear down the old structure. It had been completely gutted by the fire and, as well as having soot ingrained into the bricks, it was explained to Ajay and his mum that the structure had undoubtedly been weakened by the blaze.

It took less than three days for the brickwork to be completed. Next came the roof. Ajay was keen to go inside to see the progress, but was not allowed in as it would be too dangerous. This did not ring true as the men seemed to happily wander in and out, with nothing more than sandals, shorts and t-shirts on. But he did not argue – mainly because he did not want word to get back to Ranveer.

It was just over two weeks, as the evening meal was drawing to a close, when Ranveer announced: "Your house is ready."

There was a stunned silence from the Pandeys.

"Do you want to look at it?" he asked.

"Yes," Ajay eventually almost whispered.

All seven of them went over. Ranveer gave Mrs Pandey the key. She took one step in and was frozen to the spot. She did not recognise the place. Along one wall were fitted kitchen units with a built-in sink and cooker top. In the middle of the room was a beautiful wooden dining table and four chairs. The wall opposite the kitchen units had a TV on it. Beneath it was a PlayStation, which Nitesh immediately ran over to.

Even the walls and ceiling were transformed. So smooth and perfectly painted, they almost glistened. The floor *did* glisten. The tiles looked amazing.

But the room was shorter. At the end of it was a door. Bimala opened it. She nearly fell over. A bathroom. *A bathroom. A fully functioning bathroom with a rain shower and a sit-down toilet.* Before they had washed from a bucket beneath a cold water tap in the far corner of the kitchen, and used communal toilets. They had got used to using the bathroom at the Kaushiks but had never expected this.

Suddenly Ajay ran upstairs. The other three followed. They all stopped at the top of the stairs. Instead of one big room, there was a narrow hallway with two doors leading off it. Ajay opened the first door. The room had two single beds with a narrow but tall chest of drawers in between. All the furniture looked to be of the same high-quality dark wood the dining table and chairs were made from.

Mrs Pandey opened the second door and went in. Ajay, Bimala and Nitesh followed. The room was identical. They all hugged each other the best they could in the small space between the beds. Mrs Pandey and the two children were crying. Ajay managed to hold back his tears.

By the time they came downstairs, the Kaushiks were sitting around the dining table, grinning.

"You like?" asked Mr Kaushik.

Nitesh and Bimala ran over and hugged him, and then Mrs Kaushik.

Mrs Pandey bent and touched Ranveer's feet. When she stood up, she put her hands together and bowed her head slightly. Ranveer smiled and also put his hands together.

"Why don't you stay the night and move in tomorrow?" suggested Mrs Kaushik.

Nitesh and Bimala's faces immediately fell.

Mr Kaushik laughed. "We'll help you move your things across. There's food in the cupboards and the fridge."

Mrs Pandey looked confused. She looked at the kitchen. Beneath the counter was a fridge. *She actually had her own fridge.* She started to cry again. Ajay laughed and went over and hugged her.

It did not take long to pack. All they had were clothes, which all fitted into half a dozen carrier bags.

Ajay went over to Ranveer's house when his parents would be in bed.

"Thank you, bhaisaab," he said, handing over the money Ranveer had got out of Bhatti.

Ranveer smiled and said, "Keep it."

Ajay looked confused. That was a hell of a lot of money for anyone, and the building work would have cost much more. In truth, Ajay was worried about how he would be able to pay for it all.

"You advised me wisely, Chotu. That's your reward."

Ajay was dumbfounded.

"But you've already helped us so much, bhaisaab," he said at last.

"That's nothing," Ranveer said, looking at the money with mild arrogance. "You deserve it."

Ajay immediately understood. Ranveer had taken over Anand's operations as Ajay had advised, and things were going very well.

"Thank you, bhaisaab," he said quietly.

5

"Hello, Ajay." Ajay turned from handing the money from the latest sale to Mr Joshi, a smile ready to greet his next customer. It was so gratifying that so many people knew him by name.

He managed to maintain his smile when he saw Deepika standing there in her school uniform, but was at a loss as to what to say. The last time he had seen her was months ago. He had often thought about her, vividly remembering that brief touch of her hand, and wondering why she and her parents did not come to the temple anymore. But then Anand had come on to the scene, and she had been knocked out of his mind.

"Deepika..." he managed at last. "It's been so long. Where have you been?"

She smiled weakly. "We go to a different mandir now. My mum was not happy about the way you looked at me."

Ajay flushed.

"It's OK," she said quietly. "I've thought about you a lot since then." This was obviously an understatement.

"So have I," he replied in the same whisper.

She nodded. "My parents don't know I'm here, but I don't care."

Tears came to her eyes as she said this, but she managed to control them.

Ajay felt a tugging on his pyjama suit leg. He turned around. There was a chai waiting on the ground. He picked it up and handed it to Deepika, who took it and slowly sipped at it, closing her eyes briefly.

"What would they say if they knew you were here?" Ajay asked in a quiet tone.

She was silent.

"They haven't mentioned you since we stopped coming here," she said, her voice returning to a near normal level. It was said a little too brightly. She was lying.

Ajay just looked at her.

"They were worried for me. No parent wants their daughter to get involved with a boy." She was talking nervously, almost gabbling. This was probably what they had said to her, but Ajay and Deepika knew the truth. There was no way her parents wanted their beautiful, middle-class, high caste daughter's head turned by a dalit, slum dwelling (where else would he live?) chai boy.

Ajay felt another tug on his trouser leg. He turned to find another cup of chai. He took his time picking it up. He did not look at Deepika as he sipped it.

"It took a lot to come to see you, Ajay," she said gently.

He only then realised that he had been lost in angry thoughts, recalling Ranveer's words of how the middle-class, high caste flat dwellers looked on the likes of them as vermin.

"I know," Ajay replied, quickly coming back to his senses. "Thank you."

"Take a break."

Ajay turned to look at Mr Joshi, whose words had broken the awkward moment.

"Take a break," he repeated.

"But I have just been on a break –"

"You didn't take long enough. Take a break," he ordered with a bad-tempered flick of the hand.

Ajay smiled and turned back to Deepika, who was also smiling.

Ajay led the way to his usual, secluded resting place.

"How have you been?" she asked as they sat down on a couple of large pieces of hewn stone, a respectable but still intimate distance from each other.

"Our house burnt down," he replied simply.

"*What!*" she almost shouted, her voice going up several octaves.

Just as Ajay had hoped, it was enough to shock her out of any anger she felt towards him. He now had her full attention.

"My mother thinks she may have left the cooker on. Luckily, I smelt the smoke and got everyone out before it burnt down."

Deepika nodded, still looking shocked.

"But we lost everything... Luckily, a neighbour let us stay with him, and so many people in Paraharavi helped us rebuild." He felt himself blush more deeply than he ever had – how could he make such a faux pas as to mention he lived in a slum?

"You're so lucky," Deepika replied. "Where I live, the neighbours would sue you for being so careless."

Ajay smiled weakly. She was such a sweet girl.

"The new house is much better. The walls almost shine. My little brother and sister are so happy."

"You have brothers and sisters?" she asked enviously.

"Just one of each."

She nodded. "There's just me. It's up to me to make my father's dreams come true," she said with only the slightest resentment in her voice.

"Doctor?" asked Ajay.

"Lecturer. Dad always dreamed of being a university lecturer."

Ajay could not help but think how lucky she was. At least she did not have to be the breadwinner for her family. But he said nothing. She was clearly unhappy with what was expected of her. It was hard, and he did not have the opportunities she had, but he was proud to live up to his responsibilities.

"Do you live far away?" he asked.

She shook her head. "About a kilometre."

"Did you walk?" he asked. He also wanted to know what her home was like – was it large or small? a detached house, a bungalow or an apartment? But those were questions he could not ask.

She nodded. "I live in a flat," she said, as if she had read his thoughts. "Three bedrooms – we have more than enough space for us."

He nodded. Just as he had thought.

They chatted some more, with Ajay telling her about Bimala and Nitesh, and regaling her with the stories about fat cat American tourists, hippies and the rest. The sound of her laughter lifted his heart.

She felt boring as she told him about her father being a civil servant, and how they had just bought a new car. Her parents did not mind if she went to the mall with her friends a couple of times a week, provided she kept well ahead in her studies. They probably thought she was at the mall now.

As she talked, she put her hand in front of her on the flat surface of the stone. Ajay put his hand on top. She closed her eyes and stopped talking. Ajay edged a little closer. She opened her eyes suddenly and blushed.

"I've got to go," she mumbled.

Ajay nodded, wondering if he should apologise.

After she left, he could not get what had happened out of his mind. His previous good mood went into reverse – it took days for it to begin to lift.

But he felt his heart grow lighter when she came back to the temple the following week.

"Hello, Ajay, I'm sorry," was the first thing she said.

Ajay felt a tug on his pyjama leg. He turned around. Mr Joshi dismissed him with a flick of the hand.

They went to the secluded spot. Deepika sat closer to Ajay and put her hand out on the stone. Ajay put his hand on top. She looked at him. He shuffled forward a little. She smiled.

They talked about what had happened in their lives recently. She told him about the girls at school and what they had been up to. He told her about chai customers, other traders and what happened in Paraharavi. They made each other laugh.

She visited once a week. Mr Joshi would make them a cup of chai each and dismiss Ajay from the stall.

They got to know each other better and became closer, but physically, nothing happened other than holding hands.

A new routine was also established at home. The Pandeys went over to the Kaushiks for meals twice a week. Just like when they lived there, Mrs Kaushik and Mrs Pandey prepared the food together.

Ajay managed to get Mrs Pandey to quit her cleaning work. He told her that Mr Joshi had given him a pay rise and she did not need to work anymore (in reality, he intended to use the money from Bhatti, which was enough for the Pandeys to live in relative luxury for two years even without Ajay's wages). It did not take much persuading – Bimala had often told Ajay how tired and in pain their mother looked after a morning's cleaning.

Mrs Pandey got into the habit of inviting Mrs Kaushik over at least once a week for chai and samosas. Sometimes, Ajay could hear their laughter from down the street as he made his way home.

A little over two months after the Pandeys moved back into their own place, the Kaushiks moved to Greater Kailash.

Apparently, Ranveer had bought a house there and showed his mum and dad only when he finally owned it.

When Mrs Kaushik told Mrs Pandey, she burst into tears. So did Mrs Pandey.

"It's a beautiful house," said Mrs Kaushik. "But I'm going to miss your lovely family."

"We'll miss you as well," Mrs Pandey replied.

"You must come to visit." Mrs Kaushik gently squeezed Mrs

Pandey's hand as she said this. Both women smiled through their tears.

Later that evening, Mrs Pandey told Ajay the news. He was startled. In less than three months, Ranveer had made enough money to build a luxury house for the Pandeys *and* buy a house in Greater Kailash? He desperately wanted to see the house. Was it as large as Anand's?

Within a few days, his wish was granted. Ranveer picked them all up in his new, shiny, black Range Rover. It turned quite a few heads as they drove through Paraharavi. Ajay knew it was only a matter of time before Ranveer was wearing heavy gold jewellery.

Although the house was slightly smaller than Anand's, it was certainly bigger than any of the houses around it. It shouted, "I'VE ARRIVED!!!" There was no way anyone could look down on the person who lived there.

Inevitably, Mrs Pandey and Mrs Kaushik grew apart. Instead of meeting three or four times a week, they were lucky to see each other every ten days. Mrs Pandey's friendships with the other women in the area grew now that she was not constantly exhausted and in pain due to work, but none matched the closeness she had had with Mrs Kaushik.

Another thing happened. Ajay grew. A mixture of hormones and a much improved diet meant he shot up and broadened. His voice also broke. He was far stronger. Deepika was impressed with the change, commenting on it more than once. But it was not all good news. He could no longer attract the customers to Mr Joshi's stall with his cuteness. He was more like a slightly ungainly gorilla than a cute little kitten. Now, when he greeted temple goers, many seemed to physically back away. He tried his best, but takings fell.

He knew it was only a matter of time before Mr Joshi had no choice but to replace him.

It was not long after Ajay had come to this realisation that the

Pandeys visited the Kaushiks, and Ranveer took Ajay into a separate room towards the end of the evening meal.

"What's wrong, Chotu?"

"Everything's fine," Ajay replied lamely.

"Oh, come on, I don't think you looked this depressed even when your house burnt down. What's wrong?"

"Well, look at me..." Ajay replied, shrugging his shoulders.

"What's wrong with you? You look pretty powerful to me."

"That's the problem. I used to be a cute kitten who attracted customers to Mr Joshi's stall. Now I'm more like a wild elephant they run from."

Ranveer could not help but smile, and then laugh.

"I can see that could be a problem," he said with laughter still in his voice. "Why do you bother with that place? Come and work for me."

Ajay looked at him.

"How much do you earn?" asked Ranveer.

When Ajay told him, Ranveer looked incredulous. "How can you live on *that*?"

Ajay shrugged.

Ranveer told Ajay how much he could earn if he worked for him. It was Ajay's turn to look incredulous.

"It's easy work, Chotu. All you do is stand there, and people come to you," Ranveer reassured.

"What would I be doing?" It was a stupid question, but Ajay needed to ask it.

"Dealing in heroin," Ranveer said with controlled patience. "What do you think?"

"I know. Just had to check." Ajay looked uncertain.

"Look – Friday and Saturday are the busiest nights – you'll earn the most then. Just try those two nights for a few weeks. See how you get on."

Ajay knew it was a generous offer and, if anything went wrong, Ranveer would be there for him. He also knew that, if he turned this down now, he would be very lucky indeed to get the same chance again.

"Thank you, bhaisaab," he replied, sounding as positive as he could.

"Good. Start next week. But take my advice: learn to use a knife. You won't need it often, but you *will* need it."

Ajay felt slightly sick. But what choice did he have? Bhatti's money was not going to last forever, and he did not want to go from shit job to shit job, just about scraping by. He knew his English, with a little practice, would be as good as a Delhi University graduate's, but there were no fancy jobs waiting for *him*.

6

Ranveer made sure Ajay got his old pitch on Sadar Ganj. It was not too far from Paraharavi, and Ranveer knew he would earn good money from it.

Every evening during the week preceding the start of his new job, Ajay had gone up to his room whilst Nitesh was on the PlayStation. He had spent at least an hour practicing with the knife, following videos he found online.

All that practice had felt like a bit of a waste of time on the Friday. Most of the transactions were quick and straightforward – the customers gave him the money, and he then gave them the heroin before they quickly went on their way. It was not the time or place for small talk. However, he was repulsed and amazed by the junkies that shook like crazy, but as soon as they got the heroin, staggered into some shadows a few metres away, and were somehow able to find a vein and get the needle into it. The worst he saw was someone pass out no more than 20 metres from him after injecting themselves. They came around eventually and staggered off.

On the Saturday, he met a more tricky customer.

"I want heroin."

"Money first."

"Give it to me! I need it!" he yelled

"Money first!" Ajay rasped, trying to cover his fear.

"Just fucking give me it!" he screamed, looking as if he was out of his mind.

Ajay stepped backwards, partly from fright, partly so he could get his knife out.

The junkie was probably about 17 years old, but slightly smaller than Ajay. He lunged forward. Ajay stepped out of his way, but the junkie was determined.

Just then, the junkie went flying as someone cannoned into him, knocking him to the ground. The guy who knocked him over kicked him in the ribs a couple of times. Pausing, he went to kick him again. This just about gave the junkie the space to get up and run off.

The guy started laughing.

"Dev told me to look out for you," the guy said, getting his breath back. "Hi, I'm Rishi." He approached Ajay, hand extended. Rishi was probably about the same age as the junkie, but a lot taller and broader.

"Thanks. I'm Ajay," Ajay replied, shaking his hand.

"I know. Dev told me. I've got the spot on that corner." He pointed to a very dimly lit bit of pavement about 300 metres away. "I came running as soon as I heard that nutter. He's always around here, trying it on with new lads. He's not the only one. Have you got a knife?"

Ajay nodded.

"Good. You'll need it. Take my advice – learn how to use it. Give me a shout if you need me."

The rest of the night passed without incident, but Ajay was on his guard.

On the Friday and Saturday, he had gone to work on the chai stall as usual, and then directly to Sadar Ganj after that. On the Sunday he came home, ate and went straight to bed, barely saying a word. He was exhausted partly by the long hours, but mostly by all he had gone through. Bhatti and Anand he could handle, but crazed smack heads were in a league of their own.

Over the weeks, he got more used to the work. Rishi would sometimes come over and chat at the beginning of the night, when it was quiet. Another piece of valuable advice Rishi gave him was to injure the psychos – whatever you do, do not kill them. The police knew about the dealing in this area, but, providing it was kept low-key, they left you alone. Better it was here than in a respectable area. If dead bodies started turning up, the police would have to do something. Also, there was no money to be made from a dead junkie. Once you showed them who was the boss, they never argued. Instead, they made sure they had the money.

As time went on, Rishi told Ajay more and more about Delhi's heroin trade.

Mr Kaushik controlled everything east of the Yamuna (Ajay did not let on that he knew Ranveer). He had gangmasters like Dev up and down the area. If anyone else tried to move in, they did not live long. A cold shiver went down Ajay's spine when he heard this.

The whole of Delhi was split into areas like this, except the middle of Delhi.

"Why not the middle?"

"Too many tourists and too many cops," replied Rishi. "Going there is asking for trouble."

"But tourists have money."

"Is it worth it? 20 years in prison. There's cops everywhere. They always find out where you're dealing from. Even if you've got nothing on you, they arrest you and make your life hell."

Ajay looked thoughtful.

"You could always try dealing through the dark net," Rishi suggested after a prolonged silence.

Ajay had looked at the dark net. It was the obvious place to go to deal in anything illicit.

"Do you know how to get a SIM card without ID?" Rishi asked.

Ajay shook his head.

"If you want to start doing things in the centre, you'll need one – you don't want the cops tracing you. I can get you one."

Ajay looked at him for a while. Ajay had got to know him over the last few weeks. The price Rishi had quoted did not seem to be too out of the way. He was probably making something out of it, but that was fine. He was taking a risk – he needed a return.

"Sometimes you have to try lots of search terms until you come across anything useful. But when you do, click on it. Follow links. You'll find lots of them. Some websites charge commission – don't use them. You can be traced. Only use the ones that charge the buyer only. Don't deal in bitcoin – I've heard of people being traced. Change your SIM card and the website you deal from every week or two. The cops are clever."

"If you know so much, why don't *you* do it?" Ajay asked.

"What, and go to prison for 20 years? Dev treats me well. If I was disloyal, he'd kill me."

Ajay nodded. Some people were generals. Others were foot soldiers.

The next day Ajay had the SIM. When he got home late that night he put it in his phone and went immediately on to the dark web. He tried a number of search terms, eventually typing "heroin for sale Delhi." The first entry seemed to be of a drug dealing site. He wanted to cheer, but instead he switched the phone off and went upstairs to bed. He had to be up early the next day.

Ajay spent the next few evenings looking at websites on the dark net. He found over a hundred through which you could sell heroin, but most charged the dealer for their services, and they nearly all wanted bitcoin. But there were quite a number who only charged the customer.

Some further research showed him that the international price was over ten times what he sold it for in Sadar Ganj. But he would never get that. Westerners knew India was a cheap country. He would be very happy if he got three times as much as he currently sold it for.

The only way he would find out was to try it…

The next evening he got the metro to Paharganj. It was the first time he had been there. The only other times he had been to the other side of the Yamuna were when he had visited Anand's and Ranveer's places.

He could not believe the energy of the place. He wandered up and down Main Bazaar for a while, taking it all in. The restaurants were full of every colour of person. He was used to this from the temple but, somehow, it seemed to be amplified here.

Around the back streets were the food stalls which only locals went to. You ate your food standing up or sat on a plastic chair, joining the auto drivers.

He went back on to Main Bazaar with its shops, hotels and restaurants and their brightly lit signs. It became even busier as the street vendors set up their stalls to take advantage of the growing night time crowd. They sold everything from phone chargers to suitcases to sunglasses.

He took in the atmosphere whilst enjoying the anonymity. In the slum everyone knew your every move almost before you did. He wondered which he preferred.

The tourists in the large groups all seemed to be happy. The ones by themselves did not look anywhere near as content – quite a number looked miserable. There were some residents of Paraharavi who were unhappy, but very few compared to what he saw here. When he had seen the tourists at the temple, he had always felt a deep seated envy. But now he was not so sure. Those miserable faces were not all that different from many of the heroin addicts before they got their fix.

If he wanted to deal, this seemed the ideal area.

He decided on a website that appeared to be South American. All that time spent browsing drugs websites had taught him that North Americans put a lot of money into fighting drug dealing, but South Americans did not have the budget. He planned to wait until the following Sunday. This gave him the opportunity to get some supplies in. On the Friday he sold three grams, and on the Saturday he sold four grams. However, he told Dev that he had sold five grams on the Friday and six grams on the Saturday, paying for the shortfall out of his own pocket (his commission on sales was 10%). That gave him a stock of four grams.

He created an account on the website on Sunday morning. He deliberately kept his advert simple: "Heroin in Paharganj, Delhi. Cash. Good price. Good quality. Good delivery."

He checked regularly all day. Nothing. He could see that people were looking at the post, but that was all. He was disappointed. But things could be worse. At least he could sell what he had at Sadar Ganj next weekend.

But on the Monday he got a message. "Want 0.5g today."

A smile spread across his face when he read it. It was 4pm. He was still at the temple. The earliest he could get away was 6pm. His heart pounding, he messaged back with a price. He immediately got an "OK" back. He replied: "See you at 7.30. I tell you where."

Within 30 seconds Slim J messaged back: "OK". He smiled again.

He arrived at Paharganj at 7.10. He walked up and down Main Bazaar. Bilal's Café had some seats free.

He typed: "Come to Bilal's Café, Main Bazaar. I wear green shirt and red cap. Act like I friend. Say: Hello friend - I like cap - nice colour. Put money on bill plate and I give you birthday card with H. I there now."

Ajay went into Bilal's and ordered a can of Coke. Within three minutes a white, tall young man was sitting opposite him.

"Hello, my friend," he said enthusiastically in his North American accent. "I like the cap – nice colour. It suits you."

Ajay smiled. "Thank you."

"How are you?" continued Slim J, keeping up the pretence.

"I am fine." Ajay smiled. He caught the waiter's eye. "One Coke, and the bill."

The waiter was back in two minutes.

Ajay shifted the plate with the bill on it, so it was away from the aisle.

"I pay last time. You pay this time."

Slim J nodded, and discreetly deposited the money under the bill.

"I give tip," said Ajay. Equally discreetly, he put the money for the bill under the bill whilst removing Slim J's payment.

He handed the card over. Slim J took it out of the envelope and opened it a little. He smiled in satisfaction.

"Thank you. That's so nice of you."

"Come. We go to my house. My mother make samosa and good meal for you."

They both got their drinks and left together. They walked along for about half a minute.

"Let me know if you want more," Ajay said quietly before disappearing into the crowd.

His heart was pounding and he felt elated. He had made what would have taken him three weeks to earn at the chai stall in minutes. And this was just the beginning.

The next day he checked his phone more frequently.

"What are you doing, boy? Put your phone away. I am sick of you looking at it!" Mr Joshi reprimanded. Ajay flushed. If he carried on like this, not only would Mr Joshi get more angry, but it would attract attention, and that was the last thing he wanted.

He looked at his phone as soon as he went on his afternoon break. Slim J had put a review up: "Good stuff. Discreet and polite. Best I've had in India."

Ajay grinned from ear to ear. He was walking past a couple of stalls at the time. The stallholders gave him strange looks.

He checked again at 6pm, when he had finished for the day. *Two new orders.* He kept control of his facial features, but his heart was pounding. This was unbelievable. He sent the same reply to both: "I contact you by 7.30."

He got messages back immediately.

"OK"

"WTF! OK, but make it quick."

He looked up the meaning of WTF. He snorted.

By the time he had got to Paharganj another order had come in.

He went to a different eatery than the night before. He then sent a message to the first customer.

The deal was completed in less than ten minutes.

He went to another eatery and messaged the next one.

Again, it was all done and dusted in less than ten minutes. These junkies were desperate. Were they junkies? Ajay could not see how they could be. It would mean getting on a plane and getting here. How could they do that if they were so desperate for heroin all the time? Maybe they took it on the plane. But surely they would be searched before they got on. Maybe they just wanted to have a good time - they may have been afraid that, if they did not get there quickly, he would be gone. Anyway, it did not matter. They gave him money. That was all he cared about.

He messaged the third person: "Can you come now. I am in Paharganj."

Within three seconds he got the reply: "Yes!!!"

After completing the transaction he went to yet another eatery, but this time for a sit down and a chai. He fought the urge to grin uncontrollably and giggle by trying his best to look sullen.

He finished his chai and ordered something to eat, all the time checking his phone. By the time his meal arrived another order had come in.

He immediately messaged the price. As always, he got a prompt "OK". He replied: "Come to Sher Punjab Restaurant Rajguru Road. I wear green shirt and red cap. Act like I friend. Say – hello friend. I like cap. Nice colour. Put money on bill plate and I give you birthday card with H. Come 15 minutes. No early."

"OK" was the immediate reply.

After leaving Sher Punjab he wandered up and down Main Bazaar, checking his phone every 15 minutes. Within an hour he had another order. Another two came in quite quickly after that. As soon as he could, he went into a toilet and pulled his advert. He could not believe he had sold out in three days.

Before leaving Main Bazaar he went into a busy shop and bought twenty identical cards with an elephant on the front. He did not haggle and handed over the exact money – he did not want to draw attention to himself.

He then went into one of the many small electrical shops and bought a set of small digital scales – capable of weighing as little as 1/1000 of a gram. He also bought 500 small snap bags – the kind used for very small electrical components, but which had many other uses as well. He had been estimating and putting the stuff in torn off bits of plastic. But, if things went how he hoped they would, he needed to up his game.

His head was spinning by the time he got on the metro. In one night he had made what would have taken him nearly six months to earn with Mr Joshi.

This was amazing, but he had to keep it going. In three days, two of which were quiet, he had got through four grams. There was no way he would be able to buy the kind of quantities he needed from Dev – he would ask too many questions. He had no choice but to go to see Ranveer. He texted him.

"Bhaisaab, can I come to see you tomorrow? I need to discuss something with you."

By the time he got home he got the reply: "What time do you finish at the temple?"

"6"

"I will pick you up outside."

True to his word, Ranveer was waiting outside the temple when Ajay came out. He got straight into the Range Rover.

"Hello, bhaisaab."

"Hello, Chotu, how are you?"

"I'm fine, bhaisaab."

"What did you want?"

"Thank you for the work," Ajay said tentatively.

"That's OK. But what did you want?"

"I've got an idea," replied Ajay.

"Have you? What is it?"

"To sell to the tourists in central Delhi," Ajay blurted out.

This was met by silence.

"OK... That's really risky. There's cops everywhere. How will you do it?" asked Ranveer.

"I'll put an advert on the dark web. And I'll meet them in restaurants and bars. Tourists will pay more – much more..."

Ranveer sniggered and shook his head. "If there's anyone who could pull this off, you could. But be careful. There's cops everywhere there."

Ranveer gave Ajay a price which was 20% less per gram than the street junkies at Sadar Ganj paid. If Ajay bought 100 grams, he got an extra 20% discount.

The 20% discount for bulk buying was well worth it. But that would have to wait. He had got through three and a half grams in one night. He should get a week's worth. That would be about 25 grams. With the money from Bhatti, he could easily manage that.

"Do you mind if I don't carry on with Sadar Ganj?"

Ranveer laughed. "That was just a little baby step. I had plans for you, but it looks like your plans are better. I'll tell Dev. How much do you want?"

"Is 25 grams OK?"

"I'll meet you outside the temple tomorrow. Have the money."

Ranveer gave him a lift home and ate with them. Mrs Pandey and the children were delighted to see him. They all chatted and played on the PlayStation afterwards. It was late by the time Ranveer left. The Range Rover had drawn quite a crowd, but no one had touched it. They all knew it belonged to Ranveer.

The next day Ajay told Mr Joshi that Sunday would be his last day.

Although Mr Joshi shed a tear, Ajay could tell that he was also relieved. Ajay had grown even more, and it was getting to the point that he was driving away more customers than he was attracting.

"I'm sorry to see you go, beta. You're so good, and you've helped me so much. But things are getting hard for me now – I'm old. I need to slow down. I'll miss you. May Ganeshji bless you and your family. Good luck to beta, good luck."

On Sunday, after the children had gone to bed, Ajay told his mum that he had quit his job.

"Have you got another job?" she asked, even though she knew that he would only quit if he had something better to go to.

"I'm going into business."

"Who with?" she asked.

"Ranveer."

She looked at him as if he had slapped her.

"Don't worry, mummyji. You know I've always looked after you, Bimala and Nitesh. It's a good business – we'll be selling samosas on Paharganj." He added the last bit just to pacify her.

She looked at him doubtfully. "Be careful, my son."

"I always am, mummyji. It's just samosas. Ranveer said he was bored and he wanted to do something for fun. I said he should sell samosas to tourists. They're always friendly. He asked me to work with him. He'll pay me much more than Mr Joshi ever could."

Mrs Pandey smiled but still looked doubtful.

Before he went to bed he texted Ranveer: "Quit Mr Joshi today. Told mum am selling samosas with you on Paharganj."

He immediately got the reply: "They'll be the most expensive samosas ever!!!"

On the Monday morning Ajay ran an identical ad on another site, but this time he included the price. He was hoping that people would recognise the ad. The tactic worked: he had an order in less than two hours.

He immediately set off to Paharganj with ten cards containing half gram bags.

By the time the metro arrived he had another order. Maybe he should have brought all twenty cards.

Everything went smoothly and he got rid of all ten cards by 7pm.

A problem that he had not anticipated was that he was running out of eateries. They had to be large, busy, full of tourists and downmarket enough so it did not look out of place if you just got a cold drink. There were surprisingly few of these. He had already been to a number of them twice. If he went to the same ones every night it would only be a matter of time before somebody would smell a rat and tell the police. This area gave the traders good business – they did not want drugs spoiling it.

Before going home he went into an English language bookshop. It was the first time he had ever been in a proper bookshop. The few books he had were bought from street traders in Paraharavi. He took his time looking around – he felt completely at home. He opened a few fiction books. But then he found the section on Indian history. Before he knew it, he was totally absorbed.

"Hello, sir, are you buying?"

He looked up to see a balding man who was probably in his mid-40s, and had spoken English to him. He looked a little annoyed. Ajay looked at his phone. He had been sitting on the floor reading a single book for nearly an hour.

"Sorry," Ajay replied, also in English.

He stood up, with the book in his hand, quickly picked out three more books from that section and went over to the travel section, where he got a Lonely Planet guide to India. The man looked surprised and pleased when Ajay went to the counter and bought them all.

The bookshop had calmed Ajay down. He was able to think slowly and clearly. Ten bags *in one day*. It would have taken him over eight months to earn that kind of money with Mr Joshi.

At this rate he would run out of supplies before the end of the week. He should ask Ranveer for another delivery as soon as he could. The most he could buy was 50 grams (as far as Ranveer was concerned he was doubling his money – if he ordered more than 50 grams Ranveer may well become suspicious). That 50 grams would last him another ten days. Then he could double that.

He texted Ranveer.

"Need some more bhaisaab"

"Already!?!"

"Will run out on Friday. Can we meet Friday morning?"

"Friday 10am outside temple"

"OK. Can I have 50 please?"

He didn't receive a reply. He would take enough money and hope for the best.

When he got home he opened the Lonely Planet guidebook to about a third of the way in and cut into the pages. He also cut the bottom off a plastic drinks bottle. He inserted the bottom of the bottle into the cavity he had made in the book. He inserted a piece of clean, thin, white cardboard as a makeshift bookmark before closing it.

By the time he went to bed there were another three orders. He contacted them when he got up. By the time he left home he got two replies:

"Needed it yesterday – thought you were supposed to be fast. WTF!!"

"OK."

Fast was important to these people. But it did not matter – in the meantime another order had come in. He took 20 bags with him.

When he got to Paharganj, he messaged the one from last night. "I see you outside BK Electronics Main Bazaar. I wear red cap. You ask me where India gate. I give you book. Open and take H. Put in money wrapped in paper. My friends watching for cops and thieves. Come now."

He got no reply. He went anyway. He waited ten minutes. No one came. Maybe nobody would. He could not waste time. He messaged the next person.

"I see you outside Sher Punjab Restaurant Rajguru road. I wear red cap. You ask me where India gate. I give you book. Open and take H. Put in money wrapped in paper. My friends watching for cops and thieves. Come now. Send message if OK."

He got the reply "OK" within two minutes. He was still outside BK Electronics, but no one had turned up. By the time he got to Sher

Punjab there was someone there. The exchange was far quicker than messing around in restaurants.

Within half an hour he had another order. He messaged back, making sure the meeting place was five minutes medium paced walk from where he was, and nowhere near BK Electronics.

It was nearly 9pm by the time he had sold the final bag. It had worked well. Twenty locations well away from each other. However, he realised he had gone past some shops and street vendors several times. They were not always busy. In fact, some street vendors looked at him when he passed them the third or fourth time. Tomorrow he would work out a route which meant he would not go past the same place more than twice.

When he got home Nitesh and Bimala were in bed, but his mother had waited up for him. As soon as he came in she busied herself making him something to eat.

He went up behind her and hugged her as she rolled out a chapatti. She said nothing. He sat down.

Eventually, she brought over some dahl, okra curry and three chapattis. She sat down opposite him.

"Are you OK?" She looked worried.

"I'm fine, mummyji."

"How is your work?"

"It's good. We're just setting up. I'm helping Ranveer bhaiyaa fit the shop."

"*Please* be careful, beta."

"Please don't worry. Everything is fine."

"I don't want anything to happen to you. Promise me you'll stick to samosas..."

Ajay smiled and raised his eyebrows, trying to look confused and surprised, whilst putting his hand over hers. He hoped it came across as reassuring. "Of course, mummyji. I told you – Ranveer loves to talk to tourists. He wants to practice his English. I'm going to manage the shop for him. He'll come to see you when he can. He's paid me for the last two days." He took out some money – the equivalent of what he would have earnt in a week at Mr Joshi's chai stall. He pressed it into her hand as he gently held her hand in both of his.

"You're such a good boy. But *please* be careful…"

"I will, mummyji."

She smiled, despite looking worried and doubtful.

The next day was busier still. He got rid of his remaining 20 bags by 5pm. He took down his advert immediately and sat down for a chai by himself in one of the quieter dhabas just off Main Bazaar.

The most he reckoned he could physically shift was 40 or 50 bags a day. But he needed to be careful. People really would notice him if he was doing 50 deals a day. And the more he was caught with, the more difficult it would be. Besides, 20 bags made him nearly 18 months of wages at Mr Joshi's. How much more did he need? Maybe he should cut it down to 5 bags a day. But if he did that, there was no way he would be able to buy a house like Anand's…

Suddenly he remembered what Rishi had said about changing SIM cards. Ajay texted him.

"Need new SIM card. Kailash Park by stone gateway 2pm tomorrow?"

"Yes" came back the immediate reply.

Kailash Park was in a respectable area about ten minutes walk from Paraharavi and fifteen minutes walk from Sadar Ganj.

Ajay arrived about ten to two to find Rishi waiting for him.

"Let's find a place to sit," Ajay suggested.

Rishi nodded. He looked nervous. This was a well-to-do area and he probably felt out of place. But it was best to do this in the open. In this area, if you went into a dhaba everyone would listen.

They wandered into the park and sat down in a quiet spot. The sun was way past its fiercest, making it quite pleasant.

"If you see someone coming, talk about cricket. I'll do the same."

Rishi nodded. He then discreetly passed the SIM card to Ajay. Under the guise of a handshake, Ajay handed over the money, which Rishi immediately pocketed.

"How is business?" asked Ajay.

"Same, same. Everything is comfortable. How is business for you?"

"Good. *Very* good. Thank you for your advice."

"You're welcome," replied Rishi.

"Would you like to be more than comfortable? Maybe rich?"

Rishi laughed, "Who wouldn't?"

"You're wrong. His overarm is weak. I think he'll be dropped."

"I know what you're saying," Rishi said uncertainly, "But he's improving. You watch – as the season goes on he'll take many wickets."

Just then a woman and a small girl walked past.

"That's not true," Ajay replied. "It's the kind of weakness which you can't do anything about, no matter how much you practice."

Rishi nodded. They were out of earshot. Ajay turned to check.

"I have sold to tourists and made *a lot* of money. Now I want to expand – I need someone to help me."

Rishi looked away, deep in thought. He unconsciously stroked the pocket containing the money Ajay had given him. At last he looked up.

"The risk's too great."

"How about the risk at Sadar Ganj? Now you're OK, but it's getting bad there – the police will have to do something soon. Who do you think they'll come after – you or Mr Kaushik?"

Rishi nodded. The same thing had occurred to him.

"If you help me," continued Ajay, "We can look after each other. There'll be little risk. By standing at the same place every night you're asking for much more trouble. Work with me, and we'll be fine – I know how to cut risk to nothing."

Rishi nodded, thinking.

Ajay took out what Rishi would earnt at Sadar Ganj in a week and handed it to him. There was no one around and he made no attempt at hiding what he was doing. Rishi looked surprised but took the money and quickly pocketed it.

"I might need more SIM cards soon." Ajay's tone clearly indicated that he would want something, and that was unlikely to be a SIM card.

"Thank you, bhaiyaa."

Bhaiyaa... some respect.

Rishi stood up as Ajay stood up, and shook Ajay's proffered hand.

It was 10am on Friday and Ajay was outside the temple. Ranveer turned up just under ten minutes later.

"Hello bhaiyaa," Ajay said, getting into the Range Rover.

"Hello," replied Ranveer as they drove off.

They drove along in silence before stopping at a secluded area. Ranveer handed Ajay a carrier bag. In it was a small packet wrapped in brown parcel tape about the size of a pack of playing cards.

"100 grams. Pay me when you can."

"Thank you, bhaiyaa."

Ranveer nodded.

At 20 half gram bags a day, that lot should last him ten days.

"I'll drop you near where you live. I can't come in – business to take care of."

This suited Ajay just fine. He was itching to put a new advert up and start trading.

He spent every day in Paharganj. He always met his target of getting rid of 20 bags, but it was not long before he realised he had to be more careful. The ruse with the guidebook had worked well, but after a week or so, some of the traders had begun to give him a nod of recognition as he walked past. If he carried on like this, it would not be long before someone started spying on him just to find out what he was up to. Maybe he could arrange to meet customers in the bars in the area. He could pretend to show them a photo on his phone, which had a flip open cover. He could put the heroin on the inside of the cover. But if he did it too often, even if someone didn't directly see what was happening, it would become obvious something was going on. Maybe he could combine all three – eateries, guidebook and bars.

He was generally home by 9pm. The earliest he managed was 5pm. His mum would always have a meal prepared for him when he got home. It was just what he needed after dealing all day with largely anxious, irate people.

She would also tell him about all the comings and goings in Paraharavi. It was an endless source of fascination. The intricate dance of people's lives, interwoven with mutual support, conflict, work and the common problem of just trying to get by. It made such a change from the anonymity of Paharganj. At Paraharavi he mattered. The news of his new job running a samosa shop had been on everyone's lips for a few days. Here he was part of the fabric of the place. Yet he was so keen to leave. Was that a wise move?

7

The day after he had sold all the heroin, he phoned Rishi.
"Hello bhaiyaa."
"Hello Rishi. How are you?"
"Fine, fine."
"How is business?" Ajay asked.
"Same same."
"Can you meet tomorrow at 9am at Kailash Park?"
"Of course, bhaiyaa."

Ajay had worded it as a question, but in reality it had been an order.

"Bring a SIM card."

When they met up they warmly shook hands and found somewhere to sit. Rishi gave Ajay the SIM card. Ajay handed over the money, which Rishi promptly pocketed.

"Would you like to earn that every day?" asked Ajay.

Rishi looked startled – it was more than four times as much as he made working for Dev. After regaining his composure, he nodded.

Ajay knew this would mean he was poaching one of Ranveer's workforce, but Rishi was such a small player that Ranveer probably wasn't even aware of him.

"It will mean long hours," Ajay warned.

"No problem. All I do with my days is stay in bed and play games on my phone. I'm bored."

"OK. I'll contact you soon." With that Ajay stood up and shook Rishi's hand before going on his way. He liked Rishi, but was being careful to keep a distance. Rishi was going to be his employee, his lackey, not his friend. Ajay intended to treat him well – he knew the temple goers who treated the stallholders well always got better service - but he would make sure that there were no deep, personal bonds between them.

As he came out of New Delhi Railway Station and entered Main Bazaar, Ajay always felt slightly overwhelmed. It was mayhem. The cacophony of auto-rickshaws and cars beeping their horns and revving their engines was interspersed with the high pitched rings of cycle rickshaw bells. When the shops were open there were sarees, suitcases, jackets, shirts, blouses on display in the windows and out on the street. The bars, eateries and hotels sat happily amongst them all. Slightly set back from the front were small barber shops and people selling phone paraphernalia. It gave the area a hectic, cosmopolitan buzz. It was where the majority of tourists seemed to gather, and the businesses around there could get ridiculously busy. The traffic all the way down the road was non-stop, but the shops got less crowded as you went further down.

A few days before the meeting with Rishi, Ajay had spotted what he was looking for. It had been obscured by a pile of suitcases at one end and some racks of leather jackets at the other end, but it was ideal – a small, empty shop unit on a quieter part of Main Bazaar (it was not quiet, just not as frantic as by the railway station).

Ajay asked the neighbour selling the leather jackets about it.

"Empty for two weeks. Phone wallah from Gujarat was there for few months. We think he went bankrupt."

The steel shutter was down so there was no way to tell what state it was in. But that would be no problem – Ajay could soon sort it out.

"Do you know who the landlord is?"

The shopkeeper looked at his phone and read out a name and number, which Ajay typed into his phone.

He tried phoning the number a few times, before finally texting.

"I want to rent shop in Main Bazaar. Can I see tomorrow 9am?"

He got a reply almost immediately: "Yes. What is your name?"

Ameek Singh, the owner, who appeared to be in his 30s, turned up at 9.25 the next morning. He had slightly bloodshot eyes and, despite wearing well cut clothes, looked dishevelled, with his shirt not properly tucked in, the button of one cuff undone and a small stain on the seat of his trousers. He was also slightly on edge. Not as bad as some of the junkies Ajay had dealt with, but not far off. He opened the shutter and they both walked in.

Ajay looked around. It was dusty (this was Delhi – of course it was dusty) and had cardboard boxes strewn around. There were a couple of poorly constructed display cabinets and a desk. But the basic structure was sound. There was a WC at the back. Good – that meant there was a water supply.

"How wide is it?" asked Ajay.

"12 feet."

"How deep?"

"20 feet."

Ajay nodded. 240 square feet. He had been looking on the internet and knew prices were quoted by the square foot.

"How much?"

When Ameek told him the price, Ajay looked at him almost in contempt. He had spent a lot of time (mainly between customers) looking around on the internet, and had got a feel for the area. He knew a fair price for this end was a third of what Ameek had said.

"What is your real price?" Ajay asked.

Ameek repeated the same figure.

"I might be young, but I'm not stupid."

"How old are you?" Ameek obviously knew that you had to be at least 18 years old to take on a shop lease. He seemed almost scared to ask the question, as if he would get the wrong answer and not be able to rent the place out. It was enough to tell Ajay that he would come down in price significantly.

"18." He might be slightly baby faced, but Ajay knew his size meant he could pass for 18 at a push.

Ameek dropped the price by a third.

"Bhaiyaa, this is too much. I've got another three to look at."

"Nothing is available on Main Bazaar."

"There are ones as good on Besant Road, Rajguru Marg and Sang Trashan Marg."

Ameek said nothing. Ajay's heart was pounding. He had just made that up. As well as everything else, Ameek was clearly a lazy bastard, otherwise he would have known what was happening in the area.

Irritably, Ameek came down to half his original asking price.

In a reasonable tone of voice, Ajay offered him a quarter of his original asking price.

Ameek snorted. "The last guy was paying more than that."

"He went bankrupt."

Ameek was speechless for a moment. "What will you sell?"

"I'm thinking of opening a small samosa shop. This place is too big, but I'll take it if you do me a fair price."

"Samosas! This place is full of tourists. They love samosas!"

"They need mobile phones more than samosas. If the rent isn't right it won't work."

This was a verbal battle Ajay was winning, but he had to turn that victory into a good deal. The best way to do that right now was to keep quiet.

Ameek was looking increasingly agitated. Despite his wealth (almost certainly inherited), this was a guy who was not handling life well. It did not take a genius to work out that he needed to have an easy time more than he needed money.

"OK! Three months deposit. Pay on the first of each month." He sounded as irate as he looked.

Ajay nodded and shook Ameek's hand. He could feel it quivering as he did so.

Ameek took out a short, crumpled contract out of his pocket, which Ajay read and signed. Ajay handed over the deposit plus the rent for the remainder of the month in cash. Ameek gave him a receipt, the keys and his bank account details for future rent payments before walking off at a rapid pace. As Ajay watched him go he wondered. not for the first time, what it was like to be that on edge. He had no desire to find out.

He looked around, smiling to himself. A fridge, a couple of fryers, a prep table (preferably stainless steel – Westerners liked things like that) and a purpose made counter would all easily fit in here. It needed a good clean, and maybe a couple of coats of paint and some tiles where the fryers were going to go. It would not take long.

The WC was OK – it had a squat toilet which was not chipped, and a handbasin which only had a cold water tap. The boxes in the shop were all empty. He moved them into one corner. It would take next to no time to get it into shape – a couple of hours to clear the place, another day or so to do the painting and tiling. It would take a couple of days to build a counter, put in a sink and position the fryers, fridge and table. They would need a couple of stools as well. He could pay someone to do it all, but he did not know anyone who could start straightaway and, besides, he would enjoy it.

Oh, and he needed to learn how to make samosas...

He phoned Rishi.

"What time do you start work?" Ajay asked.

"About seven. When it gets dark. There are other boys who start earlier, but there isn't enough trade for all of us when it is daylight. I stick to nights because -"

"Yeah, that's fine." Ajay was not interested in boring detail. "I need some help to set up a samosa shop in Paharganj – 15 minutes walk from New Delhi metro. Can you be here by nine tomorrow morning?"

"Yeah. But I need to be at Sadar Ganj for seven -"

"Leave at four," Ajay said abruptly. He told Rishi he would be paid a quarter of the amount they had agreed upon until the shop was set up. His pay would go up when they started trading properly.

There was a pause. Rishi was processing what Ajay had said. "I'll be there at nine."

They spent most of the next two days cleaning, tiling and painting.

The fryers, fridge, stainless steel sink unit and stainless steel table were supplied by a catering equipment warehouse on Chitragupta Road. It was surprisingly easy to feed the water from the WC into the rest of the shop, and then split it into two so that there was hot water (thanks to a small inline water heater) as well as cold.

They then built a broad counter across the front of the shop. A part of it lifted up so you could get in and out. Once inside, you could lock it very securely. There was a drawer for the cash float, and a strong box attached to the body of the counter for excess cash. They built several small compartments into the counter.

There were two compartments, one on top of the other, that would have intrigued anyone. The bottom of the upper compartment was split into two and secured to the sides with hinges. The two halves were held together by a sliding bolt at the front of the shelf. When you pulled the bolt open, the two halves flapped down on their hinges. Below that shelf was a small but powerful burner with a robust pilot light. At easy access was a knob which you only had to rotate half a turn to get the burner to ignite instantly to its full blistering power. Both compartments were lined with stainless steel.

Rishi had been confused as to what Ajay had been doing until the burner was in position. Then he smirked.

"Will you put a pan of oil on the gas, bhaiyaa?"

Ajay nodded. He intended to keep the heroin on the shelf that split into two. Any sign of the police and he or Rishi would release the bolt and turn the gas knob. It would take less than half a second. The pan would always be warm due to the pilot light. No more than two centimetres of oil would be in the pan, meaning it would heat up almost instantly. The heroin (Ajay only ever intended to keep fifty half gram bags there) would be fried in seconds.

Just as they were finishing off the counter, the shop sign arrived, as arranged.

Dileesh's Samosa Joint
A Truly Fiery Experience

At the bottom of the sign was the website.

Ajay had called it Dileesh's because it sounded like "delicious". He had watched quite a few English and American films, and he knew that many Westerners would think of this play on words as "cheesy". Some would smile, but others would look down on it. Either way, they would remember it, and that was the most important thing. The word fiery, of course, had flames coming out of it.

As well as ordinary samosas, he was going to offer samosas which were extra, extra hot, so that not even an Indian with a mouth made of asbestos could eat them. He knew some mad Westerners would try to buy them – they may get a reputation as an eating challenge. But they would only be available if they were pre-ordered on the website, so that the person ordering them would have to sign a disclaimer for any injury caused. They could only get their samosa(s) if they showed the six digit order number sent to them, a copy of which would appear on Ajay's phone for cross-checking.

Alongside that, however, he would run adverts on the dark web. Customers would get their heroin by coming to the counter with a seven digit order number, which Ajay would cross-check. Before handing them the samosa with their "special sauce", a corner would be broken off the samosa. That way, when it was thrown away, it would not look suspicious. He knew how desperate these junkies could get though, so he planned to put in the adverts that they were not to throw away the samosa within fifty metres of the shop, or he would not serve them again.

After Rishi left each day, Ajay tidied up, locked up the shop and went home. He used his evenings to learn to make samosas.

When he first asked his mum for a lesson she had asked, just as he knew she would: "What, so you and Ranveer want to open a samosa shop, but you don't know how to make samosas?"

"Mummyji, you make the best samosas ever. Everyone says so. I need you to teach me everything. And it means I can spend more time with you," he said, hugging her.

She laughed and playfully slapped him on the back. "You're so cheeky."

He learnt and practiced over the next five evenings until, finally, he got nods of approval from his mum, Bimala and Nitesh. There was definitely room for improvement, but that would come in time. What he had was good enough for now for the tourists in Paharganj.

The next day Ajay and Rishi put the shop sign up leisurely. They then cleaned the place down and got in supplies, including two large butane canisters, which they hid behind a large wooden partition at the back of the shop – Ajay could never understand why people had those ugly things on display.

It was two o'clock by the time everything was in place. Ajay decided to make a large batch of samosas. He got Rishi to help him with the simpler tasks, such as peeling the potatoes and filling the samosas. When they had finished, he fried a couple of them until they were golden brown. After allowing them to cool for a couple of minutes, they tried them.

They were *good*. Nearly as good as his mother's.

"Bhaiyaa, I never knew you could cook," said Rishi appreciatively.

"Nor did I," replied Ajay.

They fried a couple more and put the rest in the fridge. By the time they had eaten them it was time for Rishi to leave.

Ajay wondered what to do. He could meet up with Deepika. He had not seen her since the day before he had stopped working for Mr

Joshi but, after so much hard work, the place was ready and he was fired up. He was desperate to open.

He put on his apron and hat and opened the shutter. To his surprise he got his first customer within ten minutes, and they kept on coming. What he found even more astonishing was that nobody seemed bothered that he was charging ten times as much as he could have in Parharavi. He had a few requests for extra hot samosas, but explained that they were not available as it was his first day and they would be available tomorrow, but would cost twice as much as a regular samosa. Again, this seemed to be fine. He knew there were lots of places not that far away where you could get samosas for less than a quarter of what he was charging, but those places were not at all attractive. It was amazing how much these rich people paid for something that just looked good. After all, one tasty samosa was just the same as another tasty samosa – it was not even as if they were going to stay and eat it there.

He closed just before nine, having sold all 52 samosas in four hours. He was stunned. He had set this place up as a cover to sell brown sugar. But it looked like the samosas were going to make a good profit by themselves.

The next day they made 100 mild samosas and 20 fiery ones. Rishi set off at 4pm as usual. Ajay opened up by 4.30.

By 10pm (he decided that would be the closing time for now) he had sold 56 mild samosas and 12 hot ones. Unbelievable.

They did not start each day until about 12pm and had a laugh making the samosas, especially when one of them (mainly Rishi) constructed something that looked hideous. It was a great way of teaching Rishi, learning himself and team bonding. Rishi always left at his usual time. The evenings were relaxed and even more fun. Ajay chatted with the tourists, and could feel his English rapidly improving. During the last three days of that first week he averaged about 70 mild samosas and 15 hot ones per night. If things carried on like that, it would mean he would make enough profit per month from legitimate samosa sales alone to buy a new motorbike. He laughed to himself when he worked that out. And he was only 14 years old.

On the last day of that first week Ajay left Rishi alone to make the samosas, explaining that he had some business to take care of. When he came back he asked Rishi: "Are you ready to do some *proper* trading?"

Rishi nodded.

"OK. Quit your job and we start tomorrow."

Rishi nodded again. He had been at Sadar Ganj for a couple of years. In that time he had seen a lot of boys come and go. They were replaced within hours – a day or two at the most. The policy seemed to be quite simple: if you did not turn up for work you were out. Even the ones who tried to phone Dev to tell him they were sick were replaced. Boys like him were like stray dogs – there were far too many to show any concern for any of them, even the loyal ones. He knew Dev would not give him a second thought by the end of the night.

That night Ajay put a copy of his old advert on the dark web.

When he switched on his phone the next morning, he had two orders waiting – people must have recognised the advert. He texted Rishi: "Go to shop now".

They were there for 10am. They had 47 mild samosas and eight hot ones in the fridge. He set Rishi the task of making more whilst he messaged the customers: "Wrap money in paper. Write on paper *******. NO CODE, NO SALE. Come to Dileesh's Samosa Joint, Main Bazaar. Near bottom of Rajguru Road. I will give you samosa. Packet with H next to samosa. DO NOT THROW SAMOSA AWAY UNTIL YOU ARE 50 METRES FROM SHOP OR NO MORE H"

Ajay then opened the hatch. Within 20 minutes both sales had been made.

The first customer looked as if he was desperate for a fix (like most of them) and Ajay knew the samosa would go straight in the bin. But the second customer seemed to be an occasional user who just wanted a good time. He may well appreciate a samosa he could actually eat after coming down. Ajay decided to give all the heroin customers mild samosa, but still break a corner off. (Who knows –

some might like the samosas so much that it could boost legit samosa sales...)

By the end of that first day they had sold six bags. Ajay got Rishi to serve them – Rishi's size was enough to deter any potential trouble makers. Also, those two years on the streets had made him a master of how to intimidate through looks alone.

By the fifth day Ajay got orders for more than 20 bags. This carried on increasing. On the eight day he pulled the ad.

Nearly a quarter of the people coming to the shop were buying heroin, and you had to be blind not to see most of them were addicts.

He wondered what he should do. He had to make changes, but he would be a fool to get rid of the shop – it was a great way to launder money.

Rishi had introduced Ajay to some people who were able to get fake IDs as well as untraceable SIM cards. This meant that Ajay was able to open six bank accounts in six different banks, all of which were at least one kilometre away from each other. In the first week he had made more than ten times as much money from heroin as he had made from legitimate samosa sales. He deposited nearly three quarters of this, evenly distributed amongst the accounts.

He used most of the rest to buy a used Hero HF Deluxe motorbike. Nothing too flashy. If people in Paharganj suspected he was dealing in heroin, a huge brand-new motorbike would be all the confirmation they needed. However, it was still by far the most expensive thing he had ever owned.

He needed to celebrate.

"Hello," answered a sleepy Rishi. It was 9.15am.

"Rishi?"

"Hello bhaiyaa." Rishi was rapidly coming to his senses.

"What are you doing today?"

"Working for you, bhaiyaa?" Now Rishi sounded confused as well as tired.

"No, you're not. You're going to see one of the seven wonders of the world."

"Sorry bhaiyaa?!"

"I've bought a motorbike," announced Ajay.

"What? When?"

"I picked it up this morning."

This was met by a silence.

"I'll be there in fifteen. We're going to Agra," said Ajay.

"Yeah, OK, sure... see you in fifteen."

Ajay rode push bikes in and around Paraharavi and had ridden pillion quite a bit. He had even raced clapped-out motorbikes a few times. All this meant that he had good road sense. But he had never been in charge of the throttle of something this powerful. He zipped past stationary vehicles, accelerating to overtake boring drivers who stuck to the speed limit. He was at Rishi's in ten minutes. He revved his engine on the quiet backstreet. Rishi came out immediately. He put on the helmet strapped to the back of the bike, sat behind Ajay and held on to him.

They flew past the familiar streets, and it was not long before they were detouring through immaculate avenues of bungalows with manicured lawns, where people came to their windows to see who was making that unseemly racket.

The further they went, the further they left behind the smells of smoke, diesel fumes, decay and chemically infused raw sewage. At last, they hit the Taj Express Highway. They were overwhelmed. TV and movies were OK, but they did not prepare you for the real thing.

A vast open road with a surface as smooth as marble. No potholes, no makeshift tents by the side, no cars parked on it. Just an endless expanse which takes your guts, your very being on a thrill ride as you twist the throttle as hard as you can, making the engine cry out in pain. A pain which takes your own away until, eventually, the screeching gets too much to bear. You slow down slightly, but are still incredibly grateful to leave that stale, putrid Delhi air behind and feel your senses come alive.

When they got to the Taj Mahal they felt stiff and tired, but exhilarated and ready to take on the world.

The sight was nothing new. Ajay had seen many pictures in books he had read. He knew Shah Jahan had built it as a memorial to his favourite wife, who had died during childbirth. He also knew the story that Shah Jahan had planned a Black Taj Mahal on the opposite side of the River Yamuna as his own mausoleum, and that he had the architect blinded were both myths.

They entered the complex through the main gate. Rishi was left speechless by the size and ornateness of it, but Ajay took it in his stride.

The fountains on the watercourse that ran through the avenue of trees as you approached were not flowing, meaning that the Taj Mahal was reflected in the water. Despite all the photos he had seen, Ajay was still taken aback. They stood there for a moment, just staring.

As they walked closer, Ajay realised that the size must have been imposing when it was built, but now it was dwarfed by many of the buildings in the centre of Delhi. As they got nearer they could see the carvings and, eventually, the inlaid semi-precious stones. Again, spectacular for the time, but the sparkling tiles on the floor of Ajay's bathroom were more impressive.

They went into the centre of the building. As they wandered through the grounds Ajay could see that Rishi was impressed, but he became increasingly bored. The place was big. The grounds were sprawling. It would have been amazing at one point and undeniably had some beauty, but it did nothing for him. He did not know why. Maybe because he wanted power and the best things money could buy. An outdated folly to a dead person ticked neither of these boxes.

When they went out they got a couple of samosas from a street vendor (nowhere near as good as theirs) before hitting the road.

Again, they tore down the highway, the adrenaline pumping the blood through their veins so quickly that they could do nothing but love being alive.

Ajay pulled off the highway and drove through the countryside, along the banks of the Yamuna, over a bridge, stopping only when he eventually found a roadside dhaba. They sat at a secluded table away from the building in the shade of a tree. They ordered a chai and a thali each. The food was good. The hottest part of the day had passed, leaving a pleasant, relaxing heat.

"Things are getting tricky at the shop," Ajay said, breaking the silence.

Rishi nodded. With so many emaciated, jittery foreigners coming to the shop, it would not take long for someone to put two and two together.

"I need you to sell the stuff," Ajay said. Rishi looked at him.

"Don't worry," he continued. "That's what I did before we opened the shop. Nobody will suspect a thing. Have you seen the number of people who just wander around Paharganj all day?"

Rishi had. He had begun to recognise some of them after a while and even gave them a nod of acknowledgement when they passed. To begin with he had speculated about what they were up to – some of them were quite smartly dressed – but he soon realised it was just part of everyday life in this part of town. Maybe they were social misfits whose only social contact were the smiles and nods they got from people like him.

"It'll be a lot less risky than when you were at Sadar Ganj," said Ajay. "I'll look after the shop. Take ten bags with you. When I get orders, I'll text you where to go. Take the money and give them the stuff. Simple."

Rishi nodded.

"When you run out, come back to the shop. Give me the money wrapped in paper. I'll give you a samosa with ten more bags."

Ajay knew this meant Rishi was taking all the risk. If the police raided the shop Ajay would fry the heroin. If they caught Rishi, it would be a different matter. But, as Ajay had pointed out, what Rishi would be doing was far less risky than his dealings at Sadar Ganj, and it paid over four times as much. But, more important than all that, what was the point of having a monkey on a chain and climbing the coconut tree yourself?

8

By the time Ajay dropped Rishi off it was nearly 4pm. Deepika would be finishing school around now. Ajay texted her. "Do you want to meet outside Shiva Mandir?" Shiva Mandir was the temple where Ajay had worked for Mr Joshi.

"When?" came the immediate reply.

"Ten minutes."

"OK ☺"

He arrived to find her standing by the gate. He pulled up next to her. She was looking pensive as she looked around – probably worried someone would see her here. He turned off the engine so she could hear him.

"Put on the helmet and get on," he said without removing his helmet.

She looked bewildered as she realised it was him, but quickly came to her senses. She was grinning from ear to ear as she donned the helmet and climbed on to the back of the bike. Instead of holding on to the bar behind her, she clung to him tightly as they sped through the streets. They both felt good.

They eventually arrived at Dileesh's Samosa Joint. He opened the shutter and let her in, closing it behind them.

"Is this where you work now?" she asked, beginning to wander around the place.

"I own it," he said, leaning against the counter.

She looked at him in surprise, and then a little sceptically.

"You own it?" she asked with suspicion in her voice.

He nodded. He had not anticipated her disbelief.

"It's all in my mother's name though." He had prepared this bit. She would obviously be curious how a 14-year-old could run a business like this. It would have been foolish to talk about fake IDs and multiple bank accounts – this kind of girl would not be impressed by things like that. If he mentioned Ranveer, although unlikely, she may have heard of him and his dealings – a surprising number of people had.

She still looked sceptical.

"How do you think I can afford a motorbike?"

Her expression softened a little as she weighed up what he had just said.

"Let me cook you a samosa," he said, going over to the fryer, deftly switching it on and dropping half a dozen samosas into the oil. He then put some water in a small saucepan on a cooking ring.

"Chai, madam?" he asked, putting his hands together and bowing slightly.

She giggled.

"Will madam take a seat?" With a flourish of his hand he indicated the stool next to the stainless steel table behind the wooden screen.

She giggled again before walking over to the stool.

He then proceeded to put tea, spices and sugar into the pan. As the water boiled he turned it down to a simmer before adding milk. He then went over to the fryer and lifted out the basket. He efficiently shook the samosas to get rid of any excess oil. He put them in the metal tray with a lifted mesh base on the bottom of it next to the fryers, before using tongs to put them on a plate. He was in time to catch the chai before it boiled over. He poured it through a sieve into two china cups. He then put the cups in front of Deepika before bringing over the samosas.

"Your feast awaits, madam," he said, bowing elaborately.

She could not help but giggle some more.

He got the other stool, which was by the counter, and joined her.

They sipped chai and ate in silence for a couple of minutes, both at a loss as to what to say next.

"Do you really own this place?" she asked at last. She clearly believed him now, but said it just to break the silence.

He nodded. "I own the business, but rent the building."

She nodded, acknowledging that she thought that was the case.

It had been over a month since they had last seen each other. He had missed her. He knew this was his chance to take things further, but he had to be careful, or he could foul things up.

"I started working at a restaurant in Connaught Place six months ago..."

"Six months ago!" she exclaimed. "I thought you worked on the chai stall..."

"In the evenings I got the metro to Connaught Place and worked in the restaurant."

She nodded, looking overwhelmed. She would never complain again about the amount of homework she had to do.

"The owner's English was rubbish, so I waited on the tables. My English got better and I started chatting to the customers. They started coming in just to see me, and the place got busier. The owner gave me good bonuses, but I knew I could do better. I got this place five weeks ago. Now someone works for me and we sell more than 100 samosas a day."

She nodded again, smiling and obviously impressed. The time was perfect to make his move. If he did not do it now, he never would. He got off his stool, gently put his hand under her chin, put his lips on hers and kissed her. His heart was pounding, knowing that she could freak out and this could be the end of it all. Instead, she responded in kind. He held her to him and, sliding off the stool, she did the same, their lips never parting. He was aroused and, judging by the heat coming out of her body, so was she.

When they finally parted, they looked at each other before hugging for a long, long time.

When he released her he was a little less turned on. He felt happy but slightly embarrassed as he looked at her. Judging by her expression, she felt something similar.

"Do you want me to drop you off at the mandir?" he asked.

She nodded.

When he got home the kids who lived on the street were playing out. They all flocked around to look at his bike. Seeing the commotion, his mother came out as well.

"When did you get it beta?" she asked.

"Today."

"Why aren't you at the shop?"

"I shut it. It's doing well and I wanted to celebrate," he said, grinning as he sat on his bike with the kids crowding in around him, looking at it admiringly. Despite the ride to the Taj Mahal and back, it still glistened beneath the dust.

Mrs Pandey seemed to almost let the burden of worry float away as a smile spread across her face and the crease between her eyes all but disappeared – it was the first time Ajay had seen that happen. "I wish your father could see you now."

A sudden sharp pain tore through Ajay's heart, but he kept on smiling. *So do I*, he thought, saying nothing.

At last he got off the bike, leaving the slum kids to look at it and stroke it. Nitesh and Bimala looked very proud.

He went inside the house. He left the front door open, letting the air circulate and the excited chatter of the children drift in.

Mrs Pandey made chai for both of them and got out a box of matai.

"Mummyji, do you know anyone who can make samosas for my shop?"

"I thought you and Rishi made them."

"We do, but we're getting too busy. We can't make enough."

"How many do you need?" asked Mrs Pandey.

"Up to 150 a day," he replied flatly.

Mrs Pandey looked at him, wide eyed with astonishment.

"I told you we were busy," he laughed. He had a lot of reasons to be happy these days. Life had changed almost beyond recognition.

"I can make them," she eventually said, quietly.

It was his turn to look shocked. "I didn't mean that, mummyji. I just thought you might know someone who could make them –"

"I can do it," she insisted.

Ajay was silent as he looked at her for a moment. She put her hand on his.

"Beta, I'm glad I don't have to clean anymore." She unconsciously touched her leg as she said this – the very thought of those days was enough to remind her of the pain she had had to endure just to make enough money to barely eat. "But now I'm bored. I love talking to people, but there's only so much you can say. I can sit here, make samosas and watch TV whilst Nitesh and Bimala are at school."

"But it's 100 to 150 samosas *every day*." Ajay looked doubtful. He had seen how much better his mum had looked since she had had a decent place to live and had stopped working. He did not want her to go backwards.

"Don't worry, beta. I can take my time – I've nothing else to do all day."

But he *was* worried. He knew she was not in the best of health, and exhaustion would weaken her even more.

"I'll pay you seven rupees a samosa," he said with sudden inspiration.

"You don't need to pay me – I'm your mother." Mrs Pandey sounded shocked.

"You can get a friend to help you and split the money with them," he said simply. It would cut down her workload and make the work fun instead of tedious.

It was Mrs Pandey's turn to look inspired. "You think of everything, beta. What were you in your previous life – prime minister?"

He would pay her a generous amount, but not too generous. If he was too generous, people might start questioning where he was getting his money from. However, by setting a rate that was at the upper end of fair, it would ensure that his mother could employ whom she liked, and he would get the reputation for looking after people in Paraharavi.

She squeezed his hand. "God truly blessed me when he gave me a son like you."

~

The next day, after leaving Rishi in charge of the shop, Ajay went off on his motorbike. He met up with his contact and bought half a dozen untraceable SIM cards. He then went into half a dozen phone shops and bought three smartphones and three basic phones. It was time to up his game.

He would take orders via smartphone. He would then text the details of each exchange to Rishi, who would have a basic phone. After ten days he would remove his advert from the dark web, smash both phones, break up the SIM cards and chuck the remains in the Yamuna on the way home, and start again.

He got a 100g packet of H from Ranveer. He would probably need another one before long. But he knew he could get it at short notice. And he did not want to tempt fate.

He was back at the shop by late afternoon. He let Rishi serve customers whilst he weighed out 10 bags in the toilet before putting up his usual advert on the dark web.

He emerged back into the shop, put on an apron and a hat before joining Rishi at the counter.

"Busy?"

"So so," Rishi replied, wrinkling his nose, "Eight mild, one hot."

It was 3pm. It was not great, but it did not matter. They had only been open two weeks. Trade would build up. Anyway, the money he made from samosa sales was not even loose change. But he needed it to be busy so he had a good cover. It would happen. If it did not, he could advertise his samosas. No problem.

Ajay passed Rishi a small, black carrier bag under the cover of the counter and said quietly: "Take off your apron and hat. Go to the toilet. When you come out, leave the shop."

Rishi discreetly nodded, understanding perfectly what was happening. Of course he did – you did not survive on the street as long as he had without being able to read the subtlest of cues.

Ajay extended the closing time to midnight. By then nine of the 10 bags had been sold.

The following day it was 15. The day after it reached 23… On the sixth day they had sold 50 bags. With only Rishi working for him, this was Ajay's limit. Two months ago this would have been the stuff of pipe dreams. If he got more street boys, what he could do was limitless. But, if he was not careful, he would end up like one of those movie drugs barons who had warehouses full of cash. With that amount of money, the police would be watching his every move, and every lowlife would do *anything* to get their hands on it. He could not think of anything worse.

With the amount of cash he was putting into his accounts, he was hoping questions would not be asked. When he had asked Ranveer how to hide his cash, Ranveer had advised him that cash deposits of up to 50% more than he was paying in would not raise any suspicions.

He wondered what to do with all the money he was making. He knew how unhappy Mrs Kaushik had become since moving out of Paraharavi. He did not want to do the same to his own mother. Mrs Pandey had her friends, and there may be some competition amongst them, but not much. Instead, they helped each other when they could. It was them against the world. Mrs Kaushik did not need any help. Instead, she was always talking about her neighbours showing off their latest washing machine or car. At first, she had despised this fickleness, but now she seemed to be doing it herself. He knew if they moved into a posh area, they would become like that as well.

How about Bimala and Nitesh? He could give them a good start in life with a top end private school. But he knew there was a good chance they would be despised and mocked. Even if they were not, no doubt there was a lifestyle that went along with those types of schools. Looking at Mrs Kaushik's experiences, that included judging people by the size of your house, your washing machine and your car. But it would impress Deepika – or would it? He had to remind himself he was only 14 years old – impressing Deepika would have to wait. For now he would just bank the cash, spending no more than he made at the shop. That was enough to live very comfortably and send his brother and sister to better schools.

Ajay regularly had to turn down heroin orders. Although Rishi was good at what he did, he could not handle more than 50 transactions a day. Ajay decided to put the price up by 50% - maybe that would dampen demand to something more manageable.

"Be careful, Chotu," Ranveer said. It was the second time Ranveer had sold Ajay three 100g bags – enough to last Ajay for more than a week. "If you get caught with more than 250 grams you could go to prison for 20 years."

Ajay nodded.

"I know you're under 16, but the cops will still lock you up for a long time."

Ajay almost imperceptibly jolted.

Ranveer waited for him to calm down before continuing. "You're doing all right, Chotu. Keep this up, and you'll be selling as much as some of my gangmasters." Ranveer sounded like someone who had been in his position for years. He came across as supremely confident and completely in control. That was what was needed to ooze authority. That and, Ajay speculated, the willingness to break legs and end lives.

∼

The shop was open from 10am to midnight every day except Mondays, when Ajay closed it from 3.45pm to 6.30pm. He would make sure he was outside Shiva Mandir by 4.15 so he could pick up Deepika. They would go to Hauz Khas to one of the many small eateries and coffee shops there. They avoided Central Delhi as Deepika and her parents went shopping there sometimes on weekends. They did not want an overzealous shopkeeper to blab to her parents about her being there with her male friend with the motorbike.

They talked more. Ajay learned about Deepika's friends and the pressure on her to do well at school. In turn, he told her about his brother and sister, and made her laugh with tales of foreigners who tried the extra hot samosas but immediately spat out the first mouthful into a tissue. He told her how the shop was getting more and more popular, but he did not want to open another one as it would be too much pressure. She looked disappointed when he said that – it seemed to offend her middle-class sensibilities.

He asked her how she was doing at school. It turned out she was top of her class for nearly everything (Hindi was her weakest subject - there were two girls who consistently did better than her). Her parents were pleased with her, but were also always on her back to do better. She was happy to try to be a lecturer – she loved studying - but wished her parents were less pushy.

After a few weeks, Ajay told her of his ambitions to open more shops, but he would wait until he was 18 years old. At the moment, the pressure on his mother of having everything in her name was too great for her. This seemed to please Deepika.

He desperately wanted to kiss her and hold her again, and maybe more but, whenever he suggested going to the shop, she blushed and shook her head. He just smiled and nodded, but his sense of frustration grew.

∼

Business went smoothly for the next few months. The increased price seemed to be about right. Some days they sold less than 50 bags, but not much less. On most days he could have sold more than 50, but not much more. Some customers bought more than one bag at a time, but the vast majority stuck to just one.

When Rishi had first started in his new role he had looked exhausted at the end of each day. This was not surprising. He had to make an exchange about every 15 minutes. That meant walking to a new location every time. However, the exhaustion was quickly replaced by a reduction in weight and a vigour which he could not recall ever having had.

It could also be tricky for Ajay. As well as texting Rishi every 15 minutes, he had to serve samosa customers. He made this easier by streamlining things. He did away with the internet disclaimer customers had to agree to in order to purchase a hot samosa. Instead, he made them less fiery. He got a heated cabinet so he could fry the samosas in batches and keep them warm. He also had an extremely efficient extraction system installed above the fryers. It was a high-end system, meaning that it was virtually silent. He kept it on all the time – it made the place lovely and cool.

When he had first asked his mother to make them, he was selling about 100 samosas a day. Trade increased, as he knew it would, but it made life difficult, as he also knew it would. Lunchtimes and early evenings were particularly tricky. He would often have a small queue at the counter which, thanks to the batch cooking, he could dispense with quickly. The problem was that it could reappear just as quickly. It made dealing with the heroin orders problematic.

When it got to the point that he was regularly selling over 250 samosas a day, he knew he had to do something about it. It was utterly exhausting. It would be only a matter of time before he made a disastrous mistake. He would either fall into a fryer or, far, far worse, end up destroying his heroin trade due to a stupid oversight.

He increased the price of samosas by 50%. He had thought about doubling the price, but he knew that would be outrageous. He wanted to cut demand, not destroy his business. Although he did not need the money from the samosa trade, he needed the cover of a steady flow of customers at the counter to make it look like a viable business.

The price increase did meet with a few complaints from locals, but they largely understood. Who could blame him for trying to maximise profits from tourists?

His strategy worked. Demand almost immediately fell away to little more than 100 a day. Perfect. He even had time to chat to customers during the quieter periods. Mrs Pandey reacted as expected: she was worried her son was not doing so well. But he explained to her that he had put up prices because it was exhausting him and he could not carry on at that pace. He still made good money. This seemed to placate her. She confessed that she preferred making just 100 a day. It was enough to keep her busy, but not overwhelmed.

Bimala and Nitesh told him that they would come home from school to find their mother and another woman (this had been a couple of other women when he was selling 250 samosas a day) sitting around the dining table and chatting over chai after having spent a few hours making samosas. Ajay noticed his mum smiled a lot more these days.

Nitesh and Bimala also seemed to be happier. The new school they went to had smaller class sizes and gave more individual attention to the pupils. Bimala's weakness had always been English, whereas Nitesh had struggled with maths. They were now much more confident in both. The only problem seemed to be that Mrs Pandey had to be very strict with them when it came to PlayStation and TV. She made sure they went out every day to play with other children on the street, as well as doing their studies. They were allowed an hour of TV and PlayStation on school days, and a lot more on weekends. They were both flourishing.

Whilst all this was happening Ajay's bank balance shot up.

~

"Ajay Pandey?" enquired the man on the other side of the counter. It was gone 10pm and the samosa trade was more or less over for the night. At five feet six, the man was a lot shorter than Ajay and also a lot less stocky. He was in his mid-thirties and had an air of authority about him. He was probably the food inspector. Ajay had heard that they were being more active these days in Paharganj due to an increasing number of tourists being submitted to hospital with suspected food poisoning. Apparently they worked very late as they were short-staffed.

"Yes," Ajay said, smiling. Best to keep these people on side.

"Assistant Sub Inspector Gurpreet Singh," said the man, pulling out some ID.

Ajay looked at the ID, his smile fading when he realised this was not the food inspector, but a police inspector. He thought quickly.

"Would you like a samosa, sir?"

"I am more interested in your other trade." Singh paused for effect. "Let me in."

Ajay went to the end of the counter with the door. He turned the knob on the gas ring next to the door and slid the bolt on the shelf above it, causing the remaining 11 bags of heroin to fall into the rapidly heating oil. He then slowly slid the bolts securing the end section of the counter, and then unbolted the half door at the same speed.

Singh entered and Ajay secured the half door and counter top before putting the framed notice "Back in 5 minutes" on the counter. He used this when he needed the toilet.

Singh looked around. He spotted the burner beneath the counter. He sneered and snorted to himself.

"Do you think that will save you, my friend?"

Ajay said nothing. If he kept his mouth shut, he could not say anything that this idiot could use against him.

Singh wandered towards the back of the shop, only glancing at the fryers. He walked around the screen and looked under the prep table and sink. Opening the door to the toilet, he glanced around it from the doorway.

"I know about you and your friend Mr Rishi Ghanchi," he said quietly from where he was standing.

Ajay kept his cool. He could easily employ the services of a lot of good lawyers. Singh may know it, but could he prove it?

"I've been watching you both. A couple of Mr Ghanchi's deals were to acquaintances of mine."

Oh shit! This was not looking good. Maybe he was bluffing…

"I've been filming Mr Ghanchi as he walks around Paharganj meeting up with foreigners every 15 minutes. I've even got quite a bit of video of him getting his 'samosas' plus from you." He just stared at Ajay for a while. If he was trying to unnerve him, it was not working. The killing of Anand had hardened him to anything this swaggering halfwit could throw at him.

"How old are you?" asked Singh.

"Fifteen."

Singh raised his eyebrows and nodded. He was clearly both surprised and impressed.

"Still old enough to be locked away for a year and have all your assets seized. I should take you to the cells now and beat a confession out of you."

You can try, thought Ajay, but said nothing.

"How much are you making?"

Standing perfectly still, Ajay said nothing. It was obvious what was coming next.

"Now, I could tell the sub-inspector what's happening. He's a devout man, and would be here within minutes. He *hates* drug dealers. *Really* hates them. You'd be so battered by the time he formally questioned you, you'd tell him your dead grandmother is the biggest whore in Delhi's biggest brothel if that's what he wanted you to say."

"So he believes people should *pay*," Ajay said coolly. He hoped he had emphasised the word "pay" in just the right way.

Singh nodded. "The question is, do I tell him or not?"

Ajay shrugged and said: "I'm just a businessman with regular expenses I need to pay out all the time."

Singh tentatively mentioned a figure. It was just over half that day's takings.

Ajay nodded. He went over to the counter and unlocked the strong box. He rapidly counted out the correct amount.

He came back to where Singh was standing and handed the bundle over, his heart pounding. He knew this could be an elaborate entrapment.

Singh smiled, took the money and pocketed it.

"Very good, my friend. Shall we make this a regular thing?"

Ajay nodded. That amount every week was not even ten percent of what he made.

"Good. See you next month."

Next month! Ajay struggled to keep a straight face. This guy was unbelievably stupid. He knew Ajay was selling a bag every 15 minutes. He knew what Ajay charged. *And that was all he wanted?*

After Assistant Sub-Inspector Gurpreet Singh left, Ajay looked up what someone in his position was paid. What he had asked for was between three and ten times his monthly salary. That explained it...

Singh was going to cost him less than two per cent of his monthly profit. A small price to pay to keep the police off his back. But would they stay off his back? This could be just one renegade officer who shook down drug dealers. There could be others who also covered this area. He dismissed the thought. There was no point in worrying about something that may never happen. There are some things which are best dealt with when they arise.

When Rishi came back, Ajay said to him: "I'm tired. Let's shut early."

Rishi was glad to hear this. He found the pace of work hard, and was grateful for any time he could have off.

"How was today for you?" asked Ajay.

"Fine, fine."

"No trouble?"

"No, no trouble. These foreigners are so good to deal with."

"If the police ever hassle you, say nothing. I'll get you the best lawyers, and there'll be a fat bonus if you keep your mouth shut."

Rishi nodded in satisfaction. Leaving his pitch at Sadar Ganj was the best thing he had ever done.

The next two months were smooth and uneventful, with Singh turning up at the beginning of each month for his payout. Ajay wondered how many others he blackmailed like this. He suspected he might be the only one. Of course, there were other dealers around in central Delhi, but they mainly seemed to use cryptocurrency and so were less easy to lean on without leaving a trail. If anyone started asking questions, and saw cash withdrawals about the same time as Singh visited, it would be hard to explain away. He had heard of two that had been arrested in the past week alone.

On Singh's fourth visit, Ajay let him in and they went behind the screen as usual. Ajay took out his phone and attached a set of earbuds to it. He handed the earbuds to Singh, who put them in his ears. He was bemused, but sensed he needed to do this. Ajay then set a video playing and handed the phone to Singh.

Ajay watched with a poker face as Singh's expression turned from reserved confidence to ill-disguised panic.

The video had been taken on a small CCTV camera hidden in the corner of the ceiling. It, and a very sensitive microphone had captured Singh taking the money and Ajay saying: "Thanks, inspector. Heroin dealers are getting into trouble all the time in Delhi – I heard of three being busted in the last month. Thank you for looking the other way."

Singh had replied: "That's OK, my friend. Keep the money coming and I'll make sure your heroin keeps flowing."

"I'll have the same ready for you next month, inspectorji."

Singh looked up from the phone, scared and angry.

Ajay handed him a bundle of cash – his usual amount.

Singh now looked confused.

"I don't want our arrangement to end," Ajay said. "But I want something for my money."

"Who do you think you are?" hissed Singh.

"Someone who could get you sent away for ten years," Ajay hissed back. "I'll get out after one and start again. An ex-bent cop in prison? You'll be lucky to get out alive. Who'll look after your family when you're gone? No one by the time *I've* finished."

Singh seemed to shrink. He was well aware of what happened to cops in prison. He looked at the money in his hand and then at Ajay. He almost looked like a small child who needed to be taken by the hand and delivered back to his mummy.

"All I want is useful information when you get it," Ajay said in a reasonable tone. "Am I the only dealer you're shaking down?"

Singh nodded.

"How many others are there in Paharganj?"

"You're the only one in central Delhi."

Ajay looked surprised and then suspicious.

"There are others, but they use cryptocurrency, and they come and go. We sometimes get one, but not often. I'm in charge of finding them. Your advert was easy to spot – a couple of my stooges did deals with your street boy. When your advert disappeared I just looked out for another one that was the same. That time I followed your boy and found you." Singh spoke succinctly but weakly.

Ajay nodded in satisfaction. Silently he got out a bundle of notes out of his pocket and handed them over to Singh. Singh took them but looked shocked.

"You look after me, I look after you," Ajay said matter-of-factly. "Tell me about anything I need to know and you get a bonus. This video" – he held up the phone – "will be safe if I'm safe."

Singh shoved the money in his pocket and scurried out.

9

For Ajay's 16th birthday, his mum invited Ranveer and his parents around for a small surprise party. She got Saksham to take the dining table away for the night, and replace it with a longer one. He also provided three more chairs. Although it made the room feel crowded, seven people could comfortably fit around the table.

Just as Mrs Pandey had hoped, Ajay absolutely loved it. Usually his birthday was like any other ordinary day, not acknowledged at all.

He felt overwhelmed. It was as if, at last, all the hard work for his family was being recognised.

The food and the conversation flowed freely as they sat around the table. It was as if they were back in the Kaushik's old place, but more so. The problem with the Kaushik's new place was that it was *too* nice. Slightly cramped meant intimate and cosy. It gave the feeling that they were all uniting against the common enemy – that enemy being their shared circumstances.

At the end of the meal the Kaushiks gave Ajay a suit by Hugo Boss. It looked great and fitted perfectly. A wonderful end to the day.

When the Kaushiks got into Ranveer's car, he handed Ajay a carrier bag. "Something to be opened later, Chotu," he said quietly.

When the others had gone to bed, Ajay sat watching TV. He

opened the carrier and took the small present out of it. It was wrapped in the same expensive, tasteful paper the suit had been in. He opened it. Six 100g packs of heroin. After getting over the initial shock, Ajay shook his head. Double his usual order. To think that, less than three years ago, this would have been the equivalent of 50 years of wages. He shook his head again. There was no denying life was good.

Something made him look in the bag again. There was a small envelope, which he had not seen as the present had been on top of it. Thinking it contained a birthday card, he opened it.

It was, indeed, a birthday card. In it Ranveer had written:

Happy birthday! Got a special present for you. Meet me tomorrow at 8pm at the bar at Hotel Mayur, Hauz Khas. Wear the suit.

It meant shutting the shop early, but Ajay was intrigued. It was probably no more than a posh meal at a 5-star hotel, but it would be a welcome change from his usual routine.

Ajay arrived on time, only to find Ranveer and a tall, attractive woman already there. Her long, slender neck underlined a delicate but firm jaw. Her small, dainty nose was prettily set between two cheekbones which were accentuated just enough with a discreet amount of blusher. The makeup around her eyes made them look even more striking. Her lips were truly luscious – perfect for kissing. As Ajay approached he could hear her laughing at something Ranveer had said. She had a beautiful voice and her short dress revealed legs to match. Ajay guessed she was probably a few years older than him. With difficulty he managed not to stare at her.

"Hello, Ajay," Ranveer said, standing up. This must have been the first time he had not called Ajay Chotu. "This is Natasha."

She smiled and nodded at Ajay and said, "An absolute pleasure to meet you. Ranveer has told me you're a very successful businessman, on his way to the top."

Ajay blushed.

Ranveer sat down. Ajay did the same.

"You're looking good – that suit was *made* for you," Natasha said, leaning towards him so he could see down the front of her dress. He could not help but look.

"Ranveer, why don't you order us a drink," she said without looking away from Ajay.

Just then a waiter passed by but, instead of stopping him, Ranveer got up and went to the bar.

"Have you been here before?" Natasha continued.

"No," Ajay murmured. He was feeling nervous and overwhelmed. It was a feeling he was not used to.

She laughed, sounding like the tinkling of well-tuned, lively bells. "It's absolutely fabulous here. The rooms are so large."

"I-I'm not staying," Ajay managed to say.

"Are you sure? The beds are *very* comfortable," she said in a low voice as she edged forward slightly.

By now Ranveer was standing next to them, grinning at the exchange. He bent over and whispered in Ajay's ear: "Natasha is the rest of your birthday present. Enjoy – she's yours all night." He put a hotel room key on the table in front of Ajay before quickly walking off. Ajay just stared at it.

He eventually came to his senses and looked around, but Ranveer was gone. He looked at Natasha, wondering if that was her real name, and concluding that it probably was not. She was sitting back in her chair, smiling, her legs crossed.

"Would you like to go upstairs?" she asked gently.

Ajay looked at her for a moment. He felt a lot more in control now that he knew what was going on, but he was torn. He thought of Deepika, and immediately of the kiss in the back of the shop all those months ago, and how frustrated he had felt ever since. He nodded.

Natasha reached over, took the key and slipped it into her handbag. She then took him by the hand and led him out of the bar.

When they got to the room she asked him to undo her zip. She stepped out of her dress, turned around and started to undo his belt.

He kissed her. She responded passionately whilst unfastening the button on his trousers.

Before he knew what was happening, they were both naked and on the bed. His first performance was over far too quickly. But it was the first of many.

He fulfilled many fantasies, and stuff beyond them. Why had he not done this before? Who needed Deepika...

In the morning he took Natasha's number. She told him that she had lots of willing "friends" as well.

He began to shut the shop at 10pm – he had generally sold out of H by then anyway. He would spend the rest of the evening with Natasha or one or more of her "friends". The sessions could go on all night if the friend was particularly talented, which she frequently was.

However, after a few weeks he began to feel hollow. There was no denying that the sex was good – very good – but he needed more. The intimacy he had with Deepika could not be replaced with carnal lust. He still carried on seeing Natasha and her friends, but he began to realise he was becoming depressed.

Within six months he was opening his shop until midnight again. He would go home to a meal from his mum, and see Bimala and Nitesh in the morning before they went to school. This made him much happier. However, there were a couple of nights a week when he would not go home...

Business carried on as normal, with Singh coming as regular as clockwork for his monthly handout. Each time he would tell Ajay about drugs busts they had made in central Delhi – they were all cryptocurrency dealers. He also reassured Ajay that he was still in charge of locating drug dealers in the area. Ajay was safe. The information Singh provided was nothing Ajay did not know, but he gave him a respectable bonus each month just to keep him tame.

It was on a visit about five months after his birthday that Singh announced: "A new 'samosa' shop like yours has opened on Connaught Place."

Ajay was not surprised. He had expected it to happen a lot sooner. "Whereabouts?"

"Corner of Janpath – it opened three weeks ago."

"Why didn't you tell me before?"

"It's the first time I've seen you since it opened. Anyway, it's over a kilometre away – it won't make any difference to you."

Singh was right – Ajay had not noticed any fall off in demand.

"I've just found out he's going to open more, all over central Delhi," Singh continued.

Ajay felt his heart rate speed up. "Who's 'he'?"

"Faruk Khan."

"Who's he?" Ajay had heard the name before.

"Soon to be the new MP for New Delhi."

"What's he doing dealing in heroin?" Ajay was confused.

Singh laughed slightly. "He's always dealt in heroin. That's why he's going to be an MP."

Ajay looked even more confused.

Singh perched on the edge of the stainless steel table and folded his arms, smiling a little. He was enjoying himself. "Mr Khan sahib is no gentleman, my friend. He may have gone to the finest school in the whole of Rajasthan, but he's a complete bastard. He started dealing at school – he even became the main supplier to many of the prostitutes in the local town.

"He carried on when he left school, and controlled Jaipur's heroin trade in just two years. Another few years and he controlled more than that. If he said it, it got done. He had every official on his payroll. He'd break legs for the smallest mistake. Either that or you'd be killed. Or one of your children would be kidnapped and raped. Even if people suspected he wanted something done, it got done – *immediately*. He eventually decided to run for mayor. Most of the opposition dropped out. The rest had to be 'persuaded' to stay in the race – it would have looked very suspicious if there'd been no competition – but they all ran very bad campaigns. Of course he won. They say Jaipur never ran so smoothly." Singh chuckled, probably thinking that this was no bad thing.

"Anyway, Jaipur must have been too small for our friend Mr Khan sahib. He decided to move to Delhi, after leaving the Jaipur heroin trade in the capable hands of his next in command. He still visits if he needs to do a management 'reshuffle'." The way Singh said "reshuffle", there was no mistaking that it was in any way a civilised process.

"That was over five years ago. He spent the next few months in Delhi breaking legs and fingers, and occasionally removing testicles and watching people bleed to death. Everyone thinks Laksh Dewan controls the heroin trade in Delhi. He doesn't anymore. Khan made him an offer that he didn't dare refuse. Dewan now makes more money than he ever did – Khan's supply lines are superb – but he no longer owns Delhi.

"Khan spent the next few years spreading out to Kanral, Hapur, Bhiwani, Alwar, etc, etc. That guy must earn more in one second than I do in a year..." Singh sounded wistful.

"Anyway, he's decided to run for MP and, surprise, surprise, most of his opponents have changed their minds – they've started campaigning for him instead. But his main opponent – Jaya Chawla – isn't someone who can be intimidated. That was until – rumour has it – he personally paid her a visit, doused her in petrol, and threatened to rape her daughter in front of her. She doesn't campaign much now."

"So, what's he doing opening a samosa shop? I thought he'd want to be a government minister," said Ajay.

Singh shrugged. "Maybe he's bored. Anyway, he can't be a minister – he's independent."

"*But a samosa shop?*"

Singh shrugged again. He grinned before saying: "Maybe he's had enough of all those posh dinners."

This was not funny. Ajay could see everything dissolving away in front of him. He had enough money to shut up shop now, move somewhere very comfortable and live the rest of his life in tranquillity. But that's not what he wanted. He was happy with his life. He could not let this arsehole destroy it.

"What can I do?" Ajay sounded irate.

Singh shrugged. "He travels in a bulletproof car with solid rubber tyres. He's always got at least two bodyguards with him, plus another lot hidden. He makes sure that he only gets out of his car where a sniper couldn't take a shot without being seen."

"Show me his advert."

Singh got his phone out and located one.

"Heroin in central Delhi. Cash or bitcoin. Good quality."

Bastard! He had virtually copied Ajay's ad, but made it cheaper and was taking cryptocurrency as well. Bastard, bastard, bastard! Ajay knew he was laughing at him. If he had wanted to take over Ajay's trade, he would have just paid him a visit. But, as Singh had put it, he was probably bored. He wanted to torment Ajay and, when he got bored with that, pay him a visit. Ajay was going to end up dead - if he was lucky, he and his family would not be tortured beforehand. From what Singh had said, Khan did not hang around. If Ajay wanted to save what he had, he had to act fast.

He gave Singh a very generous bonus and a burner phone.

"Keep that on you all the time," Ajay said, pointing to the phone.

Singh nodded, got up and left. Ajay shut the shop and texted Rishi. As soon as Rishi was back, Ajay gave him a week's wages and told him to take the next few days off – he would let him know when he needed him back.

It was the first time Rishi had ever seen Ajay look worried. He tried to reassure him. "Let me know if you need anything. I'll always be here for you, bhaiyaa."

Ajay nodded distractedly.

As soon as Rishi left, Ajay got out his phone and googled Faruk Khan. There were plenty of YouTube videos on him. Ajay quickly realised why he was so successful. He looked to be over six feet tall, and was handsome and charming with an engaging smile. He was a cross between an actor and a politician. He could have been Amitabh Bachchan's protégé. He certainly did not come across as a rapist and a torturer. This was a dangerous man.

There were lots of pictures and videos of him at charity dos drinking champagne. In the occasional shot a bottle could be seen. Ajay's head spun when he looked up the price of one of the bottles. He had heard of champagne, but that was all. He looked at how much champagne cost, and found the top-end stuff could be astronomical.

There was no way Ajay could bribe this man. If he offered him a partnership, he would laugh at him before killing him for being so disrespectful. Maybe he could offer to work with him, but Khan had gone out to humiliate Ajay by driving him out of business. The only terms Khan would accept would be virtual slavery.

As he researched more, he found that Khan was due at a black tie charity fundraiser at The Oberon hotel in Delhi in three days. He sat and thought for a while.

He texted Rishi: "Can you get a waiter's uniform for Oberon Hotel?"

His phone pinged almost immediately: "Yes. I'll get it tomorrow."

He knew Rishi was well connected, but he had not expected a reply until the following morning at the earliest.

"Make sure it's about my size."

"Yes, bhaiyaa," was the prompt reply.

Exhaustion suddenly swept over him. The punch in the guts from the news about Khan combined with internet research had been too much. He went home, went straight to bed and fell asleep immediately.

He was up late the next day. Bimala and Nitesh had left for school. His mum was home and was preparing things for the day's samosa manufacturing by the time he got downstairs.

"Sorry, mummyji, but I don't need any samosas for the next couple of days."

Mrs Pandey looked downcast.

"Please pay your friends. I'll give you the money."

She nodded, but still looked sad. He went over and hugged her.

"Can I have a chai please, mataji?"

She smiled, and looked a little less lost as she busied herself.

He drank the chai whilst chatting to her. She told him about how Neel, who had a small electrical shop, was going to go into phones. Bhatti was not very happy, but he could not do anything about it. Rumour had it that he was thinking of quitting and going back to his village in Punjab.

Udant, the plastics dealer, was getting old, but had found someone equally as nasty as him to work with. Everyone wondered when his apprentice would stab him in the back and take over.

Saksham's wife had managed to sell some of his furniture to a shop in Connaught Place, and they were thinking of moving out of Paraharavi.

Ajay had forgotten how much he enjoyed listening to all the gossip. Paharganj had some of this, but nowhere near enough. It helped lift him out of his worries.

Eventually he pulled himself away. He had business to take care of.

He went up to his room and phoned Rishi.

"Hello, bhaiyaa. I've got the uniform."

Ajay looked at his watch. 10:15. He *had* underestimated Rishi.

"Good. Do you still know any boys from Sadar Ganj."

"Yes. Many." It was a stupid question – of course he did.

"Are there any who are reliable and intelligent and you've known a long time?"

There was a pause as Rishi thought. "I've known two for more than five years. One for three years. Another for –"

"Can they handle trouble and keep their mouths shut?"

"They're used to trouble, bhaiyaa. You know what it's like on Sadar Ganj."

Ajay did know, but he also knew that most of the street dealers would sell their own sisters if they could make a few rupees out of it.

He needed boys like Rishi – smart, could handle trouble and, most importantly, loyal.

"Will they keep their mouths shut?" repeated Ajay.

"Of course, bhaiyaa. They know how things work. If they betray you, things could get difficult for them and their families. All they want is to make good money. They don't want to pick a fight with a tiger."

Ajay had never thought of himself as a tiger before. It made him smile. He had progressed up the jungle.

"OK, I've got a job for two of them. Arrange a meeting for two o'clock today. I'll tell you where later. Tell them I'll pay them just for turning up, and more if they do the job well."

"Yes, bhaiyaa." If Rishi was curious about what was going on, he did not show it.

Ajay got on his bike. He had contemplated upgrading it, but thought it would bring too much attention to himself. It was ridiculous. He had more than enough in the bank to buy a mansion and several limousines, but he lived in a slum and rode a 100cc bike. However, every time he thought this, he reminded himself how unhappy Ranveer had made his parents. Did he really want to live in an area where people were only interested in you when you got a new washing machine? One positive side would be Deepika's parents and their kind could not look down on him.

It did not take him long to get to the spyware shop he had found via Google on Lodi Road.

On the way back he rode past Khan's shop in Connaught Place.

Connaught Place could not have been more different from Paharganj. In the centre was a large circular park. Around the park was a road, on the side of which were beautiful white buildings with columns on the outside. The upper stories appeared to be offices or flats, but the ground levels were entirely occupied by shops and restaurants. Paharganj was where you went for a bargain: Connaught Place was where you went for class. On the ground floor the pillars supported a covered walkway, allowing browsers to look in comfort into the windows of the designer shops and the upper end restaurants. It was so far removed from where Ajay's shop was, he was sure it got a better class of junkie.

The one thing it did have in common with Paharganj was that the traffic was moving very slowly. It allowed Ajay to take a good look at Khan's shop. An ordinary samosa shop would have been out of place in such an opulent setting, but it was far from ordinary. Khan had gone to town on it. It was more of a samosa palace, with glistening tiles on the floor and a counter to match.

The guy behind the counter seemed to be in his mid-twenties. He only briefly glanced up once from his phone. From what Ajay could see, he looked intelligent enough but a little nervous. Probably a new recruit Khan was in the process of toughening up. Ajay needed to know what the street boy was like.

He parked his bike on the other side of Connaught Place and, using a new burner phone, texted the number on the ad Singh had shown him: "Need 0.5g. Cash."

He got the reply back almost immediately: "Outside Spice Mahal, Baba Singh Marg. 15 minute."

It was exactly his M.O..

He hurried over to Baba Singh Marg, arriving eight minutes early. He stood on the opposite side of the street to Spice Mahal, but a little way along, not looking out of place as he looked at his phone.

He saw someone arrive outside Spice Mahal. It was a small, weaselly looking boy, probably in his late teens. Ajay had seen lots of these on Sadar Ganj. The only loyalty they had was to themselves. They were expert liars and would betray you if there were two rupees in it for them. The only thing they responded to was serious threats they knew you would carry out. Just what he had hoped for.

The boy was doing something on his phone. Ajay got a text a few seconds later: "Where are you?"

Satisfied, Ajay walked back to his bike.

When he got to his shop the first thing he did was smash up the burner phone he had just used, and break up the SIM card it had contained. He then got out three more burner phones, and linked one to a pair of glasses which were equipped with a hidden camera. He phoned Rishi.

"Hello."

"Have you got two boys?"

"Yes, bhaiyaa."

"Send me their names and phone numbers, and meet me with them at the corner of Chelmsford Road and Connaught Circus at two."

"OK, bhaiyaa."

All four of them were on time. They walked down Chelmsford Road until they were alone, apart from passing traffic. In as low a voice as possible, Ajay explained what he wanted doing. Both guys, who were nearly the size of Rishi, nodded. It was obviously something they would have no problem at all handling.

Ajay texted in an order using one of the burners.

The reply was almost instant: "Outside Zen Coffee House, Shaheed Bhagat Singh Marg. 20 minutes."

Jaspal, the shorter one, put on the glasses. He and his accomplice, Ramesh, strode off purposefully.

The weasel turned up on time. Jaspal approached him. He saw the weasel's eyes widen as Ramesh discreetly pressed the tip of a knife into his buttock.

"Shut up and listen," Jaspal said in a low voice. "Unless you want an extra arsehole, come with us. Don't try anything."

The weasel looked terrified, just like Jaspal knew he would. You meet scum like this every day in the drugs trade.

Ramesh put away the knife and shoved the weasel slightly so he followed Jaspal. The weasel tried to run off once, but Ramesh put his arm around him as if holding a friend close. At the same time he punched him in the kidney. When the weasel exhaled sharply in pain, Ramesh said with a smile on his face: "Next time, I'll break your fingers."

They eventually got to an alley, which Jaspal led them down.

"Give me your phone – the one you use for dealing," Jaspal commanded.

The weasel got his phone out, unlocked it and handed it over.

Jaspal scrolled through the texts. They went back four days. They were all from the same number, telling him where to go next. Jaspal got out the burner phone not linked to the glasses and typed in the number.

"You're going to talk for three minutes," Jaspal told the weasel.

"What about?" He sounded panicked.

"Anything. Tell him your work phone's stopped working and you bought a new one because it'd take too long to get back to the shop. Keep him on the phone for three minutes and then pretend the work phone's started working again."

Ramesh stuck the knife into the weasel's arse, but a little harder this time. The weasel gasped and nodded. Jaspal pressed the dial button and handed the phone over after putting on the speaker.

"Hello."

Weasel: "Helloji. The phone's broken."

"What do you mean, it's broken?"

Weasel: "It just switched off. I can't get it to go back on."

"Whose phone are you using?" There was tension in the voice.

Weasel: "I just bought one. It's quicker than coming back."

"OK," the voice sounded relieved.

"Hold on," said the weasel. "I think it might be coming back on…"

You could hear the guy from the shop breathing nervously. Eventually he said: "Is it working?"

"Hold on, I think it's about to come back on…"

Jaspal nodded. It had been more than three minutes.

"It's on," said the weasel.

The line went dead.

"Tell him you smashed the new phone and broke the SIM card," Jaspal said.

The weasel nodded.

Jaspal then grabbed him by the throat with one hand and,

squeezing, lifted him up slightly. "If you ever say one word about this to anyone we'll break all your fingers one by one, and cut off your balls. Got it?"

The weasel nodded his head – which had gone the colour of dark beetroot – the best he could.

Ramesh undid the weasel's flies and lightly jabbed the knife into his right thigh. A small patch of blood spread over the weasel's trousers at the same time his tears sprang from his eyes. Jaspal let go. The weasel fell to the ground.

Jaspal and Ramesh walked away.

∽

They joined Ajay and Rishi in a booth in a coffee shop near the centre of Connaught Place. They all sat in silence. Ajay had a set of earbuds in whilst he watched the video. When he finished he discreetly handed Jaspal and Ramesh each some neatly folded banknotes. They equally discreetly counted them. They both looked up, stunned. It would have taken a month to earn that at Sadar Ganj.

"Thank you, boys," Ajay said, feeling a little self-conscious. They were both far older than him. Jaspal appeared to be in his thirties. Ajay wondered why he was still a lowly street dealer. He seemed like a smart guy. But there were lots of intelligent people in Delhi who got nowhere – Ajay had seen more than his fair share in Paraharavi. Who knew what curveballs had been thrown at Jaspal?

"Thank you, bhaiyaa," Jaspal replied. Ramesh nodded enthusiastically. If he was going to pay that much, he could call them what he wanted.

"I'll let you know if I need you again." This was clearly a dismissal. They left without another word.

"We need to go back to the shop," Ajay said, turning to Rishi.

Once at the shop, Ajay handed Rishi a bundle of cash that would have taken two months to earn at Sadar Ganj.

Rishi smiled. "Thank you, bhaiyaa."

"Where's the uniform?"

"Safe at my house," replied Rishi.

"How did you get it?"

"I know the daughter of one of the doormen."

Ajay just looked at him. He would have asked "*How?*" but did not want to get bogged down in in a lengthy explanation of how Rishi lived down the street to someone who knew a girl who went to college with a fella who etc, etc... He had long ago learned to accept that Rishi seemed to know half of Delhi through a series of mind boggling networks.

"Somebody called Faruk Khan is due there in two days. Can you find out which room he'll be in?"

Rishi nodded.

"Find out in the next 15 minutes."

Rishi nodded.

"Go to the toilet and make the call now. I've got a few things to do. Knock on the door when you want to come out. Don't come out until I say so."

Ajay knew he was behaving strangely but, when you pay enough, you can be as strange as you like. As Rishi disappeared into the toilet Ajay grabbed a stool from the front of the shop and brought it back behind the screen. Using the phone the weasel had made the call from, he began a search on the dark web. At last he found what he wanted. It was a lot cheaper to pay via bitcoin, but he opted for cash on arrival.

Rishi had knocked on the door almost as soon as he had gone into the toilet.

"OK, come out," Ajay called.

"Presidential Suite. It's on the fifth floor," Rishi announced.

"OK, I need you to be very careful now. Get me Rohypnol. Don't use anyone who knows you work for me." Just then something occurred to him. "Find out now if Faruk Khan will be using his own security."

Rishi disappeared into the toilet again. He knocked after a few minutes.

"Kanul Kapoor stayed there a few months ago. My friend had a plan to get into his room – she knows all about the security at the hotel," Rishi said, grinning.

"Well?"

"They don't allow private security, but you can have one of their security guards outside your room and they've got CCTV down every passageway, lift and stairway."

Shit! He thought his plan had been infallible. Book a room near Khan's. Use the burner phone from which the weasel had made the call to Khan's shop to book a prostitute to come to the hotel. Dress in the uniform Rishi had obtained and take a bottle of champagne to Khan when he came back to his room after the black tie do downstairs. The champagne would be laced with Rohypnol. When Khan was unconscious, Ajay would get the prostitute to Khan's room. There Ajay would strangle her, strip her naked and put her in bed next to Khan. He would make sure the burner phone had Khan's prints on it. He would put the phone under the bed where Khan would not see it, but the police would find it.

Now, when he thought about it, it seemed ridiculous. Of course there would be security and CCTV. Also, when Khan came to he would know what had happened. The prostitute's body would disappear and the room would be expertly cleaned. The plan had been childish. Also, could he have killed a prostitute? Natasha and so many of her friends had been so obliging, often going beyond the call of duty. He had got to know quite a number of them a little, and had begun to grow fond of them them. There were a few who were not that likeable, but was that enough of a reason to kill one? The idea turned his stomach. He had killed Anand, but that had almost been an accident, and he had needed to do it.

The plan had been unbelievably naïve and born of panic. He may only be 16, but he *had* to up his game.

Khan was too clever and experienced for Ajay. He would easily get out of any setup, find out who was behind it and exact horrific revenge.

Ajay closed his eyes as he thought. He could not reason with Khan, nor could he bargain, bribe, flatter, blackmail or bully him.

That only left one option – kill him. He had no choice. Either kill or be humiliated and killed by him.

Rishi wondered what Ajay was thinking about. It was fascinating. He had never seen anybody so focussed before. At last Ajay seemed to come to some kind of conclusion.

"Find out who's on reception on the evenings Khan's staying. I need to know everything about her." The order came out as a bark. Ajay had not meant for that to happen. He knew you got the best out of people when you treated them with respect.

Rishi was a little taken aback, but he nodded. He knew Ajay well enough to realise that things must be getting to him for him to act like that.

Rishi had the answer in a few minutes. "It's Mrs Gautam – starts at six and finishes at six in the morning. She's there every day. Been there for years. She rides an old Bajaj scooter which she always parks in the same place in the staff car park." Rishi had been able to find out the salary band someone of her grade and experience would be on, but he had not been able to find out anything else about her – not even whereabouts she lived. She was polite and efficient, but kept herself to herself.

"I'll phone you when I need you," Ajay said gently, giving Rishi a bundle of cash. It was a *lot* of money for doing hardly anything. Rishi could not help but leave with a huge grin across his face.

Ajay sat alone for a while on one of the stools, both of which were now behind the screen. On the far corner of the prep table was a shallow wooden box in which there were a few tools Ajay and Rishi had used when they had done the place out. They still occasionally used them for repairs. He picked up a claw hammer and held it for a few moments. He got a towel, folded it in half and spread it on the corner of the table nearest to him. Emptying the wooden box of the other tools, he put it on the folded towel. He folded another towel and put it in the box. After placing the hammer on the towel in the box, he draped a third towel over the box.

Jaspal had struck him as far smarter than Ramesh. He was also about Ajay's size, which helped a lot. Ajay phoned him.

"Hello."

"Jaspal?"

"Yeah."

"Ajay."

"Hello, bhaiyaa."

"Can you come to my shop at one in the morning?"

"Yes, bhaiyaa."

"Tell *no one* you're coming."

"Yes, bhaiyaa."

Ajay needed a car. A roomy one – not one of those silly little things. Also some large, strong plastic bags – the ones used for building rubble. And nylon rope, a torch, vinyl weights, rubber gloves, plastic sheeting and a large, very sharp meat cleaver. He went out with a considerable amount of cash. If you want things done quickly, money is the ultimate lubricant.

When Jaspal arrived Paharganj was relatively quiet. The part of the street the samosa shop was on was completely deserted.

Ajay let Jaspal in, and took him to the back of the shop.

"Turn around and face the wall. Put your arms up, hands against the wall," Ajay said firmly but pleasantly.

Jaspal looked confused.

"I'm going to search you – like the movies."

Jaspal shrugged and assumed the position.

Ajay carefully patted him down.

"OK, that's fine."

Jaspal turned around. Ajay indicated with an open hand that he should take a seat.

"You're not going to talk about anything we talk about – not even with your wife, your girlfriend, Rishi, Ramesh, your mum, your dad... Nobody. Understand?"

"Yes, bhaiyaa," Jaspal replied, almost timidly. Ajay wondered if he was always that demure. The way he walked and the way he held himself was bordering on arrogant. But was the arrogance the façade that he had had to adopt for the street, or was the timidity a show he put on for Ajay? It did not matter, providing he kept his mouth shut and got the job done.

"I need you to kill someone for me. He's another dealer who's trying to drive me out of business. Do you have a problem with that?" Ajay's heart pounded as he said this.

An icy look came over Jaspal as he shook his head. Probably not the first time he had done this type of thing. Good.

"Do you know The Oberon Hotel?"

Jaspal nodded. The Oberon was almost as synonymous with Delhi as The Taj was with Mumbai.

"There's a receptionist there. She works from 6pm to 6am. She's in her fifties, and she drives an old Bajaj scooter. Her name is Mrs Gautam."

Jaspal nodded again.

"Put this –" Ajay picked up a small disc on the prep table next to him "- on her moped. Peel off the paper and stick it on. Put it somewhere she won't find it. Don't worry, it won't come off. It's the latest satellite micro tracker. Look around the hotel until you find the staff car park. Be careful – they'll probably have cameras. And make sure you get the right scooter – there might be more than one Bajaj."

Another nod. With the help of a pin Ajay switched on the tracker and linked it to Jaspal's phone.

"When she leaves, follow her. Keep your distance. She might live in a flat. If it's a complex you'll have to see which building she goes into. If you're lucky there'll be a buzzer entry system which'll have her name next to the flat number. Otherwise, you'll have to come back later and find out – don't be obvious when you do. Push a couple of buzzers and say you've got a package for Mrs Gautam you've got to give to her in person, and ask where she lives. Keep trying – someone'll tell you."

"Yes, bhaiyaa. No problem."

"Good. Don't go back until about 12 – that'll give her time to sleep. Get her to let you in. We'll make you a fake police ID. When you're in, put this in front of her." Ajay took several bundles of banknotes out of a carrier bag. Jaspal's eyes opened wide. It was far more money than he had ever seen in one place. "It's a lot more than she makes in three years. Don't worry – you're going to make a lot more than that in the next couple of days.

"There's somebody called Faruk Khan staying at the hotel. He's going to a big, expensive party there tomorrow night. Tell her that all she needs to do is phone up to Faruk Khan's room after he leaves the party and tell him there's a complimentary bottle of Dellamotte Blanc de Blancs 2007 champagne being sent up to his room.

"She needs to find out the second he leaves the party and goes to his room – if you leave it any more than a couple of minutes he might collapse into bed. And find out about a place you can hide (tell her you'll be in full staff uniform) until you can take the champagne up. Have you got all that?"

Jaspal looked a little uncertain.

"I'll send you a photo of the champagne."

Jaspal looked relieved.

"What if she says no?" Jaspal asked.

"She won't," Ajay said confidently. "She's in her fifties and works seven days a week. She's going to be tired and desperate to retire. It'd take her years to save all that."

Jaspal was not convinced. He knew that he dealt with the scum of the earth at Sadar Ganj, but he also knew there were incorruptible people out there.

"If she refuses, threaten her. Don't hit her – just threaten her until she does as she's told. Oh, and when she does agree, tell her, if she keeps her mouth shut, she'll never see you again. Don't be nasty, but make sure she understands that it'll end badly for her if she says anything to anyone."

Jaspal did not look convinced. "But what if she refuses and threatens to go to the police?"

"Do what you need to do – but I need her to make that phone call."

A nasty look came over Jaspal's face as he smiled and nodded. Ajay felt quietly satisfied – he had picked the right person for the job.

Ajay took out his phone, got Jaspal to stand against a blank bit of wall and took a photo of him.

"What have you got - motorbike or car?" Ajay asked.

"Motorbike," Jaspal replied.

"Which one?"

"Bajaj Platina." Jaspal flushed as he said this. It was a very small machine. He had always wanted something much more powerful, but had never had the money.

"Perfect," Ajay said, almost to himself.

"Go and find another motorbike and swap the number plates. Don't leave your plates behind." Ajay gave him a screwdriver. "Come back here when you've finished."

Jaspal hurried out whilst Ajay got back on to the website he had located earlier. He cropped and imposed Jaspal's photo on a fake Delhi police ID generator. He printed and laminated the ID before putting it in the see-through photo compartment of a wallet. Jaspal was now Assistant Sub-Inspector Imran Ahmed. There was a good amount of cash in the wallet as well.

Ajay was nervous. What would happen if Mrs Gautam was incorruptible, despite Jaspal's powers of persuasion? What if his plan did not work? He would just have to cover his tracks and think of something else. There was no way some psychopathic idiot was driving *him* out of business.

It did not take long for Jaspal to message "I'm outside".

Ajay let him in. He showed him the ID and gave him the wallet.

"There's money in there. Before you call on Mrs Gautam buy yourself smart trousers and a shirt. Make sure they're on hangers and not folded into a packet. You don't want creases in them – you'll look like you've just bought new clothes so you can play a part. *Get the details right or you'll fuck it up.*"

Jaspal nodded, partly to indicate understanding, partly out of awe. He considered himself to be sharp, but this kid operated on several levels above him.

"Put these on," Ajay said, handing over the glasses Jaspal had been wearing earlier. He also gave him the phone that had accompanied them. "The camera's on. If you go to bed, take them off and make sure the camera is pointing at you. Come back here after you've visited Mrs Gautam. You're going to make a lot of money, even if she doesn't agree. But, if I find a second's recording missing, you get nothing. Don't forget – this is just the start."

Ajay put the carrier bag containing the cash to bribe Mrs Gautam into a small black rucksack.

By the time Jaspal left it was gone 3am. The Oberon was in the Sundar Nagar area of Delhi, about four kilometres away. Normally it would take anything up to an hour to get there but, at this time of night, it took less than 15 minutes.

Jaspal could not help but stare. Marble pillars supported ornate archways, the largest of which led to the imposing entrance. Lanterns made from gold filigree illuminated the white stone of the spectacularly long driveway. The details of the five storeys above the ground floor were not very visible from where he was, but each window glistened under suitably subdued lighting, as did the domes on each corner of the building and the larger one in the middle. He had heard of this place, but could never have dreamt that it was so beautiful.

After a few minutes he came to his senses and rode off. The whole place seemed to be in its own grounds, with roads between it and any other buildings. At the back was another entrance. It had a gateway with a guard, but it was nowhere near as imposing. This was reflected by the motley selection of scooters, cycles, motorbikes and unprepossessing cars just beyond it. Obviously the staff entrance.

He rode a bit more until, at last, he came to part of the metal railings that were not illuminated or obstructed on the other side with high hedging. He parked up and clambered over them, being careful not to catch himself on the spikes at the top of them.

When he got to the staff car park he realised it was less than a quarter full. Nightshift. Even the guard at the gate seemed to be dozing.

Although mostly old, there were some meaty looking motorbikes there. The thought of a hotel receptionist in her fifties riding one of these made Jaspal smile. Scattered amongst the cars and motorbikes were a number of scooters. Surprisingly, most of them were fairly new. This place must pay well. At last, he found an old Bajaj scooter. He checked carefully. It was the only one. He fixed the tracker on its underside. He looked at his phone. Yup, the tracker was still working.

He looked at the time. 4:09am. She was due to leave work in a little under two hours. He could go home – he was only about 15 minutes away – and get an hour's sleep, but it would not be enough. It would make him more tired and, even if he was able to get up, he would barely be able to function.

He climbed back over the wall and watched YouTube videos with the help of a set of earbuds, all the time keeping an eye on any scooter movement (the app was open in the corner of the screen).

At 6:14am the scooter began to move. The early morning traffic had begun to build up, so it was easy to keep her in sight without arousing suspicion.

She crossed the river, before finally coming to a stop outside a small block of flats. Jaspal parked far enough away not to be noticeable. She let herself into the block. He waited a few minutes before approaching the front door. There was an intercom with six buzzers. They had names next to them. One of those names was S. Gautam.

At last, he could go to bed.

~

A little over three hours later, after two cups of coffee, Jaspal was buying a pair of smart trousers and a shirt to match.

After breakfast and another cup of coffee he set off, arriving at the flats just before 12.

He pressed the buzzer.

"Hello."

"Hello, Mrs Gautam. Assistant Police Sub-Inspector Imran Ahmed," he said, holding up the ID to the camera. "May I come in?"

The door buzzer immediately sounded. Her flat was on the bottom floor. She had the door open, waiting for him, looking a little tired, but at ease. Jaspal was surprised, but then he realised she was used to dealing with the high and mighty. A relatively low ranking police officer would be nothing to her.

He walked in and she led him into the living room, where she invited him to sit down. She sat opposite him, with a table between them.

"How can I help you, inspector?" she asked pleasantly.

Suddenly his heart began to race as anxiety took over - this had never been a problem, but he had never impersonated a police officer before. Also, what was it about this woman that intimidated him? He did not know – he had never met anybody like her. He quickly pulled himself together. He had a job to do. It was simple. Even if she said no, he was wearing the glasses – Ajay could see for himself that he had tried his best. What was the worst that could happen – she tried to go into another room and phone the police? If she did, he would stop her. A good right hook should be enough to knock her out.

He took the carrier bag out of the rucksack and emptied the bundles of notes on to the table.

"All this is yours for doing less than one day's work. It's more than you earn in three years," he announced, looking straight at her.

She sat there, staring at the money. She seemed to be in shock. He put the bag down and his hands on his thighs, ready to spring into action if she started screaming or shouting.

It was substantially more than she earned in five years. And she worked *hard*. Over 30 years given to The Oberon. She wished she had never left Bhubaneswar – the capital of her native state, Orissa. But the big city and big wages had dragged her away. The first few years had been good. The staff at the hotel had always been friendly, and the guests nearly always courteous. It was funny, in those days the rich – the truly rich – were far more human than those who thought they were rich. Of course, the staff would always gossip about the guests, but it was good natured (unless the guests were truly obnoxious).

But then things had begun to change. India became richer. As new money flowed through the economy, the proportion of the new rich began to increase at the hotel. No longer was it frowned upon to talk about your wealth. Guests now talked about crores as if they were loose change. It became unusual for them to make requests – they demanded. They were paying good money, so they wanted good service. They did not seem to understand that politeness would get them the same good service, just more relaxed, less resentful, if a little slower. The atmosphere began to change. The hotel no longer felt like a gentleman's club, but more like a first class airport lounge.

This was reflected in the management. They talked about "efficiency", "targets" and "customer satisfaction". They no longer seemed to be bothered about service for the sake of service. The people who worked there used to start when they left school and not leave until they retired. Now staff came and went as things chopped and changed. When they talked to each other, it was more brief exchanges of information rather than conversations about the running of the hotel – you could be reprimanded for wasting time if you were found "just idly chatting". Any gossip about guests and management was almost invariably malicious. Mrs Gautam often wondered what was said behind her back. Not that it mattered – she hardly knew any of the staff now. Once she had known them all, including the names of their spouses and children.

She had planned to retire in four years. Being a careful person, she had always put a little bit aside every month, but had started saving in earnest about six years ago. Before then she had been able to cope with things, and had thought that she would end her working days in The Oberon, but things were just getting worse and worse. She could move to another hotel in Delhi, or even one in Bhubaneswar, but it was not The Oberon that was the problem (it was better than most), but the change in Indian culture. Civility had been replaced by money. She now often heard politicians and businessmen talking about "crores", "favours" and "government contracts" in the same conversation. She had even heard heroin – and worse - being mentioned.

She had never wanted to get married (she used the title "Mrs" as it gave her more respectability). She was an independent woman and always would be. But that did not mean that she had to behave like all the pushy women who treated her like dirt every day at that damned hotel. No, she planned to do her job to the best of her ability for four more years. By then, she would have enough money to comfortably retire to her home village on the peaceful coast of Orissa. Things had changed there (where hadn't they?), but it still held the values that had become increasingly dear to her: tranquillity, courtesy and community.

All that cash for something which, at the very least, would skirt on the edge of morality. But so what? It was nothing compared to the heroin dealers and corrupt politicians.

It meant she could retire now. She could move in with her sister, who had been begging her to do so ever since their parents had died nearly two years ago, and have a comfortable, relaxed life. No one in Delhi would miss her – everyone she had been close to had moved out years ago.

She looked up at Jaspal at last. "And what exactly would that work be, young man?"

Although momentarily stunned by her sudden emergence from what seemed to be a bad trip, and her authoritative, patronising manner, Jaspal soon regained control.

"It's very simple. Somebody called Faruk Khan is staying -"

"I am familiar with the gentleman." She was not trying to be off-hand, but even the mention of that man's name riled her. He was the personification of all that was wrong with The Oberon and with modernity. Every time he stayed, he had to have The Presidential Suite. If someone else was in it, he would simply offer them ridiculous sums of money to vacate it. There had been the occasion when an old lady who stayed in that suite regularly would not move, no matter how much he offered her. Rumour had it that he had got one of her men to visit her. She moved out of the hotel immediately and had never been back. His thin veneer of respectability was virtually transparent.

(The Presidential Suite had been The Aruna Asif Ali Suite – its revamping and renaming had both been completely crass.)

"Do you know he's going to a big party at the hotel tonight?"

"I am aware of that," she replied.

"The second he leaves the event and goes to his room you will tell him that the management are sending up a bottle of..." Jaspal got out his phone, brought up the photo of the Dellamotte and showed it to her. Her eyebrows raised slightly as she recognised the bottle. Questions flashed through her mind. Who was sending it? What was in it? Would Khan come to any harm? She quickly dismissed them. The only thing that should concern her was the cash on the table in front of her and covering her tracks.

"Who will take up the champagne?" she asked.

"Me."

"Do you have a uniform?"

"Yes."

This did not surprise her. With so many agency staff passing through the place, things went missing all the time. Management just looked at it as a cost of doing business. Things like that would never have been tolerated when she had first started.

"Do you have white cotton gloves?"

He shook his head.

"Name badge?"

He shook his head again.

"Have you ever opened a bottle of champagne?"

He flushed as he shook his head again. How did this dumpy, little middle-aged woman make him feel smaller than she was?

"I'll get you a badge and some gloves – you'll need them. Remember the name on the badge. Mr Khan will always summon you by your surname – he likes to boss people around." The last bit was said with just a hint of bitterness. "Come to the staff entrance around the back at

8.30pm – the rest of the staff should be in the hotel by then. Tell the guard that VP Agency sent you – he'll let you straight in. Do you have a car?"

He shook his head.

"You will have to change when you get to the hotel. A dusty uniform is not acceptable. Try not to get it creased – Mr Khan has been known to get security to remove a member of staff for looking scruffy."

Jaspal nodded his head. It was a very welcome change from shaking it.

"There will be a member of hotel security outside the room – I'll inform him that you are on the way up." Faruk Khan was famous for his own security team, whom he had tried to get into the hotel, but Mr Verma (The Oberon's general manager) had held firm. Khan had not threatened him. He no doubt knew, if he did, his name would be dirt almost immediately. Although scum, Khan was no fool.

"The staff entrance is by the car park – you can't miss it. Go in and along the corridor. The third door on the right is a storage room for towels and bed linen that the maids use in the morning. There will be a trolley with a champagne bucket full of ice there as well as a name badge and gloves. The champagne bucket is to keep the champagne chilled. Don't worry, there's a toilet opposite." All this was delivered with what appeared to be customary efficiency.

She went on to describe how to get from this room to The Presidential Suite, all the time making sure he understood her instructions. She was clearly used to training inexperienced members of staff.

"What is your phone number?" she asked.

He read out the number of his latest burner phone as she wrote it down.

"At 10pm phone me on the main switchboard –" she dictated the number as he typed it into his phone "- and say 'Mr Verma has instructed that Mr Faruk Khan in The Presidential Suite is to be sent a bottle of 2007 Dellamotte Champagne. Please phone me when he leaves the dinner.' Do you understand?"

He nodded. She smiled, knowing that what he would say would be a very crude approximation of what she had told him. But it did not matter – there were even more unrefined trainees than him at The Oberon these days.

"OK," she said briskly. "Come back in two hours and I'll teach you how to open a bottle of champagne."

He left, feeling patronised and mothered at the same time. How could you give someone that amount of cash, but it feel like they have done *you* a favour? He phoned Ajay.

"Hello."

"All done, bhaiyaa."

"Good. Come back to the shop."

"Bhaiyaa, Mrs Gautam said that the suit shouldn't be creased. Khan might not let me into his room if it is."

"OK."

Jaspal sped through the Delhi traffic the best he could, all the time aware that he was due back at Mrs Gautam's in two hours. He got to the shop in less than three quarters of an hour.

Ajay led him to the back of the shop.

"Stand against the wall, legs and arms spread," Ajay instructed, standing well back from him.

Jaspal put his hands on the wall as he had last time. Ajay patted him down.

"Give me the phone."

Jaspal pulled out the phone connected to the glasses. Ajay spent the next twenty minutes speeding through the video, only playing it in real time when he got to the interaction with Mrs Gautam. He could not help but grin through most of it. She was like the most fearsome headmistress you could ever meet.

"That's good – you did a good job," he said, keeping his face straight as he turned to Jaspal.

He reached over to the prep table, picked up a carrier bag and handed it to Jaspal.

Jaspal looked into it. It appeared to contain twice as much cash as he had given to Mrs Gautam. He looked up at Ajay, unable to hide his surprise.

"OK, now for the hard work. Tonight you're going to take the champagne to Khan and put Rohypnol into it," Ajay said, looking questioningly at Jaspal.

Jaspal nodded confidently. Sleight of hand was something anyone who worked in Sadar Ganj soon learnt. Ajay guessed that Jaspal had learnt it way before he had started there.

"When he's unconscious, kill him."

Jaspal nodded again.

"How are you going to do that?" asked Ajay.

"Break his neck." The cold hardness of Jaspal's voice was reflected in his face. Ajay nodded, also stony faced.

"How will you know he's dead?"

"I know when someone's dead, but I'll check his pulse."

This was undoubtedly something Jaspal was experienced in.

"When you've done it, come straight back here. There'll be five times that waiting for you," Ajay said, pointing to the carrier bag he had just given to Jaspal. "You're then going to get on your motorbike, leave Delhi immediately and start a new life somewhere far away."

Jaspal nodded. This was a dream come true. He could leave all his dead head "friends" behind and start somewhere new. Maybe somewhere down south – Goa or Kerala. Swap the smog of Delhi for fresh sea air and luxury, away from the filth he had had to deal with all his life.

Ajay watched the thoughts flash across Jaspal's eyes, and wondered if getting away would make any difference to him. You can take the boy out of the slum, but you can never really take the slum out of the boy? He wondered if the same applied to him.

Ajay stood up and turned to the prep table, reaching for a rucksack at one end of it. It was a solid, expensive looking item.

"Come over here."

Although riled by the tone of the command, Jaspal did as he was told. When someone was paying you that much for an evening's work, you obeyed every word.

Ajay unzipped the rucksack, removed the bottle of champagne and unclipped and took out another very solid looking bag which fitted snugly into the rucksack. Ajay unfolded it and undid the zip which ran through its middle. As he pulled back the sides, it revealed the suit Jaspal was to wear tonight. It was immaculate. Ajay did up the zip and put the suit and champagne back in before fastening the rucksack.

He then unzipped a side pocket on the rucksack and removed a clear, plastic vial with a black screw-on lid. In it was a white powder: five crushed up Rohypnol tablets. That should be enough to knock out an elephant, especially one that had been on the champagne for several hours.

"Make sure you tap it a few times before going into Khan's room so it doesn't stick together in one big lump."

"Yes, bhaiyaa," replied Jaspal, trying not to sound as if Ajay had just made the most needless statement he had ever heard.

Ajay linked the glasses to the phone again and handed them back to Jaspal, who put them on.

"Remember, if a single second of video is missing, you get nothing."

Jaspal nodded.

"You'd better go – you don't want to be late for Mrs Gautam," Ajay said, grinning.

"No, she might give me detention," Jaspal grinned back.

The traffic on the way back was worse, meaning that he arrived over 15 minutes late.

When Mrs Gautam opened the door, she gave him such a stern look that he said "Sorry, mam" before he could stop himself.

She had bought half a dozen bottles of fizzy grape juice with champagne style corks. She proceeded to drill him in the correct way to open a bottle of fine champagne.

He had never come across the stuff before. His first taste of alcohol had been some home distilled stuff flavoured with orange squash. These days he occasionally had some cheap whisky.

It had to be served chilled. If you tried to rip off the foil using the perforated tears in it you could make a complete mess – one should always use a knife to cut through the foil just below the cage so that, once it is removed, the cork and cage are exposed. She gave him a waiter's friend, telling him to keep it on his person at all times – it was invaluable. After removing the cage, cover the cork with a napkin and twist the bottle, *not* for cork. Once the cork is loose, *slowly* release it from the bottle. You are aiming for a gentle pop or, preferably, a hiss. Anything more than that is vulgar. Once the cork is removed, give the lip of the bottle a quick wipe before pouring. Always put the glass on a tray when presenting it. Avoid *any* spillages. If there are any, *always* wipe them away.

By the time Jaspal had finished, four of the bottles had been opened, and he was exhausted. Killing someone was less draining. But he did feel he was beginning to leave the crudeness of the street behind. He could get used to a bit of refinement.

It was gone four o'clock by the time he left. He went home and got some desperately needed sleep.

He was in the vicinity of the hotel just after a quarter past eight, still feeling groggy. He made sure he did not arrive at the staff gateway until 8:30. Saying that he was from VP Agency was enough to get him ushered straight into the staff car park.

He found the maids' storage room easily, making a note of the toilet opposite. In it was a chair; a trolley; a champagne bucket full of ice; a name badge; half a dozen pristine, folded, white napkins; and a pair of spotless white cotton gloves. There was also a small cool box full of ice and a spare bucket. She had told him that it was unseemly to have the bottle dripping with water. The misting of a good chill was the desired effect.

He set his alarm for 10pm, removed the champagne from the

rucksack and placed it in the bucket, and then got changed into his uniform before pinning the badge on his breast pocket, as instructed. He was now called Harish Roshan. He took a selfie. He had never looked so smart. He was beginning to get an idea of what he would do with the fortune he was about to make.

At 10pm he phoned reception.

"Hotel Oberon. May I be of assistance?" came the crisp tones of Mrs Gautam. How had someone so refined given in to the temptation of something as crude as money?

"Mr Verma has ordered that I am to take Faruk Khan a bottle of champagne. Can you phone when he goes to his room?"

"Very well. Should I use this number?"

"Yes," Jaspal said uncertainly. They had not rehearsed that bit.

"I will let you know when he leaves his dinner, and also instruct hotel security. You should have no problem accessing The Presidential Suite."

The line went dead. For the first time that evening Jaspal felt nervous. That was OK. It was good. It would give him an edge provided it did not get out of hand, which it would not.

He realised he had no idea what time the event was due to finish. He could not exactly phone up and ask. He would just have to wait.

As the adrenaline receded, tiredness swept over him. Feeling himself nodding off, he sat up straight – he could not fall asleep. He got up and paced up and down the room. But the tiredness was too much. He removed his jacket, went to the toilet and washed his face in cold water. This helped. He went back, sat down and started watching the YouTube videos on manners. It got him more into the zone.

The call eventually came through at 11.41pm.

"Mr Khan has gone up to The Presidential Suite and the security outside his room has been informed."

"Thank you, mam," Jaspal replied.

The line went dead.

Jaspal put his phone on silent, donned the jacket, quickly and efficiently changed the champagne bucket and ice, and made his way up to the fifth floor. As he emerged from the lift he spotted the security guard sitting on the chair outside a double doorway.

As Jaspal approached, the guard stood up. He looked at Jaspal's badge and then opened the door to let him in.

Jaspal tried not to look overawed. The place was *huge*. You could easily get three small houses into this room. But he quickly realised there were doors going off it – it was bigger than he thought.

Faruk Khan was sitting on the sofa some distance from the door. In front of Khan was the largest TV Jaspal had ever seen. It was not switched on.

Khan looked over to Jaspal and smiled pleasantly.

Jaspal was surprised. When Ajay had told him he was going to kill a drug dealer he expected to find someone who looked hardened. This man looked good natured, friendly and intelligent. He could have been a gentleman politician.

Jaspal wheeled the trolley over to where Khan was sitting.

"Shall I pour the champagne, sir?"

"Am I correct in thinking it's a 2007 Dellamotte?"

"Yes, sir."

"You're spoiling me," Khan replied, ever so slightly slurring. "Yes, yes, pour away."

Jaspal removed the bottle from the ice, cut the foil and carefully removed the cage before using a napkin to gently ease out for cork. It opened with the merest pop. He poured some into a glass, spilling a little over the edge. Khan was watching.

"Sorry, sir."

Khan smiled indulgently.

Jaspal used a clean napkin to wipe the glass, whilst emptying approximately half the vial into the drink. It was wise to retain some, just in case Khan was so drunk he dropped it.

He handed the glass to Khan.

Khan took a sip.

"Exquisite," he announced.

He took another sip before saying: "Pour yourself a glass."

"I can't, sir," Jaspal said meekly. Thank god he had been watching those videos on manners.

"Nonsense!" Khan boomed. "Pour yourself a glass and take a seat. I insist!" He indicated the seat opposite him with a flourish of his hand. This guy was very drunk.

By the time Jaspal had poured himself a glass, Khan had knocked his back. He passed the empty glass to Jaspal, who filled it and put the rest of the Rohypnol in. He gave Khan the glass before sitting down.

"You fellows know how to put on a good meal," Khan enthused. "It's been an absolutely first class night."

"Thank you, sir," Jaspal replied, smiling. Well, at least he would die happy.

"How long have you been here..." Khan leant forward to look at Jaspal's name badge. "Rossan." His slur had just got worse.

"Not long, sir."

"How long?" Khan said, shutting his eyes. He sounded far away and tired.

"Well, to tell you the truth, sir, it's my first day."

But Khan was not listening. He had keeled over and was fast asleep.

Jaspal got up, pulled Khan by the arm so he was sitting upright, put one hand under his chin and the other on the crown of his head. He twisted his head sharply. There was a loud, satisfying succession of cracks. He swapped the position of his hands and jerked the head in the opposite direction. There were only a couple of cracks this time, and a lot quieter. He reversed the position of his hands again. This time there were no cracks. He carefully felt for a pulse. His job was done. He laid him back down, but put a cushion under his head so it did not hang at an awkward angle.

After putting the champagne bucket on the table in front of Khan, Jaspal wheeled the trolley to the door and let himself out, shutting the door quietly behind him.

"He's had a bit too much to drink. He's asleep," Jaspal explained to the security guard in a quiet voice.

"He was staggering when he came up," the guard said, grinning. "I'll get housekeeping to sort things out."

"Let him sleep it off," Jaspal said calmly, even though his heart was pounding. "You'll make him angry if you wake him up now."

The guard grinned even more broadly and nodded. He obviously had experienced what Jaspal was talking about.

Jaspal took the trolley back to the maids' room, retrieved the rucksack from where he had hidden it (it had all his money in it – as soon as Ajay paid him, he was leaving Delhi for good), got changed and made his way briskly back to his motorbike.

He texted Ajay: "All done."

Ajay texted back: "Park BEHIND car in front of shop. Text when you are here."

He got to Ajay's at 12:53. He texted. Ajay let him in and led the way to the back of the shop. Standing back, Ajay pointed at the wall. Jaspal took his usual position.

Ajay approached, silently uncovering the wooden box and removing the hammer. He held it for a brief moment, his eyes involuntarily closing as he rocked back and forth as nausea tore through him. He had to do this. After tonight every policeman across India, and quite a few outside the country would be looking for Jaspal. He *would* be caught. When he was, there was no way this ruthless drug dealing murderer was going to be loyal to anyone except himself. He had to do it.

He opened his eyes. Jaspal was beginning to fidget. He took the hammer in both hands and swung it with all his might into Jaspal's head, causing him to promptly collapse. Ajay ran into the toilet and threw up.

He put on a pair of rubber gloves, removed the rucksack from Jaspal's back, got a short length of nylon rope, wrapped it once around Jaspal's neck and pulled as hard as he could on both ends, holding on for at least five minutes. He checked Jaspal's pulse. Nothing. Ajay felt completely drained. He sat on the floor, hugging himself and gently rocking backwards and forwards. He was a drug dealer. This was the cost of doing business. What else could he have done? Let Khan kill him? Go to prison for the rest of his life? Leave Delhi and everything he knew behind – including Deepika? He had had no choice. Back and forth, back and forth. Slowly, his breathing and his heartbeat returned to normal.

He opened his eyes and looked at his watch. Nearly two o'clock. He could not just sit here all night. He had a body to get rid of.

He picked the glasses up from where they had fallen, and searched Jaspal for the phone. He replayed the video, starting from when Jaspal had left the shop this afternoon. He skipped through it until he got to the bit where Khan passed out. He watched Jaspal break his neck. By the time he had finished it looked as if the only thing attaching Khan's head to his body was his flesh. He was definitely dead.

Ajay had to remind himself that Mrs Gautam had seen Jaspal, as had the security guard at the staff gate and the one sat outside Khan's room. He had undoubtedly been captured by the hotel's CCTV. It would be fourteen hours at the very most before it was discovered that Khan was dead, and then Jaspal's picture would be everywhere. Even if Jaspal had left Delhi, or even India, chances were that it would not be long before he was caught.

Ajay searched Jaspal again, removing anything from his pockets.

He opened the shutter and looked outside. No one was around. He unlocked Jaspal's bike and put it in the back of the car – he had lowered the back seat and laid down black plastic sheeting in preparation. He then carried Jaspal's body and dumped it on top of the bike. He covered both with a large, black plastic sheet.

After locking up the shop, he drove until he picked up the Yamuna Expressway. Speeding along it, he looked for the turnoff he and Rishi had taken on their way back from the Taj Mahal all that time ago. At last, he spotted it. He took the next exit and doubled back, coming off at exactly the same point. He went along the country roads, careful not to go too fast. He did not want to wreck everything now by coming off the road.

At last the road went by the banks of the Yamuna, just as he remembered. He parked up, got out of the car and opened the door of the boot. He had planned to use the meat cleaver to remove Jaspal's hands, feet and head. He would dispose of these here by putting them in plastic bags and weighing the bags down with vinyl weights. He would get rid of the rest of the body further down the river. But he found himself frozen to the spot. It was bad enough that he had killed Jaspal – he could not mutilate him as well.

He got back into the car.

He drove along until he could see a bridge over the river in the distance. When he had last been here, there had been no buildings anywhere near the bridge, but this was India – things changed fast. He dimmed his headlights and slowed down.

As he approached he realised that there were still no buildings in sight of the bridge. For the first time that evening he felt relieved. He drove halfway along the bridge, stopped and turned the headlights off.

He removed the body and the motorbike from the car, depositing them next to the handrail at the edge of the bridge. He tied one end of a rope around the section attaching the steering rack to the main section of the bike. He tied the other end to the waist of the body. There was no more than a metre of rope between the two.

Pausing momentarily to catch his breath, he dropped the body over the handrail of the bridge. It lifted up the motorbike, which caught on the handrail. The body dangled ghoulishly. If there had been anything left in his stomach he would have thrown up. Instead he dry retched.

He quickly managed to regain enough control to heave the bike over the handrail, his task made easier by the weight of the body pulling it. Both landed in the water with a loud splash. He shone his torch on to the water. Nothing to see apart from a few ripples.

Next he put the plastic sheeting in a bag with a couple of vinyl weights, and tied the top shut with a small section of rope before hurling it into the river.

He put his headlights on low beam, drove to the end of the bridge, turned around and came back again. When he was well away from the bridge he put his headlights on main beam and picked up speed, but still had enough of his senses about him not to go too fast.

10

That night he slept deeply, but not peacefully. He dreamt of Jaspal attacking him with the hammer and a meat cleaver, whilst Faruk Khan looked on, laughing and sipping champagne. Mrs Gautham ignored what was going on as she busied herself sorting out guests at the hotel reception, who also seemed oblivious to the bloody massacre happening only a few feet away.

He woke up feeling drained.

He slowly came round, aided by chai and stuffed paratha made by his mother. She chatted to him about what was happening in Paraharavi. Although he could not take most of it in, it helped him feel more normal. Dutifully, he showed her his latest purchase – the car. She was delighted to see how well he was doing. Normally this would have made him feel happy, but all it did was bring back his wretchedness.

Before leaving he asked her to start making samosas again.

He went to the shop and spent most of the day carefully watching the two videos Jaspal had taken the day before. Jaspal had stuck strictly to instructions, never even hinting at Ajay's identity. Ajay was relieved.

The other thing that struck Ajay was Faruk Khan's demeanour. He had expected to see some kind of bad-tempered thug. Nothing could have been further from the truth. Khan was an affable gentleman, whose M.O. was to get even the lowliest on side by treating them as friends and nearly equals. Those intelligent eyes made him look even more approachable. Could this really be who Singh had been referring to?

He watched Jaspal's interaction with Khan again and again. This guy did not bully people into respecting him. Instead he charmed them into liking him. Although he was not averse to using aggression, his first weapon of choice was charm. And Ajay had no doubt it was more effective. Any rival would not only have to fight off his covertly delivered aggression, but also the disdain of most of society, who would be on Khan's side. This was definitely the way to do business.

By the time he got around to watching news reports they were full of Khan's death. They talked of the parliamentary hopeful who had quickly become the people's favourite. Pictures of Jaspal ran alongside those of Khan. A huge manhunt was underway. At first this made Ajay's heart rate speed up, but that was quickly replaced by a sense of relief. He had done the right thing.

That evening he drove past Khan's samosa shop. It was closed.

As soon as Dileesh's Samosa Joint opened the next day, business boomed. As a one-off, Ajay brought 100 bags of heroin with him. Although Khan had been dealing in Connaught Place – a different area of Delhi – it was not that far from Paharganj. Khan would have knocked out the competition in and around Connaught Place. His customers would now be desperately looking further afield for their fix.

By the end of the day they had sold 89 of the bags. Rishi was exhausted. Many of the regulars were getting two or three at a time (obviously the lack of supply had put people on panic stations), but there were a significant number of new customers as well. Was it time to expand?

He could get more boys to distribute from the shop. But it would be too obvious. Rishi was enough. A better way would be to open more shops. Khan's place had been open for three weeks without Ajay even being aware that he had any kind of competition. If he opened one in Connaught Place, another in Chandni Chowk, and the fourth in Sadar Bazaar, they would be spread out enough for each to maintain a healthy trade.

After shutting for the day, Ajay made chai for himself and Rishi. They sat down to drink it, slowly unwinding from the frenzied activity of the day.

"I'm thinking of expanding."

"Are you, bhaiyaa?"

"Yeah. Our rival in Connaught Place has shut down."

Rishi nodded. He had heard.

"I think I'll start there. I'll need you to take over this shop – it'll mean more money for you."

"Thank you, bhaiyaa." There had been a hesitation before he spoke. He had something on his mind.

"What's up, Rishi?" It was a question Ajay knew the answer to, but he needed Rishi to bring it out into the open.

Rishi remained silent.

"Talk to me, Rishi. You're my best friend."

After a hesitation Rishi said: "No one's heard from Jaspal for a couple of days." He was barely audible.

Ajay nodded.

"It's as if he's disappeared." The words tumbled out of Rishi's mouth as if a dam of fear had unexpectedly burst. He looked petrified as soon as he stopped talking, clearly afraid he had crossed a boundary, beyond which his very existence was threatened.

"Maybe he did some work which required him to disappear. And maybe he was paid enough money to set him up for life in another part of the country?" Ajay raised his eyebrows and smiled as he looked at Rishi, as if to say: *Have you thought of that?*

It had the desired effect. The worry lifted off Rishi's face.

"Is Ramesh still around?" asked Ajay.

Rishi nodded again.

"Would he be willing to do your job for the same money I pay you?"

"Definitely," Rishi said without hesitation.

"Would you be willing to do my job for double what you make now?"

Rishi was speechless. He could do nothing but nod.

"Can you get Ramesh to start tomorrow?"

"I'll text him now," Rishi replied, getting his phone out.

Ajay sipped at his chai as Rishi typed and sent the text. The reply came back almost immediately.

"He'll be here at 9:30," announced Rishi.

Ajay nodded and smiled in satisfaction, his head still bobbing as he brought the chai to his lips.

Within a few days Ajay found premises in Connaught Place. Rishi found someone to work with Ajay. The new boy and Ajay spent several days fitting the shop out before opening it. Ajay put an advert on the dark web: "Heroin in Connaught Place, Delhi. Cash. Good quality." By the end of the first week they were trading at full capacity: 50 bags a day.

The new boy, Manoj, proved to be every bit as good as Rishi. Within a month Ajay had recruited another street dealer and left Manoj to run the shop.

The next shop was, as planned, at Chandni Chowk.

Three weeks later, he had one at Sadar Bazaar. Staff ran them all. He just made sure that they were well stocked and kept a careful eye on things.

When he had opened the Connaught Place shop, called AJs Samosas, he had asked Mrs Pandey to find someone in Paraharavi who could make samosas for it. Although he knew she could double production, he also knew it would be stressful for her. She had found someone immediately – a Mrs Pilania (it had got around Paraharavi some time ago what a generous payer Ajay was).

When it came to the shop at Chandni Chowk (Bimala's Samosas), Mrs Pilania was happy to produce the samosas for it as well.

But he was not very happy about how things were developing. He had to make two pickups every morning and, although Mrs Pilania did a very good job, her kitchen was very basic, as were nearly all the kitchens in Paraharavi. Most of his customers were tourists, who had notoriously delicate digestive systems. Having any authorities looking into his operations was a complication that was best avoided.

He contemplated opening a small factory in Paraharavi for the express purpose of making samosas. He could put Mrs Pandey in charge. He took a day off work just so he could observe the way his mum worked. He soon saw why his mum loved what she did. She and the other woman who helped her worked well together, each having their own role, but helping each other out when required, whilst chatting away to break up the monotony. The work was fun and not at all stressful. A factory would destroy all this. He would be able to get a machine to mix the dough and more machines to cut the vegetables, and yet another machine to make the samosas. It would save a lot of money. But it would also mean that his mum would not be sitting around the table, talking with her friend.

The house to the right of them was slightly smaller than theirs and was occupied by a family of five – the Shenoys. They had come to Delhi three years before and worked hard. They were the type of people whose aim was to move out of Paraharavi and into a fancy apartment as soon as possible. When Ajay offered them enough for a deposit on and six months' rent of a fancy apartment to vacate the house, they jumped at the chance. Before paying them, he bought the property from the landlord.

He approached Kamal, reminding him that he had rebuilt the Pandeys' family home when it had burnt down because Ranveer had asked him to. He told him he would like the entire ground floor of the house currently occupied by the Shenoys to be refitted so it was a large, modern kitchen to Ajay's specifications. He added that he was still firm friends with Ranveer, who had expanded his business and lived in a very impressive house not too far away.

Kamal started work on the kitchen as soon as the house became vacant – a week after Ajay had first approached the Shenoys. He had the kitchen finished in three days. It was perfect. Ajay had no doubt that dropping Ranveer's name into the proceedings had speeded things up enormously, as well as guaranteed the quality of the finished project.

Ajay had a large fridge and two large freezers installed at the far end. Along the length of the room were two stainless steel tables with two chairs around each of them. Some free standing industrial shelving held all the equipment and ambient ingredients needed for two teams of samosa makers. There was a stainless steel sink near each of the tables. Four large cooking rings with an extraction fan above them occupied the area at the opposite end of the room to the fridge and freezers.

He employed Mrs Pilania to run the kitchen. He explained that he wanted her to employ three women so there could be two teams of two, including her. He would pay them per samosa made. He added that, although Mrs Pandey was to carry on as she was in her own kitchen, and Mrs Pilania was entirely in charge of the new kitchen, Mrs Pilania was to show Mrs Pandey all the deference a boss' mother should expect.

For this Mrs Pilania was to be paid twice the rate the other members in her team were. Oh, and if Ajay heard the slightest rumour that Mrs Pilania was taking any type of backhanders or getting the other workers to hand over any of their wages, Ajay would make sure she never got the job in Paraharavi ever again.

Ajay had discussed these arrangements with Mrs Pandey beforehand. She had smiled the twinkly smile of a parent who is touched by the love and consideration of their child. He also noticed that the crease between her eyes, which had faded so much over the past few years, was now barely visible.

The new arrangement worked well. Freezing the samosas led to far less wastage, and it allowed stocks to build up, releasing any pressure should production fall off for any reason. Hygiene standards were maintained. People were desperate to work at the new kitchen, meaning that Mrs Pilania, who proved to be an excellent choice, was able to recruit industrious individuals who gelled well in their teams.

Each of the shops now had a freezer as well as a fridge, meaning that Ajay had to deliver samosas every few days at the most. However, he still spent some time at his mum's small kitchen and the larger kitchen at least every three days. He enjoyed listening to the inconsequential chatter and the occasional banter as he slowly sipped a cup of chai.

He had realised even before opening the Connaught Place shop that he could not carry on laundering money just through an enormous number of bank accounts. It would not be long before someone at a bank realised he was depositing what totalled up to incredible amounts of cash spread over a large number of branches of that bank, and told the authorities. He needed something more sophisticated.

He spoke to Ranveer, meeting him at the industrial unit where he kept his supplies.

"I'm ready to take the next step, bhaiyaa," Ajay said.

"Why, what's happening, Chotu?" Although the nickname Chotu (which also meant "little one" in Hindi) had been endearing at first, it had begun to irritate Ajay sometime ago. He was easily Ranveer's best customer, and was soon to become a far, far better one. He deserved some respect. But he smiled.

"I'm going to open a shop in Connaught Place –"

"Congratulations. You are doing well, Chotu."

Ajay smiled and carried on "- and I need a way to deal with the money that's coming in."

Ranveer nodded, knowing exactly what Ajay meant.

"Have you heard of Hawala?" Ranveer asked.

Ajay shook his head.

"It means you can transfer your money all over the world without anyone being able to track it." Ranveer took out his phone and was silent for a moment as he searched through it. "OK, take down this number."

Ajay got his phone out and typed in the number as Ranveer dictated it.

"That's the number for Vikram Rahman – he's the head of the New Delhi Financial Sector Chamber of Commerce."

Ajay looked at him a little blankly.

Ranveer laughed lightly. "You've got a lot to learn, Chotu. There are loads of chambers of commerce in Delhi. It's where 'respectable' business people meet. You make friends and do deals."

Ajay tried to look confident, but there was a glint of uncertainty and nervousness in his eyes which he could not hide.

"Let me give Mr Rahman a call. I'll find out when the NDFSCC meets. I'll introduce you to him."

From scraping by in a slum to business meetings...

The next meeting was on Saturday afternoon, three days later. As always, it was held in a large meeting room at The Oberon. Ajay had mixed feelings when he entered the hotel. He had never been before but, in many ways, he owed the upcoming expansion of his operations to this place. Was that a good thing? He still did not know.

However, he was definitely impressed by its grandeur. He could get used to coming to places like this.

As soon as they went into the meeting room, Ranveer walked towards a balding man with slightly greying hair. Slimly built and, at about five feet four inches, he looked like a child next to Ranveer and Ajay. However, his demeanour was by no means diminutive. The furrowed brow and angry eyes seemed to be a mirror to his soul.

"Mr Rahman..." Ranveer said, smiling.

Rahman looked up at him, not letting any cheeriness pollute his face. "Mr Kaushik," he replied flatly.

"This is Mr Pandey, the gentleman I told you about," Ranveer said.

Ajay felt his chest expand with pride at being referred to as Mr Pandey and as a gentleman. 'Mr Pandey' was a title which he had only known his father to carry. It was now his, as was only right and proper. He may not be considered an adult by many measures, but his financial success and his importance to many others' wellbeing meant he was more of an adult than at least 98% of so-called adults.

Mr Rahman looked at Ajay, his expression unchanging. He offered his hand. It was almost a reluctant gesture. Ajay suspected he only ever did it at the first meeting. Ajay took the proffered hand and shook it.

"Shall we go to a private room?" Mr Rahman said, leading the way before Ajay even had the chance to answer.

Once they were in the room, the door was closed and they were both seated, Mr Rahman opened with: "Mr Kaushik tells me you need money to be moved."

"Yes," replied Ajay uncertainly. He did not just want it moved; he wanted it *laundered*.

Mr Rahman let a grimace of a smile cross his face. "Mr Pandey, when you talk about certain matters, it is best to keep the language acceptable. One never knows who is listening. Of course, language alone doesn't ensure proper safeguarding, but it does lend an extra degree of security."

Ajay nodded. He had a lot to learn and, the way things were going, he needed to learn quickly. His transition to full adulthood was going to be far faster than he had thought even a few moments ago.

"Mr Kaushik tells me you've been inquiring about moving money."

Ajay nodded firmly.

"Good. Now, the traditional way to move money was via Hawala, but that is now illegal. However, there are many in Delhi and all around the globe who operate in, let's say, very, very *similar* ways to Hawala. Do you know much about Hawala?"

Ajay shook his head.

"It's quite simple. One takes one's cash to a Hawala broker. For a small commission, the broker transfers the cash to, say, Karachi. There someone picks up the cash and takes it to another Hawala broker, who transfers it to Kabul for a small commission. From there it can be transferred in a similar manner to, say, Dubai. Because records are not kept and the cash movements are made with the utmost discretion, it's virtually impossible to track the money. It's a good way for astute business people to spread out their earnings." In other words, launder black money.

Ajay smiled and nodded.

"It's wise to always use several brokers. The entire system is based on trust. Hawala, as I say, is illegal, but those who have operated such systems have always been very honourable people – I have never known any one of them to steal. But, if the quantities of great, the chances of someone along the chain being tempted are also great, and you have no legal recourse. Take my advice: use several brokers."

Ajay nodded. Rahman was obviously a man of few words. If he repeated something you would have to be a complete idiot not to take it very, very seriously.

"I can introduce you to several gentlemen who may be able to help you..."

Ajay nodded.

Rahman looked at him coldly, raising his eyebrows slightly.

Ajay started slightly, realising he had made a faux pas. He opened the small satchel he had over his shoulder, and took out five thick bundles of high denomination notes. He put them neatly on the small table between him and Rehman. It was the amount Ranveer had told Ajay to pay Rahman.

Rahman opened his briefcase and put the money in it.

"It's been a pleasure doing business with you." Rahman sounded as if he had long ago forgotten the meaning of pleasure – or had he just been born miserable? "Come with me please, Mr Pandey."

Sure enough, Rahman introduced Ajay to five excellent contacts.

By the time all four shops were operational, Ajay was using the services of the five "Hawala" agents. His money went all over the world, eventually ending up in bank accounts in Switzerland, the Cayman Islands, Panama, Bahrain and Samoa. He could not believe it. He now earned more in an hour than he used to in a year.

He developed a steady routine, delivering 50 bags of heroin to each shop every day, and delivering samosas every few days. He picked up the shops' takings daily, giving them to the Hawala agents to deal with a few times a week.

He regularly changed the sites he advertised on on the dark web. There was no denying business was good – the shops sold out of heroin every day.

However, as the weeks turned into months, he noticed a peculiar pattern developing with the Connaught Place shop. When he checked the burner phones (which he destroyed every two weeks), he found all the other shops except Connaught Place had a lot of repeat custom. This could not be explained away by it being a tourist area – Paharganj was even more touristy. Also, he found that the Connaught Place shop finished selling its stock of heroin a lot later in the day than the other shops.

He had a good idea of what was happening, but he had to make sure. He knew it was risky using web cams as the video feed could be intercepted. Instead, he got a couple of microcameras with enough memory to record for several days each. He waited until the manager, Manoj Mishra, had left for the night. He then hid them in places in the shop that gave him a good overall view of what was happening there.

He removed them three days later, and did not have to watch the recordings for long for his suspicions to be confirmed. Manoj had his own phone from which he took orders. Undoubtedly some, if not all, of those orders came from customers established via Ajay's advertisements. Although Ajay had not suffered financially, this increased activity heightened the likelihood of attracting unwanted attention. And that was after Ajay treated Manoj so well. In short, Manoj was taking the piss.

Ajay watched a bit more to see if the street boy was in on it. Every night Manoj paid him what all the other street boys working in the shops were paid. The boy was not in on the double dealing – he probably did not know that anything was amiss. As a street dealer you did exactly as you were told and kept your mouth shut when you earned that kind of money.

Ajay spent a little longer with Manoj when he next delivered samosas.

"How's business? Any problems?" asked Ajay conversationally.

"Everything is fine, bhaiyaa," Manoj replied with a wobble of his head.

"Be careful. I heard the police are cracking down in this area."

"Yes, bhaiyaa," Manoj answered, looking worried.

"If anything happens, remember that I'll look after you..."

"Thank you, bhaiyaa."

"But if you open your mouth, I guarantee you'll be dead within 24 hours." Ajay stared at Manoj, who seemed to shrink away. This guy may be devious, but he did not have the balls to back it up. Time to take him down.

Later that day, Ajay phoned Gurpreet Singh, who had recently been promoted to sub-inspector.

The next day Manoj was picked up by the police within 100 metres of his home. He was handcuffed and taken to the police station. In his rucksack, which was searched in front of him, there were 50 small snap bags, each containing small quantities of what appeared to be heroin.

Sub-Inspector Gurpreet Singh was sitting in his office when he received a call from the front desk.

"Sub-Inspector-ji?"

"Yes, what is it?"

"Manoj Mishra is ready to be interviewed," said the voice over the phone. Singh had left orders that he be informed as soon as Mishra was brought in.

"Take him to interview room three. Don't give him any water." Singh commanded.

"Yes, Sub-Inspector-ji."

Singh put the phone down and carried on with paperwork for the next two hours.

Singh entered the interview room where Manoj had been baking. It was rarely used as the heat in it was stifling.

Singh slowly walked over to the table, reading Manoj's file.

Manoj was handcuffed to the chair on the other side of the table.

"25 grams of heroin," Singh said slowly as he sat down. He looked straight at Manoj as he added: "That's ten years of hard labour, my friend. Will you survive that?"

"I want to speak to..." Manoj's voice came out hoarsely – partly due to extreme thirst, and partly because he was terrified.

Singh cut him short by rasping: "It was in 50 bags – each weighing exactly half a gram. Looked very much like you're a dealer, Mishra. You'll be lucky to get away with just 10 years."

"I want to speak..."

"All in good time, my friend," Singh said pleasantly. "But let's get some formalities out of the way... Where did you get it from?"

Manoj looked down, but said nothing.

"Co-operate now, and things might be easier for you." Singh waited a couple of minutes before continuing. "Where do you deal?"

Manoj looked up and yelled: "I want to speak to Ajay Pandey!"

Singh feigned confusion. "Mr Pandey, who owns AJs samosas?"

"Yes!"

"How would a respectable businessman like Mr Pandey know the likes of you?" Singh sneered.

"I work for him!" Manoj did not lower his tone.

"Mr Pandey is not the kind of gentleman who'd want anything to do with the likes of you," Singh said, not letting up on his sneering tone.

"I work for him! I'm not saying anything until I see him!"

Singh sat back and watched Manoj for a few minutes. He looked hot, sweaty, exhausted and frightened.

"Please, I need to speak to him..." Manoj almost whispered.

Singh watched him for more minutes before saying: "Very well, my friend. Give me his phone number."

Singh wrote down the phone number as Manoj slowly and carefully dictated it.

Singh gave the number to the constable waiting outside the cell. "Take the prisoner to holding cell four, and *then* phone this number. Mr Ajay Pandey should answer. Tell him the prisoner wants to talk to him, and ask him to come to the station."

Singh went back to his office, where he got a phone call 20 minutes later. It was the constable he had instructed to phone Ajay Pandey.

"I'm very sorry, sir, but the phone number you gave me does not connect. I've tried three times."

Oh dear, he must have written the number down incorrectly. How careless of him...

"Mishra must have given me the wrong number. Go and ask him for the number again," ordered Singh.

"Yes, sir."

Singh smiled to himself as he waited for his phone to ring.

"Sir!" came the panicked voice of the constable. "The prisoner seems to be dead!"

"Wait with the prisoner – I'll be straight down."

Singh rushed down to holding cell four, making sure he had a concerned look on his face.

The door to the cell was open, with three constables in the cell and another four outside. The five other prisoners had been herded to the back of the cell. Manoj lay on the ground at the front of the cell. Singh crouched down beside him. He appeared to be lifeless. Judging by the angle and rotation of his head, his neck had been broken.

"Call an ambulance!" bellowed Singh.

The ambulance came within 20 minutes. Half an hour after that Singh received a phone call, informing him that Manoj Mishra was dead. He appeared to have died of a broken neck. However, the exact cause of his death would have to be established in a post mortem.

It was found that the CCTV in holding cell four had stopped working several hours before Manoj had been taken there. The other men in the cell were questioned at length, but they all claimed not to have seen a thing. They were the kind of men who would only break under extreme duress – the kind that was not legal, and would damage the reputation of the police if word got out.

Any further investigation was unlikely to get anywhere. Singh decided not to take any more action. He was well aware that the consensus in the police station and in the wider community was that a dead drug dealer was a good thing, no matter what the cause.

Some formalities were carried out, but the case notes were filed away amongst the plethora of unsolved crimes that happened on a daily basis in Delhi.

Ajay did not feel upset about Manoj's death, which worried him. Although he had held it together at the time, he had felt awful about Jaspal. He had even felt bad about Anand and Khan. He felt no remorse about Manoj. He must be getting hardened. He was not sure if he liked what was happening to him.

Ajay waited a week for the news of Manoj's death to get around. He then made sure the shop managers knew that Manoj had been found with 50 bags of heroin on him, which Ajay suspected he was selling via the Connaught Place shop without Ajay's permission – he left them to work out the rest for themselves.

Ajay summoned the street boys and spoke to them individually. He told them that they should be distributing no more than 50 bags a day and, if they suspected the shop managers were doing anything wrong, they were to phone him directly. He assured them that they would not be identified as a source. They would also be richly rewarded. But, if Ajay found they ever withheld anything, losing their jobs would be the very least of their problems. The only one to look worried was the street boy from Connaught Place. In fact, he looked petrified. Ajay decided not to get rid of him – there was no way he was ever again going to keep anything even slightly suspicious to himself.

11

As the months went by, Ajay saw the money in his foreign accounts grow and grow. It was becoming a ridiculously large amount. He could set up a series of shell companies and bring it back to India but, by the time he had paid taxes etc, he would lose over a quarter of it. He decided to leave it where it was.

He contemplated moving to a house like Ranveer's – big and somewhere posh. But he was torn. His mother was happy with her life – it was the first time he had ever seen this. Bimala and Nitesh also seemed to be happy at their new school and had a good circle of friends in the local area.

He still saw Deepika every Monday afternoon. Although he made regular use of the services offered by Natasha and her friends, he had yet to meet someone whom he felt as deeply for as he felt for Deepika. It was incredibly frustrating that he had to keep their relationship a secret.

After leaving school, she wanted to go to university, but she always talked about going to university somewhere nearby – her mother and father would not be happy about her leaving Delhi. If he had a large house, maybe her parents would consent to them marrying whilst she was still studying. It was not something he had discussed with Deepika – he was waiting until he was 18, now less than a year away.

He was buying 700g of heroin a week from Ranveer. He was keen not to have too much of the stuff on him at any one point. He knew he would go to prison even if he was caught with a small amount, but the greater the quantity, the harsher the sentence. For this reason he visited Ranveer every other day at his industrial unit. It was also good to chat with him.

"I wish my gangmasters could shift as much as you," Ranveer said to Ajay on one of his visits.

Ranveer had had the office done out. Before it had been little more than utilitarian, with a safe, a metal desk and a couple of reasonably comfortable swivel chairs. Ranveer could not understand this. All that money coming in, and a shithole of an office?

Ranveer had got in an antique pedestal desk, dating back to the days of the viceroys. His chair was a top end swivel chair. On the other side of the desk were two luxurious armchairs. The safe was disguised by a darkwood cupboard, on which sat a 48 inch TV. He had also had a kitchenette area put into the industrial unit, so his security could make him chai and warm up snacks at his request.

The meetings with Ajay were always quite lengthy: there was a lot of gossip to catch up on from Paraharavi.

"Mrs Pilania is a godsend. She's clever. She keeps everyone happy, including my mother," Ajay said wistfully.

Ranveer nodded, also looking as if he could do with a bit more of that. He looked on edge and a little drawn. Ajay had noticed this more and more about him in the last few months. Ajay thought it was probably because, like him, he was bored. Yeah, he was being deluged with money, but that was all. There was nothing to get stuck into, nothing to grab him. When he had first taken over from Bakshi, he had had to learn the ropes. After that he had set up the clothing business as a cover. This took some time. Only when it was in place did he work on getting the industrial unit looking less like a tin shed and more like something he wanted to spend time in. After that there was little to do except watch his bank balance grow.

Ajay usually just phoned up and popped in. This meant that occasionally the safe was empty. One of those times was right now. But it was not a problem.

The office had six inch tall, ornate skirting boards going along the bottom of all the walls. They were tastefully stained to the same shade of dark brown as all the other wooden furniture in the room. Ranveer got up and removed a section of skirting board just behind him. To look at it, you would never guess it would come away. It fitted perfectly against the wall, with no tell-tale gaps between it and the wall or the sections of skirting board next to it. However, a light push against it led to a barely audible click as the mechanism released the board, to reveal a compartment about four inches high, seven inches deep and two feet wide. Enough to take a lot of heroin and cash.

Ranveer removed two 100g bags. Ajay suspected there were other compartments along the skirting boards. He was right – Ranveer had had five fitted in total, but this was the only one he used. Their purpose had initially been to hide the merchandise should the police try to raid the place. He had also had the external doors reinforced. It would take a heavy car quite a few goes before it got through the shutter, and several large men with a battering ram several minutes to get through the door. Enough time to put the heroin in the compartments.

Business had grown due to Ranveer recruiting more gangmasters and pressuring them all to push more product. As a result the safe had become too small for his requirements. It was at the back of his mind to buy a new safe and get another cupboard made to cover it, but he was happy at the moment to use the compartment for his overflow.

Ajay made Ranveer smile when he told him about how he had got Kamal to do an excellent job on the kitchen in double quick time by telling Kamal that he and Ranveer were still good friends.

"Why wouldn't he do a good job for you?" asked Ranveer.

"What, a jumped-up teenage samosa wallah?"

Ranveer looked confused. "Doesn't anyone even suspect what you really do?"

"No."

Ranveer looked even more confused. "A little bit of fear's good. If you make people shake with it they avoid you, but a little bit means they respect you. Things get done quicker and everyone is ever so polite."

Ajay shrugged. Ranveer was right – to an extent. He remembered the look of terror on his mum's face that night their house burned down and Ranveer offered them a room in his house. He also recalled what people had said in hushed whispers about Ranveer when he lived in Paraharavi and they thought he was a drug dealer. Mrs Kaushik may have felt she had been part of the community but, in reality, the other women had been very careful not to snub her. None of them had ever considered her a friend.

People were not so polite with Ajay. He had quite a bit of respect because of his success in running a chain of samosa shops and because he provided jobs for people in the slum. They were not rude to him, but did not feel the need for formality or to lick his boots either. Instead, they affectionately teased him and he teased them back. He had a closeness with them that would have been impossible if they feared him.

Ajay's problem was that he no longer had that drive to provide for his family. He was not even 18 years old and he had more than enough money to last him several lifetimes. He liked talking to people in Paraharavi, but he no longer felt part of it all – that feeling of it being them against the rest of the world. Boundaries had become blurred: maybe he was now part of the rest of the world.

As time went on even more money rolled in. Ranveer provided a consistent, uninterrupted supply. The shops ran smoothly – Ajay had no doubt that this was at least partly due to Manoj's death. Ranveer had been right about fear, but you had to be careful where you used it.

Singh and Ajay still met up, but it was now every two weeks. The arrangement suited them both. Each visit netted Singh a generous amount, plus a bonus if he provided something useful, which he always made sure he did. Ajay knew most of what Singh told him, but he still paid him the bonus to keep him on side.

There were small-time street dealers in central Delhi, but Ajay let them be. He knew it was pointless getting Singh to arrest them – they would soon be replaced by others equally as desperate. However, occasionally, somebody tried to move in and run small gangs of street dealers: Ajay would get Singh to stamp down on them hard.

There was one occasion when a big-time dealer, Mr Laghari, was moving in from Mumbai. Ajay leant heavily on Singh to arrest him. He paid Singh a very large bonus and strongly implied that he would make sure his career in the police would end very quickly if he did not do as he was told. The police were not the only ones who could fit people up.

Singh was quite rightly scared of Laghari – he had had several Mumbai police inspectors killed. In the end Singh ordered one of his assistant sub-inspectors to arrest him and question him, all the time making sure that Laghari did not see him.

As expected, Laghari's lawyer had him out in hours. Singh told Ajay the second he was released, as he had been instructed to.

As Laghari walked with his lawyer to his waiting car, a sniper's bullet ripped through Laghari's skull.

There was outrage. How could something like that happen just outside a police station? The media were all over the case for months, asking all kinds of questions and prying into things that were not at all related to the affair, presumably just in case anything led back to it. During this time the only communication between Ajay and Singh was via burner phones, and all conversations were very brief. Eventually things died down. When they next met Singh got his biggest bonus ever.

Singh put the money away and just stared at Ajay.

"What is it, my friend?" asked Ajay.

"You've got some balls, haven't you?" Singh asked in awe.

"What do you mean?"

"Khan *and* Laghari?" Singh said in a whisper, almost as if he was too afraid to speak any louder.

"I don't know what you mean..."

Singh just kept on staring at him, his expression a mixture of fear and respect.

"Have you got any news?" asked Ajay, briskly getting back to business.

"Nothing much. Things had been quiet since Laghari – nobody's daring to try anything. Do you blame them? If a major player gets hit outside a police station, they must all be wondering what's going on. *I wouldn't want to take on someone who'd do that.*" He was still staring at Ajay.

"Anything at all?"

"No. Er – except we're going to bust a major heroin supplier in East Delhi."

"Who?" Ajay asked a little too quickly.

"His name is Kaushik. Ranveer Kaushik. He operates out of Greater Kailash, but he covers the whole of East Delhi –"

"When are you busting him?" Ajay could feel his pupils dilating.

"Later this afternoon."

"What time?" Ajay was barely able to keep control of his voice.

Singh looked at him for a moment. "Between one and two – depending on when we can get the relevant personnel together."

"I need to know what time," Ajay said a little more forcefully than needed.

Singh was taken aback – he had never seen Ajay so riled – even when he had told him about Khan and Laghari.

"Who is this Kaushik to you?" Singh wondered if this was a wise thing to say even before the words were out of his mouth.

"Don't ever question me," Ajay said in a low, dangerous voice.

Singh could feel himself physically backing away. He had met plenty of frightening people in his life, but what Ajay had just displayed was a controlled venom that surpassed anything he had come across. No wonder Khan and Laghari were dead.

"Yes, sir," Singh said, getting up slowly so as not to inflame Ajay anymore. "I'll look into it immediately and get back to you. I should have an answer within the hour, sir."

∼

"The raid's going down at thirteen hundred hours on an industrial estate in Greater Kailash –"

"Are you sure?" snapped Ajay.

"Yes. Kaushik's always there at that time. These high level dealers have reinforced doors, so we're using the police jeep with a battering ram on it. That'll tear through anything. We've been watching the place for a while – his security team are rubbish. We'll easily overpower them –"

"How did you find out about him?" Ajay interrupted. Singh's chattiness was annoying him. He was casually talking about destroying his mentor and his best friend – someone, without whom, he could now have been homeless instead of rich.

"He's got a team of 'gangmasters' – they run the street dealers. We occasionally arrest one, but they never say anything – too scared. Well, one came into the police station a few days ago. He said he was willing to give us Kaushik. He said he had seen Kaushik murder the previous guy who ran East Delhi. Apparently he can't live with it, and he wants to see Kaushik locked up. They've been friends since they were kids or something. Thank god for PTSD." Singh said the last bit with a smile in his voice.

Ajay held his temper. Now was the time to think – anger got in the way of that. So Dev had grassed Ranveer up. "Who's leading the raid?"

"Me," Singh replied quietly. He sounded scared. And so he should be. He was about to chuck Ajay's mentor into a rotten, stinking, overcrowded Indian prison for 20 years. Ajay should have Singh tortured to death. But he was more valuable alive. If Singh was not in charge of the raid, someone else would be – someone who would not be as forthcoming.

"Good. Keep me informed."

"Yes, sir."

Ajay severed the connection. Ranveer's life would effectively be over in less than three hours. He phoned him, but it went straight to voicemail. Shit!

Ajay phoned Dilip – Ranveer's head of security. Ranveer had given Ajay his number for emergencies.

"Hello."

"Hello. It's Ajay. Where's Ranveer?" Ajay demanded.

"I'm not sure, sir. He said he had a busy morning and he'd be in by 1pm."

"Tell him to phone me as *soon* as he gets in. It's very, very urgent. Do you understand?"

"Yes, sir," Dilip replied calmly.

"He's got to phone me the second he gets my message. Do you understand?"

"Yes, sir. I will emphasise the urgency in the most assertive manner." Dilip sounded calm, but had clearly taken on board the seriousness of the situation.

Ajay paced up and down. Ranveer was probably availing himself of the services of one of Natasha's "friends". What a time to do it.

But it gave Ajay time to think. If he told Ranveer, Ranveer would probably eventually want to know how he found out. There were some things you told *nobody*. But he could not hold out on Ranveer when it came to something like this. There had to be a way of telling him without revealing his source.

Suddenly, he stopped pacing. He got out his phone and went on to the dark web. He found what he was looking for. It was a website where you anonymously put up information you have on forthcoming police raids. He put the news of Ranveer's bust on the website.

He continued to pace up and down, constantly looking at his watch. *Phone, Ranveer, phone!*

At last, at 12:43, Ranveer phoned.

"Hello."

"Hi Ranveer! Just looked on the net. The police are about to raid your warehouse! Are you there?"

"Yeah –"

"Hide the stuff and the money. It's going to happen at one. Go! You got to be quick!"

The line went dead.

Ranveer's heart was in his mouth. He looked at his watch. 12:44. Quick – think! He had rehearsed the scenario in his head so many times, but his head was fuzzy. He unlocked the safe, pressed open the hidden compartments in the skirting boards and quickly but carefully loaded in the contents from the safe. He locked the safe. 12:52. He sent a pre-prepared text to the gangmasters.

"Police raid. Smash the phone and destroy simcard. Get rid of heroin. Leave Delhi and hide. DO IT NOW. DO NOT FORGET TO DESTROY PHONE AND SIMCARD."

12:54. He opened the office door and stormed over to the two security guards.

"The police are raiding us in five minutes. Tell them nothing. Remember, all I do is sell clothes," he said, pointing to the end of the warehouse which was dominated by cases of high-end imported clothing. He barely broke even on it but, as far as the authorities were concerned, he made a very healthy profit. The taxes were high, but the money was clean. "You'll be arrested, but don't worry – I'll get you the best lawyers. Keep your mouth shut until they get there – don't say anything. They'll get you out. If you blab, I'll make sure you die in prison."

Dilip looked calm and collected. The other guard looked petrified. Although none of the guards had been explicitly told about Ranveer's real trade, Dilip had primed them enough to subtly let them know other trades were going on as well as clothing. It was therefore paramount that the warehouse was kept doubly secure at all times. If they wanted to keep their very well paid jobs and their families safe, they needed to do their jobs well and keep their mouths firmly shut.

"All you need to do is keep your mouth shut and do what the lawyers tell you. I'll look after you and your families," Ranveer said, looking at the scared guard. This seemed to be enough for him to pull himself together slightly.

"Remember, you'll be alright if –"

Just then the door and some of the wall surrounding it was ripped down as a police jeep with a battering ram attached to its front end was driven hard into it. It reversed at speed as police officers ran in, guns drawn.

Ranveer and the guards raised their hands as weapons were pointed at them. They were cuffed and led out to three separate police cars, where they were each guarded by two police officers.

The police fanned out in the warehouse and started searching it, leaving the office to Singh and his next in command, Assistant Sub-Inspector Ranbir Gupta. Singh started slowly and methodically searching the desk. Meanwhile Gupta examined the rest of the furniture.

"Have you seen this, sir?"

Singh looked up. The door to the cupboard under the TV was open, revealing a safe. Singh went over to look at it. He did not require a combination – just a key.

"Go and get the key off Kaushik," Singh commanded.

Gupta was back within five minutes.

Singh unlocked the safe as Gupta watched. They were both disappointed to find it empty.

"Don't worry, we'll find something," Singh said resolutely, and went back to the desk, leaving Gupta to look for other hidden safes and compartments.

Singh had to sound confident so that he did not rouse any suspicions, but he knew there was a very good chance that they would find nothing – Ajay had probably tipped Kaushik off. He carried on methodically going through the desk. Most of the drawers were empty. He tipped the contents of the ones with anything in them on to the desk. In the bottom drawer of the left hand pedestal there were some papers, which all seemed to be related to Kaushik's clothing business. There was also a padded envelope. He opened it and found a bag covered in brown parcel tape. The slit in it revealed a brown powder. A broad smile spread across Singh's face.

He called Gupta over.

"Standard 100 gram bag," Gupta said matter-of-factly. "More than half empty. Looks like Ranveer Kaushik is a user. Two days in a cell and he'll sell you his mother as a whore if you promise him a fix."

Singh nodded. This was not evidence of dealing, only using. But Gupta was correct. If they handled him right, he would confess to anything. However, they needed evidence to back up any charges they brought against him.

The search continued, both in the office and the warehouse, but nothing was found. Eventually they left, leaving a constable on guard. The door was replaced within hours, but the constable was not removed. Singh had a feeling about this place...

"We found the heroin," Singh said in the comfortable interrogation room – this one had air conditioning in it.

Ranveer said nothing. His lawyer, Mr C B Thakral, had told him to say the minimum possible. The police often have a little something, and will try to use it as leverage to get you to incriminate yourself to a greater degree.

"You're looking at serious jail time," Singh continued.

Ranveer still said nothing.

"You're going down, Kaushik. If you cooperate, it won't be so bad for you."

"What heroin?" Ranveer asked in a weak voice. He was also sweating a little. He had been in a cell for eight hours. Singh would have liked to have kept him there for longer, but he had to charge him or release him within 24 hours. Shame. As Gupta had said, two days locked up and he would have signed a confession saying that he had been illegally mining paneer on the moon if it meant he could have a fix.

"The heroin in your office."

"What heroin?" Ranveer asked again, gaining a little strength from the repetition.

"The stuff in your office."

"Please can you be more specific, Sub-Inspector," Thakral interjected. "You are haranguing my client, who is clearly unwell."

"The 38.2 grams we found in your desk," Singh reluctantly conceded.

Oh, shit! thought Ranveer. *How could I forget that?* But he was also relieved. He turned to Thakral and whispered something in his ear. Thakral spoke. "That was for personal use. The pressure of business has been getting to my client. He started some time ago –"

"Who's your supplier?" Singh asked, looking at Ranveer, knowing it was a pointless question.

"I pick it up next to a dustbin in Connaught Place, where I leave the money," Ranveer replied, wishing he could get that much for a bag.

"How do you contact your supplier?"

"They post a burner phone a few weeks after my pick up. I contact them when I need more and then smash up the phone."

"When will you get your next phone?"

Ranveer shrugged. "In a couple of weeks."

"What a load of rubbish. You're looking at ten years' hard prison time, Kaushik," Singh said quietly, leaning towards him.

"Six months to ten years," corrected Thakral. "When the judge looks at my client's accounts and sees the pressure he's under to make money to pay taxes, he'll see things more sympathetically."

Ranveer would have been smiling right now, but the early stages of withdrawal meant he was in pain. He knew it would get worse, and he would find it difficult to function before long. He whispered something to Thakral.

"My client is currently in considerable pain. I request that you get him some medical attention."

Singh got up and walked out of the room in disgust.

It was the next morning, and Ranveer was looking and feeling a lot better. Thank god for methadone.

"Thakral reckons I'll get six months to one year," Ranveer said. "No problem. This place is no worse than parts of Paraharavi, hey, Chotu?"

Ajay nodded, but he could feel the irritation rise in him. Ranveer needed his help, but was still being patronising.

"The only thing is Dewan won't wait for me."

"Who's Dewan?" asked Ajay.

"He supplies me. He controls 90% plus of the heroin in Delhi."

Ajay nodded.

"Can you look after things for me, Chotu?"

"Of course." Ajay managed to keep the irritation out of his voice.

Thakral had managed to get Ajay and Ranveer a private room to talk in. Thakral had told the prison authorities that Ajay was a paralegal and they needed more information from Ranveer to help with the case.

"Get new gangmasters. Do it fast. Tell Dewan what's happened to me – he'll find out anyway. Tell him that I'll take over as soon as I'm out. But get those gangmasters in *fast* – in the next two days. Work with Dilip. Dewan won't like it if he loses too much trade."

"Of course," Ajay repeated. He hesitated before tentatively saying: "The police mentioned you were having withdrawal symptoms?"

Ranveer looked embarrassed.

Ajay looked at him sympathetically. "How did it start?"

Anger flashed across Ranveer's face, but dissipated just as quickly. He seemed to realise that he was in no position to keep his problems to himself, or to expect Ajay to call him "bhaiyaa" when he so desperately needed his help. He closed his eyes and held his head in his hands.

"I don't know why, but I started a few months ago," he said quietly

– it was hard for the big man to admit to such a pathetic weakness. "I suppose I was bored. I've tried to quit..."

Ajay nodded, suspecting that Ranveer was not telling him everything, but also not knowing what to say. Ranveer looked pathetic. Ajay used it as yet another lesson to sell but never use.

Suddenly Ranveer looked up, his face flushed with rage again. "How did they find out about me? Who grassed me up?"

Ajay thought quickly. "I heard a couple of policemen talking about you – one said 'Junkies make mistakes'."

"That's crap!" Ranveer looked even more furious. "I wasn't off my face all the time. I knew what I was doing!"

"Were you ever off your face?" Ajay asked gently.

Ranveer seemed to shrink as he almost imperceptibly nodded.

"It's OK, I'll look after your business."

Early that afternoon Sub-Inspector Gurpreet Singh got a text on his police issue phone. He looked at it immediately – it could be an order from above.

"Press along ALL the skirting boards in Kaushik's office. There are hidden compartments behind them."

The texter had withheld their number, which was, no doubt, a burner.

Singh immediately set off to Ranveer's industrial unit, taking his briefcase with him.

He entered the office and started pressing on the skirting boards. Sure enough, hidden compartments started to pop open. One contained cash and heroin, three contained just heroin, and one was crammed full of cash. He emptied the contents of the one with just cash into his briefcase. He then phoned Assistant Sub-Inspector Gupta.

"I'm at the Kaushik warehouse. Come here immediately. Bring two constables."

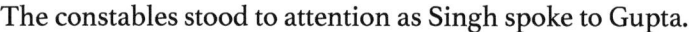

The constables stood to attention as Singh spoke to Gupta.

"I've made a thorough search here. Make sure all this powder is sent for testing, and the money goes into secure lock up. We're going to count it now. If one rupee goes missing, I'm going to hold you personally responsible, Gupta." It was a threat both of them knew that Singh had to make. In reality, the money and drugs would make it back intact to the police lock-up, where it would be logged and put in the secure area. What would happen to it after that was out of Gupta's and Singh's hands.

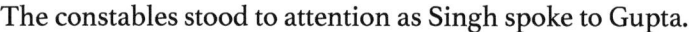

That evening Ranveer found himself in another air-conditioned interrogation room.

Singh told Ranveer how much heroin and cash they'd found hidden behind the skirting boards.

Ranveer was stunned into momentary silence. That sounded about the right amount of heroin, but it was only a small fraction of the cash. "As I've said, inspector, I don't know what you're talking about."

"That's sub-inspector, my friend," Singh corrected. He was not going to let this jumped-up slum dweller think that he could get around him with flattery. "You *do* know what I'm talking about. Why else would you have an empty safe, but cash and narcotics hidden in your office?"

"The safe's there for deliveries of jewellery, and customers sometimes pay in cash. I keep it there until I go to the bank. I don't know how the cash and narcotics got there. Maybe the people who had the place before me left it behind. I don't know what business he was in, but –"

"Don't give me that! You had the office completely gutted and done out *after* you moved in, and your prints are all over the drugs and cash."

Singh smiled broadly at Ranveer's obvious discomfort. At last, a blow that had completely knocked him off balance.

Ranveer was at a loss for words. So, the Delhi police were not as incompetent as everyone said. What should he do now?

"Sub-inspector, I haven't looked in those hiding places for years. I've never dealt in drugs, and I never would."

"So how did they get there *with your prints on them*?" Singh persisted.

Ranveer shrugged.

"Maybe I'll question your security more. You know as well as I do that they'll crack sooner or later..."

Ranveer felt sick. "There's no need to do that. These are family men. I employed them just to guard the clothing and jewellery. It's high-end and extremely valuable –"

"How about Mahesh Bakshi?"

"*What?*" asked Ranveer, thrown by the sudden change in questioning.

Singh remained silent, just staring at Ranveer.

Ranveer did not think he could feel any more uncomfortable, but the sweat began to pour off him despite the air-conditioning and a recent dose of methadone.

"I don't know what you're talking about," Ranveer finally barked, staring at Singh with open hostility.

It was time to go in for the kill. "You were followed that night all the way to the Narora reservoir. We have a team of divers searching it right now." This was not true. All Singh had was a signed statement from Dev. They had no idea whereabouts in the reservoir the body had been dumped, and the area was far too expansive to make a search viable.

The threat was enough to make Ranveer visibly crumple.

"If you confess to knowing about the heroin and cash, things won't look so bad - the judge will be more lenient. I'll even call off the search." Singh said in a conciliatory tone. He saved this technique for those who shut down when you were harsh with them, and also for those you had broken and just needed a little coaxing.

Ranveer looked at Thakral.

"May I have some time alone with my client, please?"

Singh came back 15 minutes later.

"If my client confesses to the heroin and cash you found in the office in his warehouse, will you drop all other investigations and lines of inquiry?" asked Thakral.

"I'll call off the search of Narora reservoir immediately." Singh's tone was firm and reassuring.

Ranveer wrote out and signed a confession, outlining how he had recently bought 50kg of heroin using a burner phone posted to him. He had made contact with the vendor through the dark net, but had not made any note of the website address as he had intended for it to be a one-off purchase. He had intended to use it himself and supply others. He had not sold any yet. The cash was payment for a recent clothing sale. He kept everything hidden as he felt it was unwise to trust his security too much – they were aware of the safe, and safes can be cracked by someone skilled enough.

Singh read the confession. No judge would believe the details, but it was a confession. Kaushik was going down for at least ten years – probably nearer 20.

"I'll call off the search," he said before leaving the room.

Ranveer looked and felt completely exhausted.

Ajay sat in silence.

"They know where I got rid of Mahesh's body. How do they know that?"

Ajay shrugged sympathetically.

"I need you to find out, Chotu, and then torture the bastard to death." Ranveer said the last bit through gritted teeth. "It was probably Dev – he's weak. Find him and kill him." The rage in his eyes was barely under control.

Ajay wondered if his habit had made him so volatile – he had never seen him like this before. Ajay nodded and said: "I'll look after your mum and dad as well."

This seemed to make Ranveer's anger evaporate. He looked away, forlorn.

"The worst thing is that that bastard stole nearly all the cash."

Ajay knew any cash in the office was little more than small change to Ranveer. But he knew what he meant: Singh was stealing from Ranveer, but it was Ranveer who was going to prison. He also knew that this would not be the worst thing. The worst thing would be when the authorities confiscated all his assets, which is what they did with big time drug dealers – 50kg of brown sugar put Ranveer firmly in that category.

"What am I going to do, Ajay?" Although he had regained some control, he was still breathing heavily. "I can't leave my parents homeless."

"Do you have any money in foreign accounts?"

Ranveer shook his head. Not long ago he had told Ajay that he always laundered it and had it sent back to India – he never saw the point in it being sat in an account on the other side of the world. Ranveer's deep look of regret was enough to make Ajay decide to keep a good deal of his money overseas.

Ajay was silent for a moment.

"Don't worry about your parents. I'll talk to Thakral and see if I can buy your house so they don't have to move out. I'll look after them *and* you."

Ranveer said nothing. He knew Ajay's help meant his stay in prison would be better than average. But it would still be prison and, when he got out, he would have nothing except Ajay's charity.

Ajay visited Ranveer and his parents every day. Singh had been insistent that Ranveer not be allowed out on bail as he was a flight risk – the judge had agreed. The trial itself was fast-tracked to only six weeks after arrest. Ajay convinced Ranveer that this was best – a protracted time in custody without a trial would be wearing on Ranveer's parents. Although unusual, the fast tracking was facilitated by Thakral and by Ajay giving Singh plenty of cash – more than enough to lubricate the system.

In the end Ranveer got 18 years and all his assets were forfeited to the state. Thanks to Thakral, the house was immediately signed over to Ajay, who paid the government a fair market price for it. Ajay told Ranveer's parents what had happened, and that they could stay there as long as they wanted. Mrs Kaushik burst into tears and went over and touched Ajay's feet. She looked even more haunted than Ranveer when Ajay had seen him at his worst.

Ajay visited Ranveer as often as he was allowed.

Ranveer would say the same thing every visit, virtually verbatim, with the same anger in his eyes. "It's because of *Dev* I'm here. *He* grassed me up – I *know* he did. He's weak, Ajay. He's the only one who knew where I dumped Mahesh's body. Have you found him yet?" At least he had stopped calling Ajay "Chotu".

Ajay always replied that most of the old gangmasters had disappeared. Three of them had resurfaced, and they had their old jobs back, but there was no sign of Dev. He asked everyone he could, and was still searching. When he had him, he would make him *suffer*.

In the meantime, Ajay got Singh to visit the prison governor, whom he got to accept massive bribes so that Ranveer could have his own cell, exceptionally good food, his own toilet, a TV and other luxuries. Ajay made sure Ranveer had something new before each visit – that way he could change the subject. It worked remarkably well. Ranveer talked with pride of his latest acquisition, as if he was king of the jungle. The way he spoke was as if it was all his own doing, and Ajay had not done a single thing.

Ajay just sat and listened as Ranveer went from ecstasy to rage in seconds. This was not the Ranveer he used to know. He also seemed to be more drawn and haggard each time Ajay saw him. He was obviously using even more than he had been.

After a couple of months Ranveer was transferred from Tihar

prison, Delhi to Pojapura prison, near the south tip of Kerala. Singh had managed to convince a judge to make the transfer, saying that Ranveer Kaushik was still having an undue influence on the Delhi criminal classes. He cited his treatment in prison as just one example of this. In the notoriously overcrowded prison, he had his own cell, a western style toilet, a television, a bed so comfortable Singh wished he could have one the same, a two seater sofa, etc. etc. How else could he convince the authorities to give him such luxuries, except through corruption by the Delhi underworld?

Upon hearing the news, both Mr and Mrs Kaushik burst into tears. Ajay comforted them, saying that he would pay for regular flights to see Ranveer. Or they could move to Kerala so they could visit him more often. They chose to move, just as Ajay knew they would. It meant they were nearer their son, and far, far away from those nasty, gossiping neighbours. Ajay paid the rent for a large flat in a good area of Trivandrum, as well as giving them a generous monthly allowance. It was a lot less than they had become used to when Ranveer had been running his business, but it was enough for them to live comfortably.

In the meantime, Ajay and his family moved into the house vacated by the Kaushiks. Bimala and Nitesh loved it. He saw them flourish as their learning accelerated due to the excellent nearby school. Mrs Pandey was nowhere near as happy to start with, but slowly got used to life there. She carved out a social life in the neighbourhood, even though it was not as satisfying as Paraharavi. However, she found a lot of contentment in how well Bimala and Nitesh were doing.

Maybe he would propose to Deepika in a few months, when he turned 18. Of course, he would carry on seeing Natasha and her friends. There was no way a nice girl like Deepika could do what they did for him.

It was not long after Ranveer was transferred that Singh was promoted to assistant police inspector.

"Congratulations on the promotion."

"Thank you," replied Singh in haughty tones. "This means we won't be meeting anymore. I have to be careful who I'm seen with," he added with a sneer.

"I thought you were always careful," replied Ajay, keeping his tone light and amiable.

"I am, my friend, but I no longer have time for the likes of *you*."

"That's a shame," Ajay replied, still sounding amiable. "Just like it'd be a shame if your superiors found out about the money that went into your account about the same time you raided Mr. Kaushik's warehouse."

Singh laughed. "They'll find nothing."

"But if they dig deep, they'll find an anonymous text, probably long ago deleted, on your official police phone, telling you to search behind the skirting boards in Mr. Kaushik's office."

Singh looked shocked and surprised. He felt his pocket.

Ajay held up Singh's phone. "Us slum kids know a trick or two."

"That proves nothing," Singh replied, regaining his sneer, even though it was not quite as pronounced. "It could've come from anyone."

"It could've," conceded Ajay. "But it didn't come from anyone in the police and, if you add an avalanche of social media accusations of you taking bribes for years, they will have no choice but to look at your finances *very* carefully."

Singh said nothing.

"Congratulations on the promotion," Ajay repeated, returning to his amiable tone. "That deserves a pay rise. How about double what I've been paying you?"

Singh looked at Ajay a while before saying: "I thought you said Ranveer was like a big brother to you, and without him you'd be nothing." He paused, still looking directly at Ajay. "Why did you stitch him up and get me to move him so far?"

"He was in my way," Ajay said simply.

Singh was the first to break eye contact. Not for the first time, he felt that he would rather deal with an honest bank robber or murderer instead of this devious, twisted psychopath.

12

"I'm bored," Ajay said to his mum.

It had been over a year since the Kaushiks had relocated to Kerala.

Bimala and Nitesh had moved on immeasurably. Ajay had seen their learning and intellects develop almost by the week. But, alongside that, so had their snobbery. Instead of playing out on the street and talking about what other kids said and did, they went around other kids' houses and talked about what they owned. They looked joyful when they talked about their TV being bigger and better than their friends', and sad when they talked about Ajay's car not being as good as many on the street. Nitesh seemed to be more affected than Bimala.

Ajay had thought about getting a Ferrari or maybe an antique Rolls Royce, but it would have raised eyebrows. How could a samosa wallah afford *that*? Singh was his tame poodle for now but, if Ajay brought too much attention to himself, Singh's superiors might start to ask questions and have him watched. It was wise to live not too far beyond his visible means.

Mrs Pandey had made friends in the local area. She talked about things like the new washing machine Mrs Kothare had recently acquired, or how Mrs Goyal's new cleaner was *so* good that everyone else was trying to poach her. But she added that the washing machine she had had become like an old friend she was reluctant to part with. She liked the fact that their cleaner was so bad that Mrs Pandey had to do a good hour's cleaning herself every other day – it kept her fit and gave her something to get stuck into.

She had enjoyed getting to know the women she had met in the area, making sure she made all the right noises when they showed her their latest purchases. When they asked her why she did not buy more clothes or the latest must-have household utensil, she replied that Ajay's business brought in enough money to live comfortably but not extravagantly. This approach worked well for her. The ones who were snobs soon ditched her, which saved her a job. The ones who were more genuine liked how she was lovely about their stuff despite her "straitened" circumstances. In their eyes, the fact that she showed no hint of jealousy meant that she was an exceptional person and made them want to know her all the more.

Despite the relative luxuriousness of the house in Paraharavi, life had still been hard for her there. The uneven, crowded pavements and roads made walking along them difficult. When she had visited people, she had often found herself sitting on quite uncomfortable chairs, which aggravated her hip and leg. Although they had been very careful with the water, the occasional tummy upset was inevitable. Since moving to Greater Kailash, all these concerns had become things of the past: her health had improved.

The only person who seemed to be adversely affected by the move was Ajay. The kitchen manufacturing samosas was still in the same place in Paraharavi, and he visited it every few days. He used to stay and listen to the banter and the gossip, but no longer felt part of it. The workers were friendly and respectful, but he had eventually begun to make his visits short, business-like affairs. It felt like he was an interloper if he stayed much longer. He had occasionally walked round the streets, saying "hello" to people from what now seemed like a dim and distant childhood, but had stopped doing that as it reminded him too much of what he was missing.

Business could be described as going well. He had opened a couple more shops in Central Delhi, but had stopped at that as he had saturated the area. He had good staff in all of them. The gangmasters in East Delhi also brought in good money.

Things were running smoothly – too smoothly. There was no challenge, nothing to expend his energy on.

"What should I do, mataji?" he asked, sounding almost forlorn.

"Why don't you get married? Say the word, and I'll find you a nice girl." What else would an Indian mother say?

But it made him think of Deepika. He shook his head as he thought about the plans he had had to marry her. How could he have been so naïve? He was 18 years old – far too young to settle down. He was happy sowing his wild seeds amongst the high-class whores of Delhi (some of whom still held surprises for him) and running his business, which occasionally meant taking care of rivals. Deepika was nice – too nice. She would cramp his style. He liked her – maybe he loved her. When he was with her she made him feel special, at ease, as if nothing mattered in the world except being with her. She had said that he made her feel the same. But, if that was love, it was overrated. He had a business to run and things to do – he did not want to sit around all day looking into her eyes. Yes, he was bored now, but he would be even more bored if he got married.

When he had split up with her – about six months ago – she had cried. He found it awkward and embarrassing. That was the last time he had seen her. She probably had a new boyfriend now at the University of Delhi.

When Mrs Pandey saw him shaking his head, she said: "Why don't you go to the mandir and give thanks for all you've been given?"

He was tempted to say that he had been given nothing – he had worked hard for it, but that would have led to an argument that he could never win. He smiled as he remembered his days at Mr Joshi's stall. How good he had looked in the pyjama suits and turbans. The gold cloth. The other traders. Wooing the tourists. The buzz in the temple after he had killed Anand. He wondered what it was like now. There was only one way to find out.

"I'm going out," he suddenly announced.

"Where to?" Mrs Pandey asked, taken aback.

"To the mandir. Where else?" he replied, getting up.

He drove to the Shiva mandir and just stood outside it, looking at it for some time. When he entered through the main gate he was immediately greeted by Ramesh bhai, who had sold him the white pyjama suits and whose mirror he would look in every morning when putting on his turban.

As he walked on, he was greeted by nearly all the traders, who were all still there. It was that kind of place. The hours might be long, but the money was good – too good to ever leave. Little had changed. It felt as if he had come home after being away for years.

He noticed a small boy going from stall to stall. He was probably about twelve years old, but it was difficult to tell. He looked skinny to the point of being half-starved. Maybe he was older but had never had enough to eat to grow properly. He seemed to be having brief conversations with the stallholders. All of them were dismissing him, some with a gentle shake of the head and a sad smile, some with a bad tempered flick of the hand. He reminded Ajay of himself at that age, doing the rounds in the temple just to get some work so he could make a few rupees for a little food.

Ajay went over to the boy.

"What's your name, boy?" Ajay asked.

The boy turned to him. There was anger in his eyes. Not anger from how Ajay had spoken to him, but a long-term rage at life itself.

"Vijay, sir," he replied politely. This kid may have had a raw deal from life, but he was smart enough to know how to make the best of an opportunity.

"Would you like some work, Vijay?" Ajay asked gently.

"Yes, sir. Very much, sir," Vijay answered, smiling. Despite the smile, he still looked angry. It was as if fury was permanently etched into his young features. "Which stall do you have, sir? I can do anything."

Ajay was impressed with his enthusiasm. "I don't have a stall. I used to work here, but now I deal in, let's say, stuff that you should never talk about in a mandir," he said loftily, looking around, almost sneering at the temple. He looked down at Vijay, who seemed to be barely able to control his temper.

"I have enough work, sir. Thank you," Vijay said, giving Ajay a venomous look.

"Don't worry, I'll pay you well –"

"I'm too busy working for good people," Vijay muttered, turning away.

Ajay was bewildered. Vijay obviously did not have any work. He was half-starved. Maybe he was religious, and just wanted to work at the temple. Ajay took out his wallet and extracted more cash than Vijay could have earnt in three months. He handed it Vijay.

"Keep your money!" Vijay all but yelled.

Ajay was shocked. "Take it. I'm helping you."

"I don't want your help!"

Ajay was confused and hurt.

"Who do you think you are?" Vijay virtually spat. "A big man? Where did you steal that from? Who did you kill? Who did you torture? It's blood money."

"Who do you think you are?" Ajay said angrily. "Don't talk to *me* like that!"

"An insect," replied Vijay, struggling to keep his breathing under control. "That's all I am. Delhi's full of boys like me. We're dirt. People like you tread on us without thinking. The only use we have is to make money for people like *you*. I saw my dad die working for men like *you*. They used him and broke him. Then they shot him so he couldn't tell anyone about anything he'd done." It was a speech he had rehearsed many times in his head, never realising that saying it aloud would mean he would have to fight back the tears.

Ajay was bewildered. "I just want to help you," he said in a barely audible whisper.

"What with? Blood money? It's better to die than take money like that.

"You're a mahatma. A great soul. But not a great, good soul. An evil soul. People are afraid of you, but nobody respects you. They admire you, they want to be like you, but who *likes* you? Maybe your own mother, but every other bit of respect you've got, you've paid for. People like you are everywhere, like fleas and locusts, sucking life out of everyone and everything. Kill me if you want, big man. It'll prove so much. I'd rather die than take anything from someone like *you*." Vijay ran off as tears streamed down his face.

Ajay was stunned, unable to move.

Was the boy right? If it was not for the money, Ajay would be in touch with no one he now knew except his mum, sister and brother. No one in this world is your friend; they are the friends of their needs. Or, in his case, they were friends of his money. If it was not for the money, he would still be in Paraharavi, being part of things, helping others, and them helping him. Things there had been so much more genuine. Talking to each other, having banter, gossiping were part of everyday life, but it made you feel close to other people. It meant that you could ask them for help, and they could ask you. But nobody thought of it that way – it just happened.

Now people did what he told them to because he paid them. The boy *was* right. Rishi was scared of losing his ridiculously large salary. His whole drugs network was scared of losing their money and getting their legs broken. The banks and the Hawalas were only interested in him because of the business he brought them. The neighbours at Greater Kailash were only interested in him and his family because he had a successful chain of shops – look how they had treated Ranveer's mum and dad when they had fallen from grace.

At last, he was able to move. Still in a daze, he was able to find his way to Mr Joshi's chai stall. Mr Joshi was still there, looking a little older, but still sitting on the gold cloth, making his chai.

"Is there no one to help you, bapuji?"

Mr Joshi looked up. When he saw it was Ajay, he immediately grabbed a walking stick so he could stand up. Ajay helped him.

"Ajay, beta, how are you? It's been *so* long." There was genuine concern and affection in his voice.

"I am fine, bapuji. How are you? The stick is new," Ajay added, looking down at it. The conversation was helping him return to normality.

Mr Joshi laughed. "It happens to us all, beta."

"Don't you have a boy helping you?"

Mr Joshi laughed again. "After you left, I didn't bother."

"Why not?" Ajay asked, looking confused.

Mr Joshi sat down again. Ajay crouched so he was at the same height.

"Sorry, beta, it's difficult to stand for long these days."

Ajay smiled indulgently.

"I make enough money. You didn't know, but when you were here, some bad men came and demanded protection money from me. They said they would break my legs and cut your face if I didn't pay."

Ajay felt sick. He had no idea that Anand had used him as leverage. Thank god he had killed him.

"When you left, I decided that I couldn't put anyone else through that. I'm an old man – they can do what they like to me. But you're too precious to come to any harm." He affectionately patted Ajay's left cheek as he said this.

"You know, when those men came, they took more than my money. They took everything - my dignity, my reason for living."

Ajay nodded, only now realising that he had felt the same way.

"Lots of the traders here were talking about shutting their shops and moving out of Delhi. Anand was bleeding them dry. In a few months this place would've been empty. Everyone was so happy when they heard Anand was dead."

Ajay had to steady himself. How many people would celebrate when he died? Far, far more than would mourn him.

Mr Joshi carried on talking, telling Ajay about the comings and goings at the temple. He told them about which traders had had children; about the marriages of their older children; how the temple authorities had just put up the rent of the stall, but he did not mind – everything seemed to go up every year these days; etc, etc.

With some difficulty Ajay made sure he had a smile plastered across his face as the words washed over him, very few of which he was able to take in. His mind was racing, turning over and over again the same thoughts about what he was doing with his life. He was intimidating, bullying and creating helpless drug addicts. And what for? So he could make far more money than he could spend, and die lonely and hated? And, when he did die, the only thing anybody would be interested in was his money.

At last, Mr Joshi stopped talking. Ajay got up and bade Mr Joshi farewell.

After talking to a few more traders he finally made it out of the temple.

He sat in his car. He felt drained.

He could stop dealing immediately and just live off what he had made – it was more than enough for him to live in luxury for the rest of his life. The samosa shops were doing well – they did not need the heroin trade to be viable. He could take over the running of the Paharganj one himself – he had always enjoyed talking to the customers.

In truth, he did not know what to do. It felt like someone had punched him hard in the guts. He felt sick.

He went home, and his mum made him a cup of chai. She sat opposite him, instinctively knowing not to say a word. He sat back, eyes closed, listening to his heartbeat and his breathing. Mrs Pandey silently got up, giving him the space to fill with his desolation. He eventually dragged himself upstairs. To his surprise he fell asleep immediately.

The next day he felt more able to move. He needed to get things rolling to stop himself from falling into an abyss. It would not be difficult to shut down his heroin business. If he did not put an order in with Dewan in time and did not answer his calls, Dewan would find someone else. A text would be enough to sack the gangmasters. He would tell the shop managers to get rid of the street boys, and then tell the managers that he was pulling out of heroin, and their wages were going down. He would only be able to pay them a fraction of what they earnt now, but it would still be more than they could make at Sadar Ganj, and they did not risk prison or being attacked. They would not be happy, but he doubted if any would quit. Anyway, if they did, it would not be difficult to get new staff for that kind of money. He would pay Rishi double what he would pay the shop managers – he deserved at least that.

But the first thing he had to do was tell Singh. Not only was he, by far, his most expensive employee, but he did not want any interference from the police when he went legit. Singh would be glad to be off his leash. Ajay texted him and arranged a meeting.

"I'm quitting the heroin trade," were Ajay's opening words as they sat next to each other in Ajay's car. Ajay handed over a thick envelope, which Singh stuffed into his briefcase. His final payment.

"Why, my friend? You've got a very successful business."

"I'm sick of dealing in misery and death."

Singh was silent for a few moments. "Do you think it'll all stop if you quit?"

Ajay said nothing.

"The reason I tolerated you is because, believe it or not, you're one of the good guys."

Ajay looked at him.

"We know all about Laksh Dewan, my friend, and we occasionally have to pay him a visit when he starts cutting his stuff with stupid things. But he generally behaves himself. Our main problem is people like you and those below you. When you people get greedy and start cutting with any old rubbish that you can get hold of, we end up picking up the dead bodies – that's the real reason we went for Kaushik. A few junkies died after taking his stuff, and it was getting worse. The press loves that kind of thing – it makes lovely, juicy headlines – but the director general takes a different view."

Ajay raised his eyebrows in slight shock.

"You'll be surprised how greedy people can be. I know you don't show much mercy, but you're one of the good guys when it comes to drugs.

"Having said that, it'd be better if none of you existed," Singh added, almost to himself. "You're a horrible breed – I prefer dealing with an honest bank robber or murderer. But you do exist, and we have to live with it. If you quit, I guarantee that the number of deaths will go up."

Ajay closed his eyes and sighed deeply.

"I'll see you in a couple of weeks," Singh said, getting out of the car.

Ajay sat there, not opening his eyes. What was he supposed to do? He dealt in death and misery but, if he stopped, he would make things worse. What kind of crazy, messed-up world was he living in?

He opened his eyes, slammed his car into gear and shot off. He sped through the traffic the best he could, his hand almost constantly on the horn. One auto-rickshaw wallah was lucky not to get his lights punched out. Cyclists went flying as he went far too close to them, not caring if he knocked them off their bikes.

At last, he was on the open road. He put his foot to the floor and punched the steering wheel again and again as tears streamed down his face. What kind of cunt was he? The kind that destroys lives and steals souls, who can only make this world a better place by dying.

Finally, he was where he wanted to be: on the bridge from which he had thrown Jaspal's body. Jaspal had been a good man who had just been trying to get by. Yeah, he was a drug dealer, but it was either that or the cruellest of poverty. Ajay had given him a way out, but had killed him before he could take it. It should be him who should be down there, not Jaspal. He looked down at the powerful, flowing river...

The loud horn of a lorry made him jump. He turned around.

"Move your car, you idiot! Some of us have got to work!" the driver yelled above the noise of his engine.

Ajay got into his car and drove off at speed, zipping through country lanes, taking bends and corners far too fast as he passed fields and farmhouses. At last, he felt spent. He parked up and sat awhile, his eyes closed, tears rolling down the side of his face as he leaned back into his seat.

13

For the next few days Ajay thought. He went for long walks. From a distance he watched the street boys dealing in his heroin. Some of the users looked happy to have a quick fix, but most just looked desperate.

What had he got himself into?

He had virtually no appetite, eating only when he felt weak from hunger. He avoided restaurants – the last thing he wanted was to be surrounded by people. How many of their lives had his drugs wrecked? Instead he ate from small street stalls, preferring to give his money to the likes of Mr Joshi.

It was the early afternoon of his third day when he came across a ludoo stall on a backstreet. The old man who ran it looked like he had done so for many years. Ajay bought half a dozen ludoo from him. He walked a little way away and started to eat them. He would have passed out if he had not. They were good.

A sharply dressed, well-built young man went to the stall. Ajay noticed him because he was not the kind of person you would expect to buy ludoos from a handcart on a backstreet. Ajay looked at the old ludoo wallah. He looked terrified. He handed the young man a thickish envelope, and then the young man appeared to ask for some ludoo. The old man handed them over. The young man left without paying. It did not take a genius to work out what had just happened. Ajay approached the old man.

"Who was that?" Ajay asked.

The old man looked startled. "Just a customer," he mumbled.

"No he wasn't," Ajay said gently but firmly. "A customer doesn't take ludoo and an envelope full of money and give you nothing. He's a gangster. How much did he take from you?"

The old man told him, his voice full of fear.

"What's his name?"

The old man shrugged.

"What's his name?" Ajay asked with steel in his voice.

"Haasan," the old man mumbled.

"When's he going to come back?" demanded Ajay.

"Two weeks from today – always the same time. He might be a little earlier, but never before 11. That lazy bastard just leeches off others," the old man said bitterly.

"It's only an old handcart I was given," he unexpectedly continued. "I thought it would be good to paint it and sell a few ludoo. Now that bastard takes most of what I make. It's not worth me carrying on, but he says he'll find me and break my legs if I stop." Tears were trickling down his cheeks by the time he had finished.

Ajay took out his wallet and gave the old man the exact amount Hassan had just taken from him. The old man's jaw literally fell open. Ajay walked away.

For the next six days he continued to walk around East Delhi, not going home, sleeping wherever he could find a room. It did not matter if it was a dingy hovel or a reasonable hotel. He did not care, barely taking in his surroundings.

He thought about all he had done, how he had wasted his life. His mother, brother and sister were proud of him, but he deserved no adulation. All the respect he had was based on evil deeds. How could he have *killed* people? How many people had his drugs killed? However, no matter what he thought about, his mind kept on coming back to the old man. At last, he phoned Singh and demanded a meeting. They met up the next day in Singh's car.

"There's a bastard called Haasan who runs a protection racket across the river."

Singh nodded disinterestedly.

"Well, are you going to do anything about it?" Ajay demanded incredulously.

Singh shook his head. "Not my patch."

"But you can get *someone* to do something about it?"

Singh shrugged. "The police have got better things to do."

"But he's shaking down an old man with a tiny ludoo cart. He takes most of what he makes."

Singh looked surprised and even a little shocked. "He sounds greedy. I'll tell them across the river. But, even if they bust him, all that'll happen is someone else'll come along and they might be worse."

Ajay stared at him.

"*Everyone* in that part of town pays protection. This Haasan probably killed the previous guy shaking down your old man. Someone will come along sooner or later and get rid of Haasan. They might be better or they might be worse than him. It's just the way things are."

Ajay sat there thinking.

"The police are too busy with murderers, rapists, drug dealers and burglaries in posh areas to have the time to bother with old men with handcarts.

"What's wrong with you, my friend? Have you gone soft?" Singh asked, looking confused.

Ajay looked at him with pure venom.

"If you're that bothered, take this Haasan out yourself," Singh said hastily. "But don't leave your old man unprotected – someone will move in quicker than you can blink." With that he started up the engine.

Ajay got out of the car and Singh drove off. Deep in thought, Ajay watched him disappear into the distance. It seemed the only way he could make the world a better place was not only to trade in drugs, but also move into protection. Was there any real difference between him and Anand?

A few more days of walking, observing and contemplating left him emotionally battered and tied in knots. He was thinking too much. It was time to start doing.

He phoned Rishi.

"Hello, bhaiyaa. Where are you?" Rishi sounded almost frantic.

"Have you been taking care of things?" asked Ajay. Ajay had made the necessary arrangements for Rishi to distribute the samosas and heroin to the shops should anything ever happen to him.

"Yes, of course, bhaiyaa. Dilip has managed to stop Dewan giving your territory to someone else, but it's getting difficult for him," Rishi said, still sounding tense.

Dilip had been head of security since the days of Daksh Anand. Mahesh Bakshi had not been around long enough to make any changes. When Ranveer took over he had left Dilip in place. Ajay could see why. The job was not hard, but it did require intelligence, the knack of diplomacy backed up with an iron fist, and to be connected well enough to see off any threat before it became a reality. Dilip had all these attributes in abundance.

"It's OK. I'll sort it out. Are the shops OK?" Ajay asked.

"Everything is fine, bhaiyaa," Rishi replied, beginning to sound like his old, calm self. Ajay was glad to have him on his team.

"Good. I need you to find a replacement for yourself. I've got another job for you," said Ajay.

"Yes, bhaiyaa. When do you want me to start?"

"Tomorrow. I'll pick you up at two at the shop." This would give Ajay time to go home and calm his mother, Bimala and Nitesh down.

"OK bhaiyaa. No problem."

Next stop: the industrial unit.

As soon as he entered Dilip and the security guards looked up. They had been having a tense, fraught conversation – no doubt discussing what could have happened to Ajay and what they could do about it.

It was not Dilip's shifts, but these were exceptional circumstances.

"Hello, sir. Are you OK?" Dilip asked, sounding completely calm and collected. He was good.

"Yes, I'm fine. Just had a few things to sort out. Let's talk in my office." Ajay led the way. The security guards just sat there, looking both bewildered and relieved as they watched them disappear into the office.

Ajay sat in his swivel chair and Dilip in one of the armchairs on the other side of the desk.

"How have things been?"

"A little fraught, to be honest, sir," Dilip replied with gentle calmness. "I managed to contact Mr Dewan. He was put out that it was me who was contacting him." In other words, he tore a strip off Dilip and probably threatened him and Ajay. "But I explained that you had been called away on a family emergency and had instructed that I was to place the order and pay for the delivery." Rishi was the only person except Ajay who had a key to the safe. Ajay thought it was best this way. If he had given Dilip a key there was nothing stopping him from raiding the safe and running off with its contents. Rishi, on the other hand, would need to contact Dilip before he could access it. They would both have to collude to rob the safe. They were not the types to do so. Although deeply embedded in the criminal underworld, as far as Ajay could see (and he considered himself a good judge of character) they were both deeply honourable men. All the same, Ajay made sure they had as little to do with each other as possible. He was glad to see that they had worked together, but he would have to make sure he reintroduced the distance between them. It was good to feel his brain kick into action again.

"Thank you for handling it. I'll make sure you get something extra in your pay."

"Thank you, sir," Dilip said, getting up.

Ajay spent the rest of the day making sure the money and the heroin in the safe were correct, and the shops were adequately stocked. Everything was perfect. He really did have a good team in Rishi and Dilip.

By the evening he was wondering whether to visit one of Natasha's friends. Sonam was particularly satisfying. But should he be doing that? Was it right? He thought for a moment. Natasha seemed to make sure they did OK. He always paid them directly, and they were not cheap. They probably paid Natasha commission, but they wore expensive clothes and seemed to enjoy their work. He wanted to do what was right by others, but he was not a monk. He phoned Sonam.

∾

The next day he picked up Rishi and they went somewhere quiet. He gave Rishi a thick envelope full of cash.

"Thanks," Ajay said.

"Thank you, bhaiyaa."

"There's an old man across the river who sells ludoos from a small handcart," Ajay said, getting straight down to business. "There's also a bastard called Haasan who's extorting protection money from him – he's bleeding him dry. We're going to stop him."

Rishi nodded.

"We need muscle. You know – two big guys who can intimidate..."

"No problem."

Of course it was not a problem – it was Rishi he was talking to.

∾

Haasan got up early. 10am. He stretched. After taking a leak he looked in the mirror. He did not need a shave: the stubble looked good. He flexed his biceps. *He* looked good. A strong jaw with good muscles on a broad six foot tall frame meant nobody messed with him. Especially the little old man with the big ludoos. It made him smile when he thought of him like that. He liked the little old man. With those twinkly eyes he looked like everyone's favourite grandad. It was the visit he enjoyed the most. But the old man always looked absolutely petrified – much more than anyone else. Haasan meant no harm – it was not personal, only business. He shrugged – in his world fear was the best way to get respect.

Last night had been exceptionally satisfying. Two women who were not expensive and a good bag of coke had hit the mark perfectly. He felt great. The world was his for the taking. But he did not want the world. Just payment from the old ludoo man this morning, and from the mechanic at Mandawali Road, and a final visit to the saree wallah on Vishnu Road. Tomorrow was the beginning of the weekend, which he always took off. He did not want to work *too* hard – life was for living. A great lifestyle for no more than threatening to hit people. Could things be any better?

After a good, long soak in the shower he put on a fresh shirt and trousers. He looked in the mirror again and smiled. How could you not smile at a vision like that?

He got to the old man's cart just before 1pm. He had had lunch, but had left some room for a couple of ludoos. There was no question that they were the best in Delhi.

He was smiling at the old man as he approached. So was the old man. This confused him slightly – he had only ever seen the old man look terrified and miserable. The next thing he knew was that he was surrounded by Ajay, Rishi and two of Rishi's acquaintances.

"Mr Haasan?" asked Ajay.

"Yeah…"

"We'd like to talk to you."

Haasan stood in a stupefied silence.

One of Rishi's acquaintances shoved him in the direction they wanted him to go.

Hassan found himself sandwiched between Rishi's acquaintances in the back seat of an SUV with a gun pressed into his side. Rishi drove. Ajay followed in a separate vehicle. It didn't take long for them to get to a small, abandoned barn just outside East Delhi.

Haasan tried to fight back, but he soon found himself stripped naked and tied to a chair.

Ajay was sitting opposite him, patiently waiting for him to get his breath back. Haasan's hair was a mess. But that was the least of his concerns right now. His ribs felt like they were badly bruised – maybe even cracked. He had a gash down his left calf, and his left eye was swelling into what promised to be a nasty looking black eye.

Ajay took out a flick knife out and pressed the button. A shiny stainless steel blade sprang forth. He went over to Haasan, who tried to back away. Ajay ran the razor-sharp edge of the blade lightly across Hasaan's right thigh. Hasaan cried out in pain at the same time as blood seeped out of the cut.

Ajay sat down. "Let me introduce myself, Mr Hasaan. My name is Mr Pandey.

"The old ludoo wallah tells me you visit him every month and demand money."

Hasaan carried on glaring.

"Is there anyone else you visit?"

Hasaan said nothing. Ajay got up, approaching Hasaan with the knife held in front of him.

"No!" yelled Hasaan.

Ajay sat down again.

"Now, be a good boy and answer my questions truthfully or, next time, it'll be your pretty little face. I'll cut you so badly, you'll have to pay whores just to look at you. And then I'll cut off your fingers one by one. Understand?"

Hasaan said nothing.

"Who else do you visit?"

"Lots of people," Hassan said hesitantly.

"How many?"

"About 20."

"How many?"

"60," Hassan said quietly.

"Are their names on your phone?"

Hasaan nodded.

Ajay picked up Hasaan's phone. "What's your code?"

Hasaan gave it to him.

"That's very good. Now, tell me their names."

"They're in a contact group – 'Monthly Meetings'."

Ajay fiddled with the phone briefly. It was a model he was not familiar with.

"So they are. How very generous of you - you've even put notes about them all."

Hasaan had. He might be a playboy, but there were some things in life you had to take seriously. He had all the names, phone numbers, addresses, how much they paid every month, and when the next visit was due.

"OK, you've got what you want. Let me go."

Ajay got up and walked to the door of the barn, where Rishi and the hired help were standing.

"Kill him and meet me at the ludoo wallah's," Ajay said, looking at Rishi. The words echoed in the empty space.

"No! No! You've got what you want! You've got what you want!"

Ajay continued to walk. He had given himself a headache thinking about what to do with Haasan. His initial thought was to frighten him and let him go. But he had met enough weaselling, ruthless bastards to know that they would say anything to make you believe them, but then go back to their old tricks or try to kill you. Ajay could have ignored what Haasan was doing, but he had turned a blind eye too often. Nobody else would do anything – especially the police. This world was better off without some people – Haasan was one of them. Ajay had no choice.

"You bastard! Your mother fucker! Burn in hell, you dog shit! You –"

A pistol shot echoed from within the barn. An eerie silence seemed to follow. Even though he was not religious, Ajay said a silent prayer and sent an apology to Haasan's soul.

Within an hour Rishi was dropped off next to the old man's cart. In the meantime Ajay had had time to look through Haasan's list. Singh's suggestion of taking over from Haasan so no one else could move in had not been a bad one. If Haasan had been bleeding the old man dry, he probably had been doing the same to all his other victims. They could probably afford half of what they had paid to Haasan. Ajay decided he would charge them a quarter. He could charge them nothing, but he reasoned that he needed something just to give him an incentive to carry on going around, even if it was nominal. Also, many of them would probably not be able to get their heads around someone running a protection racket without charging protection...

Rishi phoned Ajay, who joined him within ten minutes.

They approached the old man.

"Hasaan won't trouble you any more," Ajay said.

The old man nodded, but looked worried. Was he out of the red hot karai, only to find himself in the fire?

"You'll be dealing with me now." Ajay gently told him the monthly payment he expected. "Are you happy with that?"

The old man nodded, looking pleasantly surprised.

"If anyone gives you *any* hassle, text me," Ajay said reassuringly.

The old man nodded again, this time smiling.

Ajay felt good. At least there was one person who would genuinely look forward to seeing him...

Ajay and Rishi started to visit Haasan's former victims. Ajay told them what he intended to charge and gave them the choice of going with him or not. All of them paid up. He always left them with the line: "If you have *any* problems, text me."

It was his second month of doing his rounds when the saree wallah on Vishnu Road said to him: "My biggest problem is the state of the road. I've phoned the municipality many times, but the idiot who answers always says, 'Yes, we will do it next week.' I've been waiting two years."

Ajay looked out at the road. The surface was completely destroyed, and there were potholes so large that it would be impossible to drive a car down it.

"People avoid this road. Nobody comes down. It used to be a busy road – I'd watch people look at my window as they drove past, and they'd come back later. I'm going to have to shut down soon, just like Arun the phone wallah had to last month, and Mirban the cycle wallah a few weeks ago. Soon there'll be no one down here."

Ajay nodded. "Give me the number you call, and I'll see what I can do."

The saree wallah wrote it down, together with the name – Navin Puri.

The saree wallah had been Ajay and Rishi's last call of the day, so they went straight to the municipal council buildings. After some enquiries they found themselves sitting on the other side of a desk to Navin Puri.

"We will do it next week, guaranteed, sir."

"You've been saying that for two years."

"Oh no, no. It will be done. You have my word."

"You've given your word before, Mr Puri. Your word is nothing," Ajay said with ice in his voice.

"But this time I guarantee it, sir."

"Why hasn't it been done already? All the shops are shutting because no one can go down there."

"I completely understand –"

"Answer my question – why hasn't it been done already?" demanded Ajay in a tone that could not be brushed aside.

"We have other priorities, sir. Connaught Place takes a lot of our budget –"

"Connaught Place is beautiful. Too beautiful. Use some of your budget to mend the roads across the river." Ajay shifted forward in his seat. So did Rishi. "Unless you want us to see you after work and make things *very* difficult for you."

A look of fear came over Puri's face. "I-I'm very sorry, sir. Jaya Chawla, the MP for New Delhi, has told us what to do. She says it is important to keep the tourists coming in. If I try to do anything else, someone will report me and it will be stopped."

Ajay contemplated waiting for Puri after work and using more persuasive methods. He could also threaten the head of department. But it would be pointless. They would probably do some cheap job that would fall apart in a few months. It was Jaya Chawla who needed convincing.

Ajay stood up and shook Puri's hand. "Thank you for your time."

Puri looked relieved and a little bewildered.

"What now, bhaiyaa?" asked Rishi as they left the building.

"We visit Mrs Chawla." Ajay had looked up her details on the way down in the lift. She was at her offices every Monday, Tuesday and Thursday between 10am and 6pm. Today was Tuesday.

Mrs Chawla's offices were on Connaught Circus. When Ajay and Rishi entered they found themselves in a waiting room with nearly all the 25 seats occupied. They went over to the desk in the corner.

"We'd like to see Mrs Chawla," said Ajay.

"You can see Mrs Chawla or her PA. The wait for her PA is about 20 minutes. The wait for Mrs Chawla is over two hours," replied the middle-aged man behind the desk.

"We'll wait for Mrs Chawla."

The man took Ajay's name and indicated for them to take a seat.

They dozed and looked at their phones as they waited. Finally, after nearly three hours, Ajay's name was called.

"Wait here," he said to Rishi.

"Hello, Mr Pandey," was Mrs Chawla's friendly greeting. "Please take a seat."

Mrs Chawla looked as good natured and friendly as she sounded. A slightly chubby woman with long, greying hair who appeared to be in her late fifties, the saree she wore suited her. She came across as a mother/grandmother you could confide in. Ajay wondered if she had cultivated the persona. Probably. He sat down.

"Now, how can I help you?"

"The roads in East Delhi, across the river, are in a very bad state. They need mending urgently."

Mrs Chawla nodded sympathetically. "I understand what you're saying, Mr Pandey, and I appreciate your concerns. They are a very high priority, but our budget is extremely tight –"

"You have enough money for Connaught Place."

"Connaught Place attracts tourists. For every one rupee we spend, we get ten back –"

"Why can't you spend some of those rupees you get back on the roads of East Delhi?" asked Ajay.

"It's not that simple. The systems of government mean that every rupee needs to be accounted for. But you have my word, Mr Pandey, that the roads will be mended."

Ajay knew it was pointless to ask when. He also knew it was pointless to ask if she had driven to East Delhi. Both questions would be met with charming evasion and flannel. He looked at his watch.

"Your office closes in ten minutes. We can go for a drive in East Delhi after that."

Mrs Chawla looked a little shocked. "I've got to open a newly built orphanage when I leave," she said awkwardly. It was obviously a lie.

"Faruk Khan died of a broken neck," Ajay said coldly. "Many people were glad to see him go." It was still etched in his mind that Khan had doused Chawla in petrol and had threatened to rape her daughter.

"Sorry?" she replied, bemused.

"His head was wrenched one way, then another, then another until the bones in his neck were turned to dust," Ajay continued. These were details that had never been released to the media.

She looked worried and leaned forward.

"I wouldn't press that button under your desk," Ajay said in the same tone.

She froze where she was.

"I mean you no harm," he said in a much softer voice. "All I want is for you to come for a drive in East Delhi. Bring a security guard with you."

She said nothing.

"I'll leave you in peace after that."

She still said nothing. He looked at her impassively.

At last she looked at the clock on the wall. "OK, Mr Pandey, I'll get my security team and come with you."

She phoned through to the front desk and instructed that her security team meet her there.

As they walked out of her office, Ajay caught Rishi's eye. He discreetly flicked his hand to shoo him away. Rishi got up and left.

There were two very large men waiting at the desk next to whom even Rishi would look small.

All four of them walked to Ajay's car, which was in the car park at the back of the building. One guard sat on the passenger seat. Mrs Chawla and the other guard sat on the back seat.

Ajay drove through the rush hour traffic until he eventually managed to cross the river. Then, as he drove along, the ride became noticeably bumpier. Eventually, they arrived at the top of Vishnu Road, where the saree wallah's shop was.

Ajay turned to Mrs Chawla. "Has the ride been comfortable, madam?"

"It's been very pleasant, Mr Pandey. You should've seen the state of the roads when I was a girl."

"OK. Do you mind if I let this gentleman –" Ajay indicated the guard next to him with a flourish of his open hand "- drive down Vishnu Road so you can get a true feel of it?"

Mrs Chawla laughed, "Bijay's my driver. Of course I don't mind."

Ajay and Bijay got out of the car and swapped seats.

It was only a few metres before the car hit a pothole and everyone was thrown about in their seats.

"Don't worry about my suspension," Ajay reassured Bijay. He turned back to Mrs Chawla. "Please look at how many shops are closed down. Nobody comes down here."

They were all shaken violently over what felt like every centimetre of the next 20 metres.

"Stop!" shouted Mrs Chawla at last. "This is intolerable! How did things get this bad?"

Turning to her, Ajay said: "The poor taxpayers of East Delhi have been paying for the luxuries of Connaught Place."

The two security guards looked shocked. They had never heard anyone speak to their boss like that.

"I had no idea. I'll make sure something is done about it," Mrs Chawla replied, sounding embarrassed as she looked at the two closed down shops next to her window.

"Let's get out of the car and walk back up to the top of the road, and your driver can turn around and pick us up," Ajay said, knowing that the short walk would give Mrs Chawla an even better idea of the state of the road and the atmosphere of dereliction that pervaded the area.

Ajay, Mrs Chawla and the security guard who wasn't driving got out of the car. There was no denying that this boy oozed presence and authority. The guards had never seen Mrs Chawla so cowed.

Vishnu Road was completely resurfaced within a week.

When it was completed Ajay got a text from the saree wallah. "Thank you bhaisaab. There is matai and chai waiting for you. God bless you."

Ajay felt moved beyond measure.

As the months went on, more and more of the shopkeepers who paid him protection turned to Ajay with their woes. Troublesome youths were easily dealt with. Petty gangsters usually responded to a good beating. However, there were the more persistent ones – they ended up in prison for a long time thanks to Singh speaking to the right members of the constabulary in East Delhi. That was enough to deter others who could have been tempted to take their place.

What proved to be more tricky was the Municipal Corporation of Delhi. But things became easier as time went on. After a while, whenever Ajay visited Mrs Chawla he was ushered straight into her office. It had not taken her long to realise that he was a valuable asset: he told her about things that the city officials tried to hide from her, in the process opening her eyes to how much of Delhi *really* functioned.

Several months after he had sorted out Vishnu Road, Ajay was visiting the saree wallah for his monthly fee, chai and matai.

"There's a friend of mine in Shahdara who would like you to visit him," said the saree wallah.

"Why?" asked Ajay.

"He wants to pay you protection."

Ajay looked completely bemused. "Why?" he was eventually able to say.

"I've told him it's the best value for money he'll ever get."

Maybe Ajay had overdone it...

14

The heroin proved to be more of a problem. He was between a rock and a hard place. If he dropped prices, he would create more users. If he put them up, his customers would probably struggle and turn more to crime.

He thought about discussing it with Singh, but decided against it. Singh would just tell him what to do from a police point of view. He needed a humane solution.

He had heard of a place called Sanctuary, a free drugs rehab clinic in the far north of the city. He decided to visit.

It was a two storey building which looked slightly dilapidated. As he entered he came into a small room and found himself facing a slim middle-aged woman sitting behind a desk. She was dressed in plain, sensible shoes, with trousers and a blouse to match. She had kind eyes.

"Hello," he said. "I'd like to talk to someone about heroin addiction," realising that he had not thought about what he wanted from the meeting, and that he also sounded like a junkie.

"I'm very sorry, but it's over a five year wait to get on to the programme."

"Five years!"

She nodded, looking sad.

After a moment of stunned silence he said: "It's OK, I'm not an addict. I'm doing some research and just wanted to talk to someone about drugs, especially heroin. Maybe the manager."

"That's me."

"Oh, OK," he said, trying to cover his surprise. "Do you have time to talk?"

She nodded.

He sat on one of the plastic chairs facing the desk. It had been a long time since he had sat on anything that uncomfortable.

"Why are there so many addicts?" he blurted out, not knowing what else to say.

"There are so many addicts everywhere – from the USA to Europe to India. The number increases daily. The problem is partly supply – it's getting cheaper and more freely available. Add to that the internet, more disposable income, more depression, more stress, global trends... You get the picture?"

Ajay nodded.

"What can be done? Put more dealers in prison?"

She shook her head. "The prisons are overflowing, but addiction is increasing. It makes no difference. It might be making things worse. The courts throw people in prison for petty amounts. The conditions are terrible. People are coming out with worse habits than they had when they went in."

"But what about the dealers?" Ajay persisted. "Surely it's best to get them off the streets."

She shook her head again. "If you put them in prison, someone comes along straightaway to start where they left off. The problem is there's too much money to be made."

"Are drugs too cheap?" asked Ajay.

"Of course they are. But what are we supposed to do – demand the dealers pay tax? With the amount coming out of Afghanistan alone, the price is just going to go down. And, if you add fentanyl, MDNA, chitta and all the rest, heroin has to be cheap to compete.

The problem is not just heroin. The problem is great – too great..." She looked sad.

Ajay nodded sympathetically.

"Why do you have a five year waiting list?"

She laughed bitterly. "Because the government are lying hypocrites. They say they want to help people come off drugs. They say they fund us, but what they give us is a joke. And, if we complain, they threaten to cut our funding and tell us to do more fundraising. But who wants to give money to drug addicts? Rotary clubs and middle-class ladies don't even want to think about it – all they're interested in is endangered tigers and orphans."

Ajay did not know what to say.

"Take my advice," she said. "Don't ever become a drug addict. You'll be more hated than a rabid dog."

Those words rang in Ajay's ears.

"How much more money do you need?" asked Ajay.

"At least ten times more than the government gives us. Look at this place – it's falling down. We have just 12 people on the rehab courses, and only two counsellors. It's not enough. And we have to limit people to just one 30 day stay. Anyone who's worked in this environment knows that's never enough. We need more centres –"

"OK," he said, nodding.

She looked at him quizzically.

"I'll give you the money – whatever it takes. I have deep pockets," he said quietly. "And I'll buy five buildings for you to use as centres. I'll fit them all out."

She looked shocked.

"Will that be enough to start with?" Ajay asked tentatively.

"I don't know what to say, Mr..."

"Pandey."

"I don't know what to say, Mr Pandey. By the way, I'm Mrs Chopra. It's an absolute pleasure to meet you." She proffered her hand, which he shook. "It'll mean we can begin to make a real difference. I hope you don't mind me asking, but what do you do?"

It was a reasonable question. She had to be sure it was not a wind-up. She would be used to dealing with devious people who would try to use her for all kinds of purposes.

"I run a small chain of samosa shops in Central Delhi and a clothes wholesale business."

"I'm so grateful to you. Again, I hope you don't mind me asking, but what has made you seek us out? As I said, unfortunately people usually avoid us."

Ajay was silent. He looked at her. He wanted to confess that he was a drug dealer, the scum of the earth, and he wanted to make amends... But how could he say *that*?

"I've known a *lot* of people die and have their lives ruined by drugs," he said at last, his eyes moist as he thought of all the deaths and heartache he would have brought over the years.

"I'm sorry..." she said.

Ajay shut his eyes. "Maybe I can make a difference now," he said quietly. The comment was to himself – he had zoned out to everything but the pain that now tore through him, as it had so often in the last few weeks.

"You *will* make a difference. A huge difference, Mr Pandey."

He opened his eyes, startled into realising he was not alone.

Mrs Chopra had a tear rolling down her cheek.

He wiped away a tear as well.

15

"How bad is his stuff?" Ajay asked.

"It's not too bad – I've seen a lot worse," Singh replied. "Suri – Dewan killed him and took over – used to put all kinds of rubbish in. Dewan's nowhere near that bad."

"What does he put in?"

Singh shrugged. "Not sure anymore. We had to have a word with him a couple of times when he first took over and we started finding dead junkies everywhere. He was putting in caffeine and painkillers – the junkies couldn't tell when they were overdosing. That wasn't as bad as Suri – one time he was selling pure fentanyl cut with sugar and milk. The amount of people who died and ended up completely psychotic... if Dewan hadn't killed him, I would've."

Ajay looked at Singh. Singh was wily enough to know that you had to tolerate some crime, but there was a line which should never be crossed. He had become a policeman not just to throw his weight around and blackmail drug dealers, as Ajay had first thought. He genuinely wanted to make a difference.

"Can you get Dewan's stuff tested?" asked Ajay.

"We only do that if we know we've got a problem."

Ajay took a 100 gram packet out of a carrier bag. "I need this testing – it's Dewan's."

"Do you know how much a test costs?"

"A lot less than I pay you every two weeks."

Singh clenched his jaw in irritation. "I'll see what I can do."

"I want it tested properly. I want to know *exactly* what's in it. When are you going to do it?" There was steel in Ajay's voice.

"OK, OK. I'll let you know in the next couple of days."

True to his word, Singh texted Ajay within 48 hours. "20% heroin. 15% sugar. 30% milk powder. 30% talcum powder. 5% brick dust. Trace fentanyl – makes it feel like 25% heroin. Brick dust is for colour – would not advise. Talc can cause blood clots. Seen worse. Overall not too dangerous."

Ajay stared at the text. Fentanyl, brick dust and talc. What was he doing? Dealing in heroin was bad enough, but he had thought that Dewan's stuff was OK – word on the street had always been that it was.

"We need to meet," Ajay texted back.

They were sitting in Ajay's car within the hour. Ajay handed over an envelope. Singh felt the thickness, looked inside and then looked at Ajay. It was less than his usual amount.

"That's just a bonus – it's more than you make in a month. Not bad for one meeting.. Don't worry, you'll still get your payment every two weeks," Ajay said, not looking at him.

Singh put the money away.

"I don't like the shit I'm selling," said Ajay.

"It's the best you'll get in Delhi. Trust me, there's a lot worse out there, my friend."

Ajay could feel anger rise in him. "I don't care. It's not good enough for me."

"You could try importing it yourself. It's risky and you have to be careful who you're dealing with. If it goes through too many hands, they'll all cut it, and you won't know what with. We suspect Dewan's Afghan suppliers strengthen their stuff with cheap fentanyl from China and it gets cut with whatever is around. Dewan couldn't care less. All he's bothered about is making money and keeping the police off his back. God knows where the brick dust and talc came from – probably not Dewan."

Ajay felt dejected. What was he doing? He had to get out of this shitty trade.

"You could try getting it from Myanmar."

"Myanmar?" asked Ajay, sounding surprised. It seemed a long way to go.

"Our colleagues on the East Coast have the opposite problem – the stuff's too pure. Sometimes 99% heroin gets through, and it kills everyone who tries it. You'll pay more, but you can get pure stuff. They drop it on the Odisha coast. You could get one of your guys to bring it to Delhi. Cut it yourself – just stick to baking powder, sugar and milk powder."

Ajay nodded. He liked what he was hearing. But how the hell was he supposed to make connections in Myanmar?

"I'll see what I can do..." Singh said as he got out of the car. The comment startled Ajay out of his thoughts – it felt as if Singh had read his mind.

Within an hour Ajay had received a text from Singh. "___ Call this number. Mr Nayak. Middleman in Odisha. Say "Copenhagen" when he answers – password only valid for today. Only deals in clean stuff. Tolerated by police, but be careful."

Ajay typed in the number.

"Hello," said the voice at the other end.

"Copenhagen," was Ajay's reply.

"Who is this?" The reply was in English.

"Ajay Pandey, a businessman in Delhi. Mr Nayak?"

"Yes, what do you want?"

"I want to do business."

"What type of business?"

"15 to 20 kilos. Pure," replied Ajay.

There was a pause. "Where are you?"

"Delhi – I'll come to you."

"OK," Nayak said slowly. "Come to Bhabaneswar Airport tomorrow."

"OK. I'll book a ticket and get back to you."

Nayak severed the connection. Ajay was surprised at the smoothness and brevity of the transaction. The password Singh had given him obviously carried a lot of weight.

Ajay booked a flight arriving just after 4pm the next day. He texted Nayak the details of the flight, together with a photo of himself.

"Someone will meet you at the airport," was the text he got back.

He was met by a large man and taken to a car where another two large men were waiting. He sat on the back seat, where the man next to him made no attempt to hide the gun in the holster under his jacket.

An hour's drive later and he found himself in a spacious shed in a field in the middle of the Odisha countryside. Two of the men looked on as the third one searched him. When he had finished he made a phone call, speaking a language Ajay did not recognise.

20 minutes later a short, late middle-aged man and two more large men entered.

"Mr Pandey," the older man said, approaching him. "I'm Mr Nayak."

They shook hands. Nayak, without letting go, said: "I hope we can do business. But, if you betray me, I will torture and kill you and your family." His English, although heavily accented, was perfect.

Ajay nodded. Nayak let go of his hand.

"So you want to do business?" Nayak asked.

"Yes. 15 to 20 kilos pure heroin in one month." Ajay's English was good, but not as good as Nayak's. However, it was not as accented, making it easier to understand.

"Where do you trade?"

"Delhi."

"Where in Delhi?"

"East and central," replied Ajay.

"*Central?*" Nayak sounded surprised. "And the police leave you alone?"

Ajay shrugged. "I'm very careful."

"Who supplies you? Laksh Dewan?"

"Yes," Ajay replied uncertainly.

"Of course he does. He controls Delhi. Faruk Khan tried to take over, but Dewan saw him off. I don't know how he did it – Khan was a dangerous man. They said he was going to control the whole of India one day."

Ajay kept a straight face as Nayak talked. Is *that* what those in the know thought?

"Why do you want to deal with me? Laksh Dewan is a good man."

Ajay hesitated. He had not expected this degree of questioning. He quickly realised he had been naïve not to prepare for it, and began to think rapidly. If he said that he did not like what Dewan was cutting his stuff with because it was bad for his customers, Nayak and his men would laugh at him before killing him, and then probably deliver his body to Dewan as a present. If he said he wanted to take over from Dewan, he would get a similar reaction.

"I need stronger, purer stuff. A lot of my customers in Central Delhi are asking," Ajay said after only a short pause.

"Why don't you ask Dewan?"

"He gets it from Afghanistan. They cut it before sending, and then they cut it more and more in Pakistan."

Nayak nodded. Everyone knew this was true.

"15 to 20 kilos in one month?" asked Nayak.

Ajay nodded.

"How do I know you will take it?"

"I pay cash every time."

Nayak and his men laughed.

"Do you think I offer credit?" Nayak grinned.

Ajay said nothing.

"OK, young man. I'll supply you. But, remember, if you betray me, you will watch your mother being raped and tortured."

After the briefest of pauses Ajay said: "I need a sample."

Nayak nodded at one of his men. He took what looked like a 100g packet out of his inside jacket pocket, and came over and handed it to Nayak.

Nayak told him the price. Even if this stuff was 100 per cent pure, it was still more than he was paying now, and he had processing costs to add on to it.

"What purity?" asked Ajay.

"100% pure heroin."

Ajay shook his head. "Too much. I pay a quarter less in Delhi."

A tension fell over the room.

"You're arguing over a few rupees?"

"I have to pick it up, transport it and process it. It might be the best, but it's too much." Despite a composed exterior, Ajay's heart was pounding. Nayak was obviously ruthless, but did not come across as a nutcase. The worst thing that was likely to happen was he would refuse to deal with Ajay. Ajay was taking a risk, maybe even with his own life, but there was no way he was going to let Nayak think of him as some kind of young, naïve pushover whom he could piss all over.

Nayak looked at him for a while. "OK, young man, you've got yourself a 25% discount. But you'll take at least 20 kilos a month. And pay for this –" he held up the packet in his hand "– now."

When Ajay got back to Delhi, the first thing he did was call Singh.

"I've got a sample I need testing."

Singh picked up ten grams within the hour, and had the results to him the next day. "100% pure. Lab never seen anything like it."

OK. Time to get the ball rolling. He called Dilip into his office.

"I'm changing my supplier. Dewan is out."

Dilip paused before saying: "He might make things difficult, sir."

"Oh, I know he will. And our current setup isn't good enough."

Dilip was hesitant. Things were running smoothly – no one interfered with what they did. This was in no small part due to the fact that dealing with Dewan offered a certain amount of protection in itself. Dilip had a military background and the thought of a challenge brought a certain excitement, but he had got used to an easy life.

"Do you think we need to move?" asked Ajay.

"This place is fortified, sir."

"The police got through the door in less than a second," Ajay pointed out.

Dilip did not need to be reminded.

"If we stay here, we're easy targets. All Dewan has to do is wait until dark and attack fast and hard. He could easily kill whoever's on duty and burn the place out."

This was true. The industrial estate was like a ghost town at night, and they were right in the middle of it. The first thing anyone would know about it would be in the morning.

"We need to toughen up," Ajay said, hoping it would be a call to arms.

It seemed to work. He saw Dilip going from relaxed to sitting up to attention.

"Yes, sir."

"You were a lieutenant commander in MARCOS, weren't you?" MARCOS stood for Marine Commandos – the Indian navy special forces.

"Yes, sir," Dilip replied, his chest puffing out slightly.

"Are you still in touch with any of your old MARCOS buddies?"

"Yes sir. I meet regularly with a number of my old comrades."

"Do you know any who are fighting fit, know how to handle a gun and need work?"

Dilip laughed a little. "There are always men like that available."

"Good. We need two on duty at any one time, and two who can be there within seconds. They need to be invisible and keep their mouth shut."

"That's what they're trained for."

"When can you get them here?" demanded Ajay.

"Give me 72 hours, sir."

"Good. Now, I was thinking of moving operations to Paharganj."

Dilip looked startled.

"It's in the centre of town, where all the action is," Ajay continued. "One gun shot and the police will be straight there."

"But isn't it a bit too visible, sir?"

"That's the whole point. It's not as if we have junkies visiting us. I can even have an office where I can meet my clothing clients." Ajay had continued Ranveer's clothing business – it was a good cover, and it allowed him to bring back some of the money from abroad. "It'll be the perfect cover: hiding in plain sight."

Dilip nodded. It was a tactic he had used many times.

"OK. I've got details of three buildings. I need your advice – let's go." With that Ajay stood up and walked towards the door. Dilip followed.

In reality Ajay had more or less decided which building to take. It was three stories high and on Chitragupta Road. The top floor had been converted to a three bedroom flat. The two floors below were basic offices. The ground floor would be perfect for the clothing business. The back rooms could be used for storage, with proper shelving generously spaced, instead of the cramped area to one side of the industrial unit. It would add an air of professionalism. Convert the front room into a plush office, and the place would ooze legitimacy.

He planned to get the floors and ceilings reinforced throughout the building. The heroin would be stored on the first floor, which would have a reinforced entrance and two MARCOS men on duty at any one time, with the other two in the flat upstairs. The only way any of them would be allowed on any type of leave was if a replacement was there. Although Ajay had carefully thought things through he would, of course, consult Dilip and see if anything else could be put in place.

When they saw the building, Dilip agreed with Ajay.

Ajay told the estate agent he wanted the building and was willing to pay cash if it could be in his name in two weeks. The agent did not seem phased. In fact, she assured Ajay that she had done this many times before. Ajay did not quite believe her. He told her there was a very large bonus for her if she got it through in time. If not, he would pull out of the deal. Her eyes lit up. It was only then that he was convinced it would be done.

Over the next week, Ajay and Dilip planned out the middle floor and got the materials in place. Ajay got hold of Kamal, the builder from Paraharavi, and told him what he wanted. It was not something that was beyond his capabilities, although he did raise his eyebrows at the steel prison door at the entrance to the first floor.

The sale went through in nine days. Building work on the middle floor was completed three days after that. It took another two days to fit out the ground floor, and another two to paint it. They moved in the next day. It was at this point that Ajay paid off the old security guards, and Dilip got the MARCOS men in.

Ajay had kept Rishi informed of the change of premises and the increase in security, but he had kept the meeting with Nayak to himself.

Two days after moving in Ajay called Rishi into his office.

"Rishi, you're going to Odisha tomorrow…"

16

An hour after Ajay's order was due, Dewan phoned him.

"Where's your order?" he demanded. "You're late – you're going to pay an extra ten per cent. If you're late again, that goes up."

"I'm not ordering from you anymore," Ajay calmly replied.

There was a momentary silence. "*I* tell you when you stop trading, not you."

"I'm not stopping."

Another silence from Dewan. "Who do you think you're talking to? I *own* Delhi."

"You don't own East Delhi anymore."

"*What?* Who the *hell* do you think you are?" yelled Dewan.

"Someone who knows who killed Faruk Khan," Ajay said in the same calm tone.

Dewan was silent.

"You didn't kill him," continued Ajay. "He would've finished you. And you didn't have the balls to take on Laghari. You're nothing, Dewan. Just a jumped-up street dealer who sells fentanyl and brick dust."

"Who do you think you are?" Dewan repeated, but this time in a low, controlled voice. "I could have you finished off tomorrow."

"Do you want to have your neck broken like Khan, or be shot like Laghari?" Ajay asked, his voice still betraying no emotion. "Take your pick – I can arrange it."

"I don't believe you," Dewan replied.

"Try me." It was the first time Ajay's voice took on any kind of inflection. It sounded as if he was just itching to kill Dewan. It even sent a cold shiver down Ajay's own spine.

Dewan terminated the call.

∼

Ajay had a sign put above the shop.

Ajay's Unique Fashion
High End Imported Women's Clothing
Wholesale Only

He employed a shop consultant to dress the window, which she suggested changing every two weeks. She charged what many would have considered a fortune, but Ajay agreed. The fees may have been extortionate, but they were nothing to him, and having the consultant on his books gave him an added legitimacy. That added legitimacy would be the perfect cover to claim his profit had increased, meaning he could launder even more money through the clothing business.

The net result of all the changes was that his clothing sales went up 400% in less than three months. He could not believe it. Like Ranveer, he had worked on minimal margins. The purpose of the clothing business had been a cover to allow him to get some of his drugs money back into the country. But, if it carried on like this, more than enough money would end up in India very fast.

The shop consultant had told him many times that he was not charging anywhere near enough – his cheapest rival's prices were in excess of 50% more than his, and their quality was inferior. End consumers at the luxury end of the market *wanted* to pay more – it made them feel good about themselves, as if they were worth much more than those less well off than them. At the moment, the retailers were putting a massive markup on his clothes but, sooner or later, someone would come along and sell them at bargain basement prices. The unsophisticated masses would go mad for his clothes for one season, but then he would be finished.

He doubled his prices. Demand fell to virtually nothing as his customers abandoned him. But the shop consultant put a few new customers his way. They were more discerning, and they liked what they saw. They displayed his merchandise discreetly but prominently in their upmarket boutiques. Their customers liked it. Demand steadily went up as word about him spread. It levelled off below his previous peak, which suited him fine – he was making a lot more money for less work, and there was plenty of capacity to launder the drugs money. He had three staff fulfilling orders, all of them blissfully unaware of the merchandise that was a few feet above their heads.

Demand increased for heroin as well. This did not surprise him, but it troubled him. It was not what he wanted.

He had not put his prices up, fearing a spike in crime by junkies who would do anything for a fix. The gangmasters told him that the new stuff was so good, word had spread like wildfire. People were crossing the river every night just so they could score what had begun to be called "Delhi Gold". Users were reporting that the high was better, and the come down nowhere near as bad as with anything else they had tried.

Ajay did not know what to do with all the money that was rolling in. He did not want flashy cars, expensive watches and all those other trinkets. They were silly little toys which held no interest for him.

He gave enough money to Sanctuary to allow them to more than double the amount of rehab spaces they had. But demand for his heroin still kept on going up. He gave more and more money to Sanctuary. Eventually Mrs Chopra told him she could not take any more. Delhi was saturated – they had empty beds.

Why was he selling ever increasing amounts? Did people *want* to be addicts? What was he doing wrong? Whatever it was, it felt like a weight around his neck, slowly choking the life out of him.

He would go for long walks to try to clear his head, but he would come back feeling just as bad. He walked along main roads, cut into backstreets, not caring where he went. On more than one occasion he found himself near a stinking alley. There he would often see semi-comatosed junkies, the likes of which had no interest in rehab. He wondered how many of them were using his stuff.

He began to watch them from a distance. They would often be gathered near one person – their dealer. He was looking at a group like this when the dealer saw him. He came over.

"You want to try? Delhi Gold – the best in all Delhi," he said in that slimy way that these low lives use to try to ingratiate themselves. He held out a wrap which looked like a tenth of a gram.

Ajay felt his wretchedness turn to pure rage. He wanted to kick this slim ball to death but, after he managed to bring his breathing under control, he asked: "How much?"

Ajay was shocked when he heard the price. The slime ball was marking up 150%.

Ajay bought some. It was the same colour as what he supplied, but that did not mean it had not been cut.

Ajay watched the now grinning slime ball go back to the small crowd in the alley. What looked to be a ten year old boy handed him some money in exchange for a small wrap like he had sold to Ajay. Ajay walked away feeling sick.

He discussed what he had seen with Rishi, who had spent far longer as a street dealer than him.

"Oh yes," Rishi said immediately. "You see it a lot. Someone starts using, and he gets more and more addicted. He ends up needing so much that the only way he can pay for it is by dealing himself. I've seen lots of people like that. They'll sell to anyone, especially street kids. Those kids don't have anyone, and they think of him as their big brother. They'll do anything for him. Those scum love it. They give the kids drugs, and the kids give them respect, love and enough money to buy more brown sugar than they could ever use. You'll never get those type of people into rehab – heroin gives them everything they never had."

He knew this went on, but did it account for the rise in demand? He decided to visit the gangmasters to find out what was really happening.

One gangmaster after another told him the same story – the street boys were often selling two or three or more grams at a time. It was those large sales that were mainly behind the increasing demand. His stuff was all over Delhi, and even going beyond into Uttar Pradesh, Rajasthan and Haryana.

He could feel himself slipping into despair until, finally, Arun, one of the gangmasters, said: "If they weren't using Delhi Gold, they'd be using something else, and there'd be a lot more dead kids on the streets of Delhi."

"Do you know how the other dealers are doing?" Ajay asked. Arun seemed pretty switched on.

"From what I've heard, they're nearly all down. All those free rehab places are having *some* effect," Arun said dismissively, "But the main problem is that they can't compete with Delhi Gold." He added the latter with more than a hint of smugness.

Maybe Ajay was doing some good, but there was no denying that he was feeding a massive soul-destroying machine.

The lengths of his walks around Delhi increased. He frequented the back streets more, often watching the putrid alleys from a discreet distance. He would see festering street kids huddled in groups. They would come and go, always returning with money or valuables to give to their "big brother" for their next fix. Time and time again Ajay wanted to go over and kick the shit out of those bastard dealers, but he reminded himself that he was no better than them. In fact, he was worse. They were only the retailers of death and misery: he was the wholesaler.

He was lost. What should he do? He could not rescue each one of those street kids himself.

He started giving large amounts to charities that supported street kids, especially those on drugs. Although his donations increased substantially each month, so did the demand for his heroin – those bastard dealers were experts at finding victims.

He still met regularly with Mrs Chawla, bringing complaints about appalling street maintenance, insufferable sanitation, badly-run municipal departments, incompetent officials, etc, etc. He no longer charged his protection "customers" in East Delhi anything, instead offering his services for free. They frequently brought problems to his attention which did not affect them, but he was always happy to help.

He was persuasive in the extreme. A few reports of blocked drains were often enough for Mrs Chawla to order the complete renewal of the sewage system in that neighbourhood. The recording of a pillar of the community making a phone call to a well-funded municipal department, only to be put on hold for two hours before being cut off more than once led to the entire management of a branch of the Delhi government to be replaced.

But, no matter what he did, he could not find any peace. As the months turned into years the demand for his product grew. He was killing even more people and wrecking an ever increasing number of lives with his drugs, and there was no way out without making things even worse. The frequency of sleepless nights increased. He tried to lose himself in solving problems for the people of East Delhi but, however hard he worked, it was not enough.

It was after a particularly bad night's sleep that he went to see Mrs Chawla about some East Delhi shopkeepers complaining about how the rats in their area had got out of control, and they could not get the municipality to do anything about it.

"What's wrong, Mr Pandey?" she asked after he had finished outlining shopkeepers' complaints.

"I've just told you."

"You've been coming to my office for years, and I've never seen you look so bad. Rats are a common problem in Delhi, something which you've told me about many times before. They're certainly not enough to get you into a state you're in, beta."

It was the first time she had ever called him "beta". It made him smile slightly.

"The amount of street children I see on drugs makes me feel completely helpless," he blurted out dejectedly. He was surprised by his own lack of control – things must be getting to him.

"Aren't you doing enough?"

He looked up at her.

"Oh, I know about your very generous donations to Sanctuary and street kids charities across Delhi," she said shrewdly.

He just looked at her for a while. He had gone out of his way not to make a big deal of it. But of course she knew – she was that kind of person.

"What difference does it make?" he almost whispered, turning away.

"A big difference to the children and those who have tried all their lives to get off drugs."

Ajay nodded, conceding the point. "But the number of addicts just keeps growing." He shut his eyes. "Every time I give more money, more drugs are sold."

"I've been doing this job for over 20 years," she replied. "One of the first things I learnt was that there are some things you can't do anything about."

He did not open his eyes.

"Not many people know this," she continued, "But elections are due in just over a year and I've decided not to stand again."

He opened his eyes.

"Why don't you stand, Mr Pandey?"

He looked at her, bewildered. Who would vote for a 25-year-old drug dealer from a slum with next to no education?

"You're the most persuasive person I've ever come across. You know how to break down barriers with the perfect blend of charm, appealing to raw emotion, and a huge stick – to beat your opponent into submission," she said, with more than just a hint of resentment as she added the latter.

Ajay could not help but smile broadly.

"You know, some years ago I heard of an interesting experiment in Zurich – the capital of Switzerland. They got the people with the biggest heroin habits and gave them heroin on prescription. I don't know if you know, but these people sell to others to feed their habit."

Ajay nodded impatiently.

"Well, they found that the number of new users fell by 80% the following year."

Ajay stared at her, wide-eyed.

"I've been spending much of the last few years trying to persuade the Delhi authorities to do something similar but, alas, to no avail."

Ajay smiled at her old fashioned language.

"There's only one person I know who could get it done, and that's you, Mr Pandey. What do you say?"

She sat back and waited patiently, watching Ajay.

Ajay sat back and shut his eyes again. Him, MP? How? But why not? He had been in business for over a decade. Dealing with junkies, taking on business rivals, forming and expanding three separate enterprises, providing jobs, funding charities, helping to bring up Bimala and Nitesh – he had more life experience than most. But would people take him seriously? He would make them. And it was his opportunity to do something worthwhile, instead of just throwing money at things to make himself feel better. But would he have time? He was already busy. But he could get a manager in for the clothing, and get others to take over more of his tasks. Employing a good team to help with the MP's caseload would not be a problem. He would not move out of these offices – they were just right – not too fancy or depressingly dowdy either. They were not so big as to intimidate or scream opulence. But they would be too small for a decent sized team. No problem – he could get secondary offices elsewhere, which people would not need to know about. But the key thing was to have *good* people to advise him.

He opened his eyes.

"If I run, I'd need you to advise me – before I get in and after. One or two days a week – I'll pay more than you get paid now."

She shook her head. "It wouldn't look good. As sitting MP I recommend you and help you win, and you pay me so much. I'll help you as much as you need, but I can't accept anything in return. And trust me, I'll always be there. But it won't be long before you won't need me."

He nodded as a shiver of excitement went down his spine.

∼

Over the next two weeks, he got in a manager to run the clothing business, and got Rishi to distribute samosas and drugs to the shops, and pick up the cash. Dilip took a more active role in making sure the gangmasters were kept well supplied, and their takings collected. Dilip and Rishi went together to give the cash to various Hawala agents. The only active part Ajay decided to take was making sure the money arrived in his foreign accounts. Although there was no way of telling if someone was skimming off the top, it allowed him to keep some sort of track of his finances.

He visited Mrs Chawla almost daily, and learnt more and more about how Delhi really functioned. He was surprised that there was not more corruption. But he was stunned at the level of pointless bureaucracy and how it all intertwined – you had to have your wits about you to navigate your way through it.

She told him about the duties of an MP. It seemed to involve going to a lot of dinners and openings of new buildings. He decided he would cut these to a minimum.

There were people whom you had to work with, others you had to fight, and others you had to charm – just like in business. But, in politics, things were not as black and white: there was more involved than just money. However, he came away with the firm impression that Mrs Chawla stood for too much nonsense. That was not to say that he intended to be too harsh with people – he had long ago learnt that the art of getting a good job done is getting other people to do what you want them to do because they want to do it. If that failed, he would use a very big stick.

There was no denying that Mrs Chawla was popular amongst the constituents, the party, and the city officials in Delhi. This had got her far, but only so far. He had five years to make his changes work. If his drugs policies did not work in that time, he would never be re-elected. He intended to crack heads together but, after the soreness lifted, those who ran Delhi would see he was doing the right thing.

As soon as he and Mrs Chawla announced he was running for MP, and the central theme of his first term in office would be to make heroin available on prescription for long-term addicts, he had the media's full attention.

Newspaper headlines were eye-catching. They went from the lurid ("MP To Legalise Heroin"), to the absurd ("MP: 'Make People Into Junkies'"), to the more favourable ("A Better Approach To Delhi's Drug Crisis?").

There were even mentions on national TV news. "Delhi's latest parliamentary candidate announced today that he intended to make heroin available on prescription. He claims this will bring down crime and addiction rates as long-term addicts typically steal and sell drugs to others so they can feed their own addiction. It yet has to be seen how the voters will react."

He had several requests for TV interviews – most of them via Mrs Chawla's office. He decided with Mrs Chawla that it would be good to give one interview to start with. They chose New India TV's Pooja Sati's "Politics Today" show. It would give him national exposure on a popular show which had been running for well over a decade. Pooja was known for her tough but fair questioning. By agreeing to go up against her, it showed he was not afraid. The fact that the very first interview he intended to give was with a woman would appeal to the female electorate and younger voters. Quite a few men would think of being interviewed by a woman as demeaning, but dinosaurs like that would never vote for someone as radical as him anyway.

Pooja: "Good morning, Mr Pandey, and thanks for agreeing to come on to the show."

Ajay: "Thank you for inviting me." He smiled as he said this, trying to appear relaxed, but feeling the exact opposite.

Pooja: "You've made quite a splash this week with the announcement that you intend to make heroin available on prescription."

Ajay: "That wasn't my intention. I just put forward a common sense, practical policy."

Pooja: "But it's very, very controversial, to say the least. How can you possibly justify it?"

Ajay: "The amount of drug use in India is increasing rapidly. The majority of people in prison are there because of drugs – either dealing, using or because of crimes committed to get the money to pay for them. And yet drug use still goes up. Our current approach isn't working. We need something that *will* work."

Pooja: "But the reason these drugs are illegal is because of the damage they cause. Look at the devastation in China before and after the opium wars. They banned the use of cocaine in Coca-Cola because of the damage it caused. Everywhere drugs have been allowed to take hold, the results have been horrendous."

Ajay nodded. "What you're saying is true. But the opposite is also true. The United States declared a war on drugs in 1972. Since then they have spent over one trillion dollars on it. And the results? Much of Central and South America has been badly affected – over half a million people killed or gone missing in Mexico alone. And, after spending all that money, with their prisons overflowing, all that has happened is that addiction has increased."

Pooja: "I take your point – there have been some very powerful drugs barons created. But it could be argued that they would have been created anyway, and the problem would have been far worse if the US had not taken action. What you are suggesting is creating a nation of state-sponsored addicts in some vain hope that this will somehow bring down addiction rates."

Ajay: "What we have across the world is an approach that isn't working. Why are India's prisons overflowing, but the drugs on the streets increasing? Why are the number of addicts going up despite record police seizures of heroin? Delhi has too many places for free drugs rehab programmes – beds go empty – but addiction rates continue to rise."

Pooja: "I have heard that the reason that there are so many rehab places in Delhi is due to you – you provide over 95% of the funding."

Ajay was left momentarily speechless as the camera focused in on him. "I'm not sure of all the funding sources, but it's a subject I'm passionate about," he said quietly.

Pooja: "You certainly seem to be putting your money where your mouth is. But how is making drugs freely available going to create less addiction?"

Ajay: "I don't want to make drugs freely available. I want drug dealers to be punished. But the system we have is not working. It's making addicts go underground. They have to steal to make money to pay for the drugs. This destabilises communities, increases fear everywhere and funds drug dealers so they can expand their operations. It's the perfect way to make things worse.

"What I want is the worst, long-term addicts to have drugs available on prescription. These people fund their habits by selling to others and creating more addicts. They did what I'm talking about in Zurich five years ago, and the number of new registered addicts fell by 80%."

Pooja nodded impatiently: "Yes, but do we want to tolerate more addicts on the streets of our capital, or anywhere else for that matter?"

Ajay: "I am not proposing more tolerance, but more understanding. The prescription will be given only by experienced doctors who know the signs of long-term addiction. The drugs will be administered under strict conditions. The punishment for any doctor trying to sell prescriptions will be as harsh as for any other drug dealer – at least ten years in prison. Addicts will be able to go on as many rehab programmes as they need to."

Pooja (sounding incredulous): "But will taxpayers accept their money going to drug users in this way?"

Ajay: "For every rupee spent, it will save many more in terms of policing, prison and the cost of having your house burgled or your car stolen. It will make Delhi a better place to live."

Pooja: "Am I right in thinking you were brought up in a slum, your father died when you were ten years old, you helped bring up your brother and sister, and now you run several highly successful businesses?"

Ajay nodded.

Pooja: "Mr Pandey, you seem to be worldly wise at a very young age, but do you believe there is such a thing as an ethical drug dealer, or are they all vermin who feed off others' misfortune?"

Ajay: "Mrs Sati, as I've said, many people find themselves pushed into it through their circumstances. If we jump hard on them, they will turn more and more to what they know – drug dealing. If we continue to push them underground, people will continue to suffer and die from bad drugs and overdoses, as well as commit crimes. We've tried war and failed. Now it's time for something less confrontational and more helpful. We've got nothing to lose, and lots to gain."

Pooja: "You've made your point very well. May the best candidates win the elections..."

After shaking a few hands and posing for selfies, Ajay went straight back to Mrs Chawla's office.

"Have you been checking the internet?" Mrs Chawla asked as soon as he walked in.

He shook his head. He had used the car journey back to turn Pooja's last comment over in his mind. It almost sounded like she was having a dig at him about his heroin trade. Maybe she was not, but he would have to be careful. If that got out, it would be very challenging to contain the damage, to say the least.

She turned to her screen and read some quotes. "*Delhi's next MP offers new hope...Ajay Pandey to neutralise drugs menace...Pandey: a new man for a new way...Pooja Sati outranked and outclassed...*" She turned back to him. "I've never seen anyone do this before. And it was your first interview." She shook her head in disbelief.

Ajay smiled and nodded, but said nothing. He knew the interview had gone well, but he also knew that that was just the beginning.

"You did well," said Mrs Chawla. "Pooja gave you a hard time – that's her job – but you handled it better than I've seen many professional politicians do. Congratulations. Carry on like this and you'll be prime minister."

～

As soon as he left Mrs Chawla's office he went back to his premises on Chitragupta Road, where he met up with Rishi and Dilip on the first floor.

"I need you to completely take over," he said to them both. "I can't afford to be seen associating with anyone in this business."

They both nodded.

"I'm going to check that the money's arriving in my accounts. Just carry on doing what you're doing. Only contact me if there is a real, dire emergency, and then only use burner phones. Dilip, I know you already know this, but make sure no one comes up here or even knows what's here. If you hear of anyone who's planning to open their mouth about me and this trade, make sure they don't. If you see or hear about any reporters snooping about, silence them. Do what you have to do..." His heart was racing as he added the latter bit, but he knew that, unless he ruthlessly saw off any threat, everything he wanted to do could be jeopardised. Although he was giving Dilip carte blanche, he knew that Dilip would not take extreme action unless he needed to.

Dilip nodded. He would keep his ear even more firmly to the ground, and be ready to act without hesitation. But the first thing he would do is tell the gangmasters of the increased consequences of blabbing, and make sure they told the street boys. In terms of security for the first floor, he already had cameras all the way up the stairs, and sensors on each of the steps so he and his team would be alerted as soon as anyone put one foot off the ground floor. He would get an extra, very solid but attractive door put at the bottom of the staircase. He knew some MARCOS men who worked for media organisations. Loyalty to their old army buddy and the promise of a hefty payout would ensure they kept alert and let him know immediately about any curious reporter. It would not take much to stop them dead in their tracks...

"Rishi, tell Dilip if you hear *anything*. Also, we need to change things. Tell the shop managers to carry on doing what they're doing, but I'm going to replace them over the next couple of weeks. I'm only going to sell samosas from the shops. The current managers are going to carry on working with their street boys selling heroin, but not with the cover of the shops. Sort out the details and tell them that they're still going to be paid the same."

Rishi nodded.

"If I win the election, you'll both get a year's salary as a bonus."

Both their serious faces broke out into broad smiles.

By the time he got back to Mrs Chawla's office, she was waiting for him.

"Where have you been?" she demanded, looking almost frantic. "The phones are going mad! There's queues of people wanting to help with your campaign."

He looked around. Mrs Chawla had four staff members during the week. She had asked two of them to come in today as she suspected something like this would happen – both of them were on the phone. Ajay went over to where one of them was sitting. He looked at the piece of paper she was writing on. At the top was written "Wants to help AP's campaign". Below it was an impressive list of names, phone numbers and e-mail addresses.

Ajay got his phone out and looked at the social media accounts he had set up for his campaign – they were inundated too.

"You need to find bigger offices," Mrs Chawla said, standing next to him. "It's the first day of your campaign and you've already outgrown this place."

Ajay grinned. There was no doubt he would need larger offices. But he also needed to avoid a prestigious setting like Connaught Place – it would send out the wrong signal. He wanted to help ordinary people, not suck up to the rich. However, he needed somewhere central. The obvious place was Paharganj.

Using his phone, he almost immediately found somewhere that looked ideal – a large first floor office above a shop on Desh Bandhu Gupta Road, with an entrance that led directly on to the street. He carried on searching, and found a few other possibilities, but none of them looked as good.

The first thing the next day he contacted the estate agent for the DBG Road property, and arranged a viewing immediately. It consisted of a very large room, with a small room off the side of it. Perfect. The large room would be for his team of volunteers. He would use the small room for private meetings. There were four WCs towards the rear of the large room. A window ran along the entire front of the large and small rooms, affording a panoramic view of DBG Road. The air-conditioning was modern, silent and very efficient. It would be difficult to find better. He offered the estate agent a very generous bonus if contracts were signed and keys were in his hand before the end of the day. It was all done and dusted by 1pm.

He went through the lists of names that Mrs Chawla's staff had compiled, phoning around until he found six people who could come to his new offices by 3pm. In the meantime he bought six mobile phones, six laptops and a couple of printers. That was the other good thing about Paharganj – the plethora of shops meant you could get virtually anything you wanted.

When they arrived he found that the oldest appeared to be in her late twenties, and the youngest was about 17.

"Thanks for coming, guys. These are our new premises. As you can see, there's nothing here – I only got this place this afternoon. We need to get some furniture! I need you guys to split into pairs and get desks and chairs. Nothing too fancy – even old kitchen tables and dining chairs will do. Just something you can carry between yourselves up the stairs. We'll need six desks and chairs. In fact, make it 12 chairs. So, if each pair of you gets two desks and four chairs. How does that sound?"

They all nodded their heads enthusiastically.

"OK, if you can split into pairs…"

A little bit of chatter later, and they were in pairs. He gave each pair a small bundle of cash.

"Now, please don't go too mad. Go for functional. Used is better - it'll be cheaper. We need to watch the budget. But nothing too battered. Please get receipts -we need to make sure we keep a record of expenses. I'm sorry, but I need anything you don't spend back, guys. But get yourselves something to eat when you're finished – and get a receipt for that as well.

"OK, see you in a bit. Please be as quick as possible – we've got a lot to do tonight."

With that they all left, busily chatting amongst themselves.

In reality Ajay could have got the stuff delivered by now, just as he had with the printers and laptops, but he knew what he had asked them to do would be a great team building exercise.

What he had forgotten was a fridge, an electric kettle, and some snacks and drinks. The fridge and kettle could wait until tomorrow. He went out and came back with two large carrier bags full of drinks and snacks. He found himself behind two of his team carrying a desk up the stairs.

Within two hours the desks and chairs were all in situ. It was beginning to look like an office with the mismatched furniture giving it a slightly homely feel. This was added to by the hubbub of young people enthusiastically talking as they ate.

When they all appeared to have finished, he asked: "Is everyone OK for time? There's still a few things to do."

They all nodded, looking around at each other as they did so.

"OK. Thanks, guys. I need these laptops setting up." Ajay pointed to the pile of boxes in the corner. "We'll need internet access, so please link them to the phones. Also, the printers need connecting to a couple of laptops."

They all sat there, nodding.

"OK, guys, a word about how I work. If I ask you to do something, as far as I'm concerned that's it – please just get on with it. OK?"

One of them got up, and the others followed suit.

"Work in pairs – it'll be easier. Work with someone you've not worked with," Ajay called over the noise of their collective voices.

Everything was set up in less than an hour.

"This place is looking good. Thank you. I've set up social media accounts. We're going to use them *properly* – nothing underhand. First rule of politics – don't be hostile. If they go low, you go high. Remember, someone convinced against their will is of the same opinion still. Try to charm them. If they say something factually incorrect, point that out and try to give them the source of your information, but don't get into an all out argument. Did everyone see my interview with Pooja Sati?"

They all nodded.

"Well, that's my main policy. But I've also worked with Mrs Chawla - the current MP - for many years, helping to get roads resurfaced, crimes dealt with, drainage systems replaced, Delhi Municipality departments overhauled, etc, etc. It's all written down here." He waved some typewritten sheets which had details of what he had done.

"I need to start engaging with the electorate on social media straight away – we've got a few days of stuff to catch up on. Things went crazy after the Pooja Sati interview. If you get stuck on anything, let me know. If you work on a laptop each, we'll get a lot more done."

The noise was rapidly replaced by silence as they began to work through the backlog of messages and comments.

As they left at various times throughout the evening, he told them that the office would be open at 9am every day, and he would be grateful if they could come back again whenever they had the time.

The following morning five of them turned up. He bought five more phones, the numbers of which Mrs Chawla's staff gave out to anyone asking to help with his campaign. He phoned people on the lists that her staff had already compiled until he found six more volunteers who could come in later that morning.

By the end of the morning there were six helpers on social media. The rest were on the phones, taking details of potential volunteers and answering questions. Ajay was on hand for anything problematic, but it was mainly fairly basic stuff.

Over the next two days various volunteers managed to plough through the social media backlog. Also, the phones stopped ringing as much.

Ajay realised that the initial boost given by the Pooja Sati interview was fizzling out. His campaign needed a boost. At the moment, they were just compiling lists of potential volunteers, and responding to comments and queries. Apart from making heroin available on prescription, he had no real message. He needed something pithy that people could unite behind. He needed a slogan.

At 12pm on the third day he called a meeting of all the volunteers who were in the campaign offices.

"Thank you for everything you've done – it's been great. We're on top of the social media, and phone calls are being answered. What we need now is something that tells people what we are really about. We need a slogan. Something which Delhi-ites can relate to. Any suggestions?"

"Vote for Pandey. Vote for Delhi," someone called out. Ajay wrote it on the whiteboard he had got that morning.

"Getting rid of drugs in Delhi," someone else called out. Ajay wrote that down as well. As uninspiring as the last one.

"I love Delhi." This was not going well. But give it time...

"Crimefree Delhi." Ajay wrote that down, but said: "Great suggestions, but we need something to focus Delhi-ites' minds on what's been achieved in East Delhi as well as how I'm going to clean up the drugs problem."

"Keeping Delhi clean and crime-free."

"Delhi will be clean."

"Cleaning up Delhi." That sounded like it should be on the side of a refuse truck.

"We need something that'll give people hope. They need belief in a new future," said Ajay.

"A new Delhi starts here."

"From streets to solutions: a new Delhi."

"Delhi's future: brighter, bolder, better." The suggestions were definitely improving.

"Fixing what others ignore."

"Courage, clarity, change."

"From chaos to change."

"Pandey for Delhi: real solutions, real change."

"Ajay acts. Delhi changes." That was it!

"Brilliant! What does everyone think of that one?" asked Ajay.

There were nods of assent.

"Do I have a volunteer to help me design a poster?"

Four hands went up. He got them all to work together. It did not take them long to come up with something impressive looking.

Ajay Acts. Delhi Changes.
Fixing What Others Ignore

When you had problems, Ajay acted. For the past 6 years, he's been on our side:

- Fixed Our Roads, Made Them New.
- Cleaned our Streets, Improved Our Health.
- Fought Bureaucracy, Got Things Done.
- Stood Up To Crime, Brought Down Disorder.

Ajay Pandey is not just talking change; he's *been* the change, from rebuilding our infrastructure to fighting crime.

Now, Delhi faces its greatest challenge: the devastating drug epidemic.

Traditional methods aren't working. Ajay has a real solution to bring real change:

- Decriminalise & Prescribe: Breaking the dealer's grip, stopping new addictions.
- Slash Drug-Related Crime: Making our homes and businesses secure.
- Heal Our Community: Shifting addicts from criminals to patients, building a stronger Delhi.

Choose Ajay Pandey. For Real Solutions. For Real Change. For You.

Below that was a phone number (after a lot of persistence and some large payouts he had got a landline number for the office), address, a website and social media accounts. The poster had photos of: a clean road with schoolchildren walking safely, a mother thanking Ajay outside Mrs Chawla's office, a well-funded home for former street kids, a dramatic before & after of a street of which he had got the surface fixed, and Ajay smiling with a group of addicts now in recovery.

Ajay nodded his approval and immediately put in an order for 10,000 to be printed. They were to be delivered the next day. Good. He got a volunteer to phone up other people who had offered to volunteer and ask them to put the posters up around Delhi. He wondered how effective the posters would be – social media was far more focused, but not everyone had it. Also, they served a dual purpose - he was getting more people who had volunteered involved. He did not want them to think he had forgotten about them.

To his surprise, within two days, he found the posters were having a marked effect. Phone calls and social media activity increased to such an extent that he had to get another five desks, three laptops and five phone lines put in. People seemed to be happy to share desks – it gave them a buddy to work with. The enquiries were varied:

- Would he do for the rest of Delhi what he had done for East Delhi? *Yes.*
- Would his policy on drugs actually work? *Yes. It has worked where it has been tried before, and it will work in Delhi. He is passionate about it – he has personally funded over 90% of free rehab places in Delhi.*
- What would he do about the slums? *Improve the sanitation, the roads, the healthcare in them, just like he has done with nearly all of the ones in East Delhi.*

Ajay instructed the volunteers to end each call, social media exchange and email exchange with "Ajay Acts. Delhi Changes. Fixing What Others Ignore."

Of course, he went around as many religious and civic groups as he could, making speeches and shaking hands. To start with he felt nervous and out of his depth but, very quickly, he learnt how to greet people like old friends. His speeches rapidly improved until he eventually came up with a winning formula.

"Namaste, friends.

"Thank you. Thank you for being here today. Thank you for standing up—not just for me, but for something far greater: a better Delhi.

"My name is Ajay Pandey. You know me. I'm not a career politician. I didn't come from a party machine. I didn't come here to make promises – I came because for six years, I've already been doing the work.

"When your roads were cratered, I had them fixed. When your drains stank, I had them replaced. When city officials ignored your calls, I made sure the whole system listened.

"And while others held press conferences and passed blame, I funded rehab centres and shelters. Not because it looked good, but because it was right. Because you deserve better.

"But I'll be honest with you. Even after all that, we're still in crisis.

"Every day in Delhi, another teenager gets addicted to drugs.

"Every night, another mother sleeps in fear because her son might rob to feed a habit.

"And every day, drug dealers get richer while our neighbourhoods suffer.

"That ends now.

"I'm not afraid to say what others won't: The war on drugs has failed.

"We've tried arrests. We've tried raids. We've tried shaming people into quitting. And still, Delhi bleeds.

"So I'm offering something bold. Something that works in countries like Switzerland and Portugal.

"Heroin – prescribed. Safely. Legally. In clinics.

"So no one needs to buy from a dealer. So no child ever becomes a new addict. So no addict ever needs to steal to survive.

"So we can treat this crisis as a health problem – not a crime.

"Will this be controversial? Yes.

"Will some try to twist it? Of course.

"But I didn't come into politics to be comfortable. I came here to clean up what others left behind.

"And I need your help to do it.

"If you want clean streets, honest government, and real solutions – not speeches – then I ask you:

"Vote Ajay Pandey. Ajay Acts. Delhi Changes. I fix what others ignore.

"Thank you. Jai Hind."

At first audiences had greeted him with guarded scepticism. Before long they applauded as soon as he stood up to speak.

"Hello, Ajay."

He stiffened as he recognised the voice. He turned around.

Deepika…

He was speechless. How long had it been? Seven – maybe eight years?

"Hello Deepika."

"How have you been?" she said, smiling broadly. He remembered a self-conscious but attractive post-adolescent. Now she was a very attractive young woman in her prime. Any vestiges of puppy fat had disappeared long ago. Her cheekbones were so defined that any make-up would have been too much. Her broad lips and friendly eyes were just as he remembered, but her increased confidence added to their beauty.

"OK..." he said uncertainly. "And you?"

"I saw one of your posters, with you looking the same as ever."

He grinned.

"I thought I'd come down to see what you're up to. You're certainly busy," she added, looking around at the activity in the office.

"What are you doing these days?" he asked.

"Still at Delhi Uni." This did not surprise him. "I'm doing my PhD now, on gender bias in Indian politics."

"You must hate me then."

Deepika laughed. It was a carefree laugh. It reminded him of multicoloured butterflies dancing in and out of beautiful wild flowers.

"I'm taking the seat of a well-respected woman," he added.

"You haven't won yet."

It was Ajay's turn to laugh. She was as sharp as he remembered.

"Don't worry," she said. "I've not come to hassle you. I'm volunteering."

Ajay nodded. After a brief silence, he said: "Would you like to go for lunch? We can talk about it there."

They left the office and found a quiet place at the less busy end of Main Bazaar.

"Your campaign seems to be going well," she said when they had sat down.

"The volunteers are great – it'd be impossible without them," he replied.

She laughed that sweet laugh of hers again. "Modesty – that's something I don't remember about you."

Feisty.

He coloured slightly. "Oh, I know I'm good, but you've got to give credit where it's due." There was no way he was letting her belittle him.

It was on the tip of her tongue to say: "Shame you didn't think that way when you dumped me." But she held back. Those days were over. The last thing she wanted was for him to think she had looked him up to settle old scores.

"You've worked hard in East Delhi, and with drug addicts and street kids," she said instead.

"You've been doing your research."

She certainly had been. She had remembered him as cocky. He had been a nice guy until he got that wretched samosa shop of his. Then he had turned into an insufferable, arrogant idiot who did nothing but talk about himself. In a way, she had been glad when he had finished with her, even though it hurt at the time.

She had dated other boys at uni, and had hardly thought about him for years, but then had been shocked to see him being interviewed by Pooja Sati. As the press reports about him accumulated, it did not sound as if they were talking about the same person she had known all that time ago. The Ajay Pandey she had known was conceited, talked constantly about how well his business was doing and never mentioned helping anybody.

"You've changed," she said.

"Have I?"

She nodded, slowly adding: "When I knew you, you were an arrogant teenager obsessed with trying to make as much money as you could."

He was quiet for a moment as he looked at her. Had he really come across like that? All he had tried to do was show her he was not some kind of unambitious no-hoper. But he remembered, no matter how hard he tried, there seemed to be a slight air of disdain about her. He had thought it had been her middle-class snobbery. Even though he had not admitted it to himself at the time, that was the real reason he had finished with her.

"I just wanted to make a better life for me and my family in those days," he said, thinking carefully before he spoke. "Since then I've learnt that the best way to use money is to help as many people as you can." He hoped that came across OK. Of course he was cocky in those days – he was only 18 when they split up.

"Are you married?" she asked.

He shook his head. "Are you?"

She shook her head as well.

"Dating?" he asked.

She was silent for a minute. "I've seen boys, but there's no one at the moment. How about you?"

He shook his head. He had never "dated" anyone apart from her. Now that she was in front of him and he was able to think about it more clearly, he realised that the whole experience with her had traumatised him. He had loved her but he only now understood that, deep down, he had felt she thought of herself as too good for him. He had felt that, if that was love, you could keep it.

He had not seen Natasha or any of her cohort for nearly a year either. It was an abstinence initially brought about by depression and hopelessness. Since he had decided to run for election his mood had picked up, but he had felt it wise not to visit them just in case word got out.

"How are your mum and dad?" he asked, remembering that this could be a delicate subject.

"OK," she said guardedly. "They're very generous – they've paid for all my education. And how about you? How's your mum, brother and sister?"

"Mum's doing well. We live in Greater Kailash now. Bimala is studying medicine in Mumbai, and Nitesh is doing a degree in Hindi literature at Banaras University."

"How does your mum feel about you standing for MP?"

"She's pleased. But she'd be pleased whatever I did," he said, smiling.

Deepika nodded, obviously wishing she could say the same about her parents.

"So, how can I help you?" Deepika asked suddenly.

Ajay looked at her, a little bewildered, before suddenly realising that they were supposed to be discussing her involvement in his campaign.

"I can take the next five weeks out of my PhD," she added.

Ajay thought quickly. She obviously knew about politics, and was even smarter than he remembered.

"I'm trying to organise everything, manage my diary and get around Delhi to see people. I can't do everything. Do you want to be my office manager? The pay's non-existent and it's stressful, but you will get some nice meals out of it." This was not quite true. He was managing things well – nothing was overwhelming -yet… Also, in reality he could afford to pay her, but it would probably get some of the other volunteers' backs up – especially those who had turned up virtually every day since day one. Also, in light of what she had said, he did not want her to think of him as someone crass who thought money was the answer to everything.

She laughed. "Sounds wonderful. I can start this afternoon."

With Deepika's help the campaign seemed to take on additional momentum. Instead of seeing only a couple of groups a day at opposite ends of Delhi, she managed his diary so he could see anything up to six groups in one afternoon, all close to each other. He did not need to go back to the office between times to make sure everything was OK – she managed it better than he had.

As well as immediately finding roles for new volunteers, she dealt with computer breakdowns, shortages of desks, wifi problems, keeping the volunteers fed, watered and motivated, and a myriad of other things with calm efficiency.

She kept a careful eye on the media and Ajay's opponents' social media. Ajay was getting much more coverage than all his opponents put together but, as time went on, they seemed to be making more headway.

Initially, his policy of making heroin available on prescription gave him lots of favourable media attention. However, his opponents seemed to band together to launch a concerted attack on him and that policy in particular. How was giving out free heroin supposed to reduce crime? Was creating a city of addicts going to make it function better? Who ever heard of a city of junkies being world class? They used ridicule to misrepresent and undermine his flagship policy. And their strategy seemed to be working according to the polls. He had always been way ahead of the pack but, as time went on, that gap was closing worryingly fast.

One week before the election the Delhi Herald ran a short editorial which gained traction almost immediately, especially online.

"Is Pandey Naïve?

"You would have had to be living in a cave not to have heard of Ajay Pandey's interview with Pooja Sati. Few, if any interviews, have catapulted a new candidate on to the centre stage so dramatically.

"Since then Pandey has been surging ahead in the polls, using his slogan 'Ajay Acts. Delhi Changes'.

"There is no denying that he is one of the good guys. His funding of drugs rehab places and street kids charities have gained him an almost mythical status in a matter of weeks. If you cross the Yamuna and speak to anyone in East Delhi, they all know how his work has benefited the residents there.

"Now he wants to introduce heroin freely available on prescription. It sounds like it could be a good idea. Stop the most addicted - those with the biggest habits - from creating new addicts in an attempt to fund their own cravings. At the same time, reduce crime across the city.

"But is Mr Pandey being naïve? Even if he is elected, he will only be an MP. India has tough drugs laws – you cannot just overturn them. It seems unlikely that the national government will just cave into his demands. The current laws have come about after many years, with experienced justice officials writing and rewriting them so they are fit for purpose. It is beyond credulity to think that these will be torn up at the behest of a young upstart.

"Those who have met Mr Pandey are taken by his charm and charisma. There is no doubt he is capable of a lot, but is he just a young ball of energy who has far more enthusiasm than experience?

"There is no doubt he will make a great MP one day, but maybe he should gain some more life experience first."

As soon as Deepika saw the article she phoned Ajay.

"Hello."

"I've just sent you a link to a Delhi Herald article. You need to read it *now*." She sounded almost frantic.

"Yeah, of course."

She severed the connection.

He phoned back within minutes.

"Patronising bastards!" he virtually bellowed. "How can they get away with this?"

"You can't let them."

"What can I do?" he asked, beginning to sound a little panicked.

"Look, you can turn this around. There's loads of examples in politics of people coming up from behind to win. Don't let those bastards get to you –"

"Hold on," said Ajay. "Mrs Chawla's trying to get through. I'll ring you back."

"Hello," he said.

"Have you seen the article in the Herald?" Mrs Chawla asked.

"Yes – Deepika forwarded it to me. We were just talking about what to do about it. We'll have to meet up –"

"Don't worry, beta. I've spent the last few months talking to Aysha Nadeem." Aysha Nadeem was the minister of law and justice. "Later this week she's going to announce that she's happy to hold a trial of heroin available on prescription in Delhi for heavy users. You have two years to prove it works. She said that she felt the time is right to try something different to prison."

"Why didn't you tell me before?" Ajay asked, sounding bewildered.

"You were so enthusiastic I didn't want to burst your bubble. I thought the best thing I could do was let you carry on campaigning and only tell you when I managed to get Aysha to agree. I just phoned her and told her about the Herald article. It was enough to make up her mind."

Ajay felt foolish and patronised but, quietly, he said: "Thank you."

"I'll see if Aysha will bring the announcement forward to this afternoon. It'll help mitigate the article."

"Thank you," he said again.

When Aysha Nadeem gave a statement, it was featured on all the news channels which, of course, linked it to Ajay's policy. This was mirrored by the internet and the newspapers – even the Delhi Herald.

Two days after Aysha Nadeem's statement, Deepika phoned Ajay: "We've just got an email from Pooja Sati's producer. Rajendra Malhotra and Neelam Verma are challenging you to a live debate." Malhotra and Verma were Ajay's main rivals in the election.

"OK..." was Ajay's guarded response as he thought.

"What shall I tell them?" asked Deepika.

"What is the best thing we can do?"

"Well, you're way ahead of them in the polls," said Deepika. "They've got nothing to lose – you have. But, if you don't debate them, it gives them a big stick to beat you with. They'll be saying that, how can you fight the drugs epidemic when you're too scared to meet them face to face?"

"Hmm..."

"If you take up Pooja's offer," continued Deepika. "You need to insist that Delhi's drugs crisis is the primary topic. It's your strongest policy and you've made it the biggest issue of the election. If Malhotra and Verma turn down your offer, it'll be them who look like cowards."

Ajay thought for a moment. "OK. Let's do it. We're not going to have much problem persuading Pooja and her team to make drugs the primary topic – it's all anyone is talking about. I'll email her producer now."

For the rest of the week Ajay carried on his punishing campaigning schedule, snatching no more than a couple of meetings with Deepika and Mrs Chawla to discuss tactics for the upcoming debate.

∼

Pooja opened the show in her usual confident manner: "Good morning. You're watching a very special edition of *Politics Today* – an election special.

"The Delhi election has caught the country by storm. This morning, three of the leading candidates are going head-to-head to debate the most controversial issue in a generation: making heroin available on prescription.

"Let me introduce the candidates.

"Ajay Pandey, candidate for the Achchhe Log Party and civic activist.

"Rajendra Malhotra, candidate for the India First Party, for which he is also the chairman.

"Neelam Verma, policy consultant and first-time candidate from the Centrist Reform Party.

"Let's begin with the issue on every Delhiite's mind: the drug crisis.

"Mr Pandey, you've proposed prescribing heroin to addicts as part of your drug reform policy. Why should voters trust such a controversial idea?"

Ajay: "Let me start with one word: results. For six years, I've funded rehab centres, built shelters, and cleaned up the streets where dealers prey on children. But the drugs keep flowing. The deaths keep rising. That's why I propose this: prescribe heroin – under medical supervision – to registered addicts. It's not about giving up. It's about taking control. No more back-alley deals. No more crimes to feed an addiction. No more children recruited by gangs. This policy works in Switzerland. It works in Portugal. It can work in Delhi. What we're doing now isn't working."

Pooja: "Mr Malhotra, you've strongly opposed this plan. Your response?"

Malhotra: "What Mr Pandey proposes is a recipe for disaster. Heroin is illegal, addictive, and lethal. You don't solve a poison problem by handing out more poison. You need to expand policing, create youth task forces, and crack down on street-level dealers. We must enforce the law – not rewrite it."

Ajay: "Respectfully, sir – we've had an increasingly draconian system enforcing drugs laws for decades. Yet, in the last ten years alone, addiction has tripled. The current system has built walls. I want to build doors. Doors to treatment, to dignity, to a life outside crime. Let me be clear: I'm not handing out heroin. I'm replacing street heroin with medical care. That's the difference between chaos and control.

"I don't believe in easy answers. I believe in solutions that work. Arrests haven't worked. Shame hasn't worked. Sending addicts to prison hasn't worked. What I'm offering is a safer path – one that gets heroin off the streets, and puts it under medical supervision. It's not about legalising heroin. It's about taking control of it."

Verma: "May I add something? Both of you raise valid points. But this isn't about just heroin – it's about broken systems. Our municipal clinics are understaffed. Our detox services are overwhelmed. Before we talk about radical reform, let's talk about capacity: can we realistically monitor and treat thousands of addicts safely?"

Ajay: "Great question. And yes – we can. There are an excess of rehab beds in Delhi – I know because I fund them, and I will continue to fund them. The funding to monitor and treat the addicts who turn to doctors for help will come from the money saved from sending them to prison.

"And don't forget, we are not just talking about the cost to the taxpayer. How about the victims of crimes committed to fund drugs habits? And the poor parents who lose their child to drug addiction and death?

"What we lack isn't funding. It's political courage."

Pooja: "Mr. Malhotra, would you reconsider your position if it reduced crime?"

Malhotra: "I will not legalise heroin. Not on my watch. The idea is dangerous, and it sends the wrong message to our youth. Addiction is not solved with a prescription pad. Is Mr Pandey seriously proposing giving junkies free heroin while honest citizens struggle to buy medicine? What kind of logic is that?"

Ajay: "I'm going to give addicts a chance to stop dying in alleyways and start getting the care they need. Let me ask you this: Are you happy with thousands of new addicts each year? Are you proud that people are getting stabbed over drugs every day? Is our current plan working? Because I'm not proud. I've seen too many young men die of this epidemic in Delhi."

The audience applauded.

Pooja: "Ms Verma, where do you stand?"

Verma: "I believe we need evidence-based reform. I would support a pilot program with strict controls, but only alongside robust mental health funding. This is not a choice between morality and medicine – it's about outcomes. Let's act smart, not just act fast."

Ajay: "Look at Portugal. Look at Switzerland. The evidence is out there, and it's clear: *addiction is not solved by a prison cell.*

"How many addicts have the police locked up? How many of them came out clean? How many came out worse?"

Ajay turned the camera: "Let me be clear – I'm not soft on drugs. I'm smart on policy. I want to make dealers obsolete. I want to treat addicts like patients, not criminals. I want to protect your children from ever meeting a dealer in the first place. And if that makes some politicians uncomfortable – well, maybe they've been comfortable for too long."

Pooja: "Thank you, Mr. Ajay. That was... forthright."

Ajay: "You invited me to be honest. I'm not here to win points. I'm here to win lives back."

Pooja: "Let's move to closing statements. One minute each. Mr Pandey?"

Ajay: "Thank you. Tonight, you heard a clear contrast. One candidate wants more of the same. One wants to waste time trying to get more proof when no more proof is needed. I offer immediate solutions that work.

"This isn't theory for me. I've walked the streets. Sat with grieving families. Spoken with addicts who want to live but don't know how. We must be brave enough to try what works – even if it makes some uncomfortable.

"This isn't a war we can win with slogans. It's a wound we must heal – with care, courage, and compassion.

"Vote for change that goes beyond promises. Ajay Acts. Delhi Changes. I fix what others ignore."

Ajay got a standing ovation and a thunderous round of applause.

Malhotra's and Verma's closing speeches got a polite round of applause.

The net result of the debate was that Ajay leapt ahead in the polls as his opponents looked outdated and out of touch.

Two days before the election Ajay and Deepika managed to snatch a lunch together.

"The campaign's going extremely well. Thanks," said Ajay.

"We're nearly there, but we've got to be careful. They say a week's a long time in politics, but you can also make a big mess in two days. Carry on doing what you're doing, but don't get too flippant. You haven't won yet. Keep control. Meet people, shake hands, but always keep an air of slight gravitas. It's better that you come across as boring than as a clown. It might lose you a few votes, but if you make a wrong comment in an unguarded moment you could lose everything."

Ajay nodded. Deepika, as always, was right.

"What will you do when the campaign's over?" Ajay asked.

She did not say anything for a while. "Go back to my PhD," she said at last, a little too enthusiastically.

"Are you looking forward to it?" he asked gently.

"Of course," she said, keeping up the overzealousness.

"What's wrong, Deepika?"

She said nothing.

"Families are great, but they can demand too much," Ajay said, almost in a whisper.

She nodded, her eyes beginning to fill with tears. She hated being completely dependent on her parents. They were generous, but they also tried to control what she did. They allowed her to live near the university, but insisted she visit them three times a week and, every time she did, they would ask when she would finish her PhD. Her father had made it clear that he would fund her for up to five years, but then she was to get married to someone of whom he approved. In other words, an arranged marriage. She could run away at the end of her PhD, but it meant running away from everything she knew, everything and everyone she loved. She did not hate her parents, but she did resent them.

"Do you want to talk about it?"

She did. She wanted to tell someone, anyone, how, despite having a charmed life, all she wanted was just the freedom to do what she wanted to do. She knew she came across as strong and feisty, but that was just a show. All the pressure to achieve, to be something, to get married was too much. In truth, she did not know what she wanted. She could lose herself in her studies for hours and, at the end of it, feel amazing. But there had to be more to life than that, surely?

She saw how Ajay had lived his life. It was not perfect – she did not envy him having to go to work at the age of ten to support his family. But he had been true to himself. But how could she say all this, especially to him? She shook her head.

They carried on eating in silence for a while.

"If there's anything I can do, let me know," he said at last.

She nodded, not looking at him.

At last, campaigning came to an end and election day arrived. All they could do now was wait for the result.

As it was Delhi, it was one of the first constituencies to be declared. Ajay stood nervously as he waited for the result. He could not take all the figures in as they were read out, but he did hear: "I therefore declare that Ajay Pandey is the MP for Delhi" amongst cheering and applause.

He gave his acceptance speech almost on autopilot. "I have to thank everyone who has helped. It wouldn't have been possible without the army of dedicated volunteers. The people of Delhi have put their trust in me. I've always done what I have set out to do and this will be no exception. I will act. Delhi will change. Thank you."

This was met with cheers and applause.

Back at the campaign offices it was met with even louder cheers and applause. Ludoos were passed around (Ajay had put in special order to the old man with the handcart), as were lots of fizzy grape juice and champagne. Excited chatter filled the air before "Ajay Acts. Delhi Changes." was repeatedly chanted.

Ajay came off the podium in a daze.

"Did you hear the result?" Deepika asked.

He shook his head.

"You got 67% of the vote – the highest ever."

He looked at her, still unable to take it in.

"Congratulations, Ajay," Mrs Chawla said, offering him her hand.

Suddenly everything seemed to hit him with clarity. He was Delhi's youngest ever MP and he had won by the largest margin ever. Deepika offered him her hand, but he hugged her instead. She hugged him back.

"We should go back to the campaign office," she said as they held each other. "Things will *really* be happening there."

"I'd prefer to get a room with you," he whispered in her ear.

He let go and she looked at him with the faintest of smiles on her face. If it was not for Mrs Chawla and the TV cameras she would have playfully punched him on the arm. She turned to see Mrs Chawla also smiling.

"I'll see you back at the office," Mrs Chawla said with what could only be described as a twinkle in her eye. Deepika flushed.

After ten minutes of intense questions from the waiting reporters, they set off back to the office in a chauffeur-driven car that Ajay had ordered. He knew, win or lose, he would be in no fit state to drive. As soon as they were a safe distance from the building, Deepika grabbed hold of Ajay and kissed him. He did not object.

There were cheers and applause as they entered the offices, followed by cries of "Speech, speech!"

Ajay began to speak.

"Stand on the desk, we can't see you!" someone shouted from the back of the packed room.

He was helped – virtually carried – up on to a desk.

"What we've achieved tonight is truly historic. The largest margin ever. Thanks to everyone in this room, we managed to get the people of Delhi to believe in what is right. Everyone here worked tirelessly to get that message across. We now know what we're capable of. But this is just the beginning. We promised the people of Delhi to cleanse the city of the scourge of drugs. Some people say that's impossible. Nothing is impossible – we've shown that tonight. Barriers are there to be broken down, and we've proven we can do it. We've already started Fixing What Others Ignore." He said the last four words slowly, so everyone could join in with him.

A cheer went up as he was helped down from the desk.

He wandered around the room, thanking people and talking to them. After more than an hour of doing this, his hand ached from shaking so many hands, and his voice was hoarse. When he discreetly left, several people saw him go but nobody tried to stop him. He had worked hard and done his duty by coming back to speak to the volunteers. He deserved a rest.

Deepika followed a few minutes later.

The hotel suite was plush. Deepika was booked into a separate one next to it, but they both went into his. He stripped off, lay on the bed – and immediately fell asleep. She looked at him, not knowing whether to feel angry or insulted or both. In the end she laughed to herself. What else should she have expected? Six weeks of all-out pressure, virtually no sleep, followed by an adrenaline rush big enough to kill an elephant was not going to end in mind-blowing sex. She found it surprisingly easy to fall asleep as well.

The next morning they more than made up for what they had missed out on the night before. They surprised each other, each wondering where the other had learnt all they seemed to be so expert in...

17

With Deepika's and Mrs Chawla's help, Ajay immediately started recruiting advisers, researchers and administrators. Most of them were former volunteers, some of the many who had worked so enthusiastically virtually every day of the campaign. They had proven their worth and, as Mrs Chawla pointed out, if he was going to achieve everything he wanted to, he needed a smart team that would go beyond the call of duty.

After discussing it with Mrs Chawla he decided not to take over Mrs Chawla's offices. They were too small and he had become firmly associated with the DBG Road offices.

Of course, the first policy he brought in was making heroin available on prescription. The take up was massive but, to his dismay, his heroin trade continued to grow, albeit at a slower pace. Obviously the take up was not enough. As much as he wanted to, he knew the answer was not to stop trading – he knew he would be replaced by some unscrupulous bastard – but he could not let it carry on like this.

He secretly met up with Rishi, and got him to print 1,00,000 cards the size of credit cards. On one side it read:

Heroin is *free*

from your doctor

On the other side it read: "Every doctor in Delhi can make sure you get free heroin if you need it. They can also help you get off it. Talk to your doctor – they understand and will help you."

This was backed up by an enormous social media campaign. All the street boys were given a 50% increase in their commission and told to give a card *every time* they made a deal. Mystery shoppers were used to make sure they did. The ones who did not were replaced.

Soon the cards were littering East and Central Delhi. It was not long after that that they were found on the streets all over Delhi and beyond. They were talked about everywhere from family dinners, to the internet, to TV programmes. When questioned, Ajay said that it was his job to get the message to those who mattered. When he side stepped any further questions, most took this as a sign of a wily operator who knew how to get things done, and when to keep his mouth shut.

After a few weeks Ajay noticed a slight downturn in trade. This became more and more pronounced as time went on. Along with this, there was no denying that the streets of Delhi were beginning to look cleaner and better maintained.

Mrs Chawla put the newspaper on the desk in front of Ajay.

He sighed. It was inevitable that it would happen.

"3 Delhi Doctors Charged With Drug Dealing

"Is Mr Pandey's drug policy falling apart?

"Three doctors were arrested in East Delhi yesterday for illegally selling prescriptions for heroin. The police were tipped off last week, leading them to set up sting operations. The doctors, who were not known to each other, will be charged and can expect 10 to 20 years in prison each…"

He looked up at Mrs Chawla.

"Press conference," she said simply.

He nodded.

Within hours he entered the packed room. You could cut the atmosphere with a knife. This lot were out for blood.

"Is your policy falling apart?" was the first question, from a middle-aged reporter from the Delhi Herald.

"What we have here are three rogue doctors. This policy has had an enormously positive effect. The take up has been massive, and we are beginning to see the results. Not only are the police reporting a reduction in crime, but many of my constituents tell me they feel that Delhi is a safer, better functioning city to live in."

"How will you ensure this never happens again?" asked a freelance journalist.

"The three doctors in question are looking at prison sentences of between ten and 20 years. This will send out a strong message. But, if you're asking me if I can guarantee that this will never happen again, well of course I can't. But do you really want me to derail a policy that is working far, far better than anything anyone has tried? It would be short sighted to do so, to say the least."

"How many reports like this would it take before your policy is looked on as toxic and other cities, who were thinking of using it, change their approach?" This question was from a reporter from Mumbai. Ajay was surprised she had come all this way for a small press conference. His policy must be even more popular than he thought.

"I represent the people of Delhi. They already are seeing how well this policy works – lurid headlines will make little difference to them. I can't control what happens outside Delhi. If the press wish to emphasise the failings of a few doctors and potentially stop a tried and tested policy being taken up, well I feel that would be unfortunate. Personally I think headlines like "Delhi Drugs Policy Successful Despite Rogue Doctors" would be fairer reporting. It would also help improve life for the readership in the long term, which that readership wouldn't forget."

There was laughter from the room. "Are you trying to unduly influence the press?" someone shouted.

Ajay realised he was beginning to lose control of the situation. It was time for a gentler approach, for which he was known.

"All I'm trying to say is that I have implemented a policy which, however you look at it, is working extremely well. In less than six months crime has reduced by over 20%. Of course there'll be problems. Doctors are human beings, with all the shortcomings which go along with that. But, on the other hand, they are highly trained professionals who are far less likely to abuse the people they come into contact with than many in our society. Surely it makes more sense to use their expertise whilst monitoring them carefully instead of having Delhi ravaged by drugs."

"Are you going to increase the monitoring of doctors?" a TV reporter asked.

"That is inevitable," Ajay replied. "My office is drafting a new proposal, which we will discuss with the police before making an announcement."

This seemed to neutralise the atmosphere in the room and, after a few more questions, Ajay drew the conference to a close.

The new proposal was to have a team of undercover police officers trying to buy heroin prescriptions from doctors. They mainly picked their targets at random, but also focused on doctors about whom they heard rumours. It became part of standard police procedure in Delhi and, in the initial few months, another nine doctors were charged. After that there were no arrests.

Inevitably, there were deaths of addicts under the care of doctors, although these were seldom reported. It was almost impossible to establish that the doctor had caused the death. In most cases, post mortems proved that it was due to the weakened immune system or compromised vital organs due to years of drug abuse. Also, there was next to no public appetite for sympathetic reporting of the deaths of drug addicts, as had been shown via social media the few times it had happened.

In a little more than a year from coming into office, Ajay's heroin sales went down by 83%. After that they plateaued. Ajay concluded that the remaining sales must be mainly to recreational users. There was nothing that could be done about them. The only thing he hoped was that they were not committing crimes to fund themselves.

Crime in Delhi fell to less than a third of what it had been before he came to office, and the prisons gradually began to empty as those who were released at the end of their sentences outstripped those going in – something which had never happened before. Ajay was given full credit for that.

In the meantime, the turnover of his clothing business increased by 150% despite another price rise, this time by 50%. He opened another 12 samosa shops (dealing in samosas only, as were the others) called "Ajay's Samosas" – he realised he could use his name to enhance his brand image.

18

Ajay and Mrs Chawla both jumped as they heard a bang and then an ear piercing scream. Ajay got up and hurried to the door. There were three heavily built men at the top of the stairs, all with handguns. Gopal, a researcher, was lying on the floor with a red patch spreading rapidly across his chest.

Ajay took in the scene at once. He quickly shut the door and locked it, being careful not to slam it. As he did so, he heard two more bangs and more screams.

Mrs Chawla was standing up now, looking concerned, but said nothing as Ajay rushed past her and started shoving the desk towards the door with all his strength. Seeing what he was doing, she joined in. They slowed down as they reached the door, not wanting to slam the desk into the door and attract the attention of the gunmen. In the meantime the gunshots and screaming continued.

"Call the police," he ordered in a whisper, as he went to the other side of the office and got his phone out.

"Dilip, we're under attack. Three armed men. Get the team and get over here!"

Just then the door handle turned. Less than a second later three bullets went through it. The door splintered and shuddered as it was kicked hard, but the heavy desk held it in place. A volley of kicks followed. The desk began to move. Suddenly the door flew off its hinges and landed on the desk.

Two of the men blocked the doorway. There was silence in the large office. Presumably everyone there was dead.

One of the men raised his gun and shot Mrs Chawla. The bullet went straight through her head, splattering Ajay with blood as she fell backwards on to the floor.

For the first time in his life, Ajay knew what it felt like to be frozen to the spot.

The men clambered over the desk with surprising nimbleness. The third one followed.

The one who had shot Mrs Chawla smirked as he said: "Mr Dewan wants us to give you a message. This is it." He raised his gun, still grinning, aiming between Ajay's eyes.

Ajay dived to one side as the assailant pulled the trigger. Before he had time to take aim and fire again, a rapid volley of shots came from the doorway. All three men fell to the floor, with Ajay's executioner shot through the head, and the other two in the legs and arms.

Dilip and two of his MARCOS men had AK47s raised to their shoulders. They lowered them and the two MARCOS men scrambled over the desk before grabbing the pistols out of the hands of the two gunmen who were still alive. There had been no need to – their limbs were useless. Behind Dilip were the other two MARCOS men, also armed with AK47s.

Ajay got up and went over to Mrs Chawla. He could not look at her. He went over to the nearest assailant and kicked him as hard as he could. The assailant cried out in pain. Ajay then knelt down and pushed his thumb into a bullet hole in the assailant's left thigh. The man screamed.

"Where's Dewan?" Ajay said in a low but clear voice.

The man said nothing.

"You've got a choice. Die in agony knowing that I'm going to rape your wife and your mother, and torture your entire family to death, or tell me the truth and live."

"His office," he replied weakly, gasping as Ajay removed his thumb.

"Where's his office?" Despite dealing with him for all those years, the only thing Ajay knew about Dewan was his name and phone number.

"Sarojini Nagar."

"His address, you idiot."

The assailant gasped for breath. Ajay pushed his thumb hard into a bullet hole in his right forearm. The man screamed again, but much louder this time.

"His address," Ajay repeated loudly but calmly.

One of the MARCOS men typed it into his phone as the assailant said it. He immediately texted it to Ajay. Ajay looked at his phone to make sure it had come through.

He could not help but look at Mrs Chawla. Her face and head were no more than bloody pulp. He winced before going over to the other assailant and repeatedly kicking him and stamping on him.

"Keep these two alive," Ajay ordered the two MARCOS men as he went over to the dead man.

"Your leader?" Ajay called over to the man he had questioned – the other assailant was in too much pain to take in anything Ajay said. The man nodded.

Ajay searched the corpse, eventually locating his phone. Ajay got hold of his right hand and held his thumb to the screen. He then changed the settings so it was permanently unlocked, before pocketing it.

He clambered over the desk, and was surprised to see Rishi standing in the main office. He was armed with a pistol.

"Thanks for coming," Ajay said, recognising the risk Rishi – who had probably never fired a gun – had taken. Rishi nodded in acknowledgement.

"OK, we're taking this to Dewan," Ajay said matter-of-factly to

Dilip and the two MARCOS men next to him. He shut his eyes tightly for a couple of seconds, trying to rid the image of Mrs Chawla from his mind. If he was to honour her, he needed a clear mind. He needed to make Dewan *pay*.

"I'm coming as well," said Rishi.

Ajay looked at him, wondering if he would just get in the way. He knew Rishi could handle himself in a fist and knife fight, but this would probably be a shoot out. There was no time to argue or think too deeply. Ajay just nodded.

They sped to the address Dewan's goon had given them. On the way Ajay phoned Singh. "Get your men to stand down – everything's under control," was all he said before severing the connection.

It was a small bungalow in its own grounds, surrounded by a low fence – perfect for seeing anyone approaching.

They drove past and parked further down the road, out of sight. They all got out.

"You'd better stay here, sir," Dilip said to Ajay, also looking at Rishi. "Me and my men will see to the bungalow. I'll call you when we've secured it."

Ajay nodded.

Within three minutes the sustained sounds of rapid gunfire filled the air. Ajay texted Singh: "Gunfire in Sarojini Nagar. Ignore it."

It was difficult to hear much more than gunfire from where they were, but Ajay was sure he heard a couple of crashes and a man cry out in pain.

It was not long before Ajay's phone rang.

"All clear," came Dilip's strained voice.

Ajay ran to the bungalow with Rishi following.

The front door was open, revealing a scene of devastation. The walls had been peppered with bullets, and much of the furniture was in splinters. One of the MARCOS men was dead, and Dilip had been shot in his right calf. Three other men were lying on the floor. They appeared to be dead. But then Ajay noticed one of them move slightly. He went over to him.

He was breathing. Ajay reached back with his open hand. Rishi put his pistol in it. Ajay crouched down, pressing the gun hard into the man's forehead.

"He's gone to his hideout in Rohini... He thinks I don't know about it... but I do," the man said between gasps. "Bastard... coward," he added bitterly.

Ajay removed the gun from his forehead, but still held on to it.

"Get my phone," the man ordered, wincing in pain.

Ajay patted the man's pockets, quickly locating it. The man reached up, whimpering slightly, and put his thumb on the screen.

"Look under L Safe."

Ajay did as he was told. It came up with an address in Rohini.

"Kick him in the bollocks from me," the man said before shutting his eyes. He was still breathing.

"Go and get him, sir. I'll look after this," Dilip said weakly. Ajay turned to him. He had managed to tighten a tourniquet just above his knee, but his lower trouser leg was completely soaked in blood. He looked pale. "Don't worry, I'll keep him alive until it's all over," he added, nodding towards the man who had just spoken.

Ajay hesitated for just a moment. He stood up, and the other two followed him to one of the cars. They shot off to the address on the phone.

Another bungalow. Ajay pulled up out of sight. The MARCOS man got out. Ajay and Rishi did likewise. Ajay noticed a gun in Rishi's right hand – he must have picked it up from one of Dewan's dead security contingent.

"Stay behind me," ordered the MARCOS man. He did not call Ajay sir. Ajay looked at him. He was in the zone.

They crept around the back of the building, Ajay and Rishi copying the MARCOS man's movements the best they could.

They entered the short garden silently. Suddenly gunfire erupted from the house. The MARCOS man's head seemed to explode as bullet after bullet entered it. Ajay and Rishi, who had been some way behind, dived behind some bushes.

The gunfire stopped.

"Get your phone out," Ajay ordered Rishi, who was shaking slightly.

"I'm going to phone you. Answer before it makes a sound."

...

"Good. I'm going to go around to the side. When I say, start shooting at the bungalow. Keep low – don't get hit!"

Ajay crept around under the cover of the foliage until he was less than half a metre away from the broken window through which Dewan had delivered his fatal shots.

"Now," Ajay whispered, the phone's microphone millimetres away from his lips.

Rishi fired two shots towards the window, taking out some of the remaining glass.

Dewan replied by sticking his rifle through the window and discharging a volley of shots. Ajay saw his opportunity and launched himself forward, grabbing the end of the rifle and dragging it down with all his weight. Dewan let out a cry as he let go.

Ajay jumped up and crashed through the window which, by now, had very little glass left in it. Dewan, who, despite being in his fifties, of a large build and a little overweight, managed to leap out of the way.

As Ajay landed, Dewan kicked out his knee, causing Ajay to buckle down. Dewan kicked him hard in the head. Ajay felt himself go dizzy. Dewan reached behind Ajay and grabbed the pistol which Ajay had shoved down the back of his trousers. Dewan stood back and pointed it at Ajay's head.

As Ajay's head stopped spinning he looked up at Dewan's grinning face.

"You can never win," Ajay said, his voice sounding far away to him.

"*You* can never win," Dewan sneered. "Do you think you could beat *me*, you jumped up slum maggot? I own –"

His words were cut short by two bangs echoing around the room. Blood spurted out of his left eye as he fell backwards. Ajay automatically turned towards where the sound had emanated. Rishi was standing just outside the window, pistol in his hand, frozen in position.

The press seemed to be quicker off the mark than the police. When it emerged that Ajay had been attacked by Dewan, a major drug lord, but he had taken the fight to him, they could not find enough superlatives to describe Ajay's bravery. None of them questioned his connection to Dilip, Rishi or the MARCOS men. He was the hero of the moment.

The police investigation, in which Singh was a lead officer, confirmed nearly everything that was reported, noting that Ajay was acquainted with Dilip, Rishi and the MARCOS men due to his constituency work, and was thus able to call on them for assistance.

It was nearly three months later, and Ajay was taking Rishi for yet another expensive meal.

"Would you like my East and Central Delhi heroin business?" Ajay asked.

"How much?"

"I want no money up front. But there are conditions. You keep the heroin at the same strength and purity – you only cut with sugar and milk powder. You never drop the price. You fund the Sanctuary rehab clinics in Delhi so they always have spare capacity. You keep on Dilip and his men, and I can call on their services whenever I want to. OK?" Dilip had replaced his dead men with other MARCOS operatives – Ajay had given the dead men's families very generous compensation.

"Yes, bhaiyaa. Thank you."

"I like you and respect you, Rishi, but, as you know, I've worked hard to get heroin under control in this city. I'm giving you this business because I trust you. But, if you break any of my conditions, I'll kill you and take the business back."

"I know you will, bhaisaab."

19

Although trying to appear confident, the two schoolgirls were shy and a little embarrassed. They were interviewing Ajay for their school blog.

"Is it true that you started off as a chaiwallah's apprentice?" one of them asked.

Ajay looked at her blankly. She reddened.

"A chaiwallah's apprentice?" he repeated.

"Yes, sir. Sorry, sir. We read that your first job was at a chai stall at a temple. We read that you worked for an old man. We thought he was training you to take over. Sorry for our misunderstanding." She looked away, blushing even more.

Ajay looked at them for a while. When they started giggling, he swivelled his chair around and looked out of the window. He became oblivious to everything around him as he felt himself go back to those times when he had worked for Mr Joshi, greeting the customers and charming them into buying chai. He smiled when he thought of the clothes he had worn. They had been cheap, but he had thought he had looked incredible. Maybe he had. They had certainly been good enough to make the temple goers part with their money. He thought of Mr Joshi sitting on his embroidered gold cloth and wondered if he was still at the temple, selling his chai.

He turned to the girls, who were now whispering to each other. They were silent as soon as he faced them.

"I'm sorry, ladies, but I've just remembered I've got an important meeting. Why don't you come back tomorrow? You can take some photos of the office and me and my staff. Tell my secretary what sizes you are, and I'll get some clothes from my range for you."

They looked at each other, wide-eyed and speechless. Ajay smiled.

"Got to move – let's go," Ajay said, standing up.

He hurried out of the office, with the girls closely following behind. He called to his secretary: "Deepika, please write down the size of clothing these two young ladies take – we're going to sort them out with some nice clothes. Make a time for them to come back tomorrow."

Deepika smiled and nodded. She was used to Ajay's acts of breathtaking generosity. She worked there two days a week, for which Ajay paid her handsomely (her pay rate was their secret – it was more than double what anyone else in the office got). She spent the rest of her time working on her PhD. Ajay paid all her university fees. She now saw her parents every two weeks or so. If anyone asked, they would say that you have to give modern girls freedom, and she was seeing Ajay Pandey, the incredible MP who had virtually wiped out crime in the whole of Delhi. Deepika had told them that, if they did not accept Ajay, she would have nothing to do with them. They had smiled in return. The fact that Ajay now had such respect and status turned what could have been a very bitter pill into the sweetness of jalebi.

Ajay went into the street and hailed a rickshaw. Thirty minutes later he stood outside the Shiva temple.

He looked up at it and closed his eyes, remembering those days when he walked here every morning.

At last he opened them. He went inside the temple. Ramesh, the pyjama wallah, spotted him straightaway and went over to him.

"Mr Pandeyji, it's been so many years..." he said in awe.

"Ramesh bhai, it's good to see you..."

Gradually, other traders saw him and came over. It was just like the old days, but then he had been a cheeky young boy who worked hard to make himself the centre of attention. Now people flocked to him.

The traders all wanted selfies with him on their stalls. He obliged. These people had been good to him - it was the least he could do.

Eventually he asked if Mr Joshi was still there.

"Oh, yes, yes, sir. Would you like me to get chai from him?" asked a trader.

"No, it's OK. I hope you don't mind, but I'd like to see him alone – you know, for old time's sake."

They all nodded and murmured their assent.

Ajay went over to a hunched figure sitting at the chai stall.

"Bapuji?" Ajay asked tentatively.

Mr Joshi looked up and squinted.

"It's Ajay, bapuji."

"Ajay, beta! Let me stand up." Mr Joshi reached out a frail hand, feeling for his stick.

"No, no bapuji!" Ajay exclaimed, crouching down in front of him. As he did so, he noticed the embroidered gold cloth still covering Mr Joshi's cushion. It was as brilliant as it had always been. Ajay could not help but smile.

"They tell me that you're an MP now."

"Yes, bapuji, I've been in office nearly two years –"

"They say you fight with drug dealers and keep drugs off the streets."

Ajay nodded slowly.

"Is it true that you spend all your money on the street kids, like you used to be when I first saw you?"

"Maybe not all, bapuji."

"I always said someone as good as you was destined for great things, beta. You truly are a mahatma."

Ajay closed his eyes as a single tear trickled down his left cheek.